THE
RELUCTANT
CORONER

THE RELUCTANT CORONER

BOOK ONE OF THE
FENWAY STEVENSON MYSTERIES

PAUL AUSTIN ARDOIN

ISBN: 978-1-949082-01-2

Third Printing: July 2020

For information please visit:
www.paulaustinardoin.com

Cover design by Ziad Ezzat
www.ziad.ezzat.com

Author photo by Monica Toohey-Krause of Studio KYK
www.studiokyk.com

Edited by Britt Graves
Additional editing by Max Christian Hansen and Jess Reynolds

10 9 8 7 6 5 4 3 2 1

For Stacie

TABLE OF CONTENTS

PART ONE
MONDAY & TUESDAY

CHAPTER ONE

She passed the sign that said *Estancia 10 Miles* and arched her back, stretching, then jumped in her seat when the rental truck drifted onto the line separating Ocean Highway from the shoulder. She set her jaw and turned the wheel a few degrees counterclockwise. A BMW in the fast lane passed her as if she were going backward.

The truck's steering pulled to the right, and it seemed like it had only worsened during the irritating ride from Seattle. She tightened her grip on the wheel as the highway began its steady incline up to the crest of the hill, where a massive industrial complex rose to meet her field of vision. Ablaze with warm orange lights, the maze of pipes and small towers extended into the sky, steam rising around it.

She blinked and she was four years old again, in her father's Range Rover, seeing the complex lit up in the darkness for the first time.

"Gotham City!" she had screamed from the back seat, pointing delightedly.

"No, Fenway," Nathaniel Ferris had said, never taking his eyes off the road. "That's Daddy's refinery."

"You're Batman," she said definitively.

"I'm not Batman," he said, laughing. "But maybe I'm Bruce Wayne. And Mrs. Wayne expects us home soon. It's already past your bedtime."

Fenway shook her head and came back to the present. The Ferris Energy refinery, constantly spewing gray-brown fumes, was an ugly monstrosity in the daylight. But at night, the orange lights and the steam and the shadows from the pipes and antennae and towers created a scene almost as beautiful as the quaint seaside town eight miles down the coast.

Life had changed so much in the last six weeks. It started with the CLOSED sign that faced her when she went to work at the clinic. No explanation—she had to go home and read a tersely worded email to learn the clinic had lost its funding.

And that same day, her mother took a turn for the worse. She would be gone in two days.

Fenway accepted the first offer on her mother's house and moved most of her things into storage. Then, three weeks before her trip in the rental truck, tiring of applying for jobs and for apartments at the same time, she was sitting at her PC reading a rejection email when her phone rang.

It showed an unfamiliar number with an 805 area code, and she wondered if it was one of the nursing recruiters she'd sent her resume to.

"Fenway?"

She drew in her breath sharply. "Dad?"

"How are you feeling?" His voice was heavy with concern. "Is everything okay?"

"I didn't recognize the number."

"Still at work. I'm calling from a conference room."

"You weren't at the funeral." It came out before Fenway could stop it, but after all the missed graduations and state volleyball championships and birthdays, she still felt raw.

"I—I wasn't sure you'd want me there."

"Really? Charlotte didn't want to renew your vows on another of my special days?"

Silence on the other end of the line. "Look—I know you're in a tough spot with the house and with your master's program, and I want to help."

Fenway scoffed. "*Now* you want to help?"

"Yes. You're still working in the ER?"

"I moved to the free clinic last year, Dad."

He clicked his tongue. "Oh. I didn't know that."

"Yeah, well, don't keep it in your brain too long. We lost our funding. They closed a couple of weeks ago."

"I see." Another pause.

"I'm applying for jobs. Just sent a couple of résumés out. Escrow closes on Mom's house next week. I'll be fine."

"Fine? Where are you going to live?"

"I have feelers out. You don't have to worry about me."

"No—of course not. But..."

Fenway closed her eyes. He'd been so angry at her mother.

"I wonder," Nathaniel Ferris began, "if you'd consider moving down here."

"Down there? Estancia?"

"It's a beautiful part of the country. I've got a few vacancies in my apartment buildings. I could reduce the rent."

Fenway leaned back in her chair. "I don't want your charity. And besides, I'm not a licensed nurse practitioner in California. I need work."

"So pay me rent and take the next available boards."

"And what do I do for money in the meantime?"

"I know people here. A good friend runs a pharmaceutical business. Hell, the new wing of the hospital has my name on it. You could work as a pharma rep or in hospital administration and then get a nursing position when you pass your boards."

"That sounds like charity, too."

"I'll just make a few introductions. Don't think I didn't notice you were valedictorian of your BSN class. They'll be thanking *me*. You'll be hired before you can unpack."

The *no thanks* was on the tip of her tongue, but she couldn't say it. How many résumés had she sent out? How many apartments had she seen that were out of her price range? How was she going to get through the next few months without her mother? She pinched the bridge of her nose and swallowed hard. "What's the catch?"

A large exhale from the other end of the line. "Come on, Fenway, I'm not all bad. There's no catch. You're my daughter, and I thought you could use a break."

Fenway leaned forward again, reading the first sentence of the job rejection letter a few times until her eyes lost focus. "I'll think about it."

"That's all I ask."

Fighting with the pull of the steering wheel, she saw the lights of Estancia emerge before her. Bits and pieces started coming together in her memory: the beach down the road from her father's mansion, the Spanish-style architecture of the outdoor mall.

Halfway down the hill, Fenway looked down at her gas gauge. The needle hung slightly above the red line. She'd probably make it.

She yawned and turned up the radio. It was Prince, and Fenway bounced in her seat, trying to get her blood flowing again. She pressed the accelerator, and the speedometer crept up to seventy.

"It's good to see you again, Dad," she muttered. No. That sounded weird. "I'm happy you were finally there for me." No. Sarcasm wasn't the way to go, and it wasn't nearly as cathartic to say as she thought it would be. "I appreciate you getting me an apartment so quickly. I hope..."

That was a good question. What *did* she hope for? Did she hope to finally connect with Nathaniel Ferris after twenty years? Did she hope to sit on the white leather sofa in his mansion and leaf through her photo albums, pointing and laughing, him getting misty-eyed at all the memories he missed?

The low fuel light came on. She cursed quietly.

Mostly, she hoped he wouldn't have Charlotte with him.

Broadway, 1 Mile.

She glanced at the low fuel light again. Her old Sentra could go fifty miles with the fuel light on. The rental truck? No idea. She took her foot off the gas and slowed to sixty, a horn sounding behind her.

Relief washed over her as she turned off Ocean Highway. The Broadway exit emptied out onto a divided four-lane boulevard, then she turned onto Estancia Canyon Road. The next landmark was the Coffee Bean on the next corner, and the apartment complex sat two blocks further down. She pulled halfway into the driveway and stopped the truck.

She flipped down the visor and looked in the mirror. The day of driving had been unkind. Her loose curls were frizzy, and her large, dark brown eyes looked tired, but she stared firmly at her own face. "I appreciate you getting me this apartment so quickly. It's good to see you again." Almost. She softened her gaze, forcing a smile onto the corners of her mouth. "I appreciate you getting me this apartment so quickly. It's good to see you again." A solid performance. She nodded and grabbed her phone off the passenger seat.

A new voicemail. But it wasn't from her father.

"Hi, Fenway," the voice said. "This is Robert Stotsky. I work for your dad, and I also oversee his apartment complexes. He had a meeting with Japanese investors at the last minute, so he asked me to meet you and get you settled in. Come to the leasing office when you arrive."

Fenway sighed.

A horn blared; an SUV was in her rearview mirror, trying to get into the driveway. She shifted into gear and lurched forward, the SUV maneuvering around her, and Fenway pulled into an uncovered visitor space on the end of the first row.

She killed the engine and hoisted herself out the cab.

The leasing office sign was posted above a unit across the parking lot, porch light blazing. Her sneakers were silent on the asphalt as she went up and knocked.

Sounds from inside: rustling, a television turning off, footsteps getting quieter, then louder. She waited a few more seconds before the door opened.

A hulking white man stood in the doorway. Fenway was five-ten, but the man towered over her, built of muscle, perhaps going a little soft around the middle. He wore a well-tailored, expensive-looking suit—not what Fenway had in mind for the building manager.

"Can I help you?" he said. His voice, kind enough, softened his angular features but still held an edge of suspicion.

"Hi," she said. "I'm supposed to be meeting, um, Robert? He's the building manager, I think."

"Oh, *you're* Fenway Ferris?" The large man caught his surprise, but too late. Obviously, the man hadn't been prepared for Ferris's daughter to be black.

"Uh, Fenway *Stevenson*. You're Robert?" She shook his hand; he had a firm grip.

The man nodded. "Yes, Rob Stotsky. Is Stevenson your married name?"

"My mother's name."

"Sorry. I don't mean to pry."

"Not a problem. Usually I get a joke about the Boston Red Sox."

"I'm a Dodgers fan myself." He laughed and turned to a small open cabinet next to the door jamb, picking a keychain off a hook. "Okay, Miss Ferris—sorry, Miss Stevenson. Here we go. I'll show you the way."

"Thanks," she said. "I'll get my stuff."

Stotsky followed Fenway out, turning off the lights and locking the door behind him.

They walked to the truck, and Fenway grabbed her sleeping bag and a suitcase from the cab. Stotsky took the case from Fenway without being asked, lifting it easily as Fenway locked the truck.

"Thanks for your help," she said, putting her purse over her shoulder.

"That everything?" he asked.

Fenway stifled a yawn. "For tonight."

"All right. Follow me."

Fenway looked at Stotsky out of the corner of her eye as they walked past the first building and turned the corner. "You're dressed awfully well for a guy who manages apartment buildings. You going to a wedding later?"

Stotsky chuckled. "The building managers all report to me. I'm just doing a favor for your dad tonight."

"Oh—so you'd usually be at home by now?"

"Don't worry about it. Your dad and I go way back. He'd do the same for my daughter, I'm sure."

The complex was dated but otherwise passable. Bright and well lit, no peeling paint. The landscaping was basic, but care had been taken with its upkeep. In the dim light, she couldn't tell if the neutral color of the stucco was beige or grey.

"So, does my father work this late on most nights?"

"Sometimes," Stotsky said. "It depends on what the oil futures are doing. Oh—before I forget, the sheriff came by earlier, looking for you."

Fenway paused and turned back. "The sheriff?"

"You know him?"

Her eyebrows knitted. "No. I don't know who the sheriff is. The Estancia sheriff?"

"The Dominguez County sheriff. I don't see how you could have done anything wrong, though. You barely got here." Stotsky laughed uneasily.

"Anything wrong? What do you mean?"

Stotsky coughed. "Nothing. I'd be really surprised if any daughter of Nathaniel Ferris was in trouble with the law."

Fenway frowned. His light tone had a hint of darkness. Was he implying something? That he'd suspect her if she *wasn't* Nathaniel Ferris's daughter? She put her hand on the body of her purse.

"Anyway, the sheriff said he'd be by tomorrow. So keep an eye out." He turned and led Fenway up an open-air staircase, then to the third door on the left. "Here we go. 214." He turned the key in the lock and pushed the door open; the small light in the entry shone weakly on Stotsky's face as he handed the suitcase to Fenway.

"Thanks."

Stotsky handed her a business card. "Free Wi-Fi in all the apartments. Password is on the back of the card. I'm not usually onsite, but you call me direct if you have any issues."

"Hey," she said, "do you happen to know if my father is sending some people over to help me with the apartment tomorrow morning?"

"Did he say he would?"

"Yes."

"Then he will. Have a good night."

If he said he would, he will. Of course. As long as his appearances in her life could be done by proxy, he could be counted on.

She shut the door behind the large man, turned around, and stared at the empty space.

Beige carpets. Cheap linoleum floors.

No job, no friends.

A father who took a business call with investors instead of meeting his daughter her first night in town.

Fenway looked up at the weak overhead light.

All the work Fenway did at her nursing jobs, in her master's program, at her life. All the work her mother did to gain distance and freedom from her rich, controlling ex-husband. Twenty years, and it had all vanished.

Fenway picked up her suitcase and opened it on the floor of her new living room. After getting ready for bed, she unrolled her sleeping bag in the bedroom and plugged her phone into the outlet a foot away.

She got in and tried to pull the sleeping bag over her head, but she was too tall. It barely covered her neck.

She rested her head on the carpet.

———

She woke to morning light filtering through the heavy mist outside. The windows had no coverings, and despite the fog, it was bright in the room.

She rolled onto her side and picked up her phone. Half past six.

But her phone was at ten percent. It hadn't charged. She checked the plugs—they were in.

Fenway looked around and her eyes rested on the light switch next to the door. Kicking the sleeping bag off, she stood up, her back complaining from the night on the hard surface, and turned on the switch.

Beep beep beep.

Six outlets in the room, and she chose the one connected to the light switch.

And now she was well and truly awake.

It was too early to move the truck; the beeping noise when backing up would wake the whole complex. She hoped her father was bringing people to help. She wasn't sure she could get the sofa and the mattress upstairs by herself.

Fenway yawned. She needed coffee.

After donning sweats and running shoes, she shook out the loose curls that didn't quite reach her shoulders and set off to find coffee.

She thought she remembered passing a Coffee Bean the night before. It was only two blocks away, but in the gray morning light—typical for early May on the central California coast—nothing looked familiar. The wooden sign for the complex was a different shape than she'd thought. The pink house on the corner had looked gray in the darkness. She might have spent her first eight years in Estancia, but never in this quirky area. It was nothing like her father's neighborhood, whose ocean-view mansions stood well apart from each other, aloof.

A few bicyclists in brightly colored, skintight outfits passed her, headed away from the main road. They went past the *Not a Through Street* sign. Where were they going?

In five minutes, she was in line at the Coffee Bean. Only three people ahead of her. On a Tuesday morning at the beginning of the commute in Seattle, the line would have been out the door.

"Large latte," she said to the cashier.

"Sure thing," the cashier chirped, and Fenway almost jumped back with the force of the unexpected enthusiasm. "Can I get your name?"

"Joanne."

"Thanks, Joanne. That'll be right up. You have a great day, okay?"

Fenway blinked. "Sure. Yeah. You too."

Fenway settled in an overstuffed chair next to a tiny round table, staring into space. The barista had to call *Joanne* twice.

As she went to get her latte, she wondered when she could get started on her life. When could she get her furniture out of the truck? When could she start interviewing for those jobs her father promised?

Everything was dependent on him. She took a drink and sat back heavily in the chair. Accepting her father's offer had seemed logical at the time, as she barely had enough money to get through the next few weeks. Now it seemed like a bad decision. Surely she could have slept on a friend's couch in Seattle. Or maybe even stayed with an ex-boyfriend. Just until she got on her feet.

A couple of phone calls and another two days in the rental truck and she could undo this decision. She sipped her latte as two women in their late thirties, dressed in matching yoga pants, crossed in front of her.

"He promised me he'd take Ethan to his game today."

"But you *have* to come to Pilates. I'll *die* if you're not there."

"When I woke up, he'd already left for the golf course. And Ethan already missed practice on Thursday."

She'd never been a huge fan of people-watching, but this was like a cultural anthropology lesson. Compared to the bustle and diversity of downtown Seattle, Estancia was a foreign country. Another pair of white women, both in dark jeans and North Face jackets, waited for their coffee orders to Fenway's right.

"I know he said not to get another area rug, but it was on sale."

"And it's gorgeous. Does he not see how gorgeous it is?"

"I *know*. Honestly, it pulls the whole room together..."

White people in their native habitat. The voice in her head sounded like Richard Attenborough.

Then two more female voices behind her. "Are you still worried about Allan getting laid off?"

"He hasn't heard anything for sure, but I hate the rumors I'm hearing. Ferris Energy has *still* got the whole area closed for the accident investigation. Can you believe it? What's Allan going to do?"

"Better unemployed than dead, Angie."

Fenway's ears pricked up.

Nathaniel Ferris had always been the most powerful man in the county. His eponymous energy company was the largest employer, and even when oil prices fluctuated wildly, he still made his numbers, got his bonuses, made his slice of the profits.

Than dead?

Had something happened? Something to ruffle her father's unrufflable feathers? Could her rich, powerful, perfect father be at fault for an accident at his refinery? She didn't remember anything from the news, but she was a thousand miles away—and didn't pay attention to any news about her father, anyway.

But this was *interesting*.

"I think you're making too big of a deal out of it," Angie's friend said. "They did an internal investigation. Wrong place, wrong time. Allan shouldn't get laid off just because his co-workers did something stupid."

Wrong place, wrong time? Fenway leaned back, but the barista called *Angie* and then the two women were out of earshot.

Fenway tried to shift her attention to other conversations, but she couldn't concentrate.

Better unemployed than dead.

Wrong place, wrong time.

CHAPTER TWO

WHAT HAD HAPPENED AT THE REFINERY? PERHAPS THE INTERNET would have answers. Fenway reached in her pocket for her phone—but it was still charging in the bedroom.

So she left the coffee shop, her latte still half full, her curiosity bubbling out of her head.

Then another bicyclist passed her, straight down the side road, past the *Not a Through Street* sign.

Fenway stopped in her tracks and took another sip.

Okay—if she was going to find out what happened at her father's refinery, she could get the information slowly on her tiny screen or she could wait to set up her computer.

And if she was going to follow those bicyclists, she should do it before anyone arrived to help move the furniture.

Fenway walked toward the complex, then past it. The road didn't fan out into a cul-de-sac like she thought it might; it was a true dead end, with a wooden fence the width of the road, made out of four-by-four posts and wide planks painted white. Red and yellow reflectors were spaced several feet apart on each of the planks. To the right of the fence, a dirt path led off into the trees, showing fresh marks from bicycle tires.

She walked to the fence and gazed as far as she could up the path. About thirty feet farther up, it turned, revealing nothing of what might lie beyond. She threw her latte cup in the trash can next to the fence and started up the path.

After a few minutes, she passed a grove of trees and found herself hiking through a small clearing. The mist was thick here, and the branches of the trees made a canopy, keeping the thick, soupy fog at bay. On the other side of the clearing, Fenway made her way through another patch of trees. She passed a brown metal sign identifying the grove as a monarch butterfly waystation. She squinted at the upper branches through the fog. No butterflies up there today, though. Farther on, white starbursts of milkweed bloomed on each side of the patch. After a second grove—another ten minutes of walking—the trees ended abruptly.

Fenway stood at the edge of a flat, grassy plain, the misty sky uninterrupted in front of her. It was easily fifty feet from the edge of the trees to the end of the grass. There was no path through the grass, which was long but lay flat. She had to step high to walk through it.

There was a short drop-off, maybe three feet or so, to a sandy beach, and about a hundred yards farther out, the Pacific.

Fenway walked to the edge of the drop-off and stopped.

Something felt odd: she hadn't been in this spot before—not that she could remember, anyway—and yet everything was familiar: the cypress tree, windblown into its odd shape, coming out of the rock formation; the drop-off, a barstool-height drop onto ground covered with sand, shrubs, and dirt. Even the black spots on the sand, oil clumping like cat litter, waste from the offshore drilling her father was mostly responsible for.

Why did she know this place?

She closed her eyes. Insects clicked in the trees behind her, waves crashed on the shore. Ravens cawed, arguing with each other, arguing with the wind.

It felt so close. She almost had it.

She opened her eyes and looked up and down the beach. Maybe the view from the shore would jog her memory. For the next half hour, Fenway walked the beach. The frigid air and the roar of the waves kept her mind off her impending job search and her father's two decades of broken promises. But nothing else looked familiar. Still, the sight of the cypress tree growing out of the rocks burned in her brain. She knew she'd seen it before.

Fenway retraced her steps to the complex, feeling better than she had since her mother's diagnosis. Maybe even before that.

She arrived at her new apartment at seven forty-five and saw a white policeman at her door—and immediately her heart raced.

Oh—this was probably the sheriff who'd been looking for her the previous night.

He wore a black uniform with a black belt and boots. It wasn't yet eight o'clock, and there was hesitation in his body language as he raised his hand to knock.

"Can I help you?" she asked.

He flinched slightly but regained his composure as he turned to her. "Hi there. I'm looking for Fenway Stevenson."

She blinked.

His skin was pale, with a smattering of freckles on his nose and cheeks. Trim but muscular, he was a good three or four inches taller than Fenway's five-ten, and his neatly pressed short-sleeved uniform shirt showed off some healthy biceps. At first glance, he looked to be in his thirties, but the lines around his blue eyes suggested a few more years of experience.

Fenway was suddenly aware of her workout clothes and the sweat she'd worked up on the hike. She pulled off her headband and shook her hair out, hoping it wasn't too frizzy. "I'm Fenway Stevenson. Is anything wrong?"

He smiled easily, showing white teeth, a slightly crooked right front incisor, just enough to be cute. He laughed, and it sounded surprisingly genuine. "Oh, sorry."

Had he had noticed her apprehension? Or had he, like Stotsky the night before, expected the daughter of Nathaniel Ferris to be white?

He cleared his throat. "Did Rob Stotsky mention I came by last night?"

"He did."

"You're not in any trouble or anything." His face grew serious. "I just have some, uh, matters to discuss. Can we go inside?"

Fenway hesitated. "I literally got here last night. I haven't brought anything in—there's nowhere to sit. My father said he'd send a couple people to help, but I don't know when they'll be here."

The sheriff shifted from one foot to the other. "How about this—have you had breakfast?"

"Just coffee."

"You been to Jack and Jill's?"

"No."

"I'll buy you breakfast, and you call your dad to get his people to start unpacking. I bet most of it will be done when we get back."

She hesitated. "I don't even know your name."

"McVie." He gestured to the name badge on his chest. "Sheriff Craig McVie, at your service."

Fenway pulled out her phone.

Her father answered on the first ring. "Nathaniel Ferris," he said gruffly.

"Hi Dad, it's me."

His tone brightened. "Fenway! You made it! Did you meet Rob? Did he treat you all right? Listen, I've got a few of my guys coming to—"

"Hang on, Dad." Fenway cut him off. "The sheriff is here. Sheriff McVie."

"Oh, Craig's there already?"

"You know him?"

"Sure I do." His tone grew concerned. "Listen, he's got to talk to you about something serious. I know you just got in last night, but it's important."

"Weren't we going to talk about setting up some job interviews?"

"I don't want to get ahead of myself."

Fenway paused, trying to decipher her father's words. "What does that mean?"

"Just talk to Craig."

Fenway glanced up at Sheriff McVie, who was watching her closely. "Really?"

"Craig's on the up-and-up. Listen, my guys will have your stuff all set up in the apartment by the time you get back. It's the least I can do."

"I'd really rather—" Fenway began. She pictured her father rummaging through her stuff. But no, he'd never come in person. Especially to do manual labor. She clicked her tongue. "Sorry. I'd love the help. Getting the place set up sounds great. Thanks, Dad."

"You're more than welcome." He paused. "Fenway, I know this is awkward. Can we—"

"The sheriff is waiting for me. We can talk later." Fenway closed her eyes for a moment. She hoped the two of them would *never* have the conversation about how uncomfortable it was for her to be back in Estancia.

"Sure, sure. Yes, I understand. Hey—Craig's taking you to Mimosa's, right?"

"No, Jack and Jill's."

"Oh, for the love of—tell him I say to take you to Mimosa's. They have a fried egg with hazelnuts, chanterelles, green garlic, and blackberries. It's phenomenal. Jack and Jill's is just a glorified Denny's."

"Sure, Dad." Fenway's stomach rumbled; a glorified Denny's sounded excellent. "Thanks for the help."

She hung up.

"Everything cool?" asked the sheriff.

"Your choice of breakfast places doesn't meet with his approval."

"Aw, crap, did he say Mimosa's? I hate Mimosa's. It's too hoity-toity."

"He wanted me to get eggs with hazelnuts and blackberries. Oh—and green garlic." She made a face. "I don't even know what green garlic *is*."

"Garlic that's jealous it doesn't get to be in *real* food."

Fenway felt the corners of her mouth turn up slightly. "Jack and Jill's it is, then. I won't tell him if you don't."

"Deal."

Sheriff McVie led the way to the parking lot, where he opened the passenger door of the green-and-white police cruiser for Fenway before hurrying around to the driver's side.

She ran her hand over the dash. "It's nice to ride in the front seat of one of these."

He started the car and glanced over at her. "You've ridden in the back?"

"Yeah."

"Sounds like a good story." He reversed out of the parking space, then turned onto the main road, heading the opposite direction from the Coffee Bean.

"It was a long time ago. Maybe not that long ago. I was in college."

McVie pressed his lips together. "You don't have an arrest record."

Fenway looked sideways at McVie. "Oh, my father had you check up on me?"

"Maybe."

"What I think you'd call a domestic dispute, but it was just my ex-boyfriend showing up at my apartment drunk and yelling at me at three in the morning. And *I'm* the one who got taken down to the station."

"But no arrest record."

"The cop at the station believed me. Said I reminded him of his daughter."

"So you made up a sob story?"

"Oh, Sheriff, I would never lie to the police." She smiled as coquettishly as she could.

The sheriff smiled but shook his head ruefully. "I wish my daughter wouldn't lie to the police. She's sixteen, and I've already caught her lying about her boyfriend. Tell you what—don't tell me any more details about you and your ex."

Fenway glanced over. McVie had a band of gold around his left ring finger. She felt a pang of disappointment.

They rode in silence until they arrived at Jack and Jill's. The restaurant was on a frontage road next to the main highway. It looked like it had started its life out as an IHOP, complete with the telltale A-frame roof. The two of them walked in. The interiors were heavy on maple paneling, like a seventies-era Alpine ski lodge, more appropriate for Hansel and Gretel than Jack and Jill. Fenway looked at the walls and other decorations—not a pail of water or broken crown to be seen.

The smells of bacon and coffee were strong by the front register where they waited. She was glad to be here instead of the green garlic place.

The rosy-cheeked hostess approached. "Two?" she asked, holding up fingers, and the sheriff nodded. She grabbed two menus and seated them by the window.

"Your server will be right with you," she said, turning away.

Fenway opened the menu and placed her coffee cup right-side up. "So, Sheriff, what did you want to talk about?"

McVie turned his cup over too, but he kept his menu closed. "It's kind of a delicate matter. And it's not really breakfast conversation."

Fenway gave a tight smile. "You're the one who wanted to discuss this over breakfast. Besides, I have a pretty strong stomach."

"That's what your dad told me. You're a nurse, right?"

The server came up, an ochre-skinned woman of about thirty, her black hair pulled into a severe bun. She took their coffee order and stepped away, nearly bumping into a young white man dressed like McVie.

"Hey, Sheriff," the man said.

McVie looked up. "Hey, Callahan."

"The men Mr. Ferris sent need the keys to Miss Ferris's truck and apartment."

"Stevenson," she corrected before fishing the keys out of the pocket of her sweats.

"What?"

"Stevenson," she repeated. "My mom's last name. I'm Miss Stevenson, not Miss Ferris."

"Sorry, Miss Stevenson. I didn't know."

"No problem, officer. Tell them thanks. It's a big help."

Callahan tipped his imaginary hat in acknowledgment and turned to leave.

"Brian," the sheriff said, putting an arm up, "I know Mr. Ferris is an important man, but get back on scene as soon as possible, all right?"

Callahan nodded.

The sheriff watched him walk out, then turned back to Fenway. "Where were we?"

"A nurse practitioner," she said.

McVie tilted his head. "What?"

"You asked if I was a nurse. I'm a nurse practitioner." She raised her chin slightly. "What was all that about—'on scene'?"

"It's—uh, well, it's why I wanted to talk to you." He put his hands flat on the table. "Okay." He smiled. "We have a problem that came up last night, and I think you can help us out because you're a nurse. Nurse practitioner. Your whole medical background—in the emergency room, and your forensic nursing degree."

"I've got one more class to finish."

"Even so."

Fenway studied McVie's face. Her father's words from their phone conversation: *I don't want to get ahead of myself. Just talk to Craig.*

Before she'd agreed to move, she'd asked her father if he had another motive besides helping her. She kicked herself for falling for his half-truths. Now the most powerful man in the county had gotten the sheriff to do his work for him. And now that Fenway had moved to Estancia, she couldn't extract herself from the situation. Not easily, anyway, and not without it being expensive. "Dammit, Sheriff, I *knew* there was a catch."

"What?"

"My father offering to move me down here. Of course there's a catch. What does he want?" She'd at least thought her father would wait a couple of months before revealing the catch. She didn't expect it dropped on her before she even returned the truck. "Lay it on me, Sheriff."

McVie's forehead crinkled and his mouth opened slightly. It was almost adorable, but Fenway was too angry to backtrack.

The server appeared with the coffee pot. "You know what you want?"

Fenway had closed her menu, intending to order a simple two-egg breakfast. But now her day would be spent figuring out her father's agenda and playing family politics through the sheriff. She opened the menu again and found the priciest item. "I'd like the smoked salmon benedict, please. And—can you add a bowl of fresh fruit?"

"There's an extra cost," the server said, pouring coffee into McVie's cup. "You want it subbed out for the hash browns?"

"No, I'd like both, thanks."

McVie stared at Fenway a moment.

"And you, Sheriff?"

"I guess I'll have the number three. Over easy, bacon crisp, sourdough toast."

They sat in silence for a moment after the server took their menus. Fenway reached for her coffee. "My father gave you all my background, then. Transcripts, criminal record, DMV data, all that stuff. You know when I'm due for my next tetanus shot?"

"We want to appoint you to a county position, and a background check is part of that. It's routine."

"I didn't agree to anything." She set the coffee down and folded her arms. "You have to know this is a huge breach of privacy. It might not even be legal."

"Only your public records," McVie said. "We didn't even run a credit report."

"My father hasn't cared about anything I've done for the last twenty years." She tried to keep the edge out of her voice. "I should have known this is only because he wants something."

McVie opened his mouth to speak, then suddenly stopped.

"Sheriff, you know everything about me. So tell me, what do *I* need to know?"

"All right." McVie took a deep breath. "Okay. The county coroner died suddenly two nights ago."

"Oh." Fenway paused for a moment and felt a pang of regret. "I'm sorry. Were you close?"

"We were co-workers. I'd have a beer with Harry after work a few times a year." The sheriff took a drink of his coffee. "Harrison Walker. Your dad bankrolled his first campaign for county coroner about six years ago."

"That's an elected position?"

"In Dominguez County it is." McVie leaned forward with his elbows on the table. "Late Sunday night, Walker's body was found face down on the side of Highway 326." He averted his eyes. "He'd been shot. Close to the entrance of the state park."

"That's awful."

McVie nodded, still not looking at her.

Fenway hesitated but pressed on. "You said you needed my help. I'm a nurse practitioner. What are you asking me to do?"

McVie looked up. "One of my responsibilities as Sheriff is to appoint people to vacant positions. The county coroner position is vacant." He took another sip of coffee. "The next election is in November. I have to appoint someone now."

"Doesn't California have an election in June?"

"The deadline to get on the ballot has passed. We've appointed other people to elected positions before—not very often, but it happens."

"So—what? Based on my nursing background, does my father want me to assess some candidates for you?" She dropped her arms to her sides. "I haven't done that before, but if it pays well, sign me up."

"Uh, no. I want... actually... I want to appoint *you*."

Fenway blinked. "Me? I don't have an M.D."

"You don't need an M.D. to be a coroner in California. Medical examiner, yes. But not coroner. Harrison Walker was an EMT."

"Even if I technically meet the requirements, there must be a dozen other people more qualified."

McVie nodded. "I'll admit you're not the first choice. One of the county supervisors has been angling for the position. He lost to Walker in the last election. A few people are planning to run for coroner in November, but none of them can serve immediately."

"I don't have any experience at being a coroner."

"Neither did Harrison Walker."

"I still have one class to go before I finish my degree."

"A master's degree in forensics is not a job requirement. Besides, you're enrolled online. You can still finish. You've got a good five years of medical experience. You've been an ER nurse, worked at a free clinic. You can recognize the signs of drug use and domestic abuse. That's a big part of the job."

"Don't I have to cut people up and determine time of death?"

"We work with the M.E. in San Miguelito. The Park Police sent Walker's body there already. Most of your job is going to be working on drug overdose cases. People who die at home from heart attacks. Falling off ladders putting up their Christmas lights. Any homicide, suicide, accidental death—if it doesn't happen under medical supervision, your team will investigate it."

Fenway looked down at the table. County coroner. *I guarantee you'll have a job before you unpack.* She was a nurse practitioner. She was *good* at it. The forensic stuff was so she could help the living, interpreting physical evidence in victims of abuse. "I don't know." Fenway raised her head, and McVie's blue eyes stared into hers. "Why me?"

"Your dad called me up after my first choices went nowhere. He told me your background, he told me you were arriving soon, and he told me you're in the perfect position to take this full-time job, even if it's for just six months."

The server appeared and set the plates in front of them. Fenway picked up her fork and knife. "I guess he has a point. I can't take a nursing job in California until I pass the boards."

McVie nodded, picking up his fork, but didn't start. "I reviewed your job history, your transcripts. I read the recommendation letters from your supervisors and instructors. Your dad knew you were valedictorian at Western Washington, but even he didn't know you had straight A's in your master's program."

Fenway began eating.

"Look," he continued, "maybe it seems like your dad is trying to play puppet master. I was skeptical at first, too. But you qualify. And I think you'd do a good job."

Fenway took another bite.

McVie put down his unused fork. "We don't have any other options. I can't leave the position open, and you're looking for a temporary job. You'll get a decent salary and benefits. You can finish your master's. You can apply for certification in California. It's a win-win, if you ask me."

Fenway swallowed carefully, then took another sip of coffee and set the mug down.

"What do you think?" His eyes were soft; asking, but not pleading.

"I'm not sure whether to be insulted or flattered."

"Flattered." McVie smiled warmly.

She didn't want to, but she found herself smiling back. It sounded intriguing—she wanted to be angry at her father for so much meddling, but McVie's frank assessment of her situation was accurate.

And his smile was adorable.

"It sounds like there are a lot of positives. I guess I'd be interested in interviewing."

He laughed, another genuine laugh. "What do you think *this* is?"

Fenway laughed in return, but darkness crept into the back of her mind.

This seemed like a win-win, but Nathaniel Ferris didn't do anything without getting something for himself. The cynical view? He'd suggested her as coroner purely for optics. It wouldn't look good if his black daughter were to struggle financially while he was so well off. Or, even more cynical, maybe he thought Fenway would look the other way if there were deaths that could be laid at his door.

Better unemployed than dead.

Wrong place, wrong time.

She looked into McVie's face. Working in the ER, she'd gotten good at telling when people were lying.

Oh, no, I never touch my mom's Oxy.

I swear I fell down a flight of stairs.

I don't know why my kids are so sick.

Fenway took another bite of her benedict.

She'd learned how to read the physical evidence. Opioid addiction was hard to mask. Radial fractures were an easy tell. The toxicology reports were tough to read, but she learned what to look for in the kids' skin when a parent was cooking meth. And her forensic classes taught her things she thought she'd never need—how to take fingerprints, how to work a crime scene, how to talk to witnesses. Maybe those classes would be useful after all.

Yeah. She might be okay at this.

But could she trust her father?

She took another three bites before McVie said anything.

"Are you considering it?"

"I'm walking through the scenarios in my head," she said. "Do you know—"

And then she stopped. She'd almost asked about the accident at the Ferris Energy refinery. Who had died. What the results of the investigation were.

"Do I know what?" asked McVie.

The sheriff and her father were close. Close enough for McVie to consider Ferris's daughter for the open coroner position. If she didn't trust her father, she sure as hell couldn't trust McVie.

"Do you know what the next steps are?"

McVie breathed a sigh of relief. "Okay—well, first, I should take you to meet the team. Two sergeants, a paralegal, and an assistant. Pretty standard for a small county like ours."

"Wait—people would be *reporting* to me?"

McVie nodded.

"I've never managed anyone before."

McVie nodded again. "I know."

"What if the whole team quits?"

"I'm not worried. Even if you're a horrible manager, they'll all gut it out for six months."

"Gosh, Mr. Sheriff, sir." Fenway clasped her hands and fluttered her eyelashes. "You sure know how to make a girl feel special."

McVie chuckled. "I'm not going to lie to you, Fenway. I expect this will be out of your comfort zone. But I did my homework on you, and now that I've met you face to face, I bet you can do it." He leaned back. "In fact, I bet you'll be good at it."

Fenway took another bite, a big bite, and chewed thoroughly before she swallowed. The ex-boyfriend who'd shown up at her door in the middle of the night had been charming too, but he'd been a child, really. Here was a grown man, a county sheriff, telling her that she could do this.

Not like she had any other options.

Fenway nodded. "When can we go meet the team?"

"How about this afternoon?"

Once Fenway had agreed to go to the office, Sheriff McVie was visibly more relaxed. He spoke about how the sheriff and the coroner worked together, what a collaborative environment it was. How the coroner—both Harrison Walker for the last five years and the coroner who preceded him—had been vital to solving open cases. Fenway found it surprisingly easy to talk to the sheriff, and she even felt some excitement about the investigations.

When they'd finished eating, the sheriff pushed his empty plate to the middle of the table. "The community will like this. They'll like *you*. And if we get this appointment done quickly, people might actually think we have our act together."

After they paid, they got back in the cruiser. When the car doors closed, their conversation, so animated in the restaurant, just died. Fenway watched McVie's hands tapping the steering wheel.

"So, uh, Sheriff," she said, trying to sound casual. "What kind of music do you like?"

"All kinds of stuff. Funk is probably my favorite. Parliament, Sly and the Family Stone, Curtis Mayfield."

Fenway narrowed her eyes at him. Was he just saying that? For all McVie knew, Fenway could be a classical violinist. Although that surely would have been revealed in the background check.

"Maybe ten years ago," McVie continued, "I went to Reno for the weekend with a few of my buddies from Fresno State. I couldn't win a blackjack hand to save my life, so I went to the box office to see who was playing—and it was the Godfather of Soul himself."

"Get out!" Fenway said, slapping McVie lightly on the shoulder. "James Brown?"

"Yep. I couldn't believe it, but they still had tickets left. So I go running to my buddies, super excited, but no. They want to go to a sports bar instead."

"Oh no," Fenway said. "What did you do?"

"I bought a ticket and went by myself."

"You went by yourself?"

"Yep. I never go by myself to anything—I don't go to movies by myself, I don't eat out by myself, nothing."

"Did you have a good time?"

He grinned. "It was *amazing*. I didn't have to worry about whether the other guys were enjoying themselves. No one made fun of my dancing. Or my off-key singing along to 'Cold Sweat.' I danced my ass off for three hours. I bought two T-shirts. It was fantastic. One of the best nights of my life."

"Really?"

"I mean, when my daughter was born, that was amazing, too. Better. But in a different way."

"And your wedding day."

McVie nodded, unsmiling. "Also in a different way."

Huh. Maybe that ring wasn't indicative of marital bliss. She tried to banish the thought from her mind.

"James Brown passed away about six months after that Reno show. I'm so glad I didn't go to a sports bar that night."

"You're lucky," Fenway said. "I never got to see James Brown."

McVie scoffed. "I bet you've seen your share of interesting concerts."

Fenway hesitated slightly and fidgeted with her sleeve. "I was always too busy with school. And then the hours in the ER and the clinic when studying for your master's? That doesn't really gel with concerts."

McVie looked over at her.

Could he see right through that lie? Could he tell that she never had the money to go to concerts? Dance clubs, yes. Especially when guys bought her drinks. But not hundred-dollar concerts.

McVie pulled into the apartment complex. "You know he never had a number one hit? The 'Macarena' was number one for three months straight, but James Brown never had a number one hit. That's a crime right there."

As they parked in Fenway's assigned spot, she saw her mother's dresser ascending the stairs. She remembered her mother using her good charcoals to number the bottom of each drawer. A lanky Latino man in jeans and a T-shirt was on one end, and a burly white guy with a long beard and plaid shorts was on the other, awkwardly trekking to the second floor.

This was really happening. She was on the verge of accepting a coroner position—in a county where coroners got shot.

What the hell was she thinking?

CHAPTER THREE

WITH SIX PEOPLE UNLOADING, THE TRUCK WAS EMPTY BEFORE lunchtime. In another couple of hours, the apartment met Fenway's definition of livable: bed assembled; dresser, sofa, dining table and chairs in place; boxes of linens and clothes in the bedroom; plates and silverware in the proper cabinets and drawers. The sheriff stepped out a few times, probably to get updates on the coroner's murder. Every time he stepped back in, he was somber for a few minutes before helping to put a nightstand together or carrying a box into the bedroom.

Fenway offered to get pizza and beer, but all of Ferris's people said they had to get back to the refinery.

Only the sheriff accepted. "Why don't we get pizza on the way to the coroner's office?"

"I'm not meeting the staff in sweats," she said. "Give me half an hour. I'll meet you at the Coffee Bean."

She wrapped her hair and showered, then pulled out some decent clothes: her black trousers weren't great but were at least no-iron. Paired with a crisp, pale-pink Henley top with a tab collar, they looked professional. She checked herself in the mirror; the ocean air had been kind to her skin but not her hair, and there was no time to fix it. She put on a pair of black-and-white flats and headed out the door into the hazy sunshine. The fog had finally burned off.

McVie was finishing a coffee in front of the Coffee Bean, and they both got in the cruiser and drove toward downtown.

"Do you have a car?"

Fenway shook her head. "I sold it before I left Seattle. I thought I'd buy a used one once I got here."

He nodded. "If you need it, the number 14 bus stops in front of the Coffee Bean every half hour or so. Drops you off right at City Hall."

"It's nice of you to assume I'll like the office enough to take the job."

"The Owner won't take no for an answer."

Fenway turned to look at McVie. "The what?"

"Oh." He stopped. "I guess I shouldn't call him that. A lot of people call him The Owner, capital O, because he owns so much in the county: the refinery, a few restaurants, a bunch of real estate—and that includes your apartment complex."

"The Owner," Fenway said, chewing the charged words. She looked at McVie's face, but there was no malice in it.

"Yeah."

She let it go. "I've called him worse when I was growing up."

Estancia was the seat of Dominguez County, and the quaint downtown had a more sterile feel than Fenway's neighborhood. The cruiser made a left from Broadway onto Fifth Street, which narrowed into a two-lane boulevard with angled parking on each side and a median with grass and small trees. Fenway looked out the windows. An ice cream shop, a music store, a tattoo parlor, a theater with a sign for *Joseph and the Amazing Technicolor Dreamcoat*, and a bakery before the government buildings appeared.

City Hall, with its white stone façade and thick, unadorned columns, sat back about two hundred feet from Fifth Street, behind a plaza that looked like a small amphitheater with a quarter-circle of cement benches cascading up in short steps. The plaza didn't look like a serious theater space, though Fenway could envision a local Shakespeare in the Park production there on a hot summer day.

On the other side of Fifth Street were a pair of utilitarian-looking four-story office buildings, reminiscent of Spanish-style architecture. The police car turned into a short parking structure after the second building, and Sheriff McVie pulled into a designated spot for law enforcement vehicles.

"Here we are."

They emerged from the parking structure. The air was still cool, but the sun warmed Fenway's face as McVie led them to a building across from City Hall.

"Hey," Fenway said, "we didn't get pizza."

"We will afterward. There's a great place on Fourth."

"Does it have good beer?"

"I'm glad you've got such intense focus on this job," McVie said, smirking. "I feel good about recommending someone whose priorities are aligned with the people of this county."

"You promised me food and then denied me," Fenway pointed out. "I'm not responsible for what I say when I'm hungry."

"Duly noted." He held open the front door for her and smiled. Yes, that crooked front tooth was definitely adorable. "The coroner's office is Suite 150. First door on the left."

She opened the door and found the office in full swing. A young white woman carried a stack of papers to an older black woman in the center of the office. The older woman wore the same dark uniform as McVie. Two phones rang at the same time, and a thin Latino man in a burgundy shirt typed furiously at a desk to Fenway's right. An older white man with a short white beard was on the phone in the back. He wore a gray sportscoat.

"Good, everyone's back from lunch," McVie said, following Fenway in. She looked around. The suite, about a thousand square feet, had a bar-height counter near the door serving as a reception area and four modern office-style desks behind it. Beyond the desk where the older woman sat, another door led to a small, glassed-in conference room.

Three six-foot-wide metal filing cabinets lined the wall between the back window and the reception area. Fenway's eye caught the bright yellow police tape across the closed wooden door of the glass-walled office at Fenway's left. She squinted. A faux-wood nameplate next to the door was inscribed with "H. Walker" and "County Coroner" in smaller letters underneath.

Ah. Even though the body was found two nights ago, they must be waiting for someone to go through Harrison Walker's work effects. Through the windows, the office looked elegant, with dark walls, a large mahogany desk with a huge flat-screen monitor, and a commanding yet comfortable-looking brown leather chair. It was a masculine office.

But why was it still sealed?

To be fair, it had only been a day and a half—if the coroner's body had been discovered late Sunday night, perhaps they hadn't gotten to it yet. Then it hit her. *Any homicide, suicide, accidental death—if it doesn't happen under medical supervision, your team will investigate it.*

But who investigates the death of the death investigator? Everyone in this office reported directly to the dead coroner. In the early stages, maybe they all had to be treated like suspects.

That's why she needed to get on board so quickly. They didn't just need her to fill a vacancy. They needed someone to investigate Walker's homicide.

Talk about trial by fire.

The sheriff interrupted her thoughts. "Most counties on this part of the coast have a combined sheriff/coroner position. We're the only county that has the two positions separated. It's been almost ten years now."

"Did this happen pre-James Brown or post?" Fenway said.

"The election was right after the show, in fact. They've been voting for both a sheriff and coroner ever since." He cleared his throat and addressed the room. "Everyone, sorry for the interruption, but I'd like to introduce you to Fenway Stevenson."

Fenway held up her hand in greeting.

McVie indicated the young man on the right side. "This is Miguel Castaneda, our paralegal."

The young man stood up and stepped forward. His burgundy long-sleeved dress shirt was a size too large, but his black-and-gray striped tie, black slacks, and Oxfords looked professional. He had short black hair, spiked a bit on top. "I go by Migs." He shook Fenway's hand, firmly but not too hard.

"Migs makes sure we're not doing anything to get us in trouble," McVie explained. "He's getting his law degree at night."

"So he can figure out how to get the criminals we catch off on a technicality, and make a shitload of money doing it," piped up a woman behind Fenway. It was the older black woman who'd been at the desk in the center. Her keen eyes twinkled; she was probably just giving Migs a hard time. Her features were striking: large but jaded eyes, dark umber skin, hair short and cropped close to her head.

"And this is Sergeant Desirée Roubideaux." McVie gritted his teeth a little.

Sergeant Roubideaux shook Fenway's hand, then turned to McVie. "I thought you were bringing in The Owner's daughter today."

"Shut *up*, Dez," Migs said quietly.

"Oh," she said, drawing the syllable out while looking Fenway up and down. "Sorry. I was expecting a white girl."

Fenway smiled sweetly at Roubideaux. "Yeah, so were my first boyfriend's parents."

Roubideaux laughed. "You're all right, Miss Stevenson. Sorry, you'll have to excuse me. I never met a black girl named after a baseball stadium before. It threw me off my game."

"Awesome," grunted McVie. "A paragon of decorum as always, Roubideaux. All right. Over there is Sergeant Mark Trevino."

The bearded man stood. The gray sportscoat was over a white polo shirt. "Nice to meet you," he said.

"And I'm Rachel." The short white woman behind the counter raised her hand. "I'm the coroner's assistant." She must have realized she was still sitting on a work stool and awkwardly got to her feet. She wore a crushed velvet blazer and dark slacks. She reached over the counter to shake Fenway's hand. At five feet tall, she was at least a head shorter than Fenway, with high cheekbones and light brown hair. She couldn't be a teenager, although her height and slender build made her appear so.

"And that's the office," McVie said. "Two sergeants to investigate, an assistant, and a legal advisor. It's small, but it's about par for the course for these coastal counties."

"Pleased to meet you all." Fenway smiled what she hoped came across as a heartfelt smile with a touch of sympathy. "And I'm sorry for your loss."

McVie cleared his throat and addressed the room. "As you might have heard, with the tragedy that hit us Sunday night, I'm obligated to appoint an acting coroner. I'm hoping I can convince Miss Stevenson to accept the appointment so the coroner's office can get back up to full speed." The sheriff turned back to Fenway. "And, as Sergeant Roubideaux has already clued you into, folks around here already know you're Mr. Ferris's daughter. So."

Is that a good thing or a bad thing?

Sergeant Roubideaux sniffed. "Some people might like a coroner who's so well-connected. Me, I like a coroner who doesn't come to official conclusions based on what other folks want to hear."

Fenway narrowed her eyes at Sergeant Roubideaux and tilted her head. "My father and I have barely seen each other for twenty years. I don't think I'll be rubber-stamping anything for *The Owner*, if that's what you're worried about."

Roubideaux snorted. Fenway wasn't sure if the snort was amusement or annoyance. Perhaps it was a little of both. "Even if you're not rubber-stamping what your daddy wants, will you be able to stand up for us? You can't be much older than Migs."

"I've been a nurse practitioner for almost five years in Seattle, I've studied forensics for the last two years, and I'm a fast learner. You're right; I don't have twenty years' experience, and yeah, this job will prob-ably be over my head—at first. But I was under the impression no one wanted to be appointed for a job they might not keep come November." Fenway stopped. She'd started to challenge Roubideaux in front of every-one, but no—she needed to strike the right balance between tough and fair. She turned toward the others in the room. "Listen, I don't want to go into a job where I'm in constant conflict with the team. I know for sure you've investigated a ton more homicides, suicides, and accidental deaths than I have, considering I've never investigated a single one outside of my classes." She looked at Roubideaux again. "If you—or anyone else in the office, for that matter—wants the job, I'll step aside."

"Hell no." Roubideaux was emphatic. "You couldn't pay me enough to sit in that office."

No one else said anything.

Sheriff McVie clapped his hands together. "This has been a real treat, everyone." He shot Roubideaux a disappointed look, and the sergeant pointedly looked away. "I hope we'll be back tomorrow."

"Thanks," Fenway said with a tight smile. "Nice to meet all of you."

"Listen," Rachel said, "we're meeting up for happy hour at Winfrey's right after work. Do you want to come too?"

"We're still doing that?" Dez said. "With everything that happened?"

"I think we should," said Rachel. "We can drink to his memory. So how about it, Miss Stevenson?"

Fenway looked at McVie who tilted his head to the side, then turned back to Rachel. "Absolutely. I'd love to join you."

"Is Piper coming, Migs?" Dez asked.

"Shut up," Migs mumbled.

"Cool," Rachel said. "You coming too, Mark?"

"Gotta check with Randy," Mark said.

"Oh, come on," Rachel said. "Isn't he on tonight?" She turned to Fenway. "Mark's husband is Pharaoh in *Joseph*. He absolutely *kills* 'King of My Heart.'"

Mark might have blushed a little.

"Okay," Dez said, "she doesn't even work here yet and already we're dragging her out drinking. This certainly bodes well, Sheriff." She winked at Fenway.

Everyone murmured goodbyes as Fenway and McVie left the coroner's suite.

McVie closed the door behind them. "All right?"

"To be honest, I wanted more time with them. See what makes them tick. But I can get that at happy hour."

"You're okay with them?"

"It's a nice enough group of people."

"Don't let Dez get to you. She hates everyone."

"I don't know." Fenway shrugged. "She says what she thinks."

McVie let out a chuckle. "If you mean she's a real pain in the ass, I agree."

"Oh, she wasn't looking to fight me or anything."

"It didn't look like she was getting ready to sing 'Kumbaya' either. Still, I thought you did well."

The two walked over to Pizzeria Santa Lucia on Fourth Street. At the counter, Fenway ordered a beer, a local pale ale made in Paso Querido. McVie ordered a Spello Special pizza for the two of them, and a Coke for himself. Fenway gave him the side-eye.

He raised the bottle. "Still on duty, officially."

Fenway and the sheriff sat down at one of the smaller tables—smaller, even though it was still a fairly large picnic bench with a cheap red-and-white tablecloth.

"Are you still interested in the appointment?"

"Yeah, I think so." Fenway put her hands flat on the table.

"Do you think you can supervise them?"

Fenway grinned. "Hell, why not? I'm a quick study. I'm sure there's a 'for Dummies' book I can buy or something." She lifted the beer to her lips.

"You haven't read your dad's book on management?"

She stopped mid-drink, then finished her swig before setting the pint glass back on the table.

"My father's book on management," she repeated, tasting her words.

"You do know your dad wrote a book on management, right? Pretty popular. Couple of business schools even teach it."

Fenway smiled.

"No?"

"No." Fenway tapped her fingers on the side of the pint glass. *I guess neither of us know very much about what the other's been up to.* "Have you read it?"

"I bought a copy."

They were both silent. Fenway turned sideways and propped her leg up on the bench. She could feel her calf and hamstrings stretch out. "You want me to investigate Mr. Walker's homicide, don't you?"

The sheriff exhaled loudly and sat back. He put his hands behind his head. Fenway noticed his soft eyes stare off into space for a minute. Finally, he nodded. "Everyone else has a conflict of interest."

"Sure. Everyone who works for him."

"Not just them," McVie said, resting his arms on the table. "All of the crime scene techs, both here and in San Miguelito County, were working with Walker on *something*. Open case files, cause-of-death consults. Something in one of those case files could point to the killer."

Fenway nodded. "Did he have any enemies?"

McVie hesitated. "That's the problem. *Everyone* hated him. That's why no one's done any of the initial investigative work."

"Like going through Walker's office."

"You noticed."

Fenway nodded. "So you need someone to fingerprint the whole office. Check against inventory for missing files or equipment." She put her leg down. "But I don't know my way around the department."

McVie folded his hands on the table. They looked strong, with thick fingers. The gold band was his only jewelry. "I'll be working with you."

"Don't you have a conflict of interest too?"

"Yes. But I seemed to hate him less than everyone else. And I guess I have a reputation as someone who follows the rules."

Fenway's eyes dipped to his wedding ring and quickly popped back up.

A server appeared with their pizza.

Fenway and McVie reached for a slice at the same time. Their fingers touched. Fenway glanced in McVie's eyes; a smile played at the corners of his mouth.

"All yours, Sheriff," she said with a flourish of her hand.

"Oh, no, I insist."

Fenway took a slice and put it on her plate. He took the next slice over.

"Why does everyone hate him?" Fenway asked.

McVie took a bite, but the pizza was hot, and he sucked in air to cool it. It looked painful but comical, and Fenway caught his eye and started to laugh.

"I'm trying to show you I'm down to earth," McVie said through the mouthful of pizza.

Fenway shook her head, her curls moving side to side. She set the pizza down to let it cool and wiped her mouth with her napkin.

She had to be careful. He was boyishly charming, and if he *did* have a good reputation in the department, no one would think of him as the killer.

Not that she had seen anything to make her think he'd be a suspect.

Still, the forensic classes were fresh in her mind. People loved to obfuscate the truth.

McVie swallowed with effort. "It's pretty simple, really." He took a sip of his drink. "He was a mean sonofabitch. Nasty. Told everyone they were doing everything wrong unless it was his idea." He shook his head. "I probably shouldn't say this, but I think he especially hated working with Dez and Miguel. He didn't want to hire either of them, but there was a committee, and they were by far the most qualified."

"Ah. Gotta be twice as good for half the respect."

"Well." McVie shifted in his seat but met Fenway's eyes. "I wish that weren't true, but in Walker's case, it probably was."

Fenway nodded.

"Oh, and I heard an earful when he found out Mark was gay."

"The guy sounds like a prince."

McVie nodded as he took another bite of pizza.

"Sheriff, let me ask you something."

"Sure."

"Everyone seems shocked that I'm black. Does my father not"—she hesitated and her breath hitched as she chose her words carefully—"talk about me?"

"Oh." McVie looked up at the light fixture above the table.

"Wow. You're figuring out how to tell me something I don't want to hear."

"It's not that," McVie said quickly. "He talks about you. But he doesn't —I don't know. No one gets a lot of details. I didn't even know you were a nurse." He started to take another bite. "Nurse practitioner."

Fenway nodded. "Okay. I get it."

McVie frowned. "I certainly don't get it. It's complicated, and Nathaniel Ferris keeps that part of his life to himself."

"Fair enough," Fenway said, her insides roiling. She touched her slice. It had cooled down enough to eat. "You think any of Walker's employees had something to do his murder?" she said before she took her first bite.

McVie shook his head. "Personally, no. But everyone who worked with Walker needs to be considered a suspect. At least until we establish more facts of the case."

"So nothing's been done? Two days and we're starting from scratch?"

McVie nodded. "Pretty much. We got the Park Police to search the area around his car. I decided to start with the phone and financial records for the office to see if Walker was having an affair or skimming money." He took a drink of his Coke. "The memorial service is Friday."

Fenway wiped her hand on her napkin. "So I guess we're doing this."

"Yes." McVie took the final bite of his slice and stared thoughtfully into space. "I expect some people won't like it. They'll say it's nepotism, the daughter of one of the most powerful men in the county."

"It *is* nepotism."

McVie picked up a second slice and held it in the air a moment. "It's a favor for your dad."

"The Owner. And now he owes you one."

He swallowed and wiped his fingers. "I don't know what to tell you, Fenway. You're the only person in a hundred-mile radius who didn't hate Harrison Walker."

Including you. Fenway nodded and grabbed another slice, watching McVie.

CHAPTER FOUR

McVie went with Fenway to drop off the rental truck. He waited with her while the paperwork that "will just take a second" took fifteen minutes. McVie cracked jokes and talked about books. He was a fan of spy novels and political intrigue, which, while not Fenway's preferred genre, was a lot better than not reading at all.

On the way back to her apartment, McVie told Fenway he'd get everything prepped for the appointment at City Hall the next day—forms for her to sign, applications to fill out. When he dropped her off, she put her hand on his shoulder and thanked him. She hoped it came off as genuine as she felt. It was all happening fast, but she could hardly ask for a better situation.

She started to get out of the car when he stopped her. "Know how to get to Winfrey's?"

She shook her head.

"The number 14 bus I was telling you about? Picks you up right in front of the Coffee Bean. Get off at the stop after City Hall. Winfrey's is across the street. Old Victorian building. They painted it bright aqua. You can't miss it."

"Thanks, Sheriff."

He winked at her. "You'll do great." He reversed out of the space and drove off.

She took the stairs slowly, head swimming with the possibilities. A new job using the forensic techniques she had been learning for the past year and a half. She unlocked her door and was met with the unfamiliar sight of her new apartment. Two boxes labeled *Clothes* and *Office* sat in the hallway.

She opened the office box and pulled out cords and cables, then lifted the computer monitor and the minitower out, and had everything powered up in fifteen minutes. She found Stotsky's business card on the kitchen counter, and logged into the Wi-Fi. Within a few minutes, she had the number 14 bus schedule, and she pulled two-fifty in quarters out of her purse. The 4:50 bus would put her at Winfrey's a few minutes after five.

———

McVie had been right: the garish aqua color was beaconlike across from the bus stop. A handful of customers sat at the bar, and the entire coroner's office team—even Sergeant Trevino—gathered around the corner of the bar, with a couple of appetizer platters between them. Rachel caught Fenway's eye and waved.

"One more!" she said to the bartender.

"Hey everyone," Fenway said. "What are we drinking?"

"A toast," Sergeant Trevino said soberly. "Shots of Johnnie Walker to remember Harrison Walker."

"And it's Johnnie Walker Red," Dez said, raising her shot, "because he was a cheap bastard."

"And because they didn't have any whiskey called Racist Asshole," Migs said quietly.

"Hear, hear," said Rachel. The bartender gave her the extra shot and she handed it to Fenway.

They all drank.

"Was he really that bad," Fenway said to Dez, making a face at the harsh taste of the cheap scotch, "or are you all just heartless jerks?"

"Oh, Fenway," Dez said, putting her arm around her shoulders, "can't it be both?"

"You know the plan is for me to be your boss, right?"

"I'm not worried. We're union, and you'll be gone in six months. Have a spring roll." Dez handed Fenway the plate and laughed. "Seriously, though, you would have hated Walker too. Nothing we did was ever good enough. He wanted to review everything we did."

"Especially the legal stuff," Migs added. "Walker didn't have a clue about the law, but he was always second-guessing me."

"The last coroner's assistant quit," Rachel ventured.

"HR never wants to intervene," Dez said. "Mark and I were sick of it. We thought Walker was going to get unseated in last year's election, but with your daddy's money, he pulled out the win over the eye doctor."

The team began to regale Fenway with stories about Harrison Walker, and Rachel called for another round.

If any of these people had been involved in Walker's death, would they really be insulting him like this? Fenway looked around at their faces.

They might. Everyone was telling war stories. The killer might tell them too, so as not to stick out.

She watched Rachel wave the bartender down. Maybe she should be on top of her game tonight. "Cranberry and soda for me," Fenway said. "I've got a long night of unpacking ahead of me."

"The coroner is dead," Mark toasted. "Long live the coroner!"

After they had another round—everyone but Fenway with another shot of Johnnie Walker Red—the stories got a bit rowdier.

Mark told Fenway about the time Walker made a sexual joke to a female server at a catered event.

Migs started a story about Walker calling him names during an annual review, but his smile faltered. Dez rapidly changed the subject to another story: Walker realized he was late to a golf game, and as he ran out of his office with his bag, he tripped over his untied shoelaces and landed on his backside, right in front of Migs. Walker blamed the departed assistant for not letting him know how late it was.

The air had gone out of the room. Dez stared into space with a firm jaw, tapping her fingers on the table. Migs sat on his stool with his shoulders slouched. Only Rachel ordered a third shot—it might have been more than that if she'd started before Fenway arrived. Fenway glanced around at the group. Walker had disrespected each of them. HR had done nothing.

Mark got up and pushed his stool back. "I think I can get a last-minute ticket to see *Joseph* tonight. They usually don't sell out on Tuesdays."

"How many times have you seen that stupid show?" Dez said.

"Oh, be quiet, Dez. You're just jealous of how hot Randy looks in the shirtless Elvis costume."

Dez cracked up. "Yep, that's right, Mark, you caught me. Jealous of your man." She looked at her watch. "All right, happy hour's over anyway. You have fun with your Pharaoh Elvis. Wait, lemme walk out with you."

When Dez and Mark had left, Migs close behind them, Rachel hopped her five-foot frame off the barstool and stood up a little unsteadily.

"You okay?" Fenway said.

"That last shot was probably not the best idea," Rachel said. "I, uh, may need to sober up a little before I drive home."

"I took the bus. I could drive your car back to your place if you want."

"Oh, no, I couldn't ask you to do that."

"I'm offering. Come on, at my place I have to unpack another ten boxes. Give me a reason to procrastinate."

Rachel paused. "Okay."

Rachel led the way to her car behind Winfrey's. She pulled a key fob from her purse and handed it to Fenway.

"BMW?"

"Yeah. The silver one right there."

Fenway unlocked the car and got in. The leather-wrapped steering wheel was delicious underneath her fingertips. She looked for where to insert the key fob.

"Just push the button," Rachel slurred.

"Oh." She pushed the button, but nothing happened.

"You gotta put your foot on the brake first, silly. You sure you can drive?"

"*You* sure this isn't a spaceship?"

The engine hummed, the electricity pulsing from her fingertips all the way to her toes. She backed out of the space, then accelerated onto the main road.

"Easy, tiger," Rachel said through a giggle. "You must be used to driving cars with weak-ass engines." The speedometer already showed 45.

"Sorry."

"No worries. Dylan does the same thing." She yawned, then stifled a belch. "So you're gonna wanna get to Broadway. Then turn up toward the mountains."

Fenway was itching to punch the accelerator and see what the car could really do, but all the stories about Walker and the ruined mood at Winfrey's pulled like a weight at her brain. "So, you didn't get along with Walker either, huh?"

"It's stupid," Rachel said. "This whole thing is stupid. Broadway is your, uh, second right. Maybe third."

"You were his assistant, though. Did he get any weird mail? Anyone *really* hate the guy?"

"Not that I saw," Rachel said. "He opened his own mail, though. Para-noid, that's what I think. And you know, he hated everyone else a lot more than they hated him."

"Oh. Just one of those general curmudgeon types."

"If you mean 'asshole,' then yes."

As Fenway turned right on Broadway, Rachel sat up straight and put her hand on the dash. Fenway glanced over. "You okay?"

"Sure, sure. I just didn't think we were at Broadway yet. My turn is about a mile up. Make a left on Scarlet Oak Drive."

"Is it at a light?"

"Uh—no. There's a Tacos Amigos on the left just before the turn, though."

"Tacos Amigos? Is that a good place?"

"Their salmonella is delicious." Rachel made a face.

Silence.

Questions flooded Fenway's mind. If Walker had been killed because of something at work, wouldn't he have been killed closer to the office? A dark road in the middle of the night suggested that he didn't want people to know who he was meeting. Maybe Walker was having an affair. She should look at his work calendar—maybe he had put something on it.

A question was out of her mouth before she could stop it. "What do you think Walker was doing out on a dark road so late?"

Rachel sighed. "Fenway, I know they're hiring you to investigate his murder, but I have no idea, okay?"

"You didn't keep his calendar?"

"It's not like he'd have created an Outlook calendar event for *drug deal at the state park*."

"Right. Sorry." Hmm. Was Rachel just joking, or did she suspect it *was* a drug deal?

"There's the Tacos Ami-*Gross*," Rachel said. "Get in the turn lane."

The Scarlet Oaks Townhomes were narrow, two-story apartments with paint and siding mimicking separated buildings. There was an empty parking space right in front of number 19, and Fenway drove the BMW in.

They got out, and Fenway locked the car, reaching out to hand the keys over. "Here you go, Rachel. Hopefully I'll see you soon if this all works out."

"Sorry I snapped at you about the calendar thing. I know you're just doing your job."

"You just lost your boss. You were probably closer to him than anyone. I should've been more understanding."

"Come on, you heard us at happy hour. No one's that broken up about it." Rachel cleared her throat and took the keys. "Thanks for the ride. How are you getting home?"

"An Uber, I guess."

"Want to wait inside? Dylan's out for the evening."

"Your roommate?"

Rachel laughed. "My husband, boss lady. Didn't I tell you I was married?" She waved her hand at Fenway as she staggered to the front door of apartment 19. "I know, I know. I'm too young to be married. Sheesh."

Rachel got the key in the lock on her second try and opened the door. Inside the townhouse, stairs led up to the left of the door. A small tiled entry opened into a good-sized living room.

"You play?" Fenway said, motioning to the video game console on the floor in front of the television.

"Sometimes. Not often. Dylan plays with his brother."

Fenway looked at the pictures on the walls: a Georgia O'Keeffe print above the sofa, three small framed pictures of Rachel and her groom in front of—what? A Las Vegas chapel?

"Thanks for inviting me to happy hour, by the way. It was fun." Fenway smiled at Rachel, who, for several seconds, wouldn't lift her eyes from the floor. "I—I didn't mean it was *fun*. I know Walker was just killed. Sorry. That came out wrong."

Rachel burst into tears.

"Oh, hey. Hey, hey." Fenway walked awkwardly to Rachel, who leaned into her, sobbing.

Fenway had no idea what to do. Finally, she put her arms around Rachel's shoulders and waited for her to regain control. It took a minute or two of the awkward embrace before Rachel's sobs started alternating with deep breaths and sniffles.

"Ugh. Sorry. I'm so sorry." Rachel righted herself and wiped her eyes with her hand.

"That's okay." Fenway pulled a tissue out of her purse.

"No. No, it's not. It was unprofessional. I just met you and you're going to be my boss."

"It really is all right." Fenway didn't know what else to say.

Rachel sat down on the sofa. "Okay, I guess now I pretty much have to tell you what happened. Why I'm so upset. And if you do become coroner and start investigating Mr. Walker's death, you're going to find out anyway."

Fenway's eyes widened. She'd hoped to get a name from Rachel of an appointment that didn't belong in the calendar or a closed-door meeting with someone Rachel didn't expect in the office. This might be bigger.

Rachel took a deep breath. "He kept harassing me at work." She paused. Bit her lip. "*Sexually* harassing me at work." She looked down at the floor. "First it was some flirtatious talk, and I didn't really think anything of it because he's married, and he's so much older than I am, and I thought he'd get the hint I wasn't interested, and I thought he was being a creep." She paused. "But it kept getting worse."

She took a deep breath and looked up, focusing halfway across the room.

"He kept at it, and he started asking me out. And I kept saying, 'Mr. Walker'—and he kept saying, 'call me Harrison,' and I never did because I never wanted him to think I had any interest—and I kept saying, 'Mr. Walker, you're a married man. I'm a married woman. And besides, I don't date co-workers.' But then asking for dates turned into asking me away for the weekend."

"Wait. Away for the weekend when you said no to a date?"

"I know. *I know.* And he left me a silver necklace with an opal pendant on it, sitting on my desk. That's my birthstone. And I walked into his office and said, 'Mr. Walker, I really cannot accept this,' and he said, 'Rachel, I'm sure I don't know what you're talking about,' and refused to take it back. I looked under it to see if there was a card from the jeweler, so I could return it and he could get a refund. But underneath the box was a hotel keycard with a room number and a time on it."

Fenway made a face. "Ick."

"Yeah, ick. Yeah, *ICK*. And I went to HR, and Lana—Lana Cassidy, she's on the third floor—she told me she couldn't do anything without proof, and I'm like, 'He gave me a hotel keycard, it's right here.' And she's like, 'I'm sorry, there's nothing I can do.'"

She looked at her hands. "So I set up a webcam on my computer. Clipped it to the top of my monitor. Started recording stuff all the time, whenever he was around. Because I didn't think he was going to stop." She looked at Fenway defiantly. "And he didn't stop."

Fenway nodded. *Of course he didn't stop. They never stop.*

"So about three weeks ago, we had a murder-suicide out by Cactus Lake," Rachel continued. "A crappy motel out there. Drugs, parties, prostitutes. Anyway, the murder scene was messy. Walker had to go back and forth with the lab before he could finish the paperwork. By the time it was done, it was the end of the month." Her lip curled. "But he *insisted* the paperwork be filed by midnight on the thirtieth. I argued with him. We've never had an issue like that before. End of December, maybe. Never April. But Walker insisted I work late to finish.

"I cancelled plans with Dylan, and Walker left the office around five thirty. By six fifteen I was alone in the place. Then around seven, just when I was entering the last page of the report, I heard a car in the parking lot.

"A minute later, I hear the outside door, and I know, I just know it's him. So I turn on the webcam. He comes in, and he has this nasty, determined look on his face.

"I say to him, 'Mr. Walker, if you're here to help me with the filing, I'm just about finished, unless you want to take this up to the third floor.'

"He says, 'Don't play with me, Rachel. We both know what I'm here to help you with.'" Rachel raised her head and glared across the room without focusing on anything. "Then he comes over and he's *on* me."

Rachel turned her head away from Fenway. "He pulls my blouse open, he bites my neck." She shuddered. "I scream for him to get off me, but he puts his hand between my legs. He tells me I'll like it. He commands me to relax. He says no one has excited him this much in years, like it's some sort of *compliment*. I yell 'no' in his ear, and that surprises him, but he knocks my chair over with me still in it, and then he pins my arms to the ground.

"So I kick him. I get his knee, or his shin, or whatever, and it makes him let go of my right arm. Then I clock him in the face as hard as I can, and he's off me enough where I can get up."

"I get across the desk from him, and I grab my purse, and I tell him to stay the hell away from me. He's bleeding from his cheek where I hit him, and he pulls himself up and says, 'Don't bother to come in Monday, you whore.' Then he spits at me, like full-on spits, and tells me to get out. And I got out. I got out of there fast."

Rachel's voice was calm, but it broke a little as she finished her story.

Fenway was quiet.

But inside her head, it was loud.

She remembered being held down too, not being able to get away. She remembered the same *ick-ICK* feeling.

Freshman year. Her Russian Lit professor.

Fenway blinked and saw his office carpet close up. Face down on his floor, she felt him licking her face as he pushed her dress up.

Fenway blinked hard.

"I got out of there," Rachel said softly, "and I came back here. And I couldn't sleep. I came downstairs—so I wouldn't wake Dylan up. And I watched TV until the sun came up. I made myself a pot of coffee, and then I went to Wal-Mart and bought myself a USB drive. And I drove back to the office, and I copied the recording from the webcam. Then I got out of there again. I didn't know what I was going to do. I wanted to tell someone, but I didn't know who to tell. I didn't want to tell Dylan. I didn't want to tell my dad. I didn't want to tell anyone."

Rachel paused. "I didn't even want to tell Lana. But I knew I had to. I didn't think she would be on my side; I thought she'd want me to go away. But I wasn't going to let him do this to anyone else. Plus, I had it all recorded. The camera was centered on my chair, so you can see the whole thing. You can't see me when I'm on the floor, but you can hear me yelling 'no.' And you can't see me when I went around the other side of the desk, but you can hear him loud and clear telling me off. It's as airtight a sexual harassment case as you can get."

"Sexual assault."

Rachel's head tilted. "What?"

"Sexual assault. He tried to rape you. This isn't him telling a dirty joke in the office. This is a full-on sexual assault case, not sexual harassment. He would have gone to jail."

"I don't think he would have gone *anywhere*. He's too powerful."

Fenway curled her lip slightly and nodded.

"Anyway, I started thinking of all these different scenarios. Like in movies. If Lana had said, 'Is this the only copy?' and if I said 'yes,' maybe she would have smashed the drive up because she wouldn't want the county to get sued. So, I went back to Wal-Mart, and I got two more USB drives. I took them home, copied the video onto them. I kept one of them here, in the junk drawer in the kitchen."

"In the kitchen?"

"I wanted to have access to that recording. I wanted to keep it close."

"You didn't think Dylan would find it in the kitchen?"

"So what if he had? It's a USB drive in a junk drawer. No way would he ever think to see what's on there."

"You don't have a safe or anything?"

"Yeah, we have a fire safe where we keep our birth certificates and passports, but if I had put the USB drive in there, Dylan would have been like, 'What's a USB drive doing in the safe?' *Then* he would have been curious enough to see what was on there."

Fenway nodded.

"I kept the second one in my purse, and the third one is in my glove compartment. I want to be able to get to them wherever I am." Rachel sighed. "I was a mess all day Saturday. I canceled plans to go out with Kelly and Jordan, and I watched TV like a zombie. Dylan was kind of mad at me because I wouldn't really talk. I wound up taking a sleeping pill around 2 A.M. I woke up a little past noon on Sunday, and I decided I'd go into Lana's office first thing Monday morning. I thought about what I'd say, how I'd insist she take action, or I'd sue. I even thought of telling her it was the only copy just to see how she'd react. I know it sounds crazy."

Fenway shook her head. "It doesn't sound crazy." She was remembering her sleepless nights after her professor raped her. Wondering if she was going to get attacked again. Wondering how she'd ever make it through the rest of the semester in his class, as it was after the drop date; how could she be so stupid? Wondering if she could afford to take an F— or maybe she could just show up for the final and try to salvage a C. Wondering what *she* did to make him do that. "It doesn't sound crazy at all."

"You're sweet," Rachel said, "but it *totally* sounds crazy." She took a deep breath. "I forced myself to go out on Sunday night, just to be with people, not alone with my thoughts. But I couldn't go to sleep again. I couldn't keep my mind focused, not on a book, not on TV. Then Dez called me about midnight and told me Mr. Walker had been found dead, and could I come into the office by six to help her out. So I did."

"What did Lana say about the USB drive?"

Rachel shook her head. "I didn't talk to Lana. I didn't give anyone the USB drive. So I haven't told anyone about what Mr. Walker did to me on Friday night."

"Until now?"

"Yes, until now."

Fenway took a deep breath. This was a lot to tell a stranger. A lot to tell your new boss. "Rachel—"

"I'm sorry," she blurted out. "I don't know why I told you."

"Because you needed to tell someone, and I'm a good person to tell."

And then Rachel's eyes went wide. "Oh, God. I'm a suspect."

Fenway paused. "Probably. And you might have to tell that story again. Exactly the way you told me."

Rachel was fighting back tears again. "I don't know if I can do it."

"You've already shown me how strong you are. You can do it."

Rachel nodded, a tear running down her cheek. She swallowed hard to regain her composure.

"Whoever investigates this is going to ask you if you own a gun. Do you own a gun?"

"Yes. My dad gave me his Smith & Wesson Model 41 when I moved out on my own," she answered. "I don't usually carry it with me, though. It's on the top shelf of my closet."

"Okay. I don't know what kind of gun was used to kill the coroner, but I got the impression it was a larger caliber weapon."

Rachel paused, chewing her lip. "You know guns?"

"Probably not enough yet."

Rachel swallowed hard.

Fenway stood up. "Listen—do you need anything? I mean, it's only been a couple of days since it happened, and—I don't know. He did a horrible thing."

Rachel was silent.

"The county has a good health plan, right? You can see someone. Like a therapist. I bet it would help to talk to someone about this."

"Maybe."

Fenway shook her head. "No, not maybe. You need to talk to someone about this. A *professional* someone."

"Maybe," she repeated.

They had come to the end of the conversation, but Fenway wasn't sure she should leave.

"Do—do you want me to stay until Dylan gets home?"

"Oh, God, no," Rachel said. "That would just invite more questions. That's the last thing I need."

"Okay, I'll get going then."

"I'm sorry, Fenway," Rachel repeated. "I don't know why I told you all that."

"No, no. Look, if you need to talk to anyone about it some more, you can talk to me." She grabbed a pen and a notepad off the coffee table. "Here," she said, scrawling her cell phone number on the notepad. "Any time." She handed it to Rachel, who took it gingerly.

Fenway walked to the door. "I mean it. Any time."

Rachel walked her out onto the front step. "Okay."

Rachel went back inside and closed the door. She opened it again. "Wait, did you call your Uber?"

"It's not far. I like walking."

Fenway started for home, wishing with each footfall that her Russian Lit professor's face were underneath, wishing that her heel were denting, grinding, smashing it.

She remembered leaving his office when it was over, determined not to cry in front of him, not even registering the saccharine compliments he was giving her except as fresh stab wounds. She ran out into the plaza between the English department offices and the library. Her phone had buzzed in her purse—at least she remembered to pick that up—and she saw *Mom* on the screen. Her mother was the exact person she needed to talk to, but she froze. It went to voicemail.

She threw everything on her bed when she reached her dorm room, grabbed a towel and her toiletries, a pair of sweats and a t-shirt, and, even though it was five thirty in the afternoon, walked quickly down the hall into the showers. She turned on the water as hot as she could and pulled the curtain around the stall and used the rest of the bar of soap scrubbing herself. She stood under the showerhead, and she only vaguely realized the hot water wasn't good for her hair; she'd have to use her avocado oil and shea butter and maybe a wrap that night. She thought of how no one would ever believe her, and how her friends would wonder why she wasn't at dinner, and her mother would worry why she didn't return the call. She leaned her back against the cool tile and slid down until she was sitting on the floor, and she sobbed, trying to be quiet so no one would hear her.

She wondered what would have happened if she had owned a Smith & Wesson Model 41 back then. The weight of the gun in her hand, the adrenaline rush as she shot him in the back on a deserted country road, the satisfaction of seeing him dead at her feet.

Fenway shook her head and kept walking.

She arrived home as the sun dipped behind the horizon.

There were boxes to unpack, but Fenway paced around the apartment, unable to stop walking. If she'd had access to a Smith & Wesson back then, there would have been a job vacancy in Russian Lit the next day. She wouldn't have even been sorry. And had Rachel, perhaps, done what Fenway had only dreamed of doing? And if so, what would Fenway, as the investigator—

But no. She didn't even have the job yet. It wasn't up to her to investigate anything.

Officially.

In the middle of the living room, Fenway stopped pacing and sighed. She eyed all the boxes, some with clothes, one with books, one with linens, and started unpacking.

Fenway kept working until every box was empty, breaking only to grab an unsatisfying microwave burrito and a six-pack of microbrew at the convenience store. Three of her mother's paintings were hanging on the walls. Her toiletries and cosmetics sat in organizers under the sink in the bathroom, and her clothes hung in the closet.

She was breaking down the last moving box just past ten thirty when her phone rang. She hoped it wasn't her father. McVie's name flashed on her screen.

"Hey, Sheriff," she answered, a little too much enthusiasm in her voice.

"Hey, Fenway," he said. "Am I calling too late?" His voice cracked slightly. Was that nervousness?

"Nope. Just finished unpacking." She pushed the folded cardboard flat and walked into the kitchen, grabbing the open beer on the counter.

"Can you be at City Hall at seven thirty tomorrow morning?"

Disappointment panged in her chest that he was calling about business—but why else would he be calling? "Oh—the appointment's going through that early?"

"Not exactly." McVie exhaled loudly. "You have to answer questions in front of the Dominguez County Board of Supervisors."

Fenway stopped in her tracks, halfway to her bedroom. "You're just telling me this now?"

"It's been tradition for them to question any county appointee."

She tried to keep the frustration out of her voice. "You could have mentioned this at any point earlier today. The pizza place. The coroner's office. You helped me move furniture for three hours."

"I thought, given the circumstances, we might be able to skip it." McVie coughed lightly. "But one member of the board wouldn't let it go. So they called a special session for tomorrow morning."

Fenway shook her head. He *must* have found out about this earlier.

Just like her father, McVie wasn't giving her a chance to say no. She'd already tried to wrap her head around why Walker was on that dark road that night. She'd already tried to assess motives. Asked questions. She already saw herself in the job. This wasn't fair.

"Sheriff," she said evenly, "people usually have more time to prepare for confirmation hearings."

"I—It's not a confirmation hearing."

"Really? Sounds like they've got veto power."

"Well—not as such. If they have grave concerns, they can discuss them with me."

"But you're expected to follow their recommendation. So it's just semantics." She drained her bottle of beer. She had taken too long to drink it and it was warm. "Do I need to be worried?"

"No."

"Are you sure?"

"I just need to prep you. One councilmember is particularly wary of your dad. I can guess a few of the tougher questions you might get. Half an hour, forty-five minutes, tops."

"Are you suggesting we prep tonight?"

"Let's do an early breakfast. You liked Jack and Jill's, right?"

"Yeah," Fenway said grudgingly. The smoked salmon benedict had been fantastic.

"Can I pick you up at six?"

"You're paying."

"I know. I really didn't think we'd need to meet them." He paused. "So —see you at six?"

"You know, Sheriff, you can tell me uncomfortable stuff. Bad news. I can take it. But if I don't have all the information to make my decision, I start losing my trust in people."

He paused. "I'm sorry. I should have let you know it was a possibility."

"Is there anything else I need to know that you're not telling me? Was Walker sleeping with your wife? Did he convince you to make a bad investment? Kick over your sandcastle when you were a kid?"

"There's nothing else. And this is just a formality. It might be uncomfortable, but it's a formality."

"I expect full disclosure from now on, Sheriff. Don't hide things from me just because you think I don't want to hear them. That's a great way to piss me off."

"Yeah, I can see that."

"Glad I made myself clear. I'll see you at six."

PART TWO
WEDNESDAY

CHAPTER FIVE

Fenway gasped and sat up in bed, her heart pounding.

Her phone was beeping at full volume, and she fumbled for it in the darkness. She almost hit snooze before remembering she was meeting McVie for breakfast.

Reluctantly, she looked at the screen. 5:01 A.M. She swung her legs out from under the covers and padded her way to the bathroom.

She was ready a full five minutes before she saw McVie's headlights on the road.

"You're bright-eyed and bushy-tailed this morning," he said when she opened the door of the cruiser.

"Aw, thanks, mister!" She curtsied to him playfully. "You going to tell me the early bird gets the worm too?"

"I was going to say you clean up good." McVie's voice was a little gruff. Fenway glanced down at her outfit. She didn't consider herself especially dressed-up: knee-length gray wool skirt and matching blazer with a navy blouse. She was trying to look professional, down to her bone-colored flats, but maybe McVie was trying to make up for dropping the surprise on her last night.

No fog blanketed the town today, and the sky was brightening as they drove to Jack and Jill's. Fenway was quiet in the car, still smarting from the miscommunication, but felt her mood lift as the server poured coffee into her mug.

After they ordered, McVie pulled out a manila folder and started reviewing the councilmembers with Fenway.

Of the five county supervisors, two were retirees, including the mayor of Estancia, Alice Jenkins. She was the elder statesman of the group, the first black judge appointed in Dominguez County. McVie said she was serving her fourth term as mayor. Fenway bit her tongue; her research the night before said it was her fifth.

The youngest member was Barry Klein, a forty-year-old optometrist —and the one who didn't trust Fenway's father. He'd run for coroner and lost, and everyone expected him to run again in November.

"Try to casually mention to Dr. Klein that you haven't seen your father in years," McVie said. "He'll probably still try to hammer your background and probably your age. I'll bet you a hundred bucks he tries to pivot to his own election campaign."

"He should have just taken the appointment," Fenway said.

"Walker had the gall to get murdered at an inopportune time for Dr. Klein," McVie said, grinning.

"He always votes against anything related to Ferris Energy," Fenway stated. "He's going to do whatever he can to disrupt me."

"The board knows he's biased," McVie said, eying her. "And how do you know how he votes?"

"There's this thing called the internet." Fenway smiled and sprinkled some hot sauce on her eggs. "So what are the other potential issues?"

"Well—not a lot, really."

"Oh." Fenway shifted in her seat. "This was a warning about Barry Klein, then."

"He's the one demanding this meeting," McVie said. "I thought the other councilmembers would shut him down, but I guess they figured if they let him spout off now, he'd shut up later." McVie scoffed. "As if Barry Klein ever shuts up."

————

They arrived at City Hall early and had fifteen minutes to kill. In the lobby area outside the council chambers, Fenway took a seat on a wooden bench, and McVie paced in front of her. The sharp scent of pine cleaner tickled her nose. "Sit down," she said. "You're going to be on your feet for most of the meeting, aren't you?"

"Probably too much coffee," McVie said, but the worry lines at the corners of his eyes had deepened since the day before. Was it simply Klein's reaction, or was there was something *else* he wasn't telling her?

He passed in front of her, back and forth. This had to stop.

"You still going to concerts?" she asked.

"What?"

"Concerts. You told me about James Brown, but I didn't hear about anything lately."

"Oh." McVie stopped pacing and sat on the bench next to her. "Amy and I went to a country show last month at the fairgrounds in P.Q. There were five or six bands there. Amy got into it, sang along to most of the songs."

"You don't like country?"

McVie shrugged. "Hard not to hear it around here, but it's not really my thing."

"Amy—is that your wife?"

"Oh—yeah. It'll be eighteen years in June. She runs a real estate firm. Pretty successful one, at that."

Fenway nodded. McVie's tone was flat—did a happy man talk about his wife that way?

Something behind Fenway caught McVie's eye, and he flashed a look of recognition. She turned her head. Her father was coming into the lobby, taking off his sunglasses. The dark brown hair she remembered had changed to salt and pepper, and he had laugh lines around his eyes. Other than that, he didn't look much different from when her mother had taken her away from Estancia twenty years before.

Nathaniel Ferris had on a stylish and expensive-looking gray suit—the color identical to Fenway's skirt and blazer. His navy blue dress shirt, open at the collar and without a tie, matched the dark blue tank Fenway wore.

He was followed by a tall, heavyset man in a dark suit, white shirt, and a dark gray tie, the pair reminding Fenway of a Mafioso and his body-guard. The bodyguard looked familiar. She turned back toward McVie.

"Sorry," he muttered.

Fenway closed her eyes for a moment and took a deep breath. She turned around to face her father.

"Hi, Dad!" Her voice went up half an octave, and, she hoped, was enthusiastic and warm.

"Fenway!" Ferris opened his arms wide.

She stepped next to him and turned her shoulder, giving him a side hug.

"Sorry I haven't seen you since you arrived."

"It's okay, Dad." She stepped away from him and grinned. "I know how busy you are with work. Hey!" She pointed at his suit. "I see you got my message on what to wear today. We still doing the hip-hop dance routine for the board of supervisors?"

Confusion came over Ferris's face until he realized she was joking about their matching outfits. Then he laughed.

"See, Rob?" Nathaniel Ferris turned to the giant next to him, and Fenway suddenly recognized her apartment building manager from Monday night. "I told you Fenway was something else. Fenway, you remember Rob Stotsky from the night you drove in."

Rob Stotsky put out his large hand and Fenway shook it as firmly as she could.

"Good to see you again," he said.

"Absolutely," Fenway said. "When you said you worked with my father, I didn't realize it was this closely."

"All of my building managers report up into Rob's team," Ferris said. "He runs Ferris Energy's security department."

"The apartment building managers report into corporate security?"

"Safety is half their job," Stotsky said. "Camera maintenance, gates, changing door locks, making sure cars don't get broken into."

"If people don't feel secure, they rent somewhere else," Ferris said. "Rob and I have a meeting downtown in about half an hour, and I thought I'd come here and see you. The board is gonna love you."

"Thanks, Dad." She felt Ferris put his arm around her back. The smile she had plastered on was taking more effort than she thought. "I want to say thank you for getting me into the apartment." She stepped out from under his arm. "And I know we need to catch up."

His eyes softened. "Happy to do it, and yes, I'd love to catch up. Are you free for dinner?"

"Sure. Dinner."

He smiled broadly, then clapped his hands together. "Okay, I've got to get to my meeting." He put his sunglasses back on, patted Rob Stotsky on the shoulder, and turned to go out the same way he came in. Stotsky followed him out the door.

Fenway exhaled. Her heart was racing. She hoped it didn't show.

McVie was looking at her with an unusual gleam in his eye. "*Who* was that?"

"Who was what? You know my father. Don't you know his head of security too?"

"No, I wasn't talking about *them*. I was talking about *you*. You transformed into a different person."

"Please." Fenway rolled her eyes. "You of all people should know how my father wants people to deal with him."

"Yes, I do. You're going to do just fine."

"So, is that what you were worried about, pacing all over the place? My father coming in to 'support' me?"

He hesitated. "Yes. I told him if he wanted to see you, to do it *after* the board of supervisors meeting."

She cocked her head. "This is one of those things you should have told me, Sheriff. I need to know if my father is planning to see me. He has very different expectations of me than I have of myself."

"I'm sorry. You're right."

"That's twice in twelve hours, Sheriff. You sure there's nothing else I need to know before I volunteer as tribute?"

Just then, the doors to the council chamber opened.

"Nothing else," McVie said. "I swear."

Fenway followed McVie inside. All five councilmembers were seated, looking down at her from the dais. At the front table, a plastic nameplate read "Sheriff Craig McVie" in embossed block letters, and next to that, a paper nameplate read "Fennway Stevenson," fresh off an inkjet printer.

Two of the supervisors gave a start when Fenway took the seat behind her nameplate. For twenty years she hadn't had to deal with that reaction, but in the last few days she had seen it from Stotsky, McVie, Dez, and now a couple of the county supervisors. How did so many people in town not know?

She grinned at the five supervisors. "Wow, aren't there any Red Sox fans here? *Fenway* only has one N." She chuckled lightly. The mayor, Alice Jenkins, gave her a wan smile. The thin man behind the "Dr. Barry Klein" nameplate narrowed his eyes at her and frowned.

The mayor called the special session to order and gave the floor to the sheriff. He read legalese from a set of papers in front of him, announcing his intent to appoint Fenway Stevenson in the position of county coroner until the next election.

"Thank you, Sheriff," Mayor Jenkins said. "Questions for Miss Stevenson?"

Barry Klein raised his hand.

The mayor looked at the other supervisors, then nodded. "Very well. Dr. Klein has the floor."

He pulled his microphone closer with a loud scratching sound. "Good morning, Miss Ferris."

Fenway paused. Oh. So that's how he was going to play this—openly hostile from the get-go. "It's Miss Stevenson. Good morning, Dr. Klein."

He paused for a moment and pushed his glasses up. "You have an interesting résumé."

Fenway looked at Dr. Klein expectantly.

"You went to junior college for two years," he continued. "Were your grades not sufficient to get into a four-year university out of high school?"

"Here we go," McVie muttered.

"My bank balance wasn't sufficient," Fenway replied. "I saved quite a bit of money by going to Cascades for two years."

"I see," Dr. Klein said. He turned the papers over. There was no other sound in the large room. "You'll have to forgive me," he finally said. "I confess I'm not familiar with Western Washington."

"It's a top-fifty BSN program," Fenway said. "Go Vikings."

He looked up. "I'm sorry?"

Fenway cleared her throat. "I said, 'Go Vikings.' The Western mascot."

"Ah," he said. "How did you do while you were there?"

"At Western? Top in my class. I gave the valedictorian speech at graduation."

"Hm." Dr. Klein flipped two pages.

"And now you're at Seattle University."

"Yes. Completing my master's degree in forensics."

"So you haven't finished the program."

"One more class. I start next week."

"Isn't your class in Seattle?"

"They have an online option for this class," Fenway said. She had been unsure about Dr. Klein's tone at first, but now she sensed he was fishing.

"To be honest, Miss Stevenson, I'm a bit concerned you haven't completed your degree yet. And I don't have a lot of confidence in online universities."

"Seattle University is a regular university, Barry," Alice Jenkins said. "Miss Stevenson said she's taking a single class online. There's a big difference."

"I'm not sure it's a difference that matters—if they offer classes on the web, they're an online university in my book."

Fenway took a deep breath. "Can I ask, is an advanced forensics degree a requirement for the position? Have the previous two coroners had one?" Fenway knew from her research the night before the answer was no—Harrison Walker had been an EMT before running for coroner. The previous coroner had been a monitor transport technician at Cottage Hospital in Santa Barbara. Before that, the position had been combined with the sheriff's office.

Dr. Klein shifted uncomfortably. "We're not talking about the previous two coroners. We're talking about you."

"Then let me be clear. An advanced forensics degree hasn't been required for anyone else, and it shouldn't be required for me."

"That judgment isn't up to you, Miss Ferris."

"My last name is Stevenson," Fenway said.

"Don't try to pretend you're someone you're not," Klein growled. "You're Nathaniel Ferris's daughter, and I'm insulted that you're trying to hide that fact from the supervisors."

"Barry," Mayor Jenkins said sharply.

Klein ignored her. "I'm deeply concerned that you're so close with Ferris Energy. That corporation controls enough of this town as it is." Klein put his hands flat on the desk, palms down. "When a powerful person has access to the coroner's office, procedures get overlooked. Policies get selectively enforced. Personal agendas take precedence over the rule of law."

Fenway could feel her blood pressure rise but breathed evenly, in for the count of ten, out for the count of ten, then looked up at Dr. Klein.

He stared back at her.

The seconds ticked by.

Klein leaned forward, fuming. "Are you going to answer the question?"

"You've asked no question," Fenway said. "It sounds like you're making a campaign speech, but you haven't asked me a single question since you inquired whether Seattle University was in Seattle."

"Watch yourself," Klein said. "Disrespect to the board won't be—"

"Ask a damn question, Barry," Mayor Jenkins said. "And watch *your* tone."

Barry Klein glared at the mayor, then cleared his throat.

"How can you assure us that you won't be prioritizing your father's corporate interests over the needs of the county?"

Fenway sat up straight. "Nathaniel Ferris and I have barely spoken more than a couple of times a year for the last two decades," she said.

"I don't believe that," Klein interrupted.

"Check phone records, email records, whatever you want. In fact, if you have so many concerns, Dr. Klein, I'm surprised you haven't done so already. I've had less exposure to the 'Nathaniel Ferris agenda' than any other person in Dominguez County."

Klein turned to the other supervisors. "This is ridiculous. We cannot allow Nathaniel Ferris to make a laughingstock of our county government. I don't care what she says. She moved into one of his apartment buildings. She probably still gets an allowance."

Fenway crossed her arms. *I didn't see a dime.*

"You should take the job instead, Dr. Klein," Fenway said.

Klein's head whipped around. "We're not talking to you."

"You obviously want it," Fenway continued. "I heard they offered it to you first. Take it. The only reason I'm being offered this appointment is because you said no."

Could Barry Klein have anything to do with Walker's murder? Maybe he wanted Walker out of the way but didn't think things through? No, that didn't make sense. Now, if it were Nathaniel Ferris dead, Klein would be the prime suspect.

"Some of us have obligations to our patients and shareholders," Klein hissed.

"I bet you could work it out," Fenway said. "You plan to run for coroner in November anyway. Just work two full-time jobs until you can get out of your practice. Hell, I worked two full-time jobs *and* got my associate's degree."

Fenway turned her head to McVie. His eyes were wide.

"Well, Barry?" Mayor Jenkins asked.

"You know I can't take the position now, Alice."

"Got anyone else in mind who'd accept? Or are you just trying to embarrass Miss Stevenson?"

Klein was silent.

"Thank you, Dr. Klein," Mayor Jenkins said firmly. "Miss Stevenson, thank you for your time and your candor." She hesitated. "I apologize for misspelling your name. We should have caught that mistake. It wasn't professional."

Fenway tapped the nameplate in front of her. "You got my last name correct. That's more than most people around here."

"Oh, please," Dr. Klein muttered under his breath.

"You're excused, Miss Stevenson," Mayor Jenkins said. "Sheriff, let's chat for a bit before we adjourn."

"I appreciate the opportunity." Fenway bent her head, halfway between a nod and a bow. She stood up and turned to McVie.

McVie sat back in his seat, shoulders slumped, eyes wide. He looked up at Fenway. "That wasn't what I expected."

She shrugged. "I didn't have a lot of time to prepare."

She walked out of the chamber. Part of her was terrified at what she'd just said, but part of her was glad she'd claimed her space.

And then it hit her.

Her mother's cypress tree painting.

It was clear in her mind now. A four-foot-wide by two-foot-high canvas her mother had hung in her bedroom above the dresser.

She'd never had a favorite painting of her mother's because most of the ones Fenway got attached to had been sold. This painting was striking, sure, but Fenway had assumed it was of a location on the Olympic Peninsula, or maybe down farther, where the Columbia empties into the Pacific. It never crossed her mind that the landscape would be in California. In Estancia.

Her mother hadn't sold it. A few buyers had been interested, but they always bought another painting instead. Maybe her mother had *liked* that painting. Maybe no matter how bad it had been for her mother in California, inspiration and hope were never far away. Her mother had found a beautiful spot overlooking the ocean, near a butterfly grove, around the corner from a coffee shop, and she had made it hers, even from a thousand miles away.

CHAPTER SIX

After buying a mediocre latte at the coffee cart in the lobby, Fenway walked around the ground floor of City Hall, killing time until the sheriff came out of the supervisors' meeting. She'd pushed against Barry Klein hard, and maybe her father would have to introduce her to hospital HR teams after all.

She meandered past the City Attorney's office, the County Clerk and Recorder's office, and then saw McVie waving to her as he exited the chambers and walked toward her.

"I've never seen Barry Klein that speechless in a meeting before," McVie chortled. "Congratulations, Coroner Stevenson," he said warmly. "It's official."

Fenway grinned and pulled him into an excited hug. She wondered if she held on for a beat too long before they broke apart. "I thought I pushed back a little too hard."

"Honestly, that had me worried. But they loved it. Klein's been a thorn in their side for years. When do you want to start?"

"How about now?"

"Done. Let's go over to the coroner's suite."

"Oh—actually, Sheriff, do you think I could see the murder scene?"

McVie's eyes widened. "Uh, I'm not sure that's a good idea. There's some paperwork for you to fill out. I-9 forms, insurance beneficiary information, that kind of thing."

"That's all going to be here when we get back, isn't it? I mean, no one's expecting us right now."

"I *did* tell HR we'd be done this morning."

Fenway tapped her foot. "It's not even eight thirty yet. I bet we can be back here by nine thirty."

"It's a good half-hour drive."

"Eleven o'clock, then."

"I think HR wanted to do paperwork first thing."

Fenway tilted her head. "Is this or is this not my investigation, Sheriff?"

"No, you're right." He shook his head. "But I don't know what you're going to find that the Park Police didn't already bag up and ship to the lab in San Miguelito."

———

Even after stopping for another latte—this time a decent one from Java Jim's at the Highway 326 exit—they made it to the crime scene by nine. The cruiser pulled onto the shoulder, and Fenway got out of the car.

"His body was found about fifty feet past that ironwood up there," McVie said, pointing. "We've taken down the tape, so anyone could have walked on it by now."

"Did they find anything?"

"Except for the body? No casings or anything. Killer might have picked them up. Or they might be lost in the grass or down the ravine."

Fenway nodded. She walked slowly toward the ironwood, scanning the ground.

"Body was found face down?"

"Yeah."

"Which way was his head?"

McVie paused. "What do you mean?"

"Which way was he facing when he fell? Toward traffic or away from it?"

"Oh. I don't know. You'll have to get Dr. Yasuda to give you the report."

Fenway nodded. Past the ironwood, fifty feet.

She scanned the ground. No one would ever be able to tell there'd been a dead body here.

Tire tracks came off the road onto the shoulder, were heavier in a spot about twenty feet in front of where the body was found, and then went back on the road.

"Would these tracks be the Park Police?"

"No, their tracks are on the other side."

"The theory is the killer took the car?"

"Yes. Could have been a car thief, but the killer is more likely."

Fenway looked across the road, scanning the opposite shoulder, although she wasn't sure what she was looking for. "How did the killer get here?"

McVie walked toward her. "Jeez, you were serious about coming out here. It's your first day, Coroner."

"He's been dead for almost three, Sheriff. The trail's already cold." She looked up and down the road. "No bus stop for miles, right?"

McVie nodded.

"We're pretty sure the killer left in Walker's car. So how did they get here?"

McVie was silent.

"Did anyone check taxi records? Uber records? This is an unusual place to get dropped off. If you find someone who got dropped here late Sunday night, I bet you'd find your killer."

"Maybe the killer drove *with* Walker."

"Maybe." Fenway stared at the tire tracks. "It looks like the car pulled off the road, parked, then drove off. Walker was killed *behind* the car."

McVie looked from the tire indentations to the location of the body, then nodded.

"He got out to talk to someone," said Fenway.

"You don't know that."

Fenway shook her head. "You're right, I don't. This is my first murder investigation." Tingles cascaded down her spine when she said it. "So tell me why I'm wrong. Tell me what other scenarios I'm not taking into account."

McVie was silent, staring intently at the tire tracks.

"He comes to a dark road in the middle of the night. Parks. Gets out. Stands twenty feet behind his car. Gets shot. I don't know which way he's facing, and I don't know where the killer is standing. My brain is thinking botched drug deal or an information exchange of some kind. That means he's meeting someone."

McVie nodded. "That's what it looks like."

"Any tire tracks on that side of the road?"

"That's where the Park Police and all the emergency vehicles parked on Monday."

Fenway folded her arms and walked slowly up the shoulder, all the way to where it ended at a bridge over the ravine. She pointed down the steep hill. "Great place to destroy evidence," she shouted.

McVie didn't respond. Probably out of earshot.

She walked slowly back to the cruiser. McVie was leaning on the passenger-side door.

"See anything interesting?"

"Not that I recognized as important," Fenway said. "There were a couple of interesting rocks, I guess."

"Seen all you need to see?"

"I think so." She clapped McVie on the shoulder. "Thanks for humoring me."

"I called in." McVie walked around the front of the car and opened the driver-side door. "Asked to run taxi and rideshare app records for Sunday night."

Fenway shrugged and got in the cruiser. "The killer might be too smart for that, but you never know."

———

McVie had a meeting to get to, so he dropped Fenway in front of the coroner's building. It was just past ten thirty.

All the employees—Dez, Mark, Rachel, and Migs—looked up from their computers as the door opened.

"It's official," Fenway announced. "I was appointed coroner this morning."

Dez stood up and smiled. "Congratulations. You're still in one piece after meeting the supervisors, I see."

Rachel couldn't look Fenway in the eyes. "Lana Cassidy is waiting for you in the conference room." Oh. The same woman who wouldn't take Rachel's complaint about Walker. That didn't sound promising. What a way to start her new job.

Fenway walked around the counter and behind Dez's desk. A raven-haired white woman in her mid-forties sat at the conference room table with her arms folded. Her eyes were hard, and her mouth was a straight line. She had cat-eye glasses with black frames, black slacks, and a long-sleeve floral-print shirt Fenway thought was too hot for a beautiful day like today.

"You're late, Miss Ferris."

"I'm sorry?"

"I've been here with the paperwork for your first day since ten o'clock. I'm not sure what job you worked at before where you could just—"

"I was at the murder scene with Sheriff McVie. And it's Fenway *Stevenson*, not Fenway Ferris."

Lana's lips twitched. "Ah. You were the Miss Stevenson on the sheriff's voicemail."

"That's correct. Didn't he tell you we were out this morning?"

"I had no idea who this *Miss Stevenson* was," Lana said. "At any rate, now that you're finally here, we can get started."

Fenway pulled out a chair and took a seat.

"I'm the director of Human Resources." She produced a business card and handed it to her with a withering stare. "We have a lot of paperwork to sign, and I have to make sure you understand all the mandatory information."

Fenway's bad feeling about Lana Cassidy didn't go away after they sat down at the conference room table. When Fenway was ten years old, she and her mom went back-to-school shopping in downtown Seattle. She was in the changing room with a pair of jeans she liked and heard muffled voices of her mother and one of the store employees. When she opened the door, Fenway saw her mother's strange, thin-lipped smile. With a practiced hand on Fenway's shoulder, her mother steered her out of the store, ignoring the glares from one of the employees and setting down the four outfits they had picked out. "I liked those outfits, Mom. Why can't we get them?"

"Baby, they just insulted us. I'm not giving them our money."

Lana Cassidy was glaring at Fenway the same way the store employee had. They had to review an enormous amount of paperwork, and Lana rushed through it all. The employee handbook, the travel policy, the signature rules.

"And you can sign expense reports up to twenty thousand dollars." Lana turned the page quickly, but not before it registered in Fenway's brain that the document said $10,000.

"Hang on," Fenway interjected, putting her hand under the page and flipping it back. "It says right here I can only authorize payments for *ten* thousand dollars, not twenty thousand."

Lana rolled her eyes. "I didn't say twenty thousand."

Fenway blinked.

"I *didn't* say twenty thousand. Let's move on."

Halfway through the paperwork, Lana stopped and looked at her watch.

"I see it's one o'clock. I suppose we'd better break for lunch."

"Great. Are there lunch places around here?"

"I already have plans," Lana said.

Fenway looked sideways at Lana. "I didn't—I mean, I'm new in town, and I don't know what's around here."

Lana gathered up her purse. "Please be back in an hour." She was out of the conference room, slamming the door behind her.

Fenway sighed. She wasn't sure what Lana had against her. The conference room door opened gently, and Rachel stuck her head in.

"You two breaking for lunch?"

Fenway nodded.

"Where is she taking you?"

"Oh, she made it pretty clear I was on my own."

"Rude," Rachel murmured. "Okay. Let's go grab some tacos."

"A better place than Tacos Amigos, I take it."

"I swear, I will *never* take you to Tacos Amigos."

As soon as Rachel and Fenway stepped out of the building into the bright sunlight, Rachel looked behind them and, seeing no one, spoke in a low voice. "I'm really sorry."

"About Lana? Don't worry about it. Not the first time that's happened to me."

"No. About last night. What a horrible burden I dumped on you." She shook her head at herself. "And from someone who reports directly to you."

"No, no, no," Fenway said. "As your manager, I needed to know that.

It happened in the office while you were working. It affects the work-place, and you were absolutely within your rights."

Rachel was quiet for a moment. "But Mr. Walker is dead," she whispered.

"Yes. That saves me the trouble of firing him." Fenway frowned. "And you told Lana Cassidy, and she didn't do anything about it?"

"Right."

Fenway shook her head.

"I'm still sorry—"

"I don't want to hear that, Rachel. This isn't going to be a place where that kind of thing is tolerated. I'm only going to be here six months. Maybe I can shed some light on the problems."

Rachel blanched. "I don't—I don't want to make this public."

"I know."

The two continued a couple of blocks east of the parking garage, where they stopped before a hole-in-the-wall taqueria.

"Here?" Fenway said.

"Dos Milagros. Best food in Estancia." Rachel held open the door and followed Fenway in. "Carne asada? Chile verde? Chicken? Vegetarian?"

"Chicken."

Rachel ordered, in Spanish, four tacos and horchatas for the two of them. She started to pull her wallet out, but Fenway stopped her.

"Got the HR lecture on the appearance of impropriety. Supervisors always pay."

Rachel smiled. "Thanks."

Fenway paid, and Rachel found a high table with two stools. Fenway sat down.

"What number are we?" Rachel asked.

"Twenty-three. You speak Spanish?"

"Yeah, I was in the Semester Abroad program at UCLA, and I spent it in Costa Rica. My dad was freaking out the whole time at how far away it was."

"UCLA? That's a great school."

"I got into Princeton. My dad wanted me closer."

The woman behind the counter called out, "Veintitres," and Rachel went to get their tacos.

She came back and handed Fenway two tacos half-wrapped in foil.

Fenway unwrapped the first one. The tangy smell of fresh cilantro was heavenly. "You get along with your dad?"

Rachel shrugged. "He didn't much like it when I eloped."

"Yeah. I know a little about strained relationships with fathers, too."

Rachel smiled and took a drink of horchata. "Maybe our dads could compare notes. My dad has been working for Ferris Energy ever since he got out of the CHP." Rachel grinned. "And now I work for you. There's a kind of, I don't know, symmetry."

"Did your dad know what a creep Walker was?"

"Are you kidding? He would have made me quit. He thinks I can't handle myself. He didn't want me taking this job in the first place." Rachel started in on her second taco. "I got the job in the coroner's office last June, right after graduating. I'll be there a year next month. There aren't a lot of press releases to write, but I get to do two or three a month. I have to start somewhere, right?"

"Right." Fenway took a bite and chewed quickly. "Man, these are great. No wonder you like it so much."

"Honestly, the carne asada ones are way better."

"I'll keep that in mind." Fenway swallowed. "So you want to do PR?"

"Honestly," she said conspiratorially, "I'd love to be White House press secretary one day."

Fenway nodded. "That's ambitious."

"Yeah."

"So, let me ask you something. Now that I'm officially investigating his death, do you know if Walker had any enemies?"

"Only everyone."

"No one liked him and he was a horrible boss. I got that. But people don't kill because of that. I'm talking about cheating someone out of money. Or sleeping with someone who was married."

"Or sexually assaulting someone?" Rachel shuddered.

Fenway leaned forward, studying Rachel's face. "Anyone come into his office and argue with him?"

"Barry Klein. Alice Jenkins. Lana Cassidy, once. I assume that one was HR-related. Dez had a couple of screaming matches with him." She thought. "McVie."

"McVie? He seems so even-keeled."

"Yeah, if you get the Boy Scout worked up, you know you've done something wrong." Rachel wiped her hands and took another drink of horchata.

"You know what any of these screaming matches were about?"

Rachel squinted. "Uh... no."

"Maybe I could see his calendar when I'm done with Lana."

Rachel looked a little abashed. The calendar had been the thing she'd gotten snippy about last night. "He didn't keep anything personal on it," Rachel said. "He barely knew how to turn on the computer."

They walked back to work in the sunshine. Fenway marveled at the weather: it was a beautiful day, the kind of day that comes only two or three times a year in Seattle. It was warm, but Fenway was still comfortable, even wearing a blazer, and there was a nice breeze off the ocean.

Lana Cassidy was waiting for her when they got back to the office. A willowy young woman stood at the counter next to Lana, a couple of inches taller than Fenway, with long, straight red hair and pale skin with an almost cartoonish amount of freckles. She was wearing a short-sleeved green dress with black ballet flats, a laptop bag over one shoulder.

Fenway checked the wall clock—one forty-five.

"Hi, Lana. I thought you said we had an hour for lunch."

"I *assumed* you'd want to get this finished up so you could get started," she snapped. "Miss Patten and I have been waiting for you for fifteen minutes."

"Then let's get back into it."

"Piper Patten," the redhead said, shaking Fenway's hand. She had a high-pitched, almost elfin voice. "I work over in IT. I'll be setting up your laptop." Fenway thought she was kind of delightful. The way Migs kept stealing glances at Piper, it seemed he thought so, too.

The three of them went into the conference room. Piper and Fenway sat down, but Lana stayed standing, then paced around the table. Piper gave Fenway her temporary keycard, reviewed the rules and regulations documents, and gave her a username and temporary password to her department laptop. It was a three-year-old Acer with the *Escape* key missing.

"Sorry about this," she said. "It was the only loaner we had on short notice."

"I'm sure it's fine."

"Lana, can you stop pacing?" said Piper. "It's really distracting."

Lana shot eye daggers at Piper. "I've got a two o'clock. Are we done here?"

"Uh, I've got to set up her VPN." Piper looked at Fenway.

"You can set that up later." Lana was already halfway out the door. "Come on, Piper. And Miss Ferris, make sure to submit the direct deposit form by noon on Friday."

Piper's eyes widened and she looked at Fenway apologetically before following Lana out.

Fenway leaned back in her chair and stared at the ceiling. At least it was mercifully short.

Maybe something in Walker's office would give some idea of what he was doing on that road. And the medical examiner could give more information of where the killer stood and where Walker was when he was shot. She wasn't sure what it might mean, but it was a place to start.

Dez had been in the department longer than anyone. She might know how to get answers from the lab.

Fenway stood and walked to the door. "Hey, Sergeant Roubideaux," Fenway said, "can you help me with something, please?"

"Ooh, first day and I get 'Sergeant Roubideaux,'" Dez said, leaning back in her seat. "Settle down, Coroner, I ain't in my dress blues. Save 'Sergeant Roubideaux' for my Outstanding Service Award."

"Okay, *Dez*, get your ass in here."

"Hmph." She stood, unable to suppress a smile. "Maybe something in between."

Fenway shut the conference room door behind Dez. "What's the process for getting information from the lab in San Miguelito?"

"They were planning to do the autopsy this morning. They were supposed to do it yesterday, but without a coroner here, and without an investigator, they called yesterday and said they'd push it back."

"Think they've done it yet?"

"I haven't heard."

Fenway thought. "Maybe I could call them."

Dez shrugged, opening the conference room door. "Suit yourself. I hear the San Mig medical examiner is kind of a bitch."

"You would know, Dez," Migs called from around the corner.

She ignored Migs and lowered her voice. "Listen, I don't think Little Miss Cassidy has a problem with *you*, I think she has a problem with..." and she pointed to the black skin on her exposed wrist.

Fenway nodded, tight-lipped.

"So watch yourself. She won't lift a finger to help you with any insubordinate employees." Dez laughed. "Except if it's me. She *hates* me."

"Okay. Another thing, Dez—there are security cameras in this building, right?"

"In the hallways and at the entrances and exits."

"How about in here?"

She looked at Fenway a little quizzically. "In here? Why?"

"I have to search and fingerprint Walker's office. And one of the board of supervisors members thinks I'm in cahoots with my father."

"We know all about Barry Klein and his feelings about your daddy."

"Yeah, well, if Klein doesn't like the way I'm handling Walker's murder, I want to make sure I can prove there's no impropriety."

"Oh, Fenway. Thinking like a politician already."

Fenway tilted her head to the side playfully. "If HR already hates me, don't you think I need to document my behavior?"

Dez laughed. "I certainly do, Coroner Stevenson. But if there are cameras in here, I don't know about them."

"Okay, one last thing. Is there someone who can assist me with Walker's office? We don't know anything about motive or opportunity yet, but I think it goes without saying that everyone who worked with Walker is under suspicion. It has to be someone from outside this office—maybe the medical examiner from San Miguelito or a member of the staff there?"

Dez looked surprised. "I thought McVie would have told you already. You aren't just the lead investigator on the physical evidence—you're the *only* investigator. Everyone else in the office, and even the CSIs from San Miguelito, has at least one or two open files in the coroner's office. We're not stupid. He might have been murdered over some falsified information, or a cop or a tech who took a bribe. We could fly in someone from L.A. or the Bay Area, I guess, but we already have someone who studied forensics without a conflict of interest." Dez paused. "I mean *you*, by the way."

Fenway look down at the table. "McVie told me he wanted me to collect evidence from Walker's office. I didn't realize I was the *only* one who could do it."

Dez shrugged. "Congratulations?"

"All right, fine. Show me where we keep the gloves, the fingerprint kit, the evidence bags, and the cameras. I'll get started."

"Now?"

"It's only two o'clock. I'm not sitting around for a couple of hours waiting for McVie to drive me home."

"Oh man," Dez said. "Walker was a lazy, micromanaging sonofabitch. Now we've got an idealist on our hands." She shook her head. "Were you in the Young Republicans in college?"

Fenway scoffed.

"Oh, come on, I was joking. I don't know if you noticed, but I have quite the sense of humor."

Fenway chuckled.

"You're talking to the woman who wanted to get your dad a Yankees jersey to thank him for a donation to the sheriff's fund." Dez guffawed. "No one had the guts to do it, but man, I bet the look on your daddy's face would've been priceless." She leaned against the doorframe. "The key for Walker's office is across the street in the Sheriff's evidence room. There's a bunch of fingerprint kits and gloves over there, too. I'll be back in ten minutes."

"Thanks, Dez."

She grinned. "Don't mention it, rookie. I haven't had this much fun at work in a long time."

Fenway sat for a moment, then opened her laptop and searched for the number for Barry Klein's office. She picked up her cell phone and dialed.

"Klein Optometry."

"Fenway Stevenson for Dr. Klein." She was put on hold, but not for long.

Dr. Klein picked up. "Now listen, Miss Stevenson. You cannot call my place of work to harass me. Those were perfectly legitimate questions—"

"I'm calling to tell you I'm collecting evidence from Mr. Walker's office."

"What?"

"Transparency, Dr. Klein. You don't trust my father, so I'm offering an olive branch. I'll be starting my evidence collection in about thirty minutes. Send an observer if you wish. Come over yourself if you want."

"It figures they'd put you in charge." Klein's voice was low and guttural. "Your father's company is represented in many of the files in Walker's office, I'm sure. No one will notice if one or two of those files disappear, right?"

"You probably have a few Ferris employees for clients yourself." Fenway took a deep breath. "So come over and observe. Make sure everything is on the up-and-up."

"How do I know you haven't already hidden whatever evidence you have in there, and this isn't all a put-on?"

She paused. "The door is locked. The key is being held in a separate office. There are cameras in the building."

"All of which is no guarantee against tampering."

"You obviously don't trust me. I might not either if I were in your shoes. Do you have another suggestion?"

There was silence on the other end of the line. She could almost hear the gears turning in Dr. Klein's head. Finally, he spoke. "I have patients to see, Miss Stevenson. Quit wasting my time." He hung up.

Fenway smiled, shaking her head, and set the phone down.

"What the hell were you just doing?"

Fenway's head snapped up. Dez was in the doorway, scowling.

CHAPTER SEVEN

FENWAY HADN'T SEEN DEZ SCOWL BEFORE. "I WAS JUST ON THE PHONE with Barry Klein. He didn't trust me, so I offered—"

"Wow, you really *haven't* investigated any crimes before." Dez shook her head. "Did you pay attention to anything we've said? *Everyone's* a suspect. McVie, me, Mark, Rachel—everyone. And that includes Barry Klein."

"Really? But he—"

"I know you haven't interviewed him to hear where he was on Sunday night. And you have no idea if he had some sort of business or personal issue with Walker." Dez folded her arms. "Why in the world would you invite a suspect to oversee your evidence collection?"

"Well—he doesn't trust me. I thought I was being proactive."

Dez scoffed. "Look, I like you, Fenway, but you better not give a shit if Barry Klein does. That's irrelevant to you finding Walker's killer." She sighed. "I don't think McVie expected you to be done so soon. He hasn't had time to brief you on process—and it's not like you went to the academy. Hang on. I'll be right back."

Dez turned and walked away.

Fenway waited a moment, then logged into the Seattle University website and read over a few of the pages on fingerprint collection. She had a decent handle on the basics. Hopefully, the basics would serve her well enough.

Dez walked in with three boxes of blue nitrile gloves, evidence bags, ID tents, and some other equipment, as well as a manila folder.

"Is that for me?"

"Yep. But first, more paperwork." Dez pulled a sheet of paper from the folder and put it in front of Fenway. HOMICIDE INVESTIGATION CHECKLIST.

Fenway chewed on her bottom lip.

"I like that you want to get started, but we've got a right way to do this. The wrong way might get the case thrown out or get us sued." Dez glared at Fenway. "I'm too close to retirement to get sued, all right?"

"All right," Fenway muttered. She looked down at the paper and the plain numbered list.

"This is all about how to process a crime scene," Fenway said.

"You don't think you need to learn how to do that?"

Fenway shifted uncomfortably in her seat. "Not for *this* investigation. The scene has already been processed."

"Fine," Dez said, pulling out another sheet. "Page two."

Fenway took the page from her and started reading. "Did we notify the next of kin? Oh! The wife's *always* a suspect! Rachel said he was married—"

"Mark got ahold of her Monday morning," Dez said. "She was in Denver visiting her sister. They didn't have children."

Fenway nodded and kept reading. *Establish movements of deceased prior to death.* This was all the boring stuff the cop shows glossed over.

"I think a lot of this has already been done."

"I hope so," said Dez. "The Park Police sent everything to the lab."

"His wallet and ID too?"

"I didn't see an inventory list, but if he had those on him, then yes."

Fenway nodded. "Do you know what he was doing on the side of that dark road that late at night?"

Dez shook her head. "Harrison Walker and I weren't exactly tight." She took a few more pages out of the folder. "The checklist is pretty long."

"Okay."

"It's detailed, but you don't know how to conduct a murder investigation yet. This'll be a crash course for you." Dez placed the papers above the one Fenway was reading. "And as long as this document is, do you know what's *not* on here?"

Fenway nodded. "Letting Barry Klein oversee your evidence collection."

Dez smirked. "You did say you were a fast learner." She slid the boxes of gloves toward Fenway. "Read up on grid search. If you're going to be gathering evidence from Walker's office, that's what you'll have to do."

Fenway exhaled. "I learned grid search in my evidence class."

"Tell your instructor to have a unit on not being stupid around suspects. Now glove up and come on."

Fenway grabbed two blue nitrile gloves, put them on, and stood up.

"I've got someone with me," Dez said. Fenway followed her out of the conference room, taking the evidence baggies and envelopes—then hurried back for her phone, too. At the counter was a tall young white male deputy, wearing the sheriff department's black uniform, his skin pink from what looked like a mild sunburn, and a military-style short haircut. Fenway nodded to him and felt the heat in her cheeks. She wondered how much of the conversation with Dez the deputy had heard.

He took three giant steps toward Walker's office, took the key out, and unlocked the door before turning to Fenway. "Okay, ma'am, there you go."

"Thanks." Fenway ducked under the police tape. *Twenty-eight years old and I got 'ma'amed.'*

He stood there.

"You waiting for a tip?" Dez said.

"No, ma'am."

"Well, go on then."

"I'm sorry, ma'am," he responded in an even voice, "but I'm required to stay."

Dez looked shocked. "For real?"

"Yes, ma'am. Protocol."

Dez tapped her temple as the answer came to her. "Ah. You're new, aren't you? You and Fenway are probably the only two people in the whole City Hall complex who don't have a file in there."

"That's what my boss told me, ma'am."

"Awesome," Fenway said. "Officer, do you have a cell phone that can video this?"

"I have a personal cell phone, but it's not to be used for police business."

"Righty-oh," Fenway said, snapping the wrists of her gloves. "I'll get down to work."

"Okay," Dez said. "Let me know if you need anything." She nodded to the deputy and went to her desk.

Fenway surveyed the room. The massive desk took up much of the space, but the side wall contained four filing cabinets. Maybe she should concentrate her search there. But how could she tell if files were missing or had been tampered with? She stepped around the desk and tried to open the top drawer of the leftmost cabinet.

Locked.

So were all the others.

She carefully took pictures with her cell phone. No suspicious marks on any of the cabinets. She looked closely at the door jamb and found nothing.

"I don't think anyone's been in this room since Walker," Fenway whispered.

She dropped to her knees, the grid method of evidence search pinging in her head, and methodically scoured the entire floor for hairs, or fibers, or anything unusual or out of place.

The grid method might be effective, but with just one person performing the search, it took a long time. Fenway's knees ached before she was even halfway done with the floor. Huh. Maybe *ma'am* was appropriate after all.

In spite of the cool air in Walker's office, she grew warm. The carpet fibers were short but thick, and she had to work hard with her fingers to make sure she didn't miss anything.

But she found nothing.

She stood and stretched, looking out the window. Not much of a view —just a parking lot—but it sure beat the windowless clinic.

She moved to the desk next. A large paper calendar served as a desk topper, and a keyboard and mouse were in front of the monitor stand, under which a laptop docking station sat.

The dock was empty.

"Anyone know where his laptop is?" she called out.

"I haven't heard," Migs said.

She looked up to see Migs leaning against the door jamb, watching her work. The deputy still stood in front of the door stoically.

"How long have you been standing there?"

"Not that long," said Migs. "I've never seen a room searched for evidence before."

"Yeah, well, I've never searched a room for evidence either. Maybe we'll both learn something." She nodded at him. "You make sure everything we do is legal, right?"

"Right."

"Let me know if I'm doing anything questionable."

"Sure."

She searched the bookcase behind Walker's leather chair. A few old tomes on case law, a couple of medical books, an old anatomy textbook.

"Have you heard an update on Walker's car?"

"No," Migs said.

"Have any idea what he was doing out in the middle of nowhere so late at night?"

"Probably drowning puppies or eating babies," Migs said. "Do you maybe want to fingerprint the docking station in case someone stole the laptop out of it?"

Fenway nodded. "Yeah, that's a good idea. Thanks, Migs."

Migs had been holding the fingerprint kit and now handed it to her through the doorway.

She dusted and lifted on the dock first, then used the grid method on the top of the desk and the bookcase. She hesitated before brushing the dust on the door handle, spilling some of the fine dark-gray powder on the floor. It took longer than she expected, and it didn't help to have Migs staring at her hands the entire time.

She finally put the last of the fingerprint tape on a card and sealed it in an evidence bag.

"That stuff really gets everywhere." Migs motioned with his head to the desk. "Think you'll find something on the docking station?"

Fenway shook her head. "No full prints from the dock. Two partials—that was it." She looked at the empty dock and squinted. "Do you know if Walker usually left his laptop here? Or did he take it home?"

"We're not supposed to leave laptops here, but he left it here some nights. I didn't keep track, though."

Fenway sighed. "You see anywhere I missed?"

"The drawer handles of the filing cabinets?"

"Good catch. Hey, do you know where the keys to those cabinets are?"

The deputy piped up. "They're in the evidence room."

Fenway turned to the deputy. "Can you go get them?"

"You'll have to leave the room and I'll have to lock up again, ma'am."

Fenway's shoulders slumped. "Can someone else get the keys from the evidence room?"

"My lieutenant was pretty clear I was responsible for everything pertaining to this office, ma'am."

Fenway felt a stabbing pain with every *ma'am*. "Okay, fine." She looked at her cell phone. "Have I really been doing this for two hours?"

"Two and a half, ma'am."

She set her jaw. "Can you meet me back here at a quarter after five? I'll have to tell the sheriff I'm staying late tonight."

"Um..." the deputy began.

"What is it?"

"I'm sorry, ma'am, but, uh, I don't report to you. Only my supervisor can authorize overtime, and I'll hit eight hours at five o'clock."

Fenway folded her arms and weighed her options. She couldn't afford to lose any more time in this investigation, but she didn't want to get into a pissing match with another department.

She sighed. "No one expected me to get started today, I guess. Yeah, let's pack it up for the day." But she'd found nothing. No calendar. No secret meeting appointments. No messages or letters. A bunch of fingerprints, but people were in and out all day long.

"Can you meet me here tomorrow at eight o'clock with the keys for both the door and the file cabinets, and whatever other keys you have for any locks inside the office?"

"Yes, ma'am."

She smiled at him. "Perfect."

Migs and the deputy took a few steps back as Fenway ducked under the police tape and exited the office. The deputy locked the door. "Thank you, ma'am. Eight o'clock tomorrow morning." He nodded stiffly and left the suite.

Fenway took her gloves off and leaned against the front counter, chin resting in her hand.

Migs and Dez packed up and were out the door just after five o'clock.

Dez handed Fenway the folder with the steps for the homicide investigation. "Study up," she said, a twinkle in her eye. "There's a practical exam tomorrow."

Mark nodded at her as he left. "Good first day?"

She glanced up at him and smiled. "Mostly. Probably the most *interesting* first day I've ever had."

"See you tomorrow."

Fenway looked at Rachel. "You getting out of here too?"

"Yeah." Rachel blushed. "I got in a little late today. I'm staying for a few more minutes."

At a quarter after the hour, McVie walked in. "So, Coroner, how was your first day?"

"Fine," she said, walking into the conference room and grabbing her purse and laptop bag. "Got an old laptop with a broken escape key."

"'Hell is other people,'" Rachel said dryly.

McVie laughed. "Ready to go?"

"Hey," Rachel said, "how come McVie is giving you a ride home?"

"I sold my car in Seattle. I was going to buy one here, but, uh, I've been a little busy." Fenway looped the laptop bag's strap over her shoulder as McVie held the door open. "Have a good night."

They walked to the parking garage. "Any revelations about the case?" McVie asked.

"Not yet. I fingerprinted Walker's office. Took a while."

"Police work is mostly repetitive motion alternating with long periods of waiting."

"I wonder why they never show that on TV."

The fog started to roll in, and although it was still light, the breeze off the ocean picked up. McVie shivered.

"Did Lana take care of you?"

She looked at McVie. She wondered if Lana had ever said a bad word to him. Would he would even believe how rude Lana had been? "I got through all the paperwork and handbooks." She cleared her throat. "Walker's work laptop is missing."

"It wasn't in his office?"

"Not unless he locked it in a drawer or a file cabinet. I don't have the keys yet. They're bringing them tomorrow morning."

"What, you didn't put in any overtime on your first day? Man, don't let Klein hear about this." He chuckled.

She frowned. She didn't want to tell McVie about her conversation with Klein. They started up the parking garage stairs. "That laptop might be important. It might have a file that points us to the motive. Or even an email or a note that identifies who Walker was meeting Sunday night."

McVie nodded. "I'll call his wife tonight. He might have taken it home."

They reached the cruiser and got in.

Fenway put on her seat belt and closed the door. "What's the protocol here? Do we need to get a search warrant for his house?"

"No need. His wife was out of town—she's not a suspect. If she hands it over, it'll be quick and easy." McVie was quiet for a minute as he started the cruiser and backed out of the space. "We haven't found his car, though. I'm wondering if we're going to see it go up in smoke soon."

"Burning a car draws too much attention," Fenway said.

McVie looked at Fenway incredulously.

"It's true. I asked about it in my evidence class. Attracts law enforcement, and the VINs usually survive." She bit her lip. "I'd check the long-term lots at LAX and the other L.A. airports. I guess we should check the regional airports, too, just to be sure, but cars get noticed in their tiny long-term lots."

"How about the Bay Area? SFO?" McVie turned onto the freeway.

She shook her head. "Too far. The killer could have driven a couple of hours to LAX, left the car, and taken a Greyhound or Amtrak or even one of the airport shuttles back here in time to get a couple of hours of sleep and show up for work the next day. SFO is a four-and-a-half-hour drive, maybe longer, and there's no easy way to get back. The train takes at least six or seven hours. Same with the bus. With LAX, you're gone for five or six hours in the middle of the night when everyone is asleep. No one even knows you're gone. With SFO, you're gone for eighteen hours."

"Okay." McVie nodded. "Maybe I'll have someone call the airport lots."

"Hey mister," she said, a touch of playfulness in her voice, "I thought *I* was supposed to be responsible for the forensic evidence."

"Wow, and I thought *I* was a stickler for the rules." McVie laughed. "But calling LAX to find a car isn't being responsible for forensic evidence. You *can* let me help on this as long as I don't touch forensic evidence or talk to witnesses."

Fenway sat back. Right. She had help. Both the ER and clinic were always short-staffed, and she'd gotten used to dealing with everything by herself. But this was a different work environment.

She turned her head to look at McVie's face. Something about his attitude, how he was so comfortable in his own skin, how being around him made Fenway like herself more, made a smile so much easier. She cleared her throat. He was still technically a suspect in Fenway's mind— although he hadn't acted at all guilty at the crime scene. "All right, Sheriff. The laptop and the car."

McVie turned into Fenway's complex, and she got out.

"See you tomorrow," McVie said, leaning over the passenger seat. "Glad you had a good first day."

She wandered around her apartment a little, wondering if she should call her father first about their very tentative dinner plans from that morning. She wasn't hungry enough yet, but she didn't want to wait around all night.

She picked up the phone and dialed.

"Nathaniel Ferris."

She put on a bad Brooklyn accent. "Yeah, Mister Ferris, I's got a lady on the line, says her name is Wrigley or Camden or something. Wait, wait, it's coming to me—a Miss Chavez Ravine."

"Very funny, Fenway."

"Hi, Dad," she said, dropping the accent. "Calling to see if we should coordinate outfits again."

"I hope you weren't this sarcastic in your interview with the supervisors."

"I only terrorized Barry Klein, and I understand he deserved it."

He hesitated before speaking. "Careful, Fenway. He's unpredictable."

"I handled myself okay."

"So you got the job?"

"I was at the crime scene by nine."

"Wow—that's really fast."

"Oh, come on, Dad, you didn't grease the wheels?"

He chuckled. "Fenway, I may have talked to one or two people, but that's hardly greasing the wheels."

"Po-tay-to, po-tah-to."

"So you actually did work today, too? Not just sign an offer?"

"Yep. I started gathering evidence in Walker's office this afternoon, and I basically have to do it all myself because everyone else has a conflict of interest. They've all got open files or investigations they're working on with him."

"You started the Walker investigation?"

"Yes, I did, Dad. It's pretty important I look like I'm making headway."

"It would be *especially* important if you were going to run for coroner in November."

"I meant important if this town is going to maintain trust in the sheriff's office. Let's not get ahead of ourselves." She paused. "Hey—you knew Harrison Walker pretty well. Did he have any enemies you can think of?"

He laughed. "The most hated man in Estancia?"

"What? Barry Klein didn't take that award?"

"Runner-up every year." Ferris snapped his fingers. "That's it! Barry Klein killed Walker because he was sick of losing the Biggest Jerk award."

She pushed out a breath. "Closer to a motive than I came today."

"You didn't make any progress?"

She clicked her tongue against her teeth. Had she already said too much? Ferris was powerful, but this felt like one of those father-daughter conversations they'd never had. *How was school? How was volleyball practice? What was the most interesting thing you learned today?* "It's, uh, early in the process. I won't even get the keys to his files until tomorrow morning, so everything is still preliminary."

"It's still faster than anyone expected."

"It's weird, though," she continued. "Aren't the first forty-eight hours of a homicide investigation the most important? Sheriff McVie seemed more concerned with the appearance of conflicts of interest than he did about starting the investigation."

"I'm sure Craig is doing everything he can with limited resources." Ferris coughed. "Enough shop talk. Now that you're in town, I'd love to take my daughter out to dinner. Are you busy tomorrow night?"

"Tomorrow night?"

"Yes."

"Uh—didn't you tell me we'd go out for dinner *tonight?*"

"Did I? I'm sorry—I've had the wrong day in my head all day. I meant Thursday."

Fenway sighed. Maybe it was a sign from the universe to go grocery shopping. "You and Charlotte aren't doing anything tomorrow night?"

"Charlotte and I are going to a movie premiere in Hollywood this weekend," he said. "Thursday night is for dinner with my daughter."

"Tomorrow it is."

"Maxime's at eight o'clock?"

"That sounds fancy enough I won't even pretend I can afford going Dutch."

"It's my treat. I'll pick you up about seven forty-five."

They said their goodbyes and hung up.

She stared at her phone. Had she given him too much information about the investigation? No. There was nothing to tell. She didn't know anything yet.

But she could just see her mother crossing her arms and shaking her head disapprovingly. Maybe Fenway *had* trusted her father too much.

"I'm just being nice," Fenway murmured. "It's not like I have anyone else left."

She grabbed the manila folder Dez had given her, sat on the sofa, and started to read about securing crime scenes.

———

Fenway's cell phone rang.

She was asleep. The second ring woke her. The third ring made her realize it was a phone call, not her alarm. She pushed her pillow to the side, reached her hand out to the bedside table, and picked up the phone. She looked at the screen: 3:26 A.M.

"Hello?" she croaked.

"Hey, Fenway, sorry to wake you." Sheriff McVie's voice was urgent.

"Craig?" She sat up and tried to shake the sleep out of her head. "I mean, Sheriff? Something wrong?"

"We have to get to your office right away. There's been a break-in."

"A break-in?"

"Yes. A break-in like I've never seen before."

PART THREE
THURSDAY

CHAPTER EIGHT

FENWAY BLINKED HARD, CATCHING THE TENSION IN MCVIE'S VOICE. Her eyes were gummy. "Someone broke into the coroner's office?"

"I'm on my way to your place right now. Throw some clothes on and get down to the parking lot."

"Sure." She got out of bed, perching the phone between her ear and shoulder, and grabbed a bra and a long-sleeve blouse. "I hope I don't have to match."

McVie had already clicked off.

She quickly shed her pajamas and pulled on her clothes. She looked in the mirror: her hair was crazy, but she didn't have time to fix it. She grabbed a hat from her closet. It was a Boston Red Sox baseball cap, a gag gift from her clinic co-workers last year. She picked up her keys and purse on her way out the door. She managed to make it downstairs in time to see McVie pull into the driveway.

She opened the passenger door and got in.

McVie pointed to her cap once she got in the car. "Seriously?"

"Just drive."

He floored it once he was on the main road. Fenway glanced over at him; he was wearing a black tee shirt that showed off his muscular arms, flexing slightly as he gripped the wheel. She suddenly remembered fleeting images from the dream she was having when she woke up: her legs wrapped around his torso, his strong arms around her back, her breaths coming short and fast, his lips on hers. She turned her head and stared at the road, feeling the heat rise to her cheeks, trying to push the images out of her mind.

They made it to the coroner's office building in about half the time it had taken the morning before.

"You really need to get a car," he said.

He pulled around to the side of the building. Fenway's jaw dropped; there was a hole where the window to Walker's office used to be. Two police cruisers had their lights going, but no sirens sounded. Three uniformed officers were standing a few feet away from the hole in the building.

"Dammit," McVie muttered. "Dammit, dammit, dammit."

He braked hard to a stop, threw the gear angrily into park, and jumped out of the car without turning it off. "Fenway!" he barked. "See if you can tell if anything's missing."

She got out and walked over to the planter between the driveway and the side of the building. There was a messy tangle of flattened bushes and shrubs where a large vehicle—maybe a big pickup or SUV—had jumped the curb and punched a truck-shaped hole in the side of the building.

She peered inside the hole. It was dark. She used the light from her phone to get a better look inside. One of the filing cabinets was missing its third drawer from the top.

"Missing file drawer," she called.

McVie was seething. "How the hell did this happen?" he shouted. "Our coroner gets killed, we can't gather evidence for *days*, and as soon as we do, the whole crime scene gets compromised!"

Fenway stood there, not sure what to do.

"Who knew about this? Who knew you were going to look at those files today?"

"Besides you?" Her voice was smaller than she wanted it to be.

"Yes, dammit, besides me!"

"Um, everyone who was here last night. Dez. Mark. Rachel. Migs. The young officer who was watching over me—I don't think I ever got his name."

"Lana Cassidy?"

"I don't know. She knew I was investigating Walker's office, but I don't think she knew I was going to look at those files. Whoever was in the evidence room where the keys were, probably. I assume the officer talked to somebody to check out the keys from the evidence room, right?"

"Who else?" McVie pushed.

"No one else."

"Your dad?"

"No, I didn't..." Fenway trailed off.

His head cocked to the side. "You didn't what?"

"I don't know. My father called last night, and he asked about the investigation. But I was purposely vague. I told him I had just started and I wanted to make some headway."

"Did you tell him you were going through the files today?"

"I don't think so."

"You don't *think* so?"

Fenway shrugged, crossing her arms. "I don't know, okay?"

McVie paced back and forth. "Fenway, this is an active investigation. We can't tell anyone anything that's going on!"

"I know."

He exhaled loudly. "I know you know intellectually. I know what you read in your textbooks. But out here in the real world, actually keeping your mouth shut about active investigations prevents shit like this from happening."

Fenway looked down at the ground.

"This is a disaster." McVie ran his hand through his hair. "I have to get a crime scene team in here. Probably from San Miguelito, even though they have a conflict of interest, but I don't have a choice."

He kicked at the ground. "I'm going to have to wake a lot of people up."

"I can canvass," she offered. "See if there's anyone around who saw anything."

"Come on, Fenway. Look at this place. There's no one around to canvass. There aren't even homeless people around City Hall. And it's the middle of the night, in a sleepy little town. No one's around."

"Then I'll go check the security footage. A truck, or something, plowed into the side of the building, and we've got security cameras, so we must have something on tape."

"Knock yourself out," McVie said, his tone softer, almost defeated. "I'll be waking up a CSI team in the next county."

Fenway skulked around to the front of the building. She swiped the temporary card next to the reader at the door. It beeped, but flashed red. She tried it two more times with the same result. She swore softly and walked back around to the side where McVie was still muttering under his breath.

It was clear to Fenway that McVie was incensed about the entire situation. He looked tired. Fenway thought he might have been angry he wasn't at home in bed with his wife.

"My keycard doesn't work."

McVie didn't respond.

Fenway waited a few awkward seconds and then spoke again. "I think it might be because it's a temporary keycard, and it might not let you in after hours."

"Imagine that, a security protocol we've actually followed correctly," he mumbled.

"Look, Sheriff, I don't know what you want me to say. I don't know if

I messed up by saying something to my father. But last night, there were, I don't know, like, ten people who knew I was going through the files tomorrow—I mean, today—and it wasn't a secret. No one thought we should keep it under wraps." She put her hands on her hips. "So, let's try to figure out who stole the files, and not play the blame game."

"Just let me be pissed off for a little while, Fenway. Just let me *be* for a little bit."

Fenway didn't say anything.

McVie grabbed his keycard off his belt and handed it to her. "Go ahead. Go review the footage."

"I'll go with you," one of the uniforms said to her. "I was the security guard in the video room when the truck hit the building."

"You were?" McVie was surprised. "Fine then, give me back my keycard."

The officer took the card back from Fenway and gave it to McVie. "I'm Quincy." He held out his hand to her. Quincy was about two inches shorter and his skin was a couple of shades darker than Fenway. He was trim, and his uniform looked clean and neat, even after the drama of the early morning.

"Fenway." She took his hand and shook it firmly. "New coroner."

"I know."

"Okay, Quincy, lead the way. Let's go see what kind of truck or SUV this was."

They went inside, past the stairs, and through a doorway on the right. It went through a short corridor which led to a dark, nondescript door. Quincy scanned his card again, and it beeped before the door opened into the video suite.

"Okay," she said. "The cameras were all recording, right? No one messed with them?"

"Right. A few years ago, someone tried to break in, and they spray painted the lenses on a couple of the cameras. We replaced them with cameras that don't look like cameras, and moved them up higher, way out of reach of someone standing on the ground underneath." He pushed a few buttons and dialed a few knobs. "Okay, this is footage from about an hour ago, from the camera mounted on the wall closest to the impact."

They saw an empty parking lot. Quincy fast-forwarded the video a bit. With the time on the video reading *3:03*, they watched a large, black pickup truck come into the frame from the left at a high rate of speed.

"This is him," Quincy said.

"What is that? A Ford?"

"Yeah, looks like an F-350 to me." The truck turned away from the building for a second. "Duallies."

She pointed to bars covering the back of the pickup. "What are those?" The bars were also blocking most of the license plate. Fenway could make out two of the numbers and she could tell they were California plates.

"Bull bars, looks like."

She didn't ask for details. "Those look weird."

"They usually go on the front. They must have jerry-rigged it to go on the back."

"Why would they do that?"

The pickup quickly accelerated in reverse, into the bushes between the parking lot and the building. The rear of the truck disappeared out of the frame, as did most of the rest of the truck. When the truck hit the building, they could see the dust come up into the frame.

Quincy squinted. "So they could back into the building without the airbags going off."

"Okay. Let's see who this guy is."

But they could only see part of the door. It obviously opened and shut, but they couldn't see who got out—or even if anyone did.

"Could you see the driver at all?"

"The driver? No. I couldn't even see if he got out."

Fenway nodded. "And it isn't necessarily a man."

Quincy rubbed his eyes. "Let's see if we can see him when he comes back."

About forty-five seconds later, the door opened and closed again, and the truck surged forward quickly. Quincy paused it, trying to make something out from the shadowy figure in the driver's seat, but the reflections off the window, the low light, and the low quality of the camera made it impossible. There wasn't anything in the video that provided a clue as to the identity of the driver.

The truck got out of the planter and back onto the asphalt of the parking lot. Then it peeled out, as Quincy came into the frame, gun drawn. The bull bars were hanging off the back of the truck awkwardly, and the bumper and gate were smashed.

"I'm surprised it could still be driven," Fenway said.

"Yeah. The truck pretty much went through the outside wall below the window, though. Really hit half-wall and half-window. The outside wall is weaker at the window there, and the glass and a two-foot high wall is a lot easier to go through than a reinforced eight-foot wall. And those bull bars helped."

"I guess. Still seems pretty lucky."

The camera saw Quincy briefly assess the damage, then run out of the frame.

"Did you fire your gun?" she asked.

"No."

"Why not?"

"I'm not supposed to fire," Quincy said. "This is property damage and theft, not a murder, or an assault, or anything. You've been watching too many cop shows."

"I bet those bull bars fell off before they got very far."

"They might have. I watched the truck go down First Street and then make a right on Broadway. Toward the freeway."

"They could be halfway to Mexico by now," she said. "Anything else on the cameras?"

"I don't know yet, but from where the truck came from, we should get the pickup truck coming into the lot with Camera 6. If we're lucky, we could get the front plate."

"If they were that stupid."

"I've seen stupider. And this was pretty brazen. A smash-and-grab really close to the sheriff's office, in the middle of a murder investigation? That's crazy. I guess they got some important files."

"I don't know how important they were. I didn't have a chance to see them. I was going to look at them tomorrow."

"I guess you won't find out now." Quincy drummed his fingers on the table. "Not unless we can stop the truck before it gets to where it's going."

"Let's at least try," she said. "See if you can get the license plate from Camera 6."

Quincy clicked a couple of buttons, and sure enough, the truck's license plate was visible. Fenway called the sheriff.

"McVie," he answered, curtly.

"Sheriff, we have a plate number. Dually black Ford F-350." She gave him the plate.

"Okay. I'll put out an APB."

She hung up and turned back to Quincy.

"I don't think anything else is going to come up, at least not for the smash-and-grab," Quincy said. "I'll let you know if I see anyone who might have been casing the place, somebody who might have been seeing if that wall was as vulnerable as it was, anything like that."

"Yeah, that's weird. Oddly specific, right? That particular office, that particular drawer?" She tapped her chin in thought.

"Do you think the driver of the truck might be the person who murdered Mr. Walker Sunday night?"

"It's the logical place to start," Fenway said, "but plenty of people were in Walker's file cabinet. Someone might have seen this as an opportunity to expunge their record, or make sure they weren't—" She stopped.

"What is it?"

She hesitated. "What have you heard about Harrison Walker?"

"What do you mean?"

"Have you heard any rumors about him at work?"

Quincy folded his arms. "I've heard he's a creep. Saying stuff to the women who work here, making them uncomfortable. If you ask me, he's a lawsuit waiting to happen."

"Yeah, I've heard that, too."

"You? You've only been in town a couple of days."

"I know, right? So, it must be pretty bad if I've heard it already. But here's the thing: stuff like sexual harassment usually doesn't stop at sexual harassment. Usually, those assholes feel entitled to money, favors, equipment, that sort of thing." She shuffled her feet.

"Okay. So, what do you think Walker did?"

"Maybe nothing." She leaned on the wall. "But probably something. Skimming off the top. Extortion. Taking a bribe. Something. And maybe it has to do with why someone drove a truck through the building and stole a drawerful of files, or maybe it has to do with why he was killed, or maybe both."

There was a knock. Quincy opened the door.

It was the sheriff. "Plate came back. Pickup belongs to Dylan Richards."

"All right," Fenway said. "I wasn't really expecting a hit on the plate so soon. Reported stolen?"

"Nope." McVie hesitated.

"What is it?"

"You know Rachel?"

"In the coroner's office? Yeah, of course."

"Dylan's her husband."

"Oh." She covered her mouth with her hand.

"Yeah. Fenway, this isn't good. It's not good for Dylan, and it's not good for Rachel either."

"No, it's not. And we can't tell if the driver is a man or woman. It could have been Rachel."

"I know Rachel in the coroner's office," Quincy said. "It's not her. She's definitely too short to be the driver. And too petite. And she doesn't carry herself like that."

"But it could be Dylan?" Fenway asked.

"I don't know. I don't think I know Dylan."

"Do you want to come with me to the Richards' apartment?" McVie asked.

She hesitated. "Yes, I do, but yesterday you and I weren't supposed to have any contact with each other. Are you sure you want me coming with you?"

"I think a pickup truck smashing through the side of the coroner's office has changed the rules," McVie said. "It's given the case urgency. We can't wait anymore. It's all hands on deck."

Quincy promised to keep them informed if anyone was seen on video casing the building. McVie and Fenway walked out toward his car.

"Truck had bull bars on the back to make it easier to smash through the wall," she said. "Quincy thinks they jerry-rigged the bull bars to the back so when they smashed through the wall, the airbags wouldn't go off. When we saw the bull bars in the video afterward, they looked like they were about to fall off the truck. We should see if anyone can find bull bars on the side of the road between here and the freeway, or on the freeway. One or two good turns might be all it needed."

"If it's Dylan's truck, this might be a pretty fast investigation."

"It might be. Still, no stone unturned, right?"

McVie laughed a little uneasily. "I guess."

They got to the car and he unlocked the door. "Hey, before we get in, I want to say sorry. I snapped at you for telling your dad. I'm tired, and I'm frustrated."

"No, you were right," Fenway conceded. "I've got to keep that closer to the vest."

They got in McVie's car and drove to the townhouse complex where Fenway had driven Rachel two nights before.

"I've got to tell you something," Fenway said, turning in her seat to look at McVie.

"What?"

"Dylan may have a motive for killing Walker. I don't really want to tell you, because Rachel told me this in confidence." She hesitated.

"Out with it, Fenway."

"Rachel was sexually assaulted by Walker on Friday night. And she recorded it on her computer."

McVie's eyes widened. "She recorded it? Like with a camera?"

"Yeah. He asked her to work late when no one else was in the office, and she got a really weird vibe, and HR wouldn't do anything. So she set up a webcam, he made his move, and she recorded it all. She made copies of the video, and she told me she put one in her kitchen junk drawer, because she was afraid HR would confiscate the video and side with Walker."

McVie breathed out. "Ugh."

"Yeah."

"Seriously. What a piece of shit." He pulled into a driveway next to a sign that said *Scarlet Oak Townhomes*. "Okay, Dylan and Rachel live in number 19."

Fenway didn't tell McVie she drove Rachel home two nights before. "I don't see any Ford pickups."

McVie parked and turned off the car. "It might be parked on the street, but in my experience, people who commit a crime with their cars usually don't drive back home. They usually stash the car somewhere. If that's the case, Dylan's probably not even here. But you never know, some criminals really are that stupid. What did you say before? No stone unturned?"

"Fine, fine." She walked with McVie to the door of number 19 and looked at her watch. It was four in the morning.

CHAPTER NINE

McVie pounded on the door. "Dylan Richards?"

"McVie! You'll wake everyone up," Fenway hissed.

"If he's not home, this'll be quick. And if he is home, I'll quiet down as soon as he answers the door." He pounded again. She looked up as a light in the upstairs window went on.

After about fifteen seconds, they heard footfalls on the stairs, then the door opened. Rachel peered out. Her hair was messy, and she was in her pajamas.

"Sheriff? Fenway? What are you doing here?"

"Is Dylan here, Rachel?" McVie said.

Rachel blinked, confused. "Yeah, he's coming in a second. What's going on?"

"Rachel, I think you and Dylan need to come down to the station."

"What? Why?"

"Where's Dylan's truck?" McVie asked.

"What do you mean? It's right there—" she trailed off as she looked in the parking lot. "Well—Dylan parked it right there last night when we got home."

"Dylan's truck smashed through the wall of Walker's office early this morning," Fenway explained. "And they took some stuff."

A dark cloud passed over Rachel's face. "Oh God, did you tell him?" Rachel nodded to the sheriff.

Fenway was silent, and she looked down at the doormat.

Rachel put her hands over her face. "God, I'm so stupid."

"I'm sorry, Rachel," Fenway started, "but we're investigating the death of your boss, and you said I was going to find out anyway, right? And now Walker's files are gone, and it looks like your husband might be involved, and I know he might have a motive."

Rachel looked confused. "Walker's files are gone? What files?"

"Can you just get Dylan and come down to the station, please?" McVie shot Fenway a look that said, *would you keep your mouth shut?*

Rachel drew in her breath sharply. "I swear, the truck was here in the parking lot when we got home last night. And I swear we haven't left." She bit her lip. "I'll go get Dylan. Can we get dressed first?"

"Of course," Fenway said.

McVie looked at her out of the corner of his eye. "But please make it quick."

Rachel nodded, turned around and went upstairs, leaving the door about halfway open.

They were both back downstairs in a couple of minutes. Dylan was only a few inches taller than Rachel—maybe five-six or five-seven, but he looked muscular in a wiry way. He had light brown hair, fairly moplike on top. "What do you mean, where's my truck?" Dylan asked as they came down the stairs.

"I don't know, Dylan." Rachel threw up her hands. "It's not where we left it last night."

"We should probably go to the station, sort it out there," said McVie.

Rachel looked at Fenway's face, trying to read her.

Dylan came out onto the front step. "Listen, Sheriff, I left my truck here last night. Right in that space, number 19, next to that silver Toyota."

"What kind of truck is it?" Fenway asked.

"It's a black Ford F-350."

"Duallies?"

"You know it," he smirked. Fenway couldn't believe it—four in the morning with the police at his door and he's being flirtatious and cool.

"Got bull bars on the back?" McVie asked.

Dylan's eyebrows pulled in. "Bull bars on the back of the truck? What idiot would put bull bars on the *back* of a pickup?"

"So that's a 'no'?"

"Yeah, that's a 'no.'"

"You didn't have bull bars on the front either?"

"Sure, on the front. That's where they go."

"Honey," Rachel said softly, "I think you better ask to file a police report on your truck. I think it was stolen and I think someone used it last night to do something illegal."

Dylan pulled Rachel to the side and they talked in low voices. Fenway couldn't hear what they were saying. They walked back after a minute, and Dylan looked at the sheriff. "Sheriff, I think my truck was stolen. I'd like to file a report."

McVie shifted his weight from one foot to the other. "Those forms are at the station. And as you don't have a car, I guess you'll have to ride with us."

"I have my car," Rachel said. "I can drive us."

"Yeah," Dylan replied, "I think I'd rather ride with Rachel. I can meet you there."

McVie looked at Dylan and Rachel. "Okay, no problem. But please go directly there. We definitely need to speak with you. If you weren't driving your truck, you're still a material witness."

Dylan squinted. "Am I under arrest?"

"No," Rachel answered. "But a material witness means they can compel you to provide evidence."

He turned to Rachel and spoke in a low voice. "And what does that mean?"

"It means we better go to the station."

"Where are you parked?" McVie asked.

"A little ways up the street past that driveway." Rachel pointed down the road a bit.

McVie watched Rachel and Dylan walk to her BMW before motioning Fenway to get in his car. "I drove her home in that car the other day," Fenway said to McVie after she got in the cruiser. "It's really nice. Wonder how she affords it on an admin's salary."

"Her dad bought it." McVie started the car and reversed out of the space. "Listen, Fenway, I know you were trying to help, but you can't be giving that kind of information out to suspects." McVie pulled out into the street behind the BMW.

"But Rachel is—" She stopped herself from saying "my friend." She reminded herself that she had met Rachel only two days before. She supposed she felt like that because Rachel had already opened up to her so much.

"I know Rachel is an employee of the coroner's office, but Walker's sexual assault gives her a motive—and it gives Dylan a motive, too."

"I can't see her doing this."

"Oh, come on, Fenway, you've known her for all of two days. One of my buddies from high school stabbed his landlord five years ago. I never would have pegged him for it either, so *you* can't tell after two days what Rachel's capable of."

She looked out the window.

"Listen," McVie said, "when we get to the station, I'm going to sit them both in our interview room, then I'm going to take Dylan out to fill out the stolen vehicle form, and I want you to keep Rachel talking."

"What are we going to talk about? Do you want me to ask her questions about the case?"

"Yes." McVie nodded. "And ask her about those recordings, and who else knows those recordings were made, and where she was Sunday night —stuff like that."

"She owns a gun," Fenway blurted out.

"Really?"

"Yes, a .22. She said her dad gave it her for self-defense, but she's never used it."

"A .22 for self-defense?" McVie shook his head. "Her dad buys her a new BMW, but can't get her a decent gun."

"So what type of gun killed Walker? Wasn't a .22, was it?"

"No, when I was there, the CSI team said it looked to be a bigger caliber. Maybe a nine-millimeter. I mean, we won't know for sure until we get the results from the autopsy, but it was definitely bigger than a .22."

The sheriff's office was behind City Hall. They pulled in next to Rachel's BMW. Dylan and Rachel were already there, waiting for them.

The station only had one interview room, so all four of them went there. They had just sat down, Fenway across from Rachel, and McVie across from Dylan, when McVie "remembered" they should fill out the stolen car form first, so the two men left the room.

Fenway was left alone in the room with Rachel. "I wish I hadn't had to say something about the attack, Rachel."

Rachel put her head in her hands. "I'm such an idiot. I just met you. And I *knew* you'd be working on the investigation. I *gave* you a reason to suspect me."

"You gave me a motive for *a lot* of people, not just yourself."

Rachel was quiet.

"But look, when you told me what had happened, I got so pissed off at Walker, I was ready to hurt him for what he did to you. And I just met you, so I can imagine how angry Dylan is with Walker. How angry anyone who cares about you would be."

"Dylan doesn't know."

Fenway tilted her head. "Are you sure? You put one of those flash drives right where he could find it."

"I told you, he'd barely notice a USB stick in the junk drawer," Rachel insisted. "He wouldn't have given it a second thought."

"How do you know, Rachel? He had more than enough time to look through the video, get fuming mad, and kill Walker on Sunday night."

"No, that didn't happen. I'm sure that didn't happen."

"Jealous husbands do crazy, stupid things." Fenway rested her chin in her hand, her elbow on the table. "It's not much of a stretch."

Rachel looked down and didn't say anything.

"Dylan ever been jealous?"

Rachel shrugged.

"So that's a 'yes.'"

Rachel sighed, obviously conflicted. "There was a guy who hit on me at a bar a couple of months ago. Dylan was playing darts with his friends, and I was bored so I started flirting with a guy at the bar. He bought me a drink. Dylan didn't like it and threatened to punch the guy. The guy left right away. Dylan was saying he was going to follow him outside, and I told him to stay at the bar a little longer. Dance with me a little."

"Did he follow the guy out?"

"No, he stayed with me and his friends."

Fenway drummed her fingers on the table. "Has Dylan ever been in trouble with the cops before?"

"Not really."

Fenway's eyebrows raised. "What does that mean?"

"It means not for a while. Not since he was a kid. He shoplifted some stuff when he was fifteen—had to spend a night in juvie before his mom got him out. Community service."

"Is that it?"

"That's all I know."

"You're sure there's nothing in his adult record?"

"I don't think so." She shook her head. "Nothing I know about, anyway."

"Okay." Fenway stood up. "And you made three copies of the video onto USB sticks?"

"Yes."

"And you've got one in your glove compartment?"

"Yes."

"And one in the junk drawer in the kitchen?"

"But like I said, I don't think Dylan would even know what it was if he found it," Rachel answered. "And if he had, he would have confronted me about it, or at least he would have acted differently about it. He would have asked me what was going on at work."

"All right. Where's the third one, again?"

"It's in my purse," Rachel said. "I was going to give it to Lana on Monday, but now that Mr. Walker is dead, I don't know what to do with it."

"I think we need to take it for evidence."

Rachel rubbed her eyes. "I want this to go away. I don't want anyone to see that. I never wanted him to touch me. I just wanted it *over.*"

"I know." Fenway sat back down. "Believe me, I know."

Part of Fenway wanted to tell Rachel about what she went through with her Russian Lit professor. She closed her eyes and willed herself not to say anything, but as soon as she closed her eyes, she could see the professor's face, feel his tongue on the side of her face, feel his hands up her blouse. Putting a bullet in his back would have felt good.

"What did you say?" Rachel asked.

Fenway realized she spoke the last sentence out loud, and she decided to steer into the skid. "I said, 'putting a bullet in his back would have felt good.'"

Rachel looked horrified.

"Well, *I* would have liked to. Walker got what was coming to him."

"He was my *boss*. You're in his *office*."

Fenway nodded. "Yeah. I guess I've already opened my big mouth up too much for one morning." She paused. "Okay, there are at least two questions the sheriff will ask me about, and if I don't have answers for him, he's not going to like it, and I'll have to take the bus home."

Rachel still looked put off by Fenway's comments, but she nodded.

"When I was at your apartment, I told you I'd have to ask you this at some point—and it looks like now is the time I have to ask."

"You want to know where I was the night Mr. Walker was shot and killed."

"Yes. I remember you told me you forced yourself to go out, right?"

"Yeah. I cancelled my plans on Saturday, but on Sunday I went to the movies with my friend Jordan. We saw a seven o'clock showing of *The Trap Door*, and I didn't want to go home after, so I convinced her to come to Krazy Burger with me, and we got chocolate shakes and onion rings. I got home about ten o'clock and watched a couple of episodes of *Hold Your Horses* until I got the call at midnight that Mr. Walker had been killed."

"Will Jordan corroborate that?"

"Sure she will." Rachel nodded. "Jordan dropped me off and came in to take back a sweater I had borrowed a few days ago. And I probably have the movie stub and the Krazy Burger receipt. Dylan makes fun of me for not throwing any of that stuff away."

"Okay. I don't know if the sheriff is going to want any of that, but we'll need to check it out."

"I understand."

"Where was Dylan?" Fenway asked.

"He was out with his brother, I think. I was asleep when he got home."

"And then I also need to know where you were earlier this morning, between one o'clock and three thirty."

"I was in bed with Dylan until you came to wake us up."

"Can anyone else vouch that you were there?"

Rachel shook her head. "No."

"Do you know if there are security cameras set up at your apartment complex?"

"Um, no, I don't know if there are cameras. What happened this morning? You said there were some files missing? And Dylan's truck is gone?"

"The sheriff is already pissed off at me for saying as much as I said at your apartment." Fenway stifled a yawn. "You'll have to wait to get the full story."

"All right. How long are we going to be here? Am I going to make it into work?"

Fenway smiled weakly. "I think your supervisor is aware there are special circumstances regarding your attendance at work today." She looked at Rachel, but there was no reaction to Fenway's weak attempt at levity. "But, to answer your question, no, I don't think we're going to get out of here in the next couple of hours. Do you want some coffee?"

"I guess so."

Fenway got up again and left the interview room, closing the door behind her.

She took a deep breath. She had done several in-depth case studies over the course of her graduate program. She remembered in one of the studies, back in January, the victim had committed a crime. The point of the case study was to demonstrate how personal biases can affect how investigators approach cases. Fenway was trying not to let that happen now, but as McVie had said earlier, it's one thing to know the right way to act intellectually, and quite another to act in the right way in the real world. Rachel had opened up to Fenway, had told her something she hadn't told anyone else, and Fenway felt like she betrayed Rachel's trust in order to further the investigation.

But as bad as she felt about Rachel, she felt almost high from the excitement of the investigation; it was like a puzzle—and it was why she had wanted to do forensics in the first place—piecing together the mystery of what exactly happened.

Actually, that wasn't quite true. She started the forensics program because she kept seeing women in the ER whose husbands or boyfriends had beaten them. She felt like forensics could establish a measure of justice for those women. Somehow. And the more she learned about forensics—the classes on evidence gathering, witness interviews, and chain of custody—the more she found it fascinating. She loved it—the mysteries, even the case studies in her classes, were intoxicating.

She walked over to the coffee maker. It was an industrial machine, with water lines coming into the back, brewing directly into tall, thermos-style carafes that held a half gallon each. The carafes were all washed out, upside down in the sink, but Fenway didn't see any coffee or any coffee filters. She started to look through the cabinets. Sponges. Paper towels. Lysol. Paper plates. Finally, in the second to last cupboard, she found some packets of French Roast from a place in Paso Querido called *Mount Caffeinated*. The filters were behind the packets. She prepped everything and pushed the 'on' switch.

"We've got people at the front desk who'll do that," McVie said from behind her. She jumped a little at his voice and turned around. He and Dylan were standing next to each other.

She smiled at McVie. "Okay. Maybe one of them could bring Rachel and me a couple of mugs when it's finished."

"Why don't you come on back to the interview room? I've got some questions for Dylan, and you might want to sit in."

McVie left Fenway with Dylan for a moment while he went to find the officer on duty to bring the coffee when it was ready.

Dylan looked down at the floor, then looked at Fenway and pointed at her cap. "Red Sox fan?"

"My father is." She smiled back.

"My brother and I drove across the country one summer during college," he said. "We tried to hit as many major league parks as we could. We drove south first, then over to Phoenix, through Texas, then up through Missouri to Chicago and Milwaukee. But it was taking too long, so we turned around." He sighed. "I still haven't seen Fenway Park." He pointed at her. "Your dad named you after the ballpark? It's not some crazy family name?"

"Family name?"

"Sure, why not? A combination of your great-uncle Fenwick and your third cousin Hemingway?"

Fenway surprised herself by laughing. "I'm going to have to make that my story from now on," she said. "That's a lot more interesting than the Red Sox jokes I've heard all my life."

McVie came back. "Ready?"

She nodded. As Dylan walked into the interview room, she pulled McVie aside. "Are you sure you want to talk with them together? Rachel knows police procedure and rules a lot better than most people. She'll stop him from saying anything incriminating."

"I know," whispered McVie. "But it's not about their answers. I want to keep them here for another couple of hours at least, and I thought if I kept them apart, they'd insist on leaving. We woke up a judge for a warrant to search Dylan's place. They're on their way to execute it right now."

"You know you're going to find that USB drive with that video of Walker attacking Rachel."

"I know."

"But she says he didn't see it."

"Look, if it turns out he *did* do it, this goes to motive, and we have to have that USB drive in our custody. Besides, I was hoping you would be talking with Rachel separately when I was gone, and we can see if there are holes in their story."

"Yeah, I got that," Fenway said. "I've got her alibi for both Sunday night and early this morning. She was with Dylan at home asleep this morning, and she was with a friend at a movie and Krazy Burgers on Sunday."

"She wasn't with Dylan Sunday?"

"She was asleep when he got home."

"All right, let's see what he says."

They went in.

CHAPTER TEN

"OKAY, DYLAN," MCVIE SAID. "NOW THAT WE'VE GOTTEN YOUR stolen vehicle report filed, let's talk about where you were a couple nights this week."

Dylan leaned back in his chair. "I already told you, I was asleep at home. Rachel and I went to bed around eleven. And you saw the report for my stolen truck—we got back from the grocery store at about six thirty, we left the truck in my spot, and I haven't seen my truck since."

"How about Sunday night?" Fenway asked.

Dylan's face darkened, and he looked from Fenway to McVie. "Sunday night? Where did you see my truck Sunday night?"

Rachel leaned over to Dylan and spoke softly. "They aren't asking about your truck. They want to know where you were when Mr. Walker got shot and killed."

Dylan balked. "Why would I kill Walker? Because he was a shitty boss to Rachel?"

Fenway looked at Rachel, who frowned and quickly shook her head, as if to quiet Dylan. McVie saw it, too. Fenway wasn't sure McVie was going to let it go; he might dig into this line of questioning to see if it would push Dylan's buttons. But he didn't, to Fenway's surprise.

"Because your truck was caught on camera, leaving the scene of a break-in at Walker's office barely two hours ago." McVie raised his voice slightly. "And we're working under the assumption the break-in and the murder are related."

Dylan had a confused look on his face. "But my truck was stolen."

"Right, you've told me." McVie stood up and leaned on the table, looking Dylan in the eyes. "But there are lots of situations where a husband has done something stupid because of his wife. Maybe Walker was a shitty boss to Rachel. Maybe he was hitting on her and you didn't like it. Maybe she was going to get fired. Maybe she was stealing paper clips, and her boss found out, and so you took him out to the woods, or followed him out there, and killed him. And maybe her stealing paper clips was in Walker's files, so you had to take that, too."

Rachel narrowed her eyes. "You don't have any proof."

McVie straightened up and sighed. "Right. All we have to go on is video evidence of *Dylan's* pickup truck, smashing through the wall of Walker's office, and leaving with a file drawer."

Dylan shook his head. "You're crazy. Smashing through the wall? In my truck?"

"Dylan loves that truck." Rachel put her hand on Dylan's shoulder. "He'd never even park it under a tree if he thought a bird would crap on it, never mind purposely smashing it through a wall."

Dylan looked from Rachel, to Fenway, then to McVie. "I swear it wasn't me driving."

Rachel shrugged. "He wouldn't hurt that truck. Plus, we were together, in bed, asleep, two hours ago."

McVie sat back down. "Okay, so you've said that's where you were tonight. How about Sunday night? You still haven't answered. Where were you on Sunday night between eight o'clock and eleven?"

Dylan hesitated, but then leaned back in his chair again and grinned.

"I was playing video games with Parker. I got out of there about eleven thirty. I had to work Monday morning."

"What's Parker's last name?" McVie asked.

"Richards," Rachel said. "Parker is Dylan's brother."

"Did Parker have to work on Monday morning, too?"

Dylan laughed. "No, Parker's a cook at Villa Roma over in Paso Q. They're closed Mondays."

McVie leaned forward. "What video games did you play?"

"Um, I don't remember."

"You don't remember? You were playing against your brother and don't remember what you were playing?"

"We usually play *Rogue Nation 3*." Dylan swallowed. "I had a deadline at work this week. I was kind of distracted with that. I wasn't really paying attention too much."

"Oh, yeah." McVie nodded. "I get that, being distracted by work stuff. That happens to me all the time." He leaned forward and lowered his voice. "My wife gets all over my ass when that happens. She hates it when I get distracted by work stuff."

Dylan laughed a little. "Yeah, Parker was kinda ticked off that I was distracted. I wasn't playing my best."

"How do you know you weren't playing your best if you don't remember what you were playing?"

Dylan paused, his cool smile frozen on his face. "Because I remember Parker said I wasn't even trying. He called me names."

"Like what?"

"You know," he trailed off, shrugging, "names."

McVie sat back. "How about dinner?"

"Dinner?"

"Yeah, did you and Parker have dinner? I mean, sometimes people are so into their video games they just order a pizza."

"Oh, right, yeah, we ordered a pizza." A bead of sweat was on Dylan's brow, even though it was cold in the room.

"What time did the delivery guy show up?"

"Um, I don't know. Maybe seven?"

"Where did you order from?"

"Oh, uh, I'm not sure. One of the chain places, I think."

Fenway looked at Rachel, whose mouth was pursed; she didn't look like she was buying it. Fenway didn't need to remember her notes from her witness interview class to tell Dylan was lying.

She stood up. "Hey, Rachel, let's go see what's taking the coffee so long."

McVie looked at her and Fenway looked plaintively at him. She was sure if she could tell Dylan was lying, so could McVie. Even if McVie's original plan was to keep the two of them together, Fenway thought the obvious lies Dylan was telling probably required a change in strategy. Dylan might have had a reason to lie in front of Rachel—going out to a bar when he promised he wouldn't, seeing another woman on the side, going to the casino in Dominguez Pines—or maybe he didn't want to confess to killing Walker in front of Rachel.

Rachel looked at McVie, and looked at Dylan, and then stared straight ahead, tapping her foot. Finally, she relented. "Sure, let's get that coffee."

The two women walked out and saw the officer from the night desk pushing buttons on the coffeemaker. Fenway walked up next to the officer.

"Didn't it work right?" she asked.

"No," he snapped at Fenway. "The filter holder wasn't in all the way and it didn't start."

"Sorry. First time using it."

"Maybe ask for help next time."

Rachel touched Fenway's arm. "How about we go over to Java Jim's? I think they open at five. It's a couple blocks away."

Fenway looked at her watch, and sure enough, it was five fifteen.

They walked outside into the misty, early morning air. It was still dark; the morning light was about to peek over the horizon, although it would have to filter through the fog. They headed down the main avenue.

"So, what's Dylan lying about?"

"I don't know," Rachel murmured, eyes matching the mistiness of the air. "I haven't seen him like that before." She pulled her phone out of her purse and dialed a number. After a minute, Fenway could hear it go to voice mail. Rachel redialed. On the third try, someone picked up.

"Parker—it's Rachel. Yes, I know what time it is, it's early, but this is important. Where was Dylan on Sunday night?"

She paused, listening.

"Okay, good. No, it's okay. No, Dylan's car was stolen last night. We're trying to piece together where he was, where someone might have been casing the truck. No, we've called the police. We're actually down at the station now, I stepped out to get some coffee. Yeah. Okay. Yeah, I'll keep you posted. Sorry to wake you up." She hung up.

Rachel tapped her phone thoughtfully on her chin. "Parker told me he and Dylan were playing pool."

"Oh."

"Not playing video games."

They were both silent the rest of the way to Java Jim's. Fenway ordered a large latte and Rachel ordered a caramel macchiato. Fenway gave the barista a ten and dumped the change into the tip jar. They sat on two over-stuffed armchairs facing each other with a small round table in between.

Rachel drew her legs up underneath herself. "Why is he lying to the police?"

"I don't know." Fenway tapped the arm of her chair. "How long have you two been married?"

"Um, we eloped in September, so about eight months. I can't imagine..." She trailed off and fell silent for a minute. "I really don't believe he saw that video." she finally said, looking at Fenway. Her eyes were large and pleading.

"I don't know whether he did or not. But you know he's lying about something. And if he did see that video, he might be lying about going to confront Walker on Sunday night." Fenway didn't mention the other possibility in her head: Dylan was cheating on Rachel and was with the other woman that night.

Rachel's mouth was turned down in a frown, but her voice stayed even. "I just wanted Mr. Walker to stop," she mumbled. "I didn't want him dead. I just wanted him to stop."

"So, let me ask you again, was Dylan with you the whole night last night?"

"Yes," Rachel nodded, definitively. "We were asleep in the same bed, together, all night."

"Are you a heavy sleeper? Is there a possibility he could have gotten out of bed without you knowing? Gone out for a couple of hours, then come back in?"

"Maybe." She shrugged. "It's happened before. I usually wake up when he gets out of bed, but I had a couple of glasses of wine last night. I thought it would help me sleep, and it did."

The barista called *Rachel* and *Joanne,* and Fenway went to fetch the drinks. She set Rachel's drink on the table and took a sip of her own before she sat back down.

Rachel picked up her cup and warmed her hands on it. "I really thought if he saw the video, he'd talk to me about it first. I never thought he'd try to go after Mr. Walker himself."

"Even after seeing what he did in the bar? With the guy you were only flirting with?"

"I really thought he'd talk to me first," she said, sadly.

They were silent for a moment. Rachel took a slow sip.

Fenway took another drink of the latte and set it down on the table. "So, what do you want to do now?"

"I just want to drink my coffee." Rachel closed her eyes. "Let me finish this, and then maybe we can sit here awhile, and then we can go back to the station."

They sat there, mostly in silence. Fenway finished her latte, but she was still tired. She went back up to the barista to get a large drip coffee, and a scone for Rachel.

They both drank their coffees until six thirty. Rachel had only eaten a couple of bites of her scone.

Fenway checked her watch. "I think we'd better head back to the station."

Outside the coffee shop, the mist had thickened into a near-drizzle, but the light was stronger. Fenway could feel her hair getting damp and starting to frizz under her Red Sox cap. There was a wet sheen on Rachel's jacket and purse, but she didn't seem to notice.

They walked back into the station, entering the coffee area, in time to see McVie, with a couple of officers standing with him, put cuffs on Dylan.

"Dylan Richards," McVie recited, "you're under arrest for the murder of Harrison Walker. You have the right to remain silent."

Fenway looked at McVie questioningly. "Sheriff?"

"Police found a USB drive at his apartment with a video of Walker sexually assaulting his wife," McVie replied. "Goes to motive."

"I told you I don't know what USB drive you're talking about," Dylan snapped. His eyes were narrowed, and he looked angrily at Rachel.

"We found a .22 pistol in one of the bedside tables," McVie said.

"That's my gun," Rachel said.

"And to top it all off, we found a nine-millimeter Glock 26 in the bedroom closet."

"Which I haven't fired in months," Dylan seethed.

"Your brother's story doesn't match your alibi for Sunday night, Dylan," the sheriff said. "Care to explain?"

Dylan looked at the floor and was silent.

Rachel glanced up at Fenway, face stricken. "I can't stay here." She ran out the door into the early morning light and mist.

Fenway was going to go after Rachel, but McVie looked at her, shook his head slightly as if to say *don't go after her,* and finished reading Dylan his Miranda rights.

Fenway didn't know what she would have said to Rachel anyway.

CHAPTER ELEVEN

McVie took Dylan away. Fenway pictured Dylan getting fingerprinted, then placed in the holding cell at the station. She assumed McVie was going to be caught up with procedural stuff for a while.

The coroner's office wouldn't officially open until eight, and her temporary keycard wouldn't even work in the building until then, as she found out earlier; she wouldn't be able to work on anything for another hour and a half. Fenway asked the officer on duty, the one who had snapped at her for her coffee-making skills, if anyone else could let her into the building. He told her, in a rather stern voice, that she'd have to take it up with Human Resources when they got in at nine. Fenway didn't bother arguing.

She walked outside and looked up and down the street. City Hall still had its footlights on, the light shining on the American flag out front. The street was slowly waking up: the bakery a block down had its open sign lit, and a few people were arriving in the parking structure.

Fenway sighed, putting her hands a little deeper into her jacket pockets, and decided to take a look at the side of her office again. If the officers were still there, or if a crime scene unit were on scene, Fenway reasoned, she might be able to talk her way through the doors.

She arrived a few minutes later and walked around to the side. There were a couple of crime scene techs dusting the cabinet for fingerprints. A few officers were moving the furniture and equipment out of the room. Dez was standing a few feet away, arms folded. Fenway walked up next to her.

"Hey, Dez."

"Hey." She bumped Fenway's shoulder with hers in greeting. "I heard what happened and thought you'd probably be on the scene."

"I was questioning suspects with McVie. Can you use your keycard to get me into the office so I can get some work done?"

"Yeah, but let's wait till the dust clears from the CSI unit." She knelt down and looked at the tire tracks in the lawn. "So, I heard it was Rachel's husband that made this hole."

"His truck, anyway," Fenway said, noncommittally. "He says it was stolen."

"You question him yet?"

"McVie did. I was keeping Rachel occupied, mostly. McVie arrested him for Walker's murder about ten minutes ago."

Dez exhaled loudly. "Ugh. Rachel must be beside herself. Probably won't be seeing her today."

"Probably not. She ran out."

"What did they have on him?"

Fenway looked down at Dez. "We have enough for suspicion. Motive. An alibi that didn't match up. A gun that's probably the same caliber as the murder weapon."

"Hmm." Dez stood back up. "We haven't seen the ballistics report yet. I'll call the M.E. in San Miguelito first thing this morning."

"You have a good relationship with the M.E.?"

Dez looked at Fenway sideways. "What's that supposed to mean?"

Fenway was a little taken aback. "I just meant I have some new territory to cover here, and if you're on decent terms with the M.E., I might like you to introduce him to me."

Dez relaxed. "Yeah, we're not on the best of terms, but I'll see what I can do." Dez put her arms above her head and stretched. "And it's a her, by the way."

"What?"

"The M.E. It's a her, not a him."

Fenway nodded. "Oh, that's right. You said she was a bitch."

Dez chuckled. "Yep. I gotta tell you something else, Fenway. That drawer they stole was the F through G drawer in active files."

Fenway closed her eyes. "Let me guess. Ferris Energy had some active files in there."

"Yep. But F through G covers a lot of ground. Dylan's last name is Richards, like Rachel's, right?"

"Yeah."

"Well, that ain't it," Dez said.

"Maybe his mom's maiden name is Ferguson or Gatsby or something."

"Maybe, but these are active cases."

"Yeah."

"But I know for a fact there was an active file in there on Ferris Energy. There were a couple of deaths there about six months ago, and Walker still hadn't determined a cause of death."

"It wouldn't have been under the last name of the deceased?"

"Not in Walker's filing system." Dez shook her head. "When multiple deaths are related, Walker filed it under a group name. Two John Does found in Querido Park last year were filed under Q."

They both fell silent, watching the CSI team carry out the last few pieces of furniture.

"I'm not going to sweep anything my father did under the rug," Fenway said. "I don't know if that's why he suggested my name to McVie, but I'm not hiding anything. My mom and I left my father twenty years ago, and I've barely talked to him. If I have to arrest him for murder, and I get run out of town, so be it. It's not like I have any ties here."

Dez kept watching the CSI team, but she nodded slowly. "I like hearing you're not going to give your father special treatment. But don't be putting him in maximum security yet. There's nothing we've found to tie him to anything."

Fenway looked down at her feet. "Yet."

"All right, I think we can go in now. We'll figure out where they put everything, and you can go through it later."

"Later?" Fenway stifled a yawn. "I already feel like I've been on the job for a full day."

"And it's not even eight A.M."

They walked around to the front of the building, where Dez let them in with her keycard.

"I need to clue you in on something, Dez," Fenway said, "and I know I've only known you a couple of days, but I have to trust somebody, and I think if you weren't trustworthy, you'd act differently around me."

"What do you mean?"

Fenway raised her eyebrow. "You'd be a lot nicer to me, for one thing."

Dez laughed. "Honey, this *is* me being nice. Just ask the M.E. what my *not-nice* looks like." She opened the door to the office suite and they went inside.

"Okay. So, this is delicate, and given what I'm about to tell you, this whole thing is probably going to blow back on the county."

"What are you talking about?"

"First, Dez, this is between you and me." Fenway sat down at Rachel's desk, Dez perched beside her. "No Mark, no Migs. Don't even tell family members. Just you and me."

"All right."

"It's about Walker. Two nights before he was killed, he sexually assaulted Rachel in the office."

"What?" Dez asked, incredulous. "What do you mean, 'sexually assaulted'?"

"He ripped her clothes. Tried to rape her. When she fought to get away from him, he told her she was fired."

"Did Rachel tell you that?"

Fenway nodded. "And it's on video."

Dez shook her head. "That piece of *shit*. I knew he was a letch, but I didn't think he'd do *that*."

"But listen," Fenway continued, "there's more. Walker had been harassing Rachel for weeks, and she went to Lana Cassidy, and Lana blew her off. Told her she needed proof, and she couldn't file a report based only on Rachel's testimony."

"Then he escalated from harassment to rape," Dez spat. "And since Lana said she needed proof, Rachel recorded it?"

"Yep."

"And she told her husband, who went ballistic."

"Well, maybe. I mean, Rachel says she didn't *tell* him, but she left a backup copy of the video on a USB stick in their junk drawer."

"That's crazy. Why would she leave it there if she didn't want him to look at it?"

"She says he wouldn't pay any attention to a random USB stick in a junk drawer. But you never know; Dylan might have found the drive and watched the video on it anyway. That's certainly McVie's working theory —Dylan watched the video, then lost his mind with rage, and lured Walker out to the woods to kill him."

"You don't think so, though." Dez looked thoughtful.

Fenway hesitated. "It would fit really well. Except, why take the files? And you can clearly see his license plate in the cameras—it's almost like the driver of the truck *wanted* us to see the plate. The driver was wearing a ski mask, and knew enough to avoid the security cameras once he was out of the truck, but didn't think to remove the license plate?"

"So, you think someone is framing Dylan."

"I guess that's what I think. That sounds so crazy, like a conspiracy theory. Who would frame Dylan?"

"Maybe someone at his work? Maybe a family member?"

"I actually think McVie is looking to see if Rachel's involved," Fenway said. "But if Dylan did it, maybe he could say it was the only way to prevent Walker from attacking her in the future. Rachel had already reported it to HR, but it didn't stop. If that were the case, I think it's possible the county could be legally liable for Walker's murder."

"Wait." Dez put up her hand to stop her. "I totally get the county is liable if *Rachel* wants to sue us for a zillion dollars. But Walker sexually assaults a girl at work, and *his* family can sue because the county let him get away with it?"

"Yeah. I've seen this kind of thing happen in Seattle. A doctor in the ER messed up during an operation and *he* sued the hospital and won. Anything can happen once lawyers get involved, but even if the Walker family doesn't sue, you're right, Rachel sure could. She tells her story to any lawyer in the country and they'll have a lawsuit on the mayor's desk by the next morning. But my point isn't that Rachel could sue. My point isn't even that Walker's family could sue. My point is, Dylan could be found innocent, or, you know, it could be ruled a justifiable homicide, because there was no reasonable legal recourse to the sexual assault."

"You watch too many lawyer shows," Dez said.

"Maybe I do, but Lana Cassidy put us in an awkward position. I don't know why she wouldn't take Rachel's statement."

"It's all CYA, Fenway. Human Resources isn't there to protect employees; it's there to reduce the employer's liability. She didn't want to open the county up for harassment claims. If she lets Rachel file, this is a government office—that shit goes public. It makes it hard to recruit new employees. Plus, it's not like Walker could get fired. It's an elected position. Getting him out of there would've meant convincing him to resign, or to, I don't even know, impeach him."

"Lana Cassidy covering her own ass resulted in Rachel getting sexually assaulted in the office. If I were Rachel, I'd be calling Gloria Allred and negotiating book rights."

"Nice to know our new coroner is bitter and jaded like the rest of us." Dez put a hand on Fenway's shoulder and smiled.

"All right, enough jaded employee talk. I've got to figure out if Rachel sent the video file to anyone through email."

"She recorded it from her work computer?"

"Yeah. All kinds of liability issues, right?"

"Well, yeah," Dez shrugged. "But you don't know her password. You'll have to wait for Migs to come in at eight, or someone from IT."

Fenway got her laptop out of her bag and put it on the desk. "There's gotta be something I can do before the workday 'officially' starts," she mumbled.

Dez was quiet for a minute. "Is Rachel all right?"

"I don't know. I think she's angry with me because she told me all of this, and I had to tell the sheriff, which let him know Dylan had a motive. So," Fenway began to tick each point on her fingers, "she was sexually assaulted on Friday by her boss, her boss gets murdered on Sunday, she gets a new boss on Wednesday, and then Thursday morning her husband is arrested for murder because she told her new boss about her rape." She looked down at the keyboard. "*I* wouldn't be okay, if I were her."

"Someone should check in on her."

"Think you could? I'm probably not her favorite person right now."

Dez nodded, got her cell phone out, went into the conference room and closed the door.

Fenway got her cell phone out, too, and thought for a moment. She needed to ask her father some uncomfortable questions, and wondered the most tactful way to go about it. She remembered when she was six or seven, and her mother had to tell her father some bad news. She remembered wondering what her mother was doing with her eyes closed, taking deep breaths. Now, Fenway realized her mother had been preparing herself to tell him the bad news, centering herself, before picking the phone, calling him, and handling him masterfully.

She remembered her mother had made sure her father had thought the solution to whatever problem it had been was his idea, and she could turn him from angry to helpful with a few well-chosen words.

Drawing on her mother as inspiration, Fenway closed her eyes, took deep breaths, and called up her father.

It rang.

"Fenway!" he answered. "Good to hear from you. Everything okay? Are we still on for tonight?"

"Sure, Dad. Listen, I hate to do this, but I've got to talk with you about something."

"Business or personal?"

"Unfortunately, Dad, it's business." She sighed. "It turns out there are some files missing from Walker's office. And it looks like they're files on Ferris Energy."

"Ferris Energy? Why in the world would anyone take Walker's files on Ferris Energy?"

Fenway paused. She had expected her father to be surprised to learn Walker *had* files on Ferris Energy. Instead, her father expressed surprise someone *took* the files. Was it common knowledge Walker had open files on Ferris Energy? Had he heard about the break-in already? Fenway hadn't said someone *took* them—she said they were *missing*. She supposed it was reasonable to assume they were taken, but perhaps it was a strange slip-up from a man who Fenway thought was always in control.

"I don't really know, Dad. I was kind of hoping you might be able to fill me in."

There was silence on the other end of the line. Fenway wondered if her father had caught his slip.

She chose her words carefully before continuing. "It's weird, because I don't know if you've heard from the sheriff yet, but we arrested a suspect this morning in Walker's murder."

"What? That's great!" Ferris exhaled. "No, I haven't heard from the sheriff—wow, two days on the job and you've already caught the killer! I knew this was the right call. Congratulations!"

"Hang on, Dad, congratulations aren't in order for *me*; Sheriff McVie was the one who made the arrest, and he's the one who requested the search warrant."

"You don't need to be modest with me, Fenway. I bet you had a lot to do with it."

"Here's the thing." She tried to get the conversation back on track. "The missing files are the one thing that doesn't fit with the theory of the crime."

"Oh, you *are* learning something in your forensics classes." Fenway thought she heard in her father's voice that he was trying to get her to change the subject. She had been easily distracted when she was eight; she didn't think she was easily distracted now, twenty years later.

Her father was right, however. Fenway *was* learning a lot in her forensics classes. Her witness interviewing class had been difficult, and she had had to work her tail off for an A. In fact, she had used her mother as an interview subject for one of her projects. The lesson of the project was about *unspoken assumptions*. The exercise was this: the interviewer lays the groundwork for establishing if the subject has prior knowledge of a fact not yet presented. Fenway had this in her mind as she continued the conversation with her father.

"Yeah, Dad, I gotta tell you, it's great to be able to use the stuff I've learned in class. One of the things they talked about in my advanced investigation class was loose ends, and only looking at theories through the lens of your own expectations. So, I'm using it now. This guy we arrested matched the motive we theorized, but we still have these missing Ferris Energy files, and I can't figure out how they fit."

"Your suspect doesn't work for me, does he?" Ferris laughed a little uneasily.

"No. We haven't found any connection to Ferris Energy at all."

"Well," he mused, "maybe there was a file in the missing drawer that the guy *did* have a connection to. Maybe it wasn't anything to do with the company."

And there it was.

Fenway hadn't mentioned a missing drawer, or any other missing files. She tried to contain her reaction; her voice remained calm. "I suppose that could be the case. But the files didn't turn up at his apartment when we executed the search warrant. Do you know what was in the Ferris Energy file?"

Nathaniel Ferris sighed. Fenway could hear him calculating in his head how to address the contents of the file—now that he realized he had slipped up by telling her he knew of their existence. "If it's the one I'm aware of, it's probably the file on our industrial accident about six months ago. We lost a couple of workers in the refinery. Our internal review concluded it was human error—specifically, errors made by the two men who were killed, who didn't follow several safety procedures—but the county investigation was still open."

"So, you asked why anyone would take those files—who stands to gain from those files going missing?"

"Honestly, Fenway, I have no idea. Ferris Energy certainly has nothing to gain from those files going missing. Our lawyers are about to get a letter from OSHA saying we were in compliance with everything, and not at fault. And, in most of these cases, OSHA reviews any relevant files— like the one Walker had—before sending any letters like that."

"Okay." Fenway thought for a moment before continuing. "So, you're saying it wouldn't make sense for anyone from your company to steal those files."

"Right—in fact, I remember our lawyers saying those findings would make it a lot more difficult for the families to sue us. So, if anything, those files getting stolen last night *hurts* us a lot more than it helps us."

"That's good to know." She exhaled audibly into the phone. "I'm kind of relieved, frankly. Your company files getting stolen really doesn't look good for me. Especially after I told you I was going to go through the files today. I was afraid people were going to look at me sideways, as if *I* had something to do with them being stolen." She paused for maximum effect. "I wish I could convince people I'm not in your pocket."

"Fenway," Nathaniel Ferris said, putting on his pontificating voice, "with me as your father, people are always going to think you're in my pocket. Especially in this town. But I know you can do the job you need to do. And I know you can get your nursing certificate for California, and finish up your degree, and then you'll have a lot more opportunities."

"Let's not get ahead of ourselves. Can you maybe get whatever company files you have on the accident, on the families involved, and come down to the station—make an appearance—so it looks like I'm looking at you as hard as everyone else? You know, tying up the loose ends?"

He thought it was a fantastic idea. Then he gave Fenway a few more words of encouragement. She realized she had gotten more words of encouragement from Nathaniel Ferris in the last two days than she had in the last twenty-eight years.

He suggested he could come down to the station before lunch, around eleven thirty. They also confirmed their dinner plans before saying their goodbyes as Dez came out of the conference room.

"How's Rachel holding up?"

"She's not," Dez shook her head. "Girl talked my ear off. She's so quiet in the office I didn't even know she could talk for that long. She's sad, and confused, and mad as hell. I called her sister for her, and she's going over there to be with her."

"Good. I'm worried about her."

"Who were you on the phone with? Daddy dearest?"

Fenway smiled. "Yes. And I'm not sure, but I think he's involved in all this. I think he's the one who stole the files."

"He was the one in the truck?"

"No, he wouldn't actually get his hands dirty. But you know what I mean."

"Why do you think so?"

Fenway shrugged. "I was talking to him just now, and I mentioned there were missing Ferris Energy files, and he suggested maybe there was another 'file in the drawer' that didn't have anything to do with Ferris Energy."

"Mmm," Dez mumbled. "But let me guess, Miss Marple, you never mentioned the missing file drawer. You never mentioned other missing files at all."

"Bingo."

"You just outfoxed the most powerful man in the county in your first twenty-four hours on the job."

"I don't know about that." She drummed her fingers on the table. "He might be playing a long game and I don't see it yet. He's a smart guy, and that slip-up was kind of a rookie mistake. I might be playing right into his hands."

CHAPTER TWELVE

AFTER DEZ WENT BACK TO HER DESK, FENWAY STARTED RESEARCHING the files. She started by searching the web for stories on the industrial accident. She found an article from the *Los Angeles Times*, dated December 14 of last year.

Toxic fumes kill 2 oil refinery workers

ESTANCIA—Two Ferris Energy refinery workers were killed Tuesday when toxic fumes were released into an underground holding area. The incident occurred about 6:45 p.m. at the end of the employees' shifts. The two refinery employees were in a holding area when the fumes were released. Neither employee had on a protective suit, and both were found unresponsive by other employees at 7:05 p.m. They were transported to Estancia Regional Medical Center, where they were pronounced dead.

According to witnesses, alarms sounded, and automatic containment procedures were activated. EMS workers were delayed in responding to the victims because the area had to be cleared of the toxic fumes.

The fumes are no longer considered a risk for workers in the Estancia refinery. Air quality outside of the refinery during and after the incident did not register any toxicity. The names of the deceased are being withheld until their families can be notified.

Fenway finished reading the article just as the sound of the door opening made her look up. A sandy-haired blond man, who looked to be in his early-to-mid-twenties, walked through the door. He wore board shorts, a stonewashed blue T-shirt, and a shell necklace. He had a worried look on his tanned face.

"Can I help you?"

"Y-y-yeah," he stammered. "I'd like to talk to the coroner."

"That's me." Fenway offered a friendly smile.

"Okay, um, so I tried to talk to the sheriff, but he wasn't available." His words were all falling out quickly. "I mean, I know I didn't tell the truth the first time, but I didn't realize what was going on. I need to talk to someone."

"Hang on, slow down. First—what's your name?"

"Sorry, sorry." He took a deep breath. "I'm Parker Richards."

"Okay, Parker. You're Dylan's brother, right?"

He nodded.

"What did you want to talk to the sheriff about?"

"Listen, he called me earlier this morning. It was really early."

"Right." She nodded. "It must have been about five o'clock."

"Yeah, and Dylan's wife called me, like, really early, too, before the sheriff did. And she was all, 'Tell me where Dylan was on Sunday night,' and I told her Dylan and I were playing pool at the new place downtown. And then the sheriff called me up, maybe five minutes later, and he was all, 'Tell me where you were on Sunday night,' and I was like, 'I was with Dylan playing pool at the new place downtown,' and it freaked me out a little, because it was really early, and I was still half-asleep, and I thought maybe the two of them were, like, next to each other, so I had to keep my story straight." He stopped and shook his head. "I don't know, man, I don't know what Dylan was thinking. And the next thing I know Dylan is arrested, and I hear it's for killing someone."

"He was arrested for killing the coroner."

A look of confusion on his face. "I thought *you* were the coroner."

"I just got appointed to replace him."

"Did you move here from Boston?"

"What?"

Parker pointed to Fenway's hat. She had almost forgotten it was on.

"No, but did you have something you needed to tell me, sir?"

Parker's face became grim. "Listen, I don't know what went bad, but he wasn't at the pool hall with me Sunday night. I mean, neither of us were at the pool hall. He told me to tell Rachel that, if she called me. Because he was seeing another girl on Sunday night, but it was all hush-hush. He didn't want anyone to know about this other girl, or anything— usually he tells me everything about the girls he sees. But he didn't tell me hardly nothing about this girl. I was thinking maybe he's really into her, but he thought I'd make fun of him—like maybe there's something wrong with her, like maybe she's a midget or whatnot," he rambled.

"Sure." Fenway coughed and shook her head. "So, he told you he was seeing another girl, and told you to tell Rachel you were playing pool together?"

"Right."

"You told Rachel you two were playing pool, and then the sheriff called you right afterward, so you also told the sheriff you were playing pool."

"Right." He looked seriously into Fenway's eyes and put his palms face down on the desk. "But only to keep my stories straight. I would never lie to the police."

"Only if you had to keep your story straight."

"Right."

"Okay, Parker. Any idea who the mystery girl is?"

"Not really. But he gets himself kinda dressed up for her. I don't know,

I'm kinda starting to think she's sophisticated. He seems pretty into her. Like, he gets all weird about it if I ask too many questions about her."

"But you don't know who she is?"

"No."

Fenway sighed. "I don't know how helpful that's going to be, Parker. He's in a lot of trouble, and unless we can find this woman, and she vouches for his whereabouts, I'm not sure that's going to change."

A look of depression crossed Parker's face. Then Fenway saw him get visibly struck by inspiration. "Oh! I got it! Didn't they catch the Boston Strangler, or something, because of parking tickets?"

"Yeah. Son of Sam."

The look on Parker's face told Fenway he had never heard of Son of Sam. "Uh, right—anyway," he continued, "Dylan goes to spend the night with this side chick a few weeks ago, and he comes back in the morning all crazy mad because he got a *parking ticket*."

Fenway crossed her arms.

"I mean, you can check that, right?" Parker was almost pleading. "Like, you can check his license plate, and find the parking tickets he's gotten, and the addresses near there? And then maybe find her, and ask if she can say he was with her?"

Fenway blinked at him. "Yes, I think we can do that." She looked over at Dez, who was looking at her computer monitor, but clearly paying much more attention to their conversation. She saw Dez nod slightly.

Parker smiled, a relieved smile. "That's awesome. That's really awesome. Can you call me to let me know if you find her?"

"Um, probably not. But, if she vouches for his whereabouts, and it holds up, we'll probably release him, so you'll know soon enough."

"Sure!" He seemed somewhat excited by this prospect.

An awkward goodbye later, he was out the door.

Dez turned to Fenway. "Well, *that* was something."

"It certainly was," she nodded. "Can I do what I just said I could do? Check the parking tickets on his truck?"

"Sure. I don't know if they've set you up in the system yet, but I can get to it." She logged in, and Fenway gave her the license plate number—it had etched itself into her brain from seeing it on tape earlier and repeating it to the sheriff.

"All right. Here it is." Dez pointed to the screen. "April the eighth. He got a street sweeper parking ticket, six-oh-five a.m. Catalina Street and Harbor Park Court." A thoughtful look crossed her face.

"What is it?"

"Sheriff McVie lives on Harbor Park Court."

"Oh."

"And McVie has a teenage daughter."

"Right."

"McVie was at a training in L.A. in early April. I think he was gone on the seventh and eighth. And he had picked up a patrol shift for Callahan on Sunday before the call came in about Walker's body."

"So, the sheriff was away from the house both the day Dylan got a street sweeper ticket, and the night of Walker's murder."

"And Dylan was really secretive about who he was seeing."

"Ugh." Fenway suddenly got a bad taste in her mouth. "McVie's teenage daughter? Is every man in Estancia this disgusting?"

Dez raised an eyebrow. "Not just in Estancia."

"We're going to have to talk with her."

"No wonder Dylan lied to McVie about where he was Sunday night." Dez pushed herself back from her desk. "If I was screwing an underage girl, I think I'd rather get arrested for murder than deal with her father."

"Especially if her father is the sheriff."

"Especially," Dez nodded.

"Should I go interview her? Think I can get to her house before school starts?"

Dez looked at the clock on the wall. "School started half an hour ago."

"Well then, do we pull her out of class?"

"Let me get this straight." Dez pulled back up to her desk and held up her index finger. "You want to go to the sheriff's daughter's high school." Dez's second finger went up. "You want to pull her out of class." Her ring finger joined the other two. "And ask her about having sex with a twenty-seven-year-old murder suspect?" She put her hand down. "And all on the basis of a parking ticket given across the street from the cul-de-sac she lives on?"

"And the sheriff's schedule. Yes."

Dez smirked. "And what are you going to tell the sheriff and his wife after the school calls them?"

Fenway paused. "The administration would call the McVies?"

"Of course they would. They call the parents any time we question a student on campus."

"Forget that then. We'll have to figure something else out."

Dez nodded.

"Look, how about this?" said Fenway. "We canvass the neighborhood with Dylan's photo. 'Did you see this man in the neighborhood Sunday evening?' The sheriff might have been out of town, but I bet there was a nosy neighbor who's all pissed off about this big truck parked in front of his house all night. Then, if someone saw him enter the sheriff's house—"

"Then what?"

"Then we'd have a plausible reason to convince the administration not to contact the McVies, right?"

"I'm telling you, Fenway, that's non-negotiable."

Fenway leaned back in her chair. "Look, we need to follow this line of thinking, don't we? Don't we need to find out if this has the potential to blow up in the sheriff's face? I mean, there's probably enough evidence to hold Dylan, but I think it looks like he made the arrest too early. And if Dylan is having sex with his underage daughter—"

"That's a pretty big *if*."

"But if he is, that could look like McVie was trying to get revenge."

"Why not just arrest Dylan for statutory rape?" Dez asked.

"Age of consent is sixteen. Isn't his daughter sixteen?"

"You're not in Seattle anymore, Fenway. Age of consent is eighteen in California."

Fenway furrowed her brow. "Even better. For the sheriff, I mean. That convinces me that McVie didn't have any idea about it. Statutory rape is plenty bad. 'Sex offender' on your record for the rest of your life—you get wrecked in prison, right?"

Dez shook her head. "You've seen too many cop shows."

"Then educate me. If you're guilty of statutory rape, you go on the sex offender list forever, right?"

"Right."

"And that means it's hard to get a job, hard to find an apartment, hard to live anywhere..."

"Yeah."

"And other prisoners don't look too kindly on pedophiles, right? Like, don't they get beat up in prison? And don't all kinds of nasty stuff happen to them in the showers?"

"Okay, you made your point, Fenway." The look on Dez's face was like she had smelled a rotten egg.

Fenway got up. "All right. So let's go."

"Let's go? Go where?"

"Let's go get a photo of Dylan and go canvass Harbor Park Court. You'll have to drive, I don't have a car yet."

Dez shook her head. "I sure hope you get more jaded in a hurry. I can hardly stand this enthusiasm."

"I have a feeling if I tell the sheriff that the guy he arrested is sleeping with his teenaged daughter, that'll leave me feeling pretty jaded by the end of the conversation."

After getting a photo of Dylan Richards from the Records Department, and filling up two cups of coffee, Fenway and Dez headed out. They arrived at Harbor Park Court around eight forty-five.

"That's McVie's house." Dez pointed to the third house on the right of the cul-de-sac.

"The one with the Jeep in the driveway?"

"Yeah. I think McVie got that Jeep for Megan for her sixteenth birthday. She must have gotten a ride this morning."

Fenway looked at the other houses. "Where do you want to start?"

"Let's start on the left side—they'll have a better view of the house, and maybe they saw Richards."

Fenway opened the car door.

"Leave your ballcap," Dez said.

"I didn't have time to do my hair this morning."

"I feel you, girl, but bad hair is better for canvassing than wearing a baseball cap. Kind of unprofessional for peace officers."

She took the cap off and tried to fix her hair with her hands to be somewhat presentable. She decided to leave it after she at least had gotten the hat-head look to go away.

There was no one home at the first two houses. At the third house, a large white guy, approximately six-foot-eight and about three hundred pounds, with a long, well-kept beard, answered the door. Dez showed her badge and then the photo, asking if the man had seen him around Sunday night.

"Sunday night?" The large man stroked his long beard thoughtfully. "I work at a restaurant, and I was working Sunday night till about 11. But I've seen that guy before. He's in the neighborhood all the time. Always parks his big black pickup over in front of the Martins' house. I see him go to the McVies' house though. Doesn't always use the front door, either. I was thinking of calling the cops, but I saw someone inside open the front door and let him in a couple of times. I figured he was a gardener or a pool guy."

"How often is he around?" Dez asked, pen poised to take notes.

The man shrugged. "It kind of varies. Sometimes I notice him two or three times a week, sometimes I don't see him or his truck for a couple of weeks."

"You ever talk to the McVies about it?"

"Nope. None of my business." He put his hands out in front of himself, palms facing up. "Know why? Because the couple who *used* to live in the Martins' house had a bunch of parties, like every other weekend, with cars lined up for blocks. I asked them about it once, and they invited me and my wife, and it turned out to be a *key party*."

"A key party? For real? This ain't 1975," said Dez.

"Tell that to them. Apparently, they thought everyone in the neighborhood knew. I guess they thought I was angling for an invite. Or maybe they thought my wife was hot. I don't know. Anyway, now I keep my mouth shut."

"All right." Dez closed her notebook. "Thanks for your time."

"One more thing," Fenway interjected. "Did you see the truck in front of the Martins' place when you got home on Sunday night?"

The man thought about it a moment. "I can't say that I'm absolutely sure, but I think so."

Fenway looked at Dez, then back to him. "Thanks again. Have a good rest of your day."

They knocked on more doors. People were home at two other houses. Both of them had seen the truck several times before. One of them didn't recognize Dylan; one of them said she was "pretty sure" that Dylan was the driver of the truck, but didn't know which house he visited, although she did say she remembered the truck parked there on Sunday night.

"That's enough for me to think we need to talk to Megan," Dez conceded as they walked back to the car. "Maybe we can catch her after school."

Fenway looked over her shoulder back at the Jeep in the McVie's driveway. "Hey, Dez," she said, "you sure that's the daughter's car?"

"Sure, I'm sure. She's stopped by the office in that car before."

Fenway cocked her head to the side. "McVie's been in the office since early this morning—he couldn't have given her a ride. I think she might be skipping school."

Dez stopped walking and narrowed her eyes at the Jeep.

"I'm going to check," Fenway said, turning and walking quickly to the McVie residence. Dez turned with her and jogged to catch up.

They got to the front porch at the same time.

"I don't think anyone's home," Dez said.

Fenway rang the bell. Dez shifted her weight from foot to foot.

"Did you hear something from inside?" Fenway asked.

"I don't know. Maybe."

Fenway rang the bell again.

She looked at Dez. "I think she's home."

"Maybe."

Fenway counted to twenty under her breath and knocked loudly on the front door.

CHAPTER THIRTEEN

THE TEENAGED GIRL WHO OPENED THE DOOR WAS A PRETTY BLONDE with alabaster skin, and a smattering of freckles, like her father. She wore light blue cotton shorts that were quite short, with a navy tank top with her bra straps showing a little.

"Hi Megan, I'm Sergeant Roubideaux. We've met a couple of times before. I work with your dad." Dez motioned to Fenway. "And this is my colleague, Miss Stevenson."

Fenway gave a small awkward wave and smile.

"Sorry for bothering you at home," Dez continued, "but we need to ask you a couple of questions."

"I got sick at school and came home." Megan offered, eyeing them warily.

"Okay," Dez said.

"Did Dad send you here to check up on me? I'm not skipping school."

"We don't really care about any of that," Fenway said. "We just have a couple of questions."

"You recognize this man?" Dez pulled the photo of Dylan out of the folder and handed it to Megan.

Megan glanced down at the photo, then looked up at them, trying to read their faces. "Is this some kind of joke?"

Dez looked at Fenway, then back at Megan. "No, it's not a joke. This man has been seen on your street regularly, and we have a witness who has him going inside your house on more than one occasion."

"You mean whenever my dad's not home?" Megan snapped.

"Well," Dez said carefully, "we haven't put the timeline together, but yeah, we're pretty sure he comes over when your parents aren't home."

Megan looked from Dez's face to Fenway's face then back to Dez's face. Then she blanched. "Ugh. Eww. You think he's having sex with *me*?"

Dez nodded slowly.

"He's banging my *mom*," Megan sneered. "My mom doesn't think I notice, because I'm in my room all the time, and they stay in the back of the house. But of course I notice. I think she used to do it only when I was at volleyball practice, or at a game. I'd find—*stuff*—in the trash can of the guest bathroom." She shuddered a little. "And then when the season ended, she kept trying to get me to go out for other sports. But then when my dad works late, or is on a business trip, *that guy* comes over."

Dez nodded again. She looked a little pained.

"I don't think my dad knows. And frankly, Mom is too busy with her new boyfriend to really pay attention to me having *my* boyfriend over, so I guess it has its benefits." She shrugged. "But eww, he is not with me. He's so *old*."

"Wow, that's a relief!" Fenway burst out, following it up with a small laugh. Megan looked at her, surprised.

"I'm sorry," Fenway caught herself and stopped her laugh short. "It's not funny. I mean, *relief* is the wrong word. We were so convinced he was, uh, with you. I don't know why it never occurred to us your mom would be home. Or that, you know, she was the one who was with him."

Dez put her hand on Fenway's shoulder and looked at her with a serious face. Fenway stopped rambling. Dez turned back to Megan. "Was he, uh, *visiting* your mom here on Sunday night?"

Megan shrugged. "I was out on Sunday night. My boyfriend and I were studying in the afternoon, and then we got some dinner and we went to a movie. I didn't get back here until after midnight."

"On a school night?"

"It's not like my mom cared."

Dez cleared her throat. "Did you notice a big black pickup truck parked on the street when you got home?"

"Nope."

"No, it wasn't there, or no, you didn't notice?"

"I was paying attention to whether or not my mom was going to hear me coming in late."

"Did she?"

"Nope. I snuck in and she didn't notice a thing."

Fenway nodded. "Okay. Anything else, Sergeant?"

Dez shook her head. "We'll let you get back to...whatever you're doing."

"Don't tell my mom I know." Megan's eyes were wide. "I don't want to deal with any kind of *serious talks* from her."

"Okay," Fenway agreed.

She turned away and started inside, then quickly turned back. "Don't tell my dad either. He'd freak."

Dez nodded. "Thanks for speaking with us, Megan."

She stepped inside and closed the door behind her.

"That was *crazy*," Fenway said, turning with Dez to walk back to the car.

"This is all kinds of messed up."

"Looks like we've got ourselves a cougar." She let out another small giggle.

Dez shot her a sharp look. "That's not funny."

Fenway stopped giggling. They were silent as they crossed the street to Dez's car.

"All right, what are we going to do?" Fenway asked. "This is material, isn't it? The guy the sheriff locked up for Walker's murder might have been at the sheriff's house that night, having relations with his wife."

"Don't call it *relations*, Fenway." Dez's face scrunched up. "It sounds like you're in a damn Jane Austen movie."

"Whatever. A booty call."

Dez ignored Fenway's comment. "The stuff you said earlier about revenge is sounding kind of dangerous now."

"I know, right? Maybe the sheriff *did* know about Dylan and his wife."

They got in the car. They sat for a minute, Dez not starting the engine.

"You okay, Dez?"

"I don't know, Fenway. This feels weird. Parts of this feel really planned out—like someone was trying to get rid of Walker for a long time—and then parts of it feel like a crime of passion. Shooting someone in the back. Making Walker's car disappear. The incredibly audacious smash-and-grab. It's weird."

"There's something here we're not seeing."

"Maybe it's time to talk to some folks at The Own—uh, your daddy's company. Usually, when there's some convoluted shit going on, Ferris Energy is in the middle of it."

"And my father knew a lot more than he's letting on. He knew the files were missing because someone *took* them *last night*. Not that they might have been misfiled, or that someone might have checked them out. Or that they could have been stolen a while ago. And he knew the whole file drawer was missing, not just a couple of files."

"He's coming to the office later?"

"Yeah," Fenway nodded. "I managed to convince him this looks bad, that his files are missing, and to come in and give a statement. He said he'll come in right before lunch."

"We've got a couple of hours before that happens," Dez sighed as she started the car.

When they got back to the office, Migs was at his desk.

Dez set her notebook on her desk. "Migs, have you seen Mark this morning?"

"Yeah, he was in for a few minutes. We got the message from the sheriff we can all work on the case now. Mark called San Miguelito because the autopsy results still aren't here, if you can believe it. The M.E. wanted to talk to either the coroner or the sheriff—didn't want to courier the results. She asked for you too, Dez." Migs shrugged. "I think Mark left McVie a message. And then he got a call from the LAX airport police—they found Walker's car in one of the private long-term lots by the airport. He decided to drive down there to see it for himself."

"LAX long-term parking, huh," Fenway muttered. "Wonder where that idea came from."

Dez sat at her desk. "Walker's car. Big break."

"I wonder if his laptop will be in there."

"We can hope."

"Hey Migs," Fenway said, "can you get a file off Rachel's machine?"

Migs looked quizzically at her. "I guess so, but why don't you ask her? She should be in any minute now."

Fenway shook her head. "I don't think she's coming in today."

"Why? Did she call in sick or something?"

"Something like that."

Migs frowned. "Yeah, I've got the admin passwords. I think I can get into her machine." He walked over to Rachel's computer and leaned down over the keyboard, but froze before he touched it.

"How long has that light been on?" Migs' eyes were wide.

"What light?"

"The light on the camera, right there." Migs pointed to the webcam perched on top of the monitor.

"I don't know. Can we get the file off the machine, or not?"

Migs knocked the camera off the monitor. He grabbed at the camera's cord going into the back of the machine and yanked it out. Then he pulled out the PC's power cord, too.

"Hey!" Fenway yelled. "What are you doing? I need to get that file."

"Not now you don't." Migs hurriedly pulled all the cords out of the back of the computer. "I'm going to take this over to IT right now. Like, right now. I think someone's been spying on us."

"What?"

Migs looked over his shoulder at her. "That camera was on, Fenway. The computer looked like it should have been asleep, but the camera was *on*." He was disconnecting all the cables going into the machine.

"Someone was watching us?"

"Maybe. And maybe listening, too. And I'm taking it over to IT right now." He picked up the tower and went out the door.

Fenway looked at Dez. "I saw that on one of those cop shows. Some guy had taken over his classmate's laptop camera so he could watch her change clothes. He ended up dead, I think."

"Was your experience watching television cops at all helpful in determining that *we've* been watched all morning?" Dez deadpanned.

"How do you know it was just this morning? It could have been for months."

Dez was silent for a few seconds. "Man, technology sucks. My mouth gets me in enough trouble as it is. If those hackers even caught half the shit I say and post it on YouTube, I'll be so out of a job."

"Well, I, for one, welcome our benevolent robot overlords."

Dez shook her head, trying not to laugh.

"Check and see if your PC has a light on its camera," Fenway said, nodding to the machine in front of Dez.

"Nope. I don't even *have* a camera."

Fenway opened her laptop. "My camera light isn't on. Migs would have noticed if there was something on his machine, right?"

"I guess so. Man, this whole case gets weirder and weirder."

"You think Rachel's camera has something to do with the case?"

"What, Fenway? You don't?" Dez started counting on her fingers. "Rachel gets the camera to record Walker's sexual harassment. Walker gets murdered. Someone takes *that* machine over in order to spy on the office. You don't think it's all connected?"

"I guess it would be a pretty big coincidence if it weren't."

"Damn right." Dez stifled a yawn. "I gotta go get some more coffee. Some *real* coffee. You want anything?"

Fenway nodded. "A latte, please."

"A regular latte? No flavors, or soy foam macchiato, or magic beans?"

"Oh, but Dez, espresso beans *are* magic."

She laughed. "Fine, a regular latte, coming up."

"Actually, make it a large latte. I'm dragging."

Fenway grabbed her purse, but Dez waved her off. She was out the door before Fenway could protest about the HR policy.

Fenway stood and stretched. She took off the Red Sox cap for a moment, ran her hand through her loose curls, and put the cap back on. She sat back down and adjusted her chair a little bit. First thing on her agenda for the rest of the day was to do some more research on the industrial accident at the Ferris refinery.

She opened a browser on her laptop and searched for stories that identified the employees who were killed. She found a link to another *Los Angeles Times* story, published two days after the first one. Fenway clicked on it, and the page started loading.

Suddenly the door to the office burst open.

Lana Cassidy stormed through.

"You're not even here one day and you're already making a mockery of the department!" Lana screeched, slamming the door behind her.

"What?"

Lana pointed a finger at Fenway. "You know damn well what I'm talking about. You show up out of the blue, and someone happens to drive through the wall that very night and steal Walker's files?"

Fenway was taken aback. "How is that my fault?"

Lana stormed over to Fenway's desk and got up right next to her. She leaned down, keeping her face only about six inches from Fenway's; the bill of Fenway's cap was almost touching Lana's forehead. "Your father put you up to this," she said quietly. "But I'm onto you. You're not getting away with anything."

"Lana, I have no idea—"

Lana spit in her face. Fenway recoiled, disgusted.

"You might think you're better than everyone else because you're rich, but your daddy can't help you now."

Fenway was roiling with anger inside, but made herself stay calm. She looked down to her purse and reached into it for her cell phone.

"Don't you dare!" Lana screamed.

Fenway had been planning to call security, or maybe record Lana on her cell phone, but she looked back up to see Lana had a snub-nosed revolver drawn on her, holding it in both hands.

"What the hell are you doing?" Fenway yelled, putting her hands up, Lana's spit running down her cheek. Fenway stood up, her legs pushing the chair backwards. She didn't know how good of a shot Lana was, but given the short distance, it probably didn't matter.

"I'm going to shoot you before you shoot me."

"I don't have a gun! Are you crazy? I was getting a Kleenex to wipe my face!" Fenway was lying, but thought Lana might have been just as angry about a cell phone as a gun.

"Don't lie to me! It's probably the same gun you used to shoot the coroner so you could take his job."

"I wasn't even in the state when he was killed!"

Lana sneered, "Oh, sure, play stupid, *Miss Ferris*."

"You obviously think I'm planning something with my father, but I'm not. He *abandoned* me and my mom years ago—I've barely seen him the last twenty years!"

"You're as good of a liar as he is, too." She cocked the gun.

Just then, the door opened. Lana turned her head slightly.

Fenway rushed her.

She put her hands straight out and ran at Lana as hard as she could.

Fenway grabbed Lana's hands—the hands holding the gun—drove her head down into Lana's solar plexus, and forced her hands up.

Lana was off-balance and stepped backward. The gun went off.

Lana fell on her back; Fenway landed hard on top of her.

Lana was still holding the gun in her right hand, and Fenway held her wrist to the floor. Lana gasped for breath.

Fenway picked up Lana's right hand, slammed it against the floor, and Lana dropped the revolver. It fell to the floor, out of reach.

Fenway could see Dez's pants and shoes, and the dropped coffee cups on the floor. Dez was standing above them, pistol drawn.

Fenway tried to catch her breath and looked up at Dez. "Give me your handcuffs."

Dez shook her head. "I leave for five minutes and anarchy erupts. Jeez, I gotta keep you in my sight at all times. You're worse than a rookie cop. How about you let me take care of the handcuffs."

Fenway pulled herself onto her knees and helped Dez roll Lana onto her stomach. Lana was still out of breath. Dez pulled Lana's arms behind her, her wrists together, and cuffed her.

Two officers appeared in the doorway. "Is everything all right?" the tall one shouted into the room. "We heard a gunshot."

Dez helped Fenway up, then got Lana to her feet and started the Miranda warning. "Lana Cassidy, you are under arrest for assault with a deadly weapon. You have the right to remain silent. Anything you say can, and will, be used against you in a court of law. You have the right to an attorney. If you cannot afford an attorney, one will be provided for you. Do you understand the rights I have read to you?"

"Damn," the short officer muttered under his breath.

Lana struggled against Dez's hold, and screamed at Fenway, "You and your father will pay! This isn't over!"

"Lana!" Dez yelled in her ear, and Lana was quiet. "You know how this works. You need to answer me. Do you understand the rights I have—"

"Yes, yes, I understand my rights," Lana sneered.

Fenway sat down slowly in the chair at her desk. She looked around. Her cap was lying on the floor next to her desk; it had come off her head in the struggle. She picked it up. There was a bullet hole through the bill of the cap.

She set the cap down and noticed her hands were shaking.

The *Times* article she had clicked on before Lana came in was on the screen.

ESTANCIA—The two employees killed by toxic fumes in Tuesday's industrial accident at the Ferris Energy oil refinery have been identified as Carl Cassidy, 46, and Lewis Fairweather, 37, both of Estancia...

"All right." The short officer stepped into the room. "We've got to secure the scene. Mike, you take Mrs. Cassidy to the sheriff's office and book her for assault." Mike, the tall officer, nodded, and led Lana out of the office.

"Why aren't you going with them?" Fenway said to Dez.

"Scott's going to treat this like an officer-involved shooting, even though neither of us fired a weapon, but he heard a shot. He doesn't know who fired it, even if we both say it was Lana. So, he's being cautious. Probably a good idea, considering we're in the coroner's office."

Scott nodded. "Yes, ma'am. And since I'll be treating this like an officer-involved shooting, I'll need you and Miss Stevenson in separate rooms so you can't compare stories."

Dez turned to Fenway. "See? We hire Boy Scouts here."

"I guess so."

Dez grabbed a few tissues off the desk and handed them to her. "You've got something on your face."

"She spit on me."

Dez's mouth tightened.

Scott asked Fenway to go into the conference room and wait for someone to take her statement. She grabbed her purse and went, closing the door behind her. She tried to calm herself. She sat at the conference table and stared at the wall.

It started slow at first, the tightness in Fenway's chest, and then a tear ran down her cheek. And then the tightness released and Fenway was sobbing.

CHAPTER FOURTEEN

THE TEARS STOPPED AFTER A FEW MINUTES. FENWAY TOOK SOME DEEP breaths. She dabbed at her eyes and her face with the tissues, which she hoped would get rid of both the spit and tear streaks running down her face. She pulled the compact out of her purse and checked herself in the mirror. She hadn't had time to put on any makeup or do her hair at three in the morning—and the ball cap could only help so much. Especially with a bullet hole in it. Fenway thought she looked ragged and worn out.

Fenway thought about how her mother would react to news that she had been shot at. How she would tell her mother to minimize the shock. Then a wave of loneliness cascaded over her like an avalanche and almost knocked the wind out of her. She didn't have anyone to call here in Estancia. No one she trusted, no one she wanted to open up to. Maybe McVie.

She had to wait about fifteen minutes before there was a knock at the door. A female detective came in.

"Miss Stevenson?"

"Fenway."

"Fenway, I'm Deputy Celeste Salvador. You can call me Celeste." She was medium height, a few inches shorter than Fenway. She looked to be in her early thirties, with umber-colored skin, and had her shoulder-length dark hair pulled back into a ponytail. Celeste had a strong chin, and dark brown eyes with heavy lids. She was wearing a black sheriff's uniform. She offered her hand in greeting.

"Hi, Celeste." Fenway shook her hand.

Celeste glanced at her. "Are you all right?"

"Yes." Then Fenway paused. "No. I've never been shot at before."

Celeste nodded. "I'll tell you something. I've got ten years in law enforcement, and I've never been shot at before either. Not once."

"I've got less than twenty-four hours in law enforcement, and I've already got you beat."

Celeste laughed softly. "Listen, Fenway, we need a statement from you, and I need to record it. Are you ready to do that now?" When Fenway responded with a nod, Celeste put a small recorder in the middle of the table and hit the red button.

"Deputy Celeste Salvador interviewing Dominguez County Coroner Fenway Stevenson. May sixth. The time is ten twenty-three a.m."

Fenway shook her head. It wasn't even eleven o'clock yet.

Celeste asked Fenway to describe what happened in detail. She went over it, starting with Dez going out to get coffee because of their busy morning, Fenway starting the Google search on the toxic fumes, and then Lana bursting in, yelling. Celeste didn't ask questions about what happened before, and nodded in a few places.

"Do you think you might have done something to antagonize Lana?" she finally asked.

"When?"

"I was thinking before she spit in your face."

"I don't think so. But Lana didn't like what I was saying about not knowing anything."

"Do you have any idea what Lana was referring to?" Celeste said.

"I didn't then." Fenway rested her elbows on the table. "But afterwards I saw my search found an *L.A. Times* article where a man named Carl *Cassidy* was one of the people killed in the accident. I assume Lana Cassidy and Carl Cassidy were related? She probably blames my father, and I guess she thinks I'm trying to cover it up. If she had walked in literally thirty seconds later, I would have known why she was so upset. I might have been able to talk her down."

Celeste nodded. "Let's get back to what she did after she spit at you."

Fenway relayed the rest of the story. Celeste interrupted when Fenway said she bull-rushed Lana.

"Why did you go after her like that?"

"Because I thought she was going to shoot me, and I couldn't run away. My only option was to try to get the gun away from her." Fenway ran her hand over her face. "Honestly, I didn't really think, I just did it. As soon as her attention was off me, and on Dez coming through the door, I just did it."

Celeste had a couple of follow-up questions after Fenway's story was done, but seemed satisfied enough with the answers. They shook hands and Celeste left.

Fenway stayed in the conference room for a couple minutes more, clearing her head, trying to gain her composure. Once she did leave the room, she saw the other deputy was finishing up with Dez. Fenway walked out of the office and into the ladies' room.

She grabbed a few paper towels and washed her face with water, which got, she hoped, the rest of the tear streaks and spit off her face. She decided against trying to put makeup on now. She gave herself a once-over in the mirror, and decided she looked all right for someone who had just been assaulted with a deadly weapon. She left the ladies' room and walked back to the coroner's office. It looked like the deputy had left, and Dez was sitting at her desk.

Fenway went over to Dez. "Did you give your statement?"

"Yep. They told me they had everything they needed. Seems like Lana listened to her Miranda warnings, and is keeping her mouth shut for the time being."

"Celeste seemed like a good cop."

"One of the best." Dez sighed. "She needs to get promoted, or go to L.A., or something. She's too talented to get stuck here."

Fenway paused, took a deep breath, and let it out. "Shall we go get another coffee? Somebody dropped ours all over the floor."

She laughed. "You're buying."

"I get shot at *and* I have to buy the coffee? Some morning."

They started the short walk down to the coffee shop. "Hey, Dez, did you know one of the guys who died in the toxic fumes at Ferris Energy was Carl Cassidy?"

She looked at Fenway. "Yes, of course. Didn't you?"

"No, I had no idea. Any relation to Lana?"

Dez cocked her head to the side. "I forget you don't know this town. Yes. Carl and Lana were married. Had been for almost twenty years. Lana didn't come back to work for about two months after Carl died. She was devastated. They have a son, Shane, who's about to graduate high school. Estancia High—the same school Megan McVie goes to."

They arrived at Java Jim's. The morning rush had died down long before, and Dez and Fenway were the only customers at the counter. Dez ordered a drip coffee and Fenway got her large latte, and they sat down on the same overstuffed chairs Fenway and Rachel had sat in earlier that morning.

"Estancia High is the only high school in town, right?"

"Some parents send their kids to Saint Benedictine's over in Paso Querido. And there's the continuation high school. But, yeah, almost all the kids in town go to Estancia. I heard Shane took his dad's death pretty hard. He struggled this year; almost didn't graduate. I think he's got to go to the community college instead of going right to USC now."

"And Lana blames my father for everything—for killing her husband, for her son not going to the college of his choice."

Dez shrugged.

"And that's why she came after me, after finding out the Ferris Energy accident file was stolen."

"Well, rookie, let's say that's the primary theory of the case, as it stands."

Fenway sighed, heavily. "This is so messed up."

"It's weird, Fenway. I've been working in the coroner's office for about eight years, and I've investigated a bunch of deaths. Mostly suicides and drug overdoses, of course, but a few weird accidental deaths, and a handful of homicides every year." She stood up and stretched. "But I've never seen anything like this. There's never been a homicide of anyone in the office—unless you count the drunk driver who ran over one of our officers a few years ago. The homicides in this county are usually pretty straightforward: a drug deal gone wrong, or a husband killing his wife or his wife's lover. Whoever killed Harrison Walker went through a lot of trouble to hide their motives, and there's a lot of misdirection here."

"So, you don't think it was Dylan."

"No, I don't. I think Dylan was with McVie's wife when Walker was murdered."

"Me too." Fenway took another drink of her latte.

"And I don't think he would have been smart enough to ditch Walker's car in a long-term lot at LAX. I think he would have taken it into the forest and abandoned it, or set it on fire, or something."

Fenway nodded. "Yeah, good point. Stashing the car at a long-term lot seems like something someone would do who's seen that kind of thing before; maybe someone with a police background, or a relative who's a cop."

"Or a career criminal who's had a lot of experience making cars disappear. Or someone like you who watches too much *CSI*," Dez teased. "Don't be blaming cops for this."

"Sorry."

Dez finished the last of her coffee. "We should get back." They both stood up. Fenway drained her cup too, and they started out the door, back to the office.

"Dez, do you think it might have been Lana? Her gun looks like it might have been the right caliber to do it. Not like a .22. Lana had a serious gun."

"I guess it could have been Lana. A lot more people in this town have guns than you might think, and obviously Lana's not scared to pull the trigger. But I don't think it was Lana. What's her motive?"

"Jeez, Ferris Energy is all over this, aren't they?" Fenway asked, though it was more like a statement. "Hey, that reminds me, my father is coming in before lunch to talk about the files."

The door to the office was open when they got back, and Migs had returned. He stood up as they came in.

Migs' face was full of concern. "How you doing, boss? I heard what happened. That's all kinds of messed up."

Fenway smiled weakly. "I'm fine, Migs. Well, honestly, I'm a little shaken up. But I'll be okay."

"I was in IT when Scott told us the story. He said you were kind of a bad-ass."

Fenway laughed uncomfortably.

"You *were* kind of a bad-ass, Fenway," Dez said. "Going right up against someone who had a gun trained on you like that?"

"Oh." Fenway blushed slightly. "Thanks, Dez."

"So," Dez said to Migs, "did you find anything out with Rachel's computer?"

"Yep, I was right—Piper found RAT software on it."

"I've heard of that." Fenway tapped her forehead and tried to remember where. "It's like a virus where someone else can remotely take over your computer, right?"

"Yeah. I mean, technically, it's a Trojan horse, not a virus. But it looks like whoever the hacker is, they could see and listen to everything going on in the office. Whoever was on the other end of Rachel's camera feed was basically live-streaming everything happening in the office."

"You find out who it was yet?"

"No, we don't know definitively who it is yet. Whoever set up the software did a decent job of concealing the recipient's IP address. But the cybercrimes unit is working on it."

"You mean *Piper* is working on it." Dez elbowed Migs.

Migs' ears got a little red. "Yeah. She's the one who does cybercrimes stuff for the sheriff's office."

"Does Piper have a timeline for when we'll have some info back?" Fenway asked.

"She said it might be a day or two. She's great, though. She can work pretty fast. I've heard she got address info out of a spearphishing email in under an hour."

Fenway nodded. "Okay. I guess we wait and see."

"There's something else."

"Besides the IP address?"

"Yeah. See, we've got this IT admin, Bradley Watermeier. Stanford dropout, rich parents; great with computers, though. He's the admin for all the firewalls, and RAT software like that takes a huge amount of bandwidth. Bradley's in charge of monitoring that kind of stuff, and he should have seen the huge amount of bandwidth being taken up by the video going through—and it wasn't just during the day—there was a huge amount of data going through on Friday night, after hours."

Fenway's brow knitted. "Could he have missed it?"

"No way." Migs vehemently shook his head. "First of all, he's super smart—so he wouldn't miss it, not if he was even paying the slightest amount of attention. But, second of all, somebody reconfigured the firewall *specifically* to hide the RAT data in the reports the IT team was getting."

"You've got more than one person looking at all the reports?" she asked.

"We do. Best security practices."

"So the reports said nothing was wrong?"

"Yep. And Bradley is really the only person who has access to both the firewall *and* those reports."

"Bradley was the one who reconfigured the firewall?" she asked.

"Piper *thinks* so. He's got the knowledge, and he's got the access. I guess there are a few other people who might know how to do that— Piper definitely does—but she doesn't have access to the firewall."

"Then why does Piper think it's him?"

"Because right before I brought Rachel's machine into IT, Bradley got a text on his cell phone, and he left the office, said he had to deal with a family emergency. Piper told me he actually grabbed a few of his personal items off his desk before he took off. When I came in and told them I thought there was spyware, and the camera was compromised, they tried calling his phone to get access to the firewall, but there was no answer. I mean, it's pretty suspicious considering whoever was watching us on Rachel's camera saw we had discovered it, and could have called Bradley to get out of the office."

Dez nodded.

"And then later, they tried to go into Bradley's computer, and Bradley's machine was being *wiped.*"

"Being wiped?" Dez asked.

"Yeah, there are computer programs that will overwrite the hard drive with random data, to make it hard to retrieve the original files. It was in the middle of its second pass."

Fenway's pulse jumped. "Was everything deleted?"

"Everything."

"Can you get it back?"

"Maybe. I mean, they're working on it. But Bradley knew how to destroy files—I wouldn't hold my breath."

Fenway swore in her head. "Are we thinking he was the one who put the virus on Rachel's PC?"

"He probably was the one who actually *did* it, but with the phone call that came in, I'm sure he was doing it *for* someone else," Migs said. "I don't think he had a motive to be the one behind the whole thing. I don't think Rachel knew Bradley—she knew him enough to say 'hi' in the office, but they never hung out, or anything. I guess he could be stalking her. But personally, I think someone wanted to see what was going on in the office, and paid Bradley off."

Dez leaned forward. "I'll get a warrant for his financials. What we've got should be compelling enough for a judge to sign. Do you know if he bought a new car recently, or anything like that?"

"I don't know him very well." Migs shook his head. "I say 'hi' to him when I go over there, like Rachel does. That's it. He's come over here a couple times to set up computers. He actually set up Rachel's PC."

"So he might have set the RAT software up ever since she started here," Fenway said.

"Yeah, but the thing is, the video feeds only started about two weeks ago. We don't know how long ago Rachel's machine was compromised, but before two weeks ago, there was no video."

Fenway nodded. "That's when Rachel bought the camera." She paused, then asked, "What was the hacker getting before? Were they listening to audio?"

"I don't know. I didn't ask. Piper would know, probably. Or could research it. I could ask her."

Dez leaned back in her chair, a thoughtful look on her face. "Okay, we know someone was spying on this office through Rachel's camera for the last two weeks, and probably had access to files or audio for a while before. I think we should look for a motive of *why* someone would do that."

"Do you think it might be related to the theft of the file drawer?" Fenway asked.

"It might *all* be related. But we probably need to go through the rest of those files in Walker's office to see if anything jumps out at us. By the way, Fenway, the officer who was here yesterday—with the keys to Walker's office—agreed to meet you at eight, which was over three hours ago. He might still be waiting for you wherever they moved the files."

Dez's phone rang.

"Roubideaux." She paused. Then, covering the mouthpiece, exasperation in her voice: "Oh, calling on behalf of the all-knowing *medical examiner*, eh?" Another pause. "We've been waiting for the results for days. Will we be able to see them? Oh, right after lunch?" She looked at her watch. "Yeah, I guess I can get Fenway there."

"You can get me where?" Fenway asked, watching Dez hang up.

Dez rolled her eyes. "The San Miguelito M.E.'s office. She wants you to come down and take a look at the body."

"They want me to look at Walker?"

"Apparently."

"After lunch?"

"Yeah, it's eleven thirty, so we can't get there till—"

"Oh *shit*!" Fenway exclaimed. "My father was supposed to be meeting me over at the sheriff's office to discuss the files at eleven thirty. I've gotta get over there *now*." She grabbed her purse and headed out the door.

"Fenway—we've gotta be at the M.E.'s at one," Dez called after her.

She had no idea if San Miguelito was ten minutes away, or an hour and ten minutes away, but Fenway had to talk to her father. There were too many mysteries about the file: why Harrison Walker wouldn't share it, why insurance companies wouldn't pay until they saw it, why a widow had threatened Fenway's life because of it. Maybe Fenway could use the confrontation with Lana to her advantage in her talk with her father; his only daughter almost got killed because he had information he didn't give up.

Fenway crossed the street to the sheriff's office. When she opened the door, two figures—Nathaniel Ferris and the imposing figure of Rob Stotsky—were there waiting for her.

CHAPTER FIFTEEN

"Fenway." Nathaniel Ferris's arms were folded and his mouth was drawn tight. "You're late."

"Yes, Dad." She walked up to Ferris and Stotsky. "You'll have to forgive me. I was shot at this morning by the widow of Carl Cassidy." She looked from her father's face to Stotsky's, watching for their reactions. "I understand Carl was one of the employees killed in the accident at the oil refinery six months ago. And I believe he was the subject of the missing file."

Stotsky's face registered determination.

Ferris's face registered horror. "You were *shot at?*"

"Yes, Dad," Fenway snapped. "Carl's widow thought I was working with *you* to cover up her husband's death. She thought I was behind the theft of the files. She accused *me* of killing Walker on Sunday night."

Stotsky put his hand up. "Did she say that?"

"Yes, she did. Right before she pulled the trigger." She suddenly noticed the interested glances of the cubicle dwellers. "Now, let's go into the interview room before we broadcast this to the whole West Coast."

Fenway motioned her father and Stotsky to go in the interview room ahead of her, and she followed them in, slamming the door behind herself. Her father jumped a little bit.

"I don't want anyone in there watching us." Stotsky pointed to the one-way mirror.

"Relax." Fenway did a hand-wave in front of the mirror. "I didn't tell anyone I was coming over here, and everyone is either dealing with the arrest of Dylan Richards, or the fact that someone tried to shoot me." She turned toward the mirror and made silly faces. "See? No one's there."

She motioned for them to take a seat on the side of the table farthest away from the one-way mirror. She sat on the near side and pulled her chair in. It made a grinding noise on the floor.

Fenway cleared her throat. "Now, tell me, Dad, why in the world would anyone think there was a cover up with the accident? And why would they think *I* was involved?"

Nathaniel Ferris looked at Stotsky's face and started to mirror the look of steely determination in his own. "I promise, Fenway, I'll get to the bottom of this. You aren't going to have to worry about your safety."

"No, Dad." She shook her head. "You are not going to get to the bottom of *anything*. You are not investigating Walker's homicide. *I am*. You're not figuring out what those files have to do with Walker's death. *I am*."

Fenway looked at Stotsky. His eyes were thin slits. His mouth was pursed. His face was getting red with anger.

"What is it, Mr. Stotsky? Do you have any knowledge about these files? Is there anything you might have mentioned to me yesterday morning that would have lowered my chances of getting shot today?"

"Come on now, Fenway." Ferris's voice was chiding.

"What, Dad? What is it? I *shouldn't* get angry that people all over this county think you're covering something up?" Fenway folded her arms. "And worse, they think *I* had something to do with the missing files. I didn't think you were covering anything up before, Dad. I'm starting to think maybe I was wrong."

Fenway wasn't sure this line of questioning was doing a lot for father-daughter relations, but she noticed Stotsky was getting angrier by the second.

"Mr. Ferris." Stotsky stood and gathered himself up to his full height. Fenway thought for a minute he was going to hit his head on the ceiling. "I believe we ought to head out of here before Miss Stevenson says something she regrets."

"Nonsense, Rob. Sit down. Fenway has every right. She was shot at today."

Stotsky turned to face Ferris, his back to Fenway. "And perhaps it's making her overly emotional. Now, Mr. Ferris, I know she is your only daughter. Her life was just put in danger. I understand you might be so concerned for her safety you feel, shall we say, more open to discussing things of a confidential nature if you think it's going to keep her safe. But, as your head of security, I'm obligated to point out these files should not be discussed with anyone outside of the company." He cleared his throat. "If Miss Stevenson wishes to file a court order, or get a subpoena, we'd be happy to supply our findings, but absent that, I can't allow you to discuss the contents of those files."

Ferris looked at Stotsky, and his eyes flashed in anger for a moment, but then he softened. "Rob is right, Fenway. Were you hurt? Are you okay?"

Fenway looked at her father, and in that instant, saw the concern and caring she had missed her whole childhood. She found it hard to maintain her cool. Not only because she really wasn't okay, but because she also didn't have anyone to turn to in town for support.

But Fenway also really wanted, and needed, to discuss those files. And perhaps, Fenway thought, letting herself be vulnerable right now would work to her advantage. Maybe she didn't have to push down those emotions. If she played it right, maybe their dinner together tonight would be the right time to get some information on the contents of the files, without the head of Ferris security looming over their conversation.

So Fenway gave into her vulnerability.

"No, Dad, I'm not okay." Her voice broke. "I'm not even on the job twenty-four hours, and I got shot at! I'm scared. And I'm furious at you for not telling me about these files. I'm furious at you because if I had known about the files, I would have known why she was so angry with me. I could have talked her down."

"I'm sorry, Fenway. I'm really sorry." He stood up, came around the side of the table, and gave her an awkward hug while she was still sitting down. She could feel the hot tears start to sting her eyes and she let them fall.

Stotsky tapped his fingers on the table. "Perhaps there will be another opportunity for a more productive discussion at a later time."

Ferris looked at Stotsky, then shifted his eyes to her. "Fenway—look, we were planning on dinner tonight. Let's have dinner. You can talk about how angry you are at me, and I'm sure it's not—" Ferris stopped and cleared his throat. "It's not just because of the files. I'm sure there's a lot from the last twenty years, too. I wasn't a good father. Let's just have dinner tonight."

Fenway looked down at the table. "Okay."

Ferris went back around and clapped Stotsky on the shoulder. "Okay?"

Stotsky moved to open the door. Ferris went out first, Stotsky following.

Fenway pulled the phone out of her purse, sniffling, but getting under control. She started to text Dez that she was heading back over.

The door opened again. It was Rob Stotsky.

"Forgot my pen." He saw Fenway texting and closed the door behind him. He leaned forward, placing his fists knuckles-down on the table; the table groaned slightly under his weight. "I need to have a chat with you, Miss Stevenson." She looked up at him. His determined look hadn't faded, and she couldn't help but think he looked much the opposite of the helpful man she had first met when she pulled into her new apartment complex. "You haven't lived here in twenty years, but you're messing with the reputation of the most powerful man in the area—maybe even the state. And it's my job to protect him. You can't accuse Mr. Ferris without proof. The innuendo and leading questions might be one of your investigative techniques, and you might be able to get away with it with him because he's your father, but they don't do any good to his reputation or his business."

Stotsky stood back up and straightened his suit jacket. "You're his daughter, so of course he wants to protect you, and this coroner job was a way he felt he could help." He cracked his knuckles. "Now, you may think you're just doing your job, but I'd advise you to take another route in your investigation. Otherwise, you may find you've killed the goose laying your golden eggs." He adjusted his tie and walked back out.

Fenway sat there for a moment, taking it all in. The blood was pounding in her ears, and her heart was racing. Any tears of sadness or self-pity were gone. She took a few deep breaths.

The door opened again, and Sheriff McVie walked in. He nodded at her. "That was pretty impressive."

"Stop." She was still looking down at the table. "I didn't think anyone was watching."

"Ah, Fenway, someone's always watching."

She was silent.

"I'm not being snarky when I say what you did was impressive. Using your vulnerability to not only get your dad to open up, but also to push Stotsky's buttons. Coming across as genuine, because it was genuine. That was hard to do. And admirable."

"Thanks, I guess."

"I talked to Dez, and if it's okay with you, I'm going to drive you to San Miguelito to see the M.E."

Fenway shook her head. "I'm sorry, but can we maybe push it to tomorrow? This day has been rough. I don't know if I can handle playing politics with an M.E. over a dead body."

"I hate to say this, Fenway, but no, we can't push it till tomorrow. First of all, someone needs to personally deliver Dylan's gun to the forensics lab. And secondly, we need those autopsy results. It's been over 72 hours, and I don't want the trail getting any colder."

"That makes two of us."

"I talked to the M.E. and she said there are a couple of things she'd like us to see for ourselves. I didn't talk to Mark this morning, so I never asked him to take Dylan's gun to the San Miguelito lab. I can drop you off at home afterward, but I really think you need to see this too."

"This is the longest day ever."

"Yep, for me too. But if those ballistics match the gun we found in Dylan's closet, we can all go home and sleep for a while."

Fenway realized Dez hadn't informed the sheriff about Dylan's truck possibly being seen away from the crime scene, or about Dylan and McVie's wife. She wondered if Dez was hoping Fenway would talk to the sheriff about all of those things, or if Dez would prefer her to follow Megan's request to tell her father nothing. Fenway figured she would decide when they were on the road.

"I definitely need to eat." Fenway picked up her purse.

"We can grab something on the way."

He stopped at the evidence locker and retrieved a black case, signing it out.

"Is that Dylan's gun?" Fenway asked.

"Yep."

They went through a burger drive-through—yet another regional fast-food place Fenway hadn't heard of. She ordered a spicy grilled chicken sandwich, McVie a deluxe burger.

"This law enforcement diet isn't going to work too much longer for me," Fenway said, but she was hungry. She had only had two large lattes all day. She ate her sandwich quickly and drank her diet soda.

McVie looked over at her. "You're quiet."

"I was hungry. And I'm exhausted."

"You can nap if you want. It'll be a good forty-five minutes."

Fenway leaned the seat back and fell asleep almost immediately.

When she woke up, they were pulling into a parking space at the San Miguelito County Medical Examiner's office.

"Morning, sunshine."

Fenway grunted, waking slowly and sitting back upright.

McVie retrieved the gun case from the trunk, and they walked into the office. They checked in at the front desk and sat in chairs with brown plastic seats and metal legs that probably had once been shiny.

"So, Sheriff, I know this may not be the place to say this, but this is going to be my first autopsy."

"Didn't you have to deal with cadavers in your classes?"

"Yeah, but those people all donated their bodies to the greater good. This is my first dead body of someone who didn't think they'd be getting cut up when they died."

"Walker probably didn't think he'd get shot in the back, either. Death is full of surprises."

A short Asian woman with closely-cropped black hair came out. She wore light blue scrubs. "Michi," McVie said. "Good to see you again."

"Good to see you too, Craig." She shook McVie's hand. "Dez didn't make it?"

"No, she needed to stay on the case back home."

Her face registered disappointment, but quickly changed. "Give her my best when you see her."

"Will do, Michi. So let me introduce you two: Dr. Michiyo Yasuda, this is our new coroner, Fenway Stevenson."

"Fenway? Like the ballpark?"

"No, I was named after my great uncle Fenwick and my third cousin Hemingway. Sort of a mash-up."

Dr. Yasuda stared at her.

Fenway cleared her throat awkwardly. "Yeah, sorry, not really. My father's a big Red Sox fan." Fenway gave Dr. Yasuda a weak smile.

Yasuda nodded. "Okay—let's take you back." She turned and was gone so quickly McVie and Fenway had to run to keep up with her.

They went through a couple of hallways to a staircase leading into the basement. After a left turn, there was a set of double doors labelled MORGUE. She swiped her keycard on the black pad next to the double doors, and there was an audible, low-pitched *click*. She pushed the door open and led them inside.

There was a body on the table under a sheet, and as Yasuda pulled the top of the sheet down and folded it back, Fenway could see it was a Caucasian male, roughly 50 years old, lying supine.

"All right," Yasuda began, "Before we get to the gunshot wound, I want to show you a couple of things." Yasuda pointed at Walker's left cheek. "In his beard, right here, two lacerations are healing. The bruising around the edges are consistent with fingernails." Yasuda pulled the sheet up from the bottom next, so Fenway could see Walker's left knee. There was a big knot an inch below the kneecap which was badly bruised. "And there's this hematoma. It's more difficult to tell what made contact here. This was done a couple of days before he was shot and killed, about the same time as the lacerations."

"Kicked and scratched." McVie crossed his arms.

"That conclusion would be consistent with the evidence," Dr. Yasuda agreed.

"I know who kicked and scratched Mr. Walker," Fenway said. "It happened at roughly seven o'clock on Friday night."

Dr. Yasuda looked up from the body. "I guess the investigation is progressing."

"I don't believe the woman who did this is the killer, however. She has an alibi for Sunday night."

Dr. Yasuda turned back to Walker's body. "Getting back to Sunday night, the bullet was a low-velocity 10-millimeter round. Sheriff, if you could assist me."

Using the sheets as leverage, McVie and Dr. Yasuda turned Walker's body onto its stomach. Dr. Yasuda pulled the sheet down to expose Walker's back; there was a hole from a gunshot on his left side.

Fenway looked closely at the hole. "Shot through the heart?"

Dr. Yasuda nodded. "And here's something interesting I wanted to make sure you saw." She picked up a three-foot long fiberglass rod and inserted it in the bullet hole. The angle was about five or ten degrees shy of being perpendicular. "Now, Mr. Walker was five-foot-nine. As you can see from the angle, the shot was fired from slightly above. I believe the gun was roughly three feet away, as there was stippling on the wound, but no burns or soot on Walker's clothes. It appears the murderer would have been a bit higher than the victim. The killer may have been tall, or Walker could have been on his knees."

"Aren't there pretty steep hills around there?" said McVie. "That might account for the angle."

"No, not where the body was found."

"What if the body was moved?" asked Fenway.

"There's no evidence of that," Yasuda said. "Blood has pooled everywhere I expect it to pool when a dead body stays in place."

Fenway nodded.

"And, no drag marks were found on the ground around his body or feet, no torn clothing or scuffs on his shoes." Dr. Yasuda pulled some photos of Walker's clothing out. "See, there are no drag marks on the clothing, just dirt on his shoulders, arms, and legs consistent with being dead before you fall forward onto the ground."

"What are we looking at?" McVie asked. "Does this narrow the height of the killer down at all?"

"Yes. Based on the gunshot residue and the stippling pattern, I estimate the shot was fired from roughly three feet away. Assuming the killer was holding the weapon at a normal height, I'd estimate the killer to be anywhere from six feet, two inches to six feet, six inches."

"And if Mr. Walker had been on his knees?"

Dr. Yasuda checked her notes. "The length of his crus measures fourteen and one-eighth inches," she said.

"His what?" McVie whispered to Fenway.

"Crus. Lower leg from the knee to the ankle," she explained.

"Subtracting the length from his full height," Dr. Yasuda continued, "Walker would have been about four feet seven inches tall on his knees. If the killer was standing—which, in my experience, isn't always the case when the victim is kneeling—the killer is right around five feet tall, give or take."

McVie chuckled. "We're either looking for a really tall or really short person."

"If the killer was standing."

McVie walked around to the other side of the table. "Okay. Anything else we need to know?"

Dr. Yasuda picked up a file folder. "The rest of it is in the autopsy report and my notes. I wanted you to see the trajectory for yourself. It's tough for the photos and descriptions to do it justice."

Fenway nodded again. "Sure, thanks."

McVie held up the gun case. "And I've got Dylan Richards' gun here."

"Let's go up to the ballistics lab." Dr. Yasuda pulled the sheet up over Walker's head, then turned and was out the door. Fenway and McVie were caught lagging behind again; Dr. Yasuda was up the stairs so quickly McVie and Fenway were breathing hard by the time they hit the ground floor. A turn down a hallway, and another fifty feet later they were at the lab.

Yasuda walked up to a technician behind a microscope. "Okay, Trevor. Richards' firearm is here."

McVie was still breathing a little heavily. "Great." He hoisted the gun case up onto the counter, got his keys out and unlocked it. "I'm going to have to have you sign this for the chain of custody—"

"Hold on. This is a Glock 26," Dr. Yasuda cut in.

Trevor nodded, looking at McVie.

McVie nodded. "Right. And we need to see if—"

Dr. Yasuda interrupted him. "This is a nine-millimeter weapon. I told you the murder weapon fired a ten-millimeter bullet. There are several weapons that could have fired that bullet, but a Glock 26 isn't one of them. This isn't the murder weapon."

McVie's face fell.

Fenway piped up. "Aren't there some cases where bullets can be used in different caliber weapons?"

Dr. Yasuda gave her a disapproving look. "Yes. A ten-millimeter gun could potentially fire a nine-millimeter bullet, albeit less accurately. But if you try to fire a ten-millimeter bullet from a nine-millimeter gun, the barrel could prohibit the bullet from going forward, and the gun could explode. And even if it doesn't, the markings on the outside of the bullet would make it clear it was fired from a nine-millimeter weapon." The doctor shook her head definitively. "No, this is a ten-millimeter bullet fired from a ten-millimeter weapon."

Fenway was quiet.

"Thanks, Doctor." McVie looked a little embarrassed. "I appreciate the time."

"Certainly." Dr. Yasuda nodded curtly. "And when you find the ten-millimeter firearm you think did the job, bring it here and I'll make sure it gets fast-tracked."

"Absolutely." McVie clicked the gun case closed. Trevor hadn't even taken the Glock out.

Fenway and McVie walked back down the corridor and out through the main doors. McVie was fuming silently all the way to the parking lot. When they got in the car and closed the doors, he let out a loud stream of profanity.

Fenway was silent. He finally fell silent too.

He started the car and they started down the road, back to Estancia.

"I thought we had him, Fenway."

"I don't know what to tell you, Sheriff. Dylan's got the motive, for sure, not to mention he lied about where he was on Sunday night, his truck crashed through the wall, and the people in the truck stole those files. The evidence might be mostly circumstantial, but it all points to him."

"Exactly."

"But his gun didn't match. And his height doesn't match either."

"He could have been crouching or leaning over Walker. Michi's autopsy didn't tell us nearly as much as I was hoping."

"Maybe the car will point us in the right direction. You heard they found Walker's car in long-term parking at LAX, right?"

"Yes. I meant to tell you earlier. Thanks for giving us the idea to look there. I asked Mark to make some calls yesterday."

"So, Dez and I were talking. And a couple of things bother me. Like, do you think Dylan Richards has the intelligence, or experience, to get rid of a murder victim's car in a long-term lot at LAX?"

McVie was quiet for a second, and Fenway could see him thinking it over. "I don't know."

"I mean, we're thinking this is a crime of passion, right? Sometime between Friday night and Sunday afternoon, Richards watches the video of Walker sexually assaulting his wife, and he's so pissed off, he lures Walker to a wilderness area, where he gets Walker on his knees and executes him."

"Yeah, that's my theory."

"Okay, I can see that. And then what does he do? He's 27, he doesn't have a record. He leaves the body. He gets in Walker's car, drives it to LAX, takes the train back, takes a taxi, or an Uber, or something from the Estancia station back to his car, which he's left on the side of the road for six hours?"

McVie was silent.

"And the car was in a place where you didn't find it," she continued, "because you had already found Walker's body by then, right?"

"It was dark, and we didn't do a real search for Walker's car until the morning."

She nodded. "Did you find anything in the morning? Someplace where it looked like someone had hidden a car, and driven through bushes and stuff on the side of the road?"

"No." McVie thought a minute. "Richards might have had an accomplice. Someone to follow him to LAX and drive him back. Maybe Rachel."

Fenway shook her head. "I don't think so, Sheriff. She has an alibi, and receipts, and I'm sure there are people who saw her at the movies."

"Maybe his brother."

"Parker? Yeah, I guess it's possible. He's not the sharpest knife in the drawer, so I guarantee you he didn't think about the LAX long-term parking, but it's possible."

"We still have motive and opportunity. We don't have the weapon, but that doesn't mean Dylan didn't shoot him."

Fenway hesitated for a second. "Sure."

McVie looked at her. "You don't think it was Dylan."

"Well..."

McVie turned back to the road. "So, if it wasn't Dylan, who do you think it was?"

Fenway sighed. "Honestly, Sheriff, I don't have any better suspects right now." She shifted in her seat. "I do think my father's company has —well, *something* to do with this. I'm not sure if it's Harrison Walker's murder, but I'm pretty sure it has something to do with the stolen files."

"Obviously—you didn't bring your father to the interview room for nothing. You were talking about what was in those files."

"Yep." She moved the seat back a little bit. "My father knew way too much about them. I told him Walker's file on Ferris Energy was missing, and he asked if there was another file in the drawer the thief might want. And he also knew the files were taken last night. He was acting like I had said, 'Hey, Dad, someone stole a whole drawer of files from Harrison

Walker's office last night,' when all I told him was, 'There's a Ferris Energy file missing.'"

McVie turned down the corners of his mouth. "I wonder if he got the information from somewhere else. It's not like we kept it secret."

"No, I guess not. Maybe he heard on the radio there was a break-in, or maybe the reporters gave out information. But I don't think so. I don't think there was enough time to see what was out there. I mean, maybe there's someone in the office feeding him information, so maybe he doesn't have anything to do with the break-in...but it sure feels like he knows something he's not telling me."

McVie drummed his fingers on the wheel and exhaled loudly through his mouth. "I've been trying to make this all fit with Dylan Richards, but even I have to admit I don't think it was him crashing through Walker's office."

"Too—what was the word you used?—brazen?"

"Yeah. But I was thinking if he *had* broken through the wall of the office, he didn't have a whole lot of time. He'd need to get rid of the truck, get back to his apartment, change clothes, and pretend like we woke him up. It was, at the most, forty-five minutes between the time he sped out of the parking lot and we knocked on his door. I mean, it's possible, but it would be cutting it really close."

"And he didn't seem like he had been up," Fenway said. "Maybe he's a great actor, but he and Rachel both seemed like they had been awakened from a dead sleep."

"Dammit." McVie continued drumming his fingers.

She was quiet. The Pacific Coast Highway met with US 101 here, and the Pacific Ocean appeared suddenly on their right. She stared out the window at the sun dancing on the blue-green water; the mist, a looming grey cloud in the distance, waiting for the late afternoon fog to overtake the coast again.

Fenway wondered if she should bring up Dylan's *real* alibi. She wondered how McVie would take it. Part of her suspected that McVie already knew—and she wondered how much of it he knew. Did he suspect his wife was cheating on him? Did he know Dylan was the other man?

She turned her head to look from the ocean to McVie's face, the creases around his eyes, his jaw almost permanently set in determination. She couldn't see him arresting Dylan on such thin evidence if he knew about Dylan and his wife—it didn't seem smart, it seemed petty. But maybe Fenway just didn't want to see the sheriff as petty.

They passed a sign that read *Estancia 7 Miles*. Fenway made up her mind.

"Sheriff." Her voice was soft. "I don't want to ask you this, but I think I have to." She shifted uncomfortably in her seat. "Do you know anything about the relationship between Dylan and your wife?"

McVie didn't say anything for a minute. He squinted his eyes at the road. Then he ran his hands through his hair and pressed his lips together before he finally spoke.

"That doesn't have anything to do with why I arrested him."

"Dylan's truck was seen in your neighborhood on Sunday night. The neighbor wouldn't swear to it, but I was pretty convinced. I think it's why Dylan lied about his alibi."

"You asked my neighbors?"

She was quiet.

McVie leaned back in his seat. "Who else knows?"

Fenway closed her eyes. "Dez."

McVie ran his hand over his face, from his forehead to his chin, and exhaled loudly. "Who else?"

She paused briefly, then went on. "No one else in the department—not that I know of, anyway. I'm not planning on telling anyone else, and I don't think Dez will say anything either. But your neighbors have seen his truck, and they're not stupid. And if the neighbors have seen his truck, I don't know that your wife has done a very good job of keeping it from Megan."

McVie looked pained and tightened his grip on the wheel.

"Look, it's really none of my business. Except you arrested the guy, and now it looks like he's not the one who did it."

McVie was quiet again.

They passed a sign that read *Estancia Next 4 Exits*.

McVie turned on his blinker and exited onto Broadway, heading for Fenway's apartment. "Get some rest. You've got dinner with your dad tonight, and I think you should be ready with a strategy to figure out what's in those files."

She gave a small, polite smile. "Thanks. What are you going to do about Dylan?"

"I'll take care of it."

He pulled into her apartment complex's parking lot. Fenway gave him a sad smile and got out of the car. She checked her phone—a little past three o'clock. She had five hours to get ready for a white linen tablecloth dinner, and a strategy for making the most powerful man in the county give up his secrets.

She walked in the door, threw her purse down, kicked her shoes off, and fell asleep on top of the covers of her bed.

CHAPTER SIXTEEN

SHE HAD A DREAM WHERE SHE WAS IN HER BED—BUT IT WAS IN HER bed at her mother's house in Seattle. It was raining, and she sat up, lightning flashed, and Lana was standing at the foot of her bed with a big Dirty Harry-style gun.

"You're nothing but a dirty whore," dream-Lana sneered, and fired the gun with a blinding muzzle flash.

Fenway woke with a start. It was still light outside. She checked the time; it was almost six. She had enough time to find a dress in her closet, do her hair, and get ready. She shook the cobwebs out of her head. She didn't feel she was ready to talk to her father, but she didn't want to spend the night in, either. She was wary of being alone with her thoughts of Lana, and getting shot, and her Russian Lit professor swarming her mind.

She was ready a little after seven thirty. Fenway picked a high-necked, purple A-line dress with long sleeves, with a hem ending at her knees. There was a shift dress in her closet she liked more, but she thought it was a little too casual for Maxime's. It also needed to be ironed, and she didn't have the time. She put her hair up and remembered she had left her Red Sox cap, with the bullet hole in the bill, in the office.

There was a knock at her door at about seven-forty. It was her father.

"Hi, Fenway." He leaned in and kissed her cheek. "You look beautiful."

"Thank you," she said, taking a step back. He was in the same suit and tie she had seen him in during the meeting before lunch. "Did you just get off work?"

"Yes. No rest for the wicked."

Fenway gave a tight smile. "Are you ready to go?"

"Yes. Are you sure you're okay? After the day you've had?"

"I napped. And it will be good for me to get out of the apartment and take my mind off this."

"I'm glad. Plus, I have a surprise for you."

"Today has been full of surprises; I'm not sure I can handle another one." They stepped out and she locked the door behind them.

"I think you might like this one."

They walked down the stairs to the parking lot. There was a black Mercedes S500 in the visitor's space, which Fenway assumed was his car; there was a man in a dark suit behind the wheel, who was probably Ferris's driver. But in her assigned parking space—which had been empty up to this point—was a silver Honda Accord. Her father went over and stood next to it.

"Surprise." He reached in his pocket and pulled out a black car remote and key.

She balked. "You got me a car?"

"Now look, I know you think I'm trying to buy you off with this—"

"Well—"

"Let me finish," Ferris said.

Fenway clamped her mouth shut.

"You literally just got to town, Fenway. You've barely had time to unpack, and you've been dumped in the middle of this time-sucking investigation. You're going to have to get to City Hall every day, you have to interview people all over the county, you'll probably have to drive to see the M.E. in San Miguelito; you can't have the sheriff constantly shuttling you around. And I know you, you're stubborn enough that you'd take the bus, but that won't work with how much time this investigation is going to take. And this way, you don't have to spend the time you don't have haggling with some dealership and spending three hours filling out paperwork."

It was all true, Fenway had to admit.

"Now, I was going to buy you a Lexus, or a BMW, but Charlotte thought you'd think it was too showy, and everywhere your fancy car went, people would look at it and think I bought the coroner's office. Plus, she said you wouldn't want the insurance payment on an expensive car."

Fenway didn't want to admit Charlotte was right.

"So, I got a deal on this Accord. Now you'll have to indulge me a little, it *is* the top-of-the-line model; great sound system, leather seats, navigation, all the safety features. But no one's going to look at a Honda and think I bought you off, right?"

"I guess not."

"So, look, if you don't want it, if you think you shouldn't take it, I understand. Drive it until the investigation is over, then give it back to me. I can always use a car like this in my fleet. You need a car right now, and I hope this helps get you and me off on the right foot."

Fenway had conflicting emotions. She knew her father could buy his way out of most situations—and he hadn't lifted a finger to help either her or her mother in the last twenty years, with his lawyers making sure he paid almost nothing in child support or alimony. She wasn't sure if he was genuinely trying to help or not.

Whatever her father's reason, Fenway realized she needed a car. She needed to find and follow up on the evidence, and she couldn't keep relying on Dez and McVie to drive her around. She suspected her father, as he often did, had an ulterior motive, but she needed a car too much to refuse.

Fenway nodded. "Thanks, Dad. I *do* need a car for this investigation. It's the kind of car I would have picked for myself." She paused. "I probably would have gotten one that wasn't fully loaded, because I can't afford it, but I do appreciate it."

"You're very welcome."

Fenway looked at the car for a minute. She had been good at the fake smile so far this evening, but she couldn't do it for any longer.

"Dad?"

"Yes?

She looked back to her father. "Why now?"

Nathaniel Ferris stopped and looked down at the ground.

"I mean—I appreciate the car, Dad. I need it. And I really needed someplace to go after what happened with Mom, so I appreciate you helping me find the apartment. But—why now?"

"I guess because you're my daughter."

She pursed her lips and shook her head. "But I was your daughter before. I was your daughter when Mom and I had to go on food stamps. When Mom took the shelves out of the kitchen pantry and slept on a cot because she could only afford a one-bedroom." Fenway was looking back at the car, and her voice was getting stronger. "I was your daughter when you didn't show up at my high school graduation. I was your daughter when I was valedictorian at Western. And you didn't show up to that, either."

"No," he said softly. "No, I sure didn't."

"I had to work two jobs during college to be able to afford my crappy little Nissan Sentra. And the day I bought it, mom told me you bought a jet. A jet! A ten-million-dollar jet, all the bells and whistles, can get you from coast to coast in six hours. And I had to struggle to get a Sentra that could barely get me up to Bellingham."

Ferris looked down.

"I can count on one hand the number of times I saw you after we left. Why?"

He cleared his throat. "I'm not sure I have a good answer for that. I know I was really mad at Joanne."

"We were on food stamps, Dad."

"I didn't know that," he said lamely.

"What did you think was going to happen? Mom couldn't afford to keep fighting your lawyers even though everyone knew she'd get enough to keep us comfortable, even if she didn't get half of everything."

He was quiet.

"Did she cheat on you?"

He started pacing slowly. "Did your mother ever tell you how we met?"

Fenway shook her head.

"Your mother was a brilliant painter."

"I know."

"I hear she had started selling her paintings again, before, you know."

"Right."

He sighed. "The company had just moved into a new headquarters building," Ferris said. "It's the one we're in now, where Santa Clarita Street hits 326, and it was huge. I'd hired interior designers to arrange the space, but all the artwork they'd picked for the walls didn't do it for me. So, one Saturday, I'm having breakfast downtown, and I decide to walk around. There used to be a little boho-type gallery over on Fourth, and I'm passing by, and I see it."

Fenway looked at her father. He had a faraway look in his eyes, and a smile even touched his lips.

"It was a painting of the Three Sisters Rock Arches north of Point Dominguez," he continued. "She captured the light perfectly, reflecting off both the rocks and the ocean. She got the color of the water absolutely perfect too. It was surreal, but at the same time, it was... I don't really know. It spoke to me. It spoke to me the way a good jazz record speaks to me. The electricity I felt was like watching Nomo pitch the ninth of his no-hitter in '01. It was special."

He shuffled his feet. "I had to have that painting on the wall of the front lobby. The first thing everyone would see when they came in. I had to buy it." He put his hands in his pockets. "And your mother was in the gallery. We talked about the painting, and the winding road to get to Three Sisters, and at the end of the evening I had a new painting and a date for the next night."

Ferris smiled wistfully. "And I came home late one night from the office—what was it, ten, twelve years later? And Joanne was gone. And you were gone. And your clothes were all gone; all your toys, your bed, the spare couch in the playroom..."

He cleared his throat again. "Look, I worked a lot. I probably never paid attention to Joanne as much as I did the night I bought her painting. But she never gave me a reason why she left. She never told me why she took you. She moved a thousand miles away, for God's sake. I wasn't going to let her steal away in the middle of the night with my only daughter, and take my money, without at least an explanation."

He folded his arms. "So, when I heard what happened to her a few weeks ago—and I'm not proud of this—the first thing I thought was, *I'm never going to know*."

"I thought you'd moved on. You married Charlotte," Fenway said quietly.

"I don't know what to tell you, Fenway. The first thing I thought was, *I'm never going to know*. And just like that—it was like a blindfold being taken off. I realized I had a daughter whose childhood I had completely missed because I was so enraged at her mother."

"And you want to make up for it."

"Of course I *want* to make up for it. But I'm not stupid. I know I'll never make up for it. But you were in a rough spot, and I could help. You were in a rough spot before, and I could have helped then, and I didn't. But I will now."

"It still hurts."

"Yeah." He paused. "Do you still want to go to dinner?"

She nodded.

"Good." Nathaniel Ferris opened the rear door of the Mercedes, and she got in and slid over. Her father slid in next to her, and the driver started up the car.

Fenway enjoyed the smooth ride of the S500, although it made her feel like a poseur in her twenty-five-dollar dress from Target. The leather was buttery soft. She had her own air vents and seat controls. The sound of a gong followed by the quick yet mournful notes of a tenor saxophone filled the car before the music settled down into a four-note bass riff.

Fenway turned to her father. "Coltrane."

"That's my girl. Know the tune?"

"*A Love Supreme.*"

He smiled. "One thing that's always going to stick with me is that Coltrane almost died from drugs, and then he turned his life around and he wrote this album. He had put out some great albums when he was high all the time, but then he cleaned himself up, discovered what was really important, and created this masterpiece. Probably the best thing he ever did."

Fenway wondered where her father was going with this, but continued to listen.

"I had a blind spot for the last twenty years. I was as blinded by my anger toward your mom as Coltrane was blinded by his drugs. And I did some amazing things with my company. I even found love again. But I was blind to what was really important."

They were quiet for a couple of blocks.

"Fenway, you remember when you were little, and you and I used to watch all those recorded Red Sox games from the '86 season?"

"The season they went to the World Series," Fenway said.

"You were absolutely fascinated they had a pitcher named Oil Can

Boyd. He was probably the ace of that great pitching staff. You kept asking me, who would name their kid 'Oil Can'?"

Her father turned the music down a little. "Oil Can pitched some great games, but I read an article a few years ago and he said he was high on weed, or cocaine, or crack for every single game he pitched. It even started in Little League for him. How screwed up does your perspective have to be when you need to get high before every game you pitch?"

His voice turned wistful. "He was a great pitcher, but I always think how great he would have been if he had cleaned himself up. He could've had a masterpiece of a season that would have been his equivalent of *A Love Supreme*. If he hadn't been so messed up, I might not have had to wait another eighteen years for them to win the World Series."

"I remember reading that article, too, Dad," Fenway said. "I remember how I couldn't believe his parents named their kid 'Oil Can.' It never occurred to me how ironic it was that I was questioning a guy's weird name, when you named me 'Fenway.' And then I found out 'Oil Can' was just his nickname."

They got to the restaurant as the first section of *A Love Supreme* concluded—Fenway's favorite part, where Coltrane plays the main riff in every single key. They walked up to the hostess stand, and the maître d' nodded to her father and took them to a table in the back secluded from the rest of the restaurant.

"This is your usual table?" She sat down across from him.

Ferris bobbed his head noncommittally, acknowledging both that this was his usual table, and that he knew Fenway was too self-consciously spartan to be impressed by it. "You have any special dietary restrictions? Vegan? Gluten-free? Anything like that?"

"No, nothing special. And anything here would have to be better than the fast-food chicken sandwich I ate on the way to the M.E.'s today."

"Well, the chilled corn soup here is phenomenal, and I recommend the pheasant. Although the lamb is good, if a bit heavy. And the steaks, of course, are excellent." He called the server over and ordered an old fashioned with some rye bourbon Fenway hadn't heard of before. The server complimented him on his choice before disappearing.

Nathaniel Ferris soon lost his sadness from their earlier talk, and settled into his *let-me-show-off-my-daughter* mode. He introduced Fenway to Eric The Sommelier—Fenway heard it as if he were a great Viking wine leader. Ferris agreed to a couple of expensive glasses of German Riesling to go with the pheasant he ordered, and appeared both surprised and delighted with Eric The Sommelier's non-wine suggestion of a coffee-infused pale ale to go with the chilled corn soup. "Do they let you keep being a sommelier if you recommend beer with the starter?" Ferris hooted. Eric The Sommelier provided a big belly laugh in return. Fenway smiled, trying to keep her eye-rolling internal. Her father ordered his second old fashioned.

Fenway had to admit the pale ale with the chilled corn soup was fantastic. She thought of the corn chowder her mother would make on chilly Seattle days.

After they cleared the plates and flatware from the starter course, and they brought her father his third old fashioned—he had chosen against the beer—Fenway cleared her throat. "Dad, first of all, I want to say thank you. This is a great place. And I'm glad you and I have a chance to reconnect."

"Uh, oh. We've entered the business discussion portion of our evening."

"Look, it's just you and me now. No police interrogation room. No hulking security guy."

Nathaniel Ferris leaned forward. He must have been feeling quite good with the bourbon flowing in his veins. "I know! Rob is *huge*, right? I bring him to some negotiations with me when the other guys are really trying to put one over on me. One time, I had him stand behind me and crack his knuckles, and just *stare* at the guy. Rob is so old-school." He laughed. "Poor guy didn't know what to do. He thought he was in a mafia movie. And everyone pays their rent on time in the building, too."

Fenway tried to get her father back on track. "Right, so, just you and me. But let's be serious for a minute. If I had known Carl Cassidy had gotten killed in that accident six months ago, I might have been able to talk my way out of that situation with his widow earlier today. But I didn't know anything, and that made her angrier. Angry enough to shoot at me."

That seemed to sober him up a bit. "Fenway, I'm so sorry. I never for a minute thought you'd be in danger. I thought maybe some people would be like, 'oh, he's giving his daughter a job,' but I never thought anyone would be upset enough by it to try to hurt you in any way."

"I believe you." Fenway folded the corners of her napkin in. "I haven't always believed everything you've said, but I believe you on this."

Ferris stared down into his glass.

"But, it also means whatever is in those stolen files, you need to tell me about. I don't care how relevant you think the details are, or whether I have a subpoena. There are people out there who, literally, are ready to kill over what's in those files. And I can't prove it yet, but that might be why Harrison Walker was murdered."

He squinted at her. "I heard you have someone in custody."

"We do."

"And you think he killed Harrison because of what's in the stolen files?"

"I don't know. Like I told you earlier, the stolen files don't fit with the theory of the crime. I mean, they *might* fit, but right now, we're not seeing the connection."

Nathaniel Ferris picked up his glass and swirled the big ice cube around in it. Then he sighed. "I'll tell you something Rob uncovered during our insurance review of the accident." He lowered his voice. "I probably shouldn't say anything about this, but I guess it might affect your case, and, uh..."

"I'm listening."

"We were going through the two employees' files. Trying to match things up. It didn't make sense—someone had to physically vent the toxic fumes into that room the two of them were in. We can't figure out who had access to that room except for the two of them. I don't know if it was a weird murder-suicide, or what, but that's what I was told was the only theory that held any water."

"So, you're saying one of the dead employees vented the toxic fumes into that room on purpose, killing both of them?"

"I know." Her father took another drink. "It doesn't make any sense, except when you look at every other explanation. Carl Cassidy had been using his EAP—for couples' counseling." He picked up his fork and turned it around a full turn. "We asked some of the members of his team what was going on. One of his buddies said Carl and his wife were going through a rough patch; Carl thought his wife was cheating on him. Even hired a private investigator to follow her when he went on trips to Houston and Alaska. The guy took pictures of this black pickup truck in front of their house when he was away on trips, and pictures of her entering a motel room in P.Q. with the same truck parked out front."

"P.Q.?"

"Sorry, Paso Querido. About half an hour down the coast highway. Neat little hippie town."

"And that boyfriend was Dylan Richards?" Fenway guessed.

"No, not Dylan Richards. That's not what I heard. There was a black pickup that belonged to this young hotshot who worked on a competing project, name of Lewis Fairweather."

Fenway remembered reading the name. "The other guy who died in the accident."

"Right." Ferris nodded. "Rob said he was talking to our PR team about whether it was better to see if we could call it a tragic one-off accident, where the workers made a mistake in the ventilation system, or if it was better to suggest the theory of the murder-suicide publicly. But we had absolutely no evidence Carl had *actually* done anything to kill himself and Lewis."

He sighed and drained the rest of his drink. "Ultimately, we decided to call it an accident, and the families were going to be getting the insurance payouts. We have quite good accidental death coverage for our employees, so the life insurance was taken care of, but given it was on our property, we negotiated an additional settlement going to Carl's widow and Fairweather's parents. Our insurance company needed the coroner to sign off on the paperwork, though, and Rob kept telling me there was a problem getting Harrison's sign off on it. I had actually called Harrison twice, and he kept saying he was finished except for a couple of bureaucratic items."

A host of servers suddenly appeared, startling Fenway. Eric The Sommelier excused himself for the interruption and regaled them with the story of the German winemakers who made their Reisling in a town near the Black Forest. A woman introduced herself as the sous chef and wove a tale of the wild pheasant taking over the Black Rock wildlife reserve in the Santa Ynez valley, and how they made the journey from overpopulation to Maxime's kitchen. The pastry chef discussed the wild blackberries in the highly recommended fruit tart. They all gave slight bows as they left. Fenway couldn't imagine what this meal was costing her father.

Fenway didn't want their conversation to lose traction, so she continued even before the servers left. "So, why would anyone steal those files?"

"I don't know." Ferris took a big bite of pheasant and kept talking. "I haven't seen them, but as far as I know, everything in those files closes the case for us. It absolves us of wrongdoing, and it doesn't mention the murder-suicide theory, or the affair between Lewis and Carl's wife. And it allows the families to get their money. It's a win for everyone on all sides."

"Except Carl Cassidy and Lewis Fairweather," Fenway muttered.

Ferris didn't notice the aside. "If the murder-suicide thing was in there, I guess Carl's widow might want to steal the file. And, I guess, if it were in there, neither Carl nor Lewis would want it out there. But they're both dead."

Fenway saw another possibility to pique her father's interest as she swallowed a bite of sweet potato purée. "What if it wasn't Lewis who was having the affair with Carl's wife? What if it had been with another guy who drove a black pickup?"

"Like who? Like that Dylan Richards guy you mentioned? He's the one you have in custody, right?"

"Yes. And he drives a black pickup. What if those files had his truck's license plate listed, or the private investigator's photos were of him and not Lewis Fairweather?"

"Well, then," Ferris said, "I guess you'd want to find those files."

Fenway's mind was already working.

He talked about the files a little more, but she realized he only knew the information he had heard secondhand—and most of it was from Rob Stotsky.

They changed subjects a couple of times after that. Her father wanted to talk about Coltrane some more. Fenway talked about how much she liked *Blue Train*. He talked about how much Coltrane had screwed up his life with heroin when he was on tour with Miles Davis. She talked about her last forensics class she was taking online.

Ferris ordered dessert, eschewing the recommended fruit tart for a butterscotch panna cotta. She had a bite of his, but she was full. She had a coffee, and although she was a little concerned about getting to sleep, she figured her body was so exhausted it wouldn't matter.

When Nathaniel Ferris dropped her off at her apartment at ten thirty, she was still feeling full. Her head was swimming with how they would get to the bottom of whether or not Dylan Richards and Lana Cassidy had been having an affair. Her father was relaxed in the back seat, eyes half-closed, humming out of tune to *Psalm*. He didn't see the sheriff's car parked in one of the visitor's spaces.

CHAPTER SEVENTEEN

FENWAY LOOKED AT HER PHONE. SHE HAD MISSED A COUPLE OF TEXTS from McVie. *Call me when you're done with your dad* at about nine o'clock and *ETA?* at about ten.

She said goodbye to her father, then walked upstairs. McVie was sitting on the walkway in front of her door.

"Hey, McVie."

"Hey, Fenway. Wow, you look great. Nice dress."

"Thanks." She picked at the hem, considering. "I felt like it wasn't expensive enough to get in my father's Mercedes." She looked closely at him. His smile lines weren't smiling, and there was a sadness in his eyes she couldn't quite place. "Is everything okay?"

He paused. "I came over to give you a whole bunch of news. Mark—uh, Sergeant Trevino—located Walker's missing laptop. It was under the seat of the car."

"Wow, that's great news. Any prints or usable evidence?"

"Not from the car itself—not yet, anyway. The steering wheel, doors, and windows were wiped clean. But the crime scene unit is looking to see if there are any hairs or anything. You can't drive two and a half hours and not drop hair, or skin particles, or something with DNA."

"That's good news about the laptop. Did you find anything on it?"

"Not yet. IT is going to be looking at it starting tomorrow."

"Is Piper taking the lead on this?"

"You got it."

"Migs knows her pretty well, from what I hear. Says she's good."

McVie nodded. "We've also got an investigator going through Bradley's financials. He was making regular three-thousand-dollar deposits in cash every month since July. Three weeks ago, the cash deposit changed to six thousand, and there was another six-thousand-dollar deposit on Monday. We're trying to see where the money is coming from. I went to the Watermeiers' house earlier tonight—Bradley's parents swear the payments weren't from them. They've got a guest house on their property, but Bradley isn't there."

"Any luck on the RAT software? Did Piper figure out where it was coming from?"

"No." McVie shook his head. "But not for lack of trying. If we can find Bradley, though, we might be able to find who paid him."

"I've got some information, too."

"Great. I could use good news."

"So, it turns out the stolen files *might* have been taken by Dylan after all. Or at least, he might have had a motive for taking them. The internal investigation at Ferris Energy uncovered that Lana was having an affair with a guy who drove a black pickup."

"Dylan does go for the older women," he replied, his voice flat.

"Yeah." Making McVie think about his wife's affair with Dylan probably wasn't the good news he was hoping for, she thought. Fenway plowed past it. "Anyway—Walker wasn't releasing the files for some reason. It might be that the files have Dylan identified as Lana's boyfriend, and that's why he didn't want the files given to the insurance investigators."

McVie rubbed his chin. "I don't know if that makes sense."

"It might not. In fact, the other guy who died also drove a black pickup. But don't you think we can check Dylan and Lana's phone records for the last year or so? If they were having an affair, don't you think there'd be a record of phone calls, either to each other, or some unknown burner phone if they thought they were playing it smart?"

"Sure." McVie nodded. "Sure, we can do that. We might be able to check those phone calls between Dylan and Lana as early as tomorrow. And at least it's a reason to justify keeping Dylan locked up for one more night."

Fenway thought her idea that McVie was above pettiness might in fact be misplaced.

"Plus," McVie said, "I think copies of those stolen files might also be on Walker's laptop."

"Really? Don't those get backed up to a shared server or something?"

"Please don't start on our antiquated data retention policies. That will depress me more."

"More?"

McVie leaned his head back and closed his eyes. "I talked to Amy tonight when I got home. Told her I knew about her and Dylan. She accused me of locking him up out of spite." He heaved a sigh. "Megan came in and screamed that she hated both of us. It wasn't pretty. I grabbed a suitcase with a few changes of clothes. Gotta figure out where I'm going to stay tonight."

"Oh. Oh, Sheriff, I'm so sorry." Fenway sat down on the concrete next to him with her back against the wall. "That really sucks. Can I do anything?"

"Honestly? I could use a drink."

"I think I've got a couple of beers left. Would that work?"

"Sure."

He stood up first, and then he helped her up, the biceps in his arms flexing as he pulled her to her feet. She saw his eyes linger on her thighs as her dress rode up her legs slightly.

Oh, Fenway thought, *he might be kind of into me too.*

Her dress was still riding up, showing a good part of her thighs, and she pulled it down, but not as much as she could have.

She unlocked the door and let them inside. McVie went to the sofa and sat down. She got two beers out of the fridge and walked over to join him. She was aware he was making an effort not to look at her body, but he was only partially succeeding. And, purposefully or not—she wasn't sure herself—when she gave him his beer, she touched his hand. "Here you go, Craig." Not *Sheriff*, and not *McVie*.

Fenway's mind was racing. She was running on adrenaline and still buzzing a little bit from the wine at dinner. *Well*, she thought, *it has been two years since I've been with anyone.* Her mind presented the facts: she had invited a married man in for a drink at almost eleven o'clock on a work night, right after his cheating wife had kicked him out; she *just* realized he was attracted to her; she had a couple of drinks already in her system; and, by her estimate, Craig was at least fifteen years older than she was. To top it all off, he was the closest thing she had to a supervisor.

But Fenway realized she didn't really care. Tonight, she might get to feel his body, his muscular arms, and she might get to look in those kind, sorrowful eyes. *And tomorrow*, Fenway thought, *he'll go to couples' counseling with his wife, and he'll think, 'yeah, you screwed a twentysomething guy, and I found out, but I screwed a twentysomething girl, and you'll never find out.'* Part of her liked the idea.

She didn't like the idea of straining their working relationship, however, but they were only going to work together until election day, and then she would get a regular nursing job, wouldn't she? It might not even be in Estancia. Life is short. At least that's what she told herself.

"So, what's going to happen to Lana?" Fenway sat down right next to Craig on the couch and put her hand on his knee. "Doesn't it depend on if I want to press charges?"

He cleared his throat. "No. It's pretty cut-and-dried. We have the evidence of Lana's gun, a bullet fired in the office, and witness testimony.

I'm not sure we'd be able to prove intent for attempted murder, so we'll probably charge her with assault with a deadly weapon."

Fenway's brows knitted. "Out in six months? A misdemeanor?"

"Nope." He shook his head, taking a swig of beer. "One, she assaulted a peace officer, and two, she used a firearm. That's a felony, and it's a four-year minimum."

"I'm not a peace officer." Fenway scooted back, turning herself sideways until her back was against the arm of the sofa, and folded her legs in front of her. Her calves were touching his leg. She pulled the hem of her dress down a little, but not enough to stop him from looking.

He smiled. "Coroners might not be peace officers in Washington state, but in California they are."

"So, you're saying I should send my direct deposit forms to someone else besides Lana?" Fenway smiled, one of her flirty, disarming smiles.

"I'm glad you can laugh about it."

The conversation changed to music, then his experiences in the sheriff's academy. Fenway moved forward and sat a little too close to him. Halfway through one of his academy stories, she stretched her bare leg out over his lap. She could feel him tense a little.

"Okay, Fenway." He set the empty beer down on the coffee table after a few more minutes. "The investigation is going to be going into overdrive tomorrow, so I better head out to a motel."

She reached out and took his hand. "You don't have to go, Craig."

He paused, looking at her hand holding his. He didn't pull away, but he didn't squeeze her hand either. Fenway could feel the seconds ticking away and she could hear her heart beating in her ears.

"Fenway," he said, "you are smart and beautiful, and you're also funny and feisty, and I really like the way your mind works. If I were twenty years younger—and single—and if we didn't work together, I'd definitely take you up on your, um, offer." He paused for a beat. "But this is such a bad idea for so many reasons."

"We'll only be working together until November," she said, trying to sound casual. "And you might be married, but, you know, turnabout is fair play."

He flinched a little.

"Sorry," she said, putting her other hand on his shoulder. "I just meant you don't need to feel guilty about anything that happens between us tonight."

"I think if I stayed over, you'd regret it tomorrow morning."

"No, I wouldn't."

He swallowed. "Tell you what. Let's put this conversation on pause. When we're done with this investigation, when I figure out a little better where Amy and I stand, and if you still look at me the way you've been looking at me tonight—and not the way you look at me during the day— then we'll see."

Fenway squeezed his hand gently. "Sorry. I didn't mean to make this weird."

"You don't need to feel sorry. Part of me—a big part of me—feels pretty great you're hitting on me. But I can't right now."

"I understand."

She sat there a minute, leg still draped on his lap, feeling his resolve crumble. Willing it to.

He shifted in his spot. "We don't have to make this weird, Fenway," he said lightly. "Want me to pick you up tomorrow morning?"

"I actually got a car. It's the silver Accord parked down there."

He smiled and put his hand on her calf. "Oh. Nice. Good, you needed a car."

Fenway pulled herself closer to him. "Last chance," she whispered in his ear. She pressed her body against his. She felt him take a really deep breath, and as he exhaled, the rest of his defenses left his body.

He turned his head and Fenway kissed him. It was slow at first, until he kissed her back. His mouth tasted like beer, and she knew hers did too, but it was a good kiss.

"This is a bad idea," he murmured.

"I want to do it anyway." She bit his ear softly, and she pulled him on top of her.

A nagging voice in Fenway's head kept repeating *this is a bad idea*, but after being awakened at three o'clock that morning, seeing a truck-sized hole in the wall of her office, getting shot at, viewing the trajectory of a bullet into a dead rapist, and having an awkward dinner with her father—after all of that, Fenway thought spending the night with a man who liked that she was smart and feisty probably wasn't the worst way to end the day.

PART FOUR
FRIDAY

CHAPTER EIGHTEEN

WHEN FENWAY WOKE, IT WAS STILL DARK, AND MCVIE WAS NO longer next to her. She checked the clock—it was a quarter to six. She pulled back the curtain beside her bed and saw the fog blanketing the apartment complex, making ghostly halos around the orange lights between the buildings.

She walked through the small apartment in seconds, and there was no McVie to be found, but there was a note that read *F—Thanks for last night. See you at the office. Service for Walker at 5 PM.—Craig*

Fenway wasn't sure she liked that he left early, but she thought it was a good sign that they stayed on a first-name basis. Or a first-initial basis. She thought briefly about what her mother would say, and she knew a relationship with a married man (even if he had been wronged) would have disappointed her mother greatly. But, strangely, Fenway wasn't feeling bad about it. She figured she'd be able to act professionally around him, as if it hadn't happened. She told herself she knew what she was getting into.

She looked at McVie's note again and decided she would attend Walker's memorial service that evening. She pulled a black dress out of the closet; it was sleeveless, a little short and a lot low-cut—more appropriate for a club, or dancing, than a professional environment. For a second, Fenway pictured herself walking into the sheriff's office with that dress on and seeing Craig's jaw drop. She found the heels she had bought originally to go with the dress. They were the highest heels she owned, strappy and sexy.

Fenway hung the dress back on the rod; it certainly wasn't appropriate for a memorial service, and she knew it. She selected a more modest dress in the closet, with a higher neck, the hem ending at the knee, and cap sleeves. She thought it would look good with the gray cardigan near the top of her sweater stack. Both pieces were only a little wrinkled, but she hung them up in the bathroom while she showered to freshen them up a bit. She paired the dress and cardigan combo with some black flats that were a little scuffed, finished getting ready, and ate a bowl of cereal. She noticed a bowl washed in the kitchen sink, figuring McVie had probably had a bowl of cereal too, before he left.

She picked up her car keys—to her *new* Honda—but before she went out the door, she changed into the strappy high heels.

The new car was nice. It was much nicer than her old Nissan she had driven in Seattle; much nicer than anything she would have gotten for herself. The leather seats were not as buttery as her father's S500, but they were comfortable, and the heated seats took the chill off the foggy morning. The engine roared to life on the first turn of the key, and the odometer read *000036*, a number that had never been so low on a car Fenway owned. It wasn't flashy, it wouldn't draw attention, but it was nice, and it was hers.

She drove to the office and parked in the structure. The fog was already starting to thin, and Fenway thought it would be another beautiful day. She left the gray cardigan in the car and went to Java Jim's to get herself a latte. She also ordered a large drip coffee for Dez, whom she expected to already be at the office. It was nearly seven thirty when she walked into the building, and, sure enough, Dez was already there, behind her desk.

"Hey, Dez. Isn't it a beautiful—" Fenway stopped when she saw the grim look on Dez's face. "What's wrong?"

Dez raised her head. "Fenway, Dylan Richards was found dead in his cell this morning."

Fenway set the cups down, slowly, on the counter and felt a knot of sympathy in her stomach—not for Dylan, but for Rachel. "What happened?"

"It looks like he hung himself with a nylon cord."

"Oh no. Who found him?"

"Sheriff McVie." Dez looked at Fenway pointedly. Fenway felt the sergeant's eyes boring through her. *She knows*, Fenway thought, *she knows the sheriff stayed with me last night, and she doesn't want to believe it*. Fenway didn't know how Dez knew—was she that transparent?

She broke her eyes from Dez's stare. "Has the body left yet? Are they sending it to Dr. Yasuda?"

"I'm not sure. CSI is probably still on the scene."

"Why didn't they call me?" Fenway said. "I'm supposed to be in charge of the physical evidence."

"I'm not sure why the sheriff didn't call you. Although he was busy trying to resuscitate the victim, and then assisting the crime scene unit; he might not have thought of it."

"Why didn't *you* call me?" Fenway snapped at Dez.

Dez looked up, displeased. "Now, honey, you know you don't want to take that tone with me."

Fenway looked down at the floor. "Sorry," she mumbled. She passed the cup to Dez. "Here, I brought you some good coffee."

"Thanks, honey." She stood up and took the cup from Fenway as if nothing had happened.

"Do you think I should I go over to the jail?"

"Probably not a bad idea. You *are* the coroner. Though you're dressed a little fancy to get in front of the inmates." She glanced down. "Especially in those shoes."

"Walker's funeral is this afternoon. My flats were all scuffed up."

Dez screwed up the corner of her mouth, suppressing a smile that made Fenway nervous.

The county jail was behind the sheriff's office. Fenway went back to her car and got her cardigan. *No sense in poking the bears*, she thought. She walked as quickly as she could across the street and to the entrance of the jail. She had to go through the metal detector, sign in, and then wait at the entrance for the guard. As she saw the guard approach, she saw McVie walking behind him.

The guard buzzed him out. "You coming in?" he asked her.

She looked between the guard and the sheriff. "I don't know—one second. Sheriff?" She stepped toward him. "Anything for me to see in the cell?"

He shook his head. "Techs are cleaning up now. Body's on the way to San Miguelito."

"Is Dr. Yasuda doing the autopsy?"

He nodded.

"Thanks," she said to the guard, "but it looks like I don't need to go in after all."

The guard tipped his hat and closed the gate.

McVie looked shaken. Fenway touched his hand. "You okay?"

"Not even close." He pulled his hand away and ran it through his hair. "That kid shouldn't have died. And a nylon cord! How the hell did he get that in there?"

"He was hanging from the ceiling?"

"From the top bunk. I've read about prisoners hanging themselves from the top bunk before. It's never happened in this jail before, though."

"I'm so sorry."

"And not only am I upset Dylan killed himself, I'm pissed off he did it on my watch and I didn't stop it." He shook his head, as if trying to rid himself of what he had seen. "But, if I'm being completely honest, I'm having a little pity party for myself too, because I'm screwed about twenty ways from Sunday."

Fenway held the door open for him and they stepped outside.

"Let's not go back to the office for a minute. Let's take a walk." As soon as the words were out of her mouth, Fenway regretted the suggestion; her shoes were not made for comfortable walks. "Maybe to the plaza. Find a place to sit and talk this out."

McVie was so beside himself with anger he was walking and seething aloud. "It's going to come out that Dylan was having sex with my wife, and it's going to come back and bite me in the ass." He fumed. "Arresting him on circumstantial evidence, having him fill out a car theft form and then arresting him anyway. Looks bad. If that comes out, people are going to question if it was really a suicide—they're going to think I had something to do with it."

"You know I'll vouch for where you were last night."

McVie pursed his lips. "It can absolutely *not* get out that we were together last night." McVie looked around as they entered the plaza, but no one was nearby. He looked Fenway right in the eyes, seriousness radiating from him. "How is it going to look that I slept with the woman I appointed coroner? Not to mention, my wife would kill me. My daughter would kill me. Your father would kill me."

Fenway crossed her arms. "Thanks. I had a great time too."

"Damn it, Fenway, this is exactly what I was talking about with this being a bad idea!"

"*This* is what you were talking about?" She leaned into his space, her tone acerbic. "That you shouldn't fuck me because you knew you'd have to come up with an alibi for killing a suspect?"

McVie glared at Fenway.

She looked down at McVie's shoes, taking a calming breath. "Sorry. I'm really sorry. That was out of line."

"Damn right that was out of line." He took a couple of steps back. "I need to take a walk to clear my head. Please don't follow me." He turned and walked quickly away.

Fenway was standing in the plaza, the fog quickly burning away, the sun dappling her face. It didn't seem like such a beautiful day anymore. She stood there for a few minutes, wondering if she should follow him anyway. She shook her head, not quite believing it was already almost as crazy of a morning as yesterday.

She walked back through the plaza and across the street to her office building. The side of the building had been boarded up, over the truck-sized hole, and it looked like they had also put up rebar and galvanized steel chain-link fencing to discourage further intrusion.

Fenway went back into the office. She picked up her now-lukewarm latte from where she had left it. "Dez, I'm going to go to San Miguelito for Dylan Richards' autopsy. But there are a few things I need done."

"All right." Dez picked up her notebook. "And did you hear about the other gun?"

Fenway stopped. "What other gun?"

"We got an anonymous tip last night; a call from a burner phone. Asked us if we had looked in the Richards' backyard."

"But Dylan and Rachel are in a townhouse. Do they even have a backyard?"

"It's tiny, but yes. They've got a few plants and a vegetable garden back there. And, lo and behold, we found a Smith & Wesson 4006 buried under the zucchini."

"What kind of ammo does that gun take?"

"Ten millimeter."

"Registered to Richards?"

Dez shook her head. "Numbers have been filed off. We sent the gun to the San Miguelito lab along with the body."

"Okay." Fenway nodded.

"Something else was found, too. Underneath one of the outdoor chair cushions."

"What?"

"A parking stub from an LAX long-term lot."

"What?"

"That's right. A parking stub. From the lot where we found Walker's car. It was time-stamped late Sunday night—about three hours after the murder."

Fenway paused. "Doesn't that seem awfully...I don't know, *convenient* to you?"

"Yep," Dez said. "Awfully convenient."

"Did Mark tell you he found the laptop in Walker's car?"

"Yeah. He told me it was wedged in a spot under the passenger seat. He actually wasn't the one to find it—the crime scene team found it when they were searching it for skin and hair from the supposed killer. They removed the seat, and there it was. We think Walker might have used that spot for a laptop hiding place a lot."

"It feels like we're getting a lot of breaks."

"Except for the prime suspect being murdered," Dez pointed out. "That wasn't too much of a break, especially for McVie."

Fenway looked down again. "It must be especially rough on Rachel."

Dez sighed. "I don't think anybody's told her yet. I guess I can be the one to tell her, but man, I sure don't want to."

"Did anyone tell her that her husband was having an affair with a married woman?"

"As if her husband committing suicide isn't bad enough? I should have a bottle full of Xanax ready when I break all of this to her."

They were silent for a minute. Fenway wanted to say something comforting, but she couldn't think of anything. She finally changed the subject.

"Hey, who all knows about Dylan and McVie's wife?"

"There's you and me. And Megan and Amy McVie. I don't know if Dylan told any of his friends."

"If he was hiding it from his brother, seems logical to think he didn't tell anyone at all."

"Yeah."

"And the sheriff knows, too," Fenway added.

Dez looked surprised. "You told him?"

"He already knew."

"He knew before he made the arrest?" she asked, then shook her head. "Ooh, that's not right."

"I know, it's a conflict of interest, right?"

"Well," Dez reasoned, "what's he supposed to do? Not arrest a suspect just because he's sleeping with his wife?"

"I don't really know the ethics of this. I'm a newbie."

Dez scoffed. "Oh, please. Try that 'newbie' crap on someone else."

Fenway smiled. "One more thing, Dez. So—it's possible the missing files pointed to an affair between Lana Cassidy and Dylan Richards."

"What?" Dez said skeptically. "You've gotta be kidding."

"No. My father took me to dinner last night and I grilled him about the files."

"Girl, didn't you say he might be setting you up?"

"Yeah, he might be, but I don't think so. I played the *I'm your only daughter and I was shot at because I didn't know what was in those files* card. He seemed genuinely concerned for me, and plus, he had about three bourbons in the first half hour. Even if he had wanted to put one over on me, I'm not sure he could have."

Dez still looked skeptical, but nodded slowly. "All right. So, what do you want me to do? Phone records? Maybe see if I can get text messages, emails, that sort of thing?"

"Absolutely. I was going to ask for phone records, but if you can get that other stuff too, that would be awesome."

"Will do, boss. Who's giving you a ride up to San Miguelito?"

"I got a car last night. I'll be okay getting there on my own."

"Aw, that's sweet, our little coroner got her own car and is all grown up." She laughed. "Okay then. Get good intel. I'll text you if anything comes up."

Fenway didn't feel the need to tell Dez her father had, in fact, gotten her the car. "Thanks, Dez."

Fenway went out to her new Accord and drove to San Miguelito. She used the navigation system to get there, and she was really glad she had it —she had slept through the trip with McVie, so she didn't notice a poorly marked split in the highway about halfway to San Miguelito. The navigation system beeped to go left at the split, thankfully; there wasn't even a signpost for the San Miguelito turnoff.

Fenway had never owned a new car before, and neither had her mother all the time they were in Seattle. They got a great deal on an old Corolla her mother drove for years. Fenway learned to drive on it. When Fenway bought the used Nissan Sentra after college graduation, she remembered how disappointed she had felt that she couldn't afford anything nicer.

Her phone rang, breaking her from her memories.

"This is Fenway."

"Hey Fenway, it's Miguel Castaneda."

"Hey Migs. Everything okay?"

"I called to tell you they arrested Bradley Watermeier."

"Oh good. Hopefully he can tell us something. Where did they find him? Was he at his parents' cabin? Maybe a girlfriend's house?"

"He was at a craps table in Vegas. He was up ten thousand dollars when they made the arrest."

"Ooh, tough luck, Bradley."

Migs laughed.

"Is he coming back to be interviewed?"

"Yes, they're bringing him back, but the state trooper I talked to estimated the drive to be about six hours. They put him on the road already, though. He should be here by about two o'clock."

"Okay. I hope I'll be back by then, but I don't know how long this is going to take. I hope Dr. Yasuda will do the autopsy soon, but I guess it depends on how backed up it is—"

Migs interrupted her. "Oh, I have an update on that, too. The sheriff called Dr. Yasuda. She promised him first priority, and she's going to put a rush on the ballistics for the gun."

"Oh, good! Thanks, Migs."

"You're welcome."

There was silence for a moment, then Fenway said, "Hey—any word on the RAT malware, or Walker's laptop yet?"

"No progress on either front. Piper's going to set aside the RAT stuff for now and focus on the laptop. Unfortunately, we're down half of the IT staff who can work on projects like this. Piper is pretty busy."

"I think Walker's laptop is the right priority. Piper's the one who set up my laptop? She seems good."

"Yeah, she's pretty awesome," Migs said, a little moonily. "Okay, I have to get going. Officer Huke and I are going over the rest of the files from Walker's office."

"Who?"

"Officer Huke. Donald Huke. The one who has the keys to Walker's office—he was going to meet you at eight o'clock yesterday morning, but you flaked on him."

It dawned on her. "Oh, the really uptight one."

"Um, Fenway, you're on speakerphone."

"Good morning, ma'am," said Officer Donald Huke.

"I really didn't like that he kept calling me 'ma'am.'" she continued, a little louder. "I'm twenty-eight. He made me think I needed an AARP card."

"Maybe *he* didn't like that you didn't learn his name," Migs offered.

"*Huke* is kind of a funny name, don't you think?"

"I'm *right here,*" said Officer Donald Huke.

"Nice to talk to you again, Officer Huke," Fenway deadpanned.

"Same here, ma'am—I mean Miss Stevenson."

"God, *Miss Stevenson* is worse. I sound like a high school math teacher with thick glasses and a severe bun. Like one of those buns that's pulled so tight it looks like you got a face lift."

Migs coughed. "Hey, hang on, Fenway."

A moment passed. Fenway heard rustling. Then Migs spoke again.

"Sorry about that." He cleared his throat and took a deep breath. "Seriously, Fenway, he's upset that you didn't bother to learn his name."

"What? Really? He was just—"

"For someone who gets angry every time she's called *Fenway Ferris*, I thought you'd understand."

Fenway scoffed. "This is totally different."

"Yeah? Well, this is the kind of shit that Walker used to pull with us. Making us feel like we didn't matter. He didn't have our back. Honestly, I'm rooting for his killer to get away. I thought you were different."

Oof. That was a punch to the gut.

"Fire me if you want, Fenway, but I'm not going to spend another six months getting treated like something you're scraping off the bottom of your shoe."

"I—I wasn't—"

"It wasn't me *this* time. Take the time to learn your co-workers' names. Especially when they're helping you."

Fenway was quiet for a moment.

"Sorry, Migs."

"Don't apologize to me. Apologize to Donald. Or even better, just learn his damn name."

Migs clicked off.

Wow. She didn't think Migs had that in him.

The worst part was that he was right.

A few minutes later, the GPS dinged, and the voice instructed her to exit the highway. She found a parking spot on the street three blocks away from the M.E.'s office. She hurried—as much as she could in those damn strappy heels—and then waited in the outer office on the same brown plastic chairs she had been in the day before.

There was a beep at the desk after about fifteen minutes, and the woman at reception looked up. "Miss Stevenson. Dr. Yasuda is ready to see you. Follow me, please."

The woman led her down the stairs to the basement, and she used a keycard to open the door for Fenway. Dr. Yasuda was there with Dylan Richards' body. His body was cut open at the throat, and Dr. Yasuda had gloves on, and was examining inside the throat.

"Hello again," Dr. Yasuda kept working on Dylan, but her tone was civil enough, if grim. "Sheriff McVie tells me this is the prime suspect in the killing of Harrison Walker."

"Right."

"I got a little bit more background on you from our call this morning. I must apologize for yesterday; I thought you were an experienced coroner, and you were missing things, or not paying attention. I didn't realize you were forced into this job when Mr. Walker was killed."

"*Forced* is kind of a strong word for it, but yeah, I'm babysitting this position until the November election." Fenway shrugged. "No one wanted to quit their day job just to work a handful of weeks."

"Have you ever performed an autopsy?"

"I've done practical work on cadavers in both my nursing and forensics programs. But I haven't done a real autopsy, no."

"It's too bad that I was well on my way with Mr. Richards before you got here. I miss teaching sometimes. But there are some things I can point out to you." She put some spacers in the wound to keep it open, then removed her hands and looked at Fenway. "First of all, Mr. Richards had been dead for between three and five hours by the time he was found."

"So, time of death between one a.m. and three a.m.," Fenway said.

"Yes. I don't like having such a wide range in time, but the temperature fluctuates in that jail quite a bit overnight. We should be able to narrow it down once we get some test results back." Dr. Yasuda pulled off her gloves, threw them away, and made a note on her laptop. She picked up a Hagedorn needle, came back to Richards' body, and pointed out the hyoid bone in the middle of his neck, under his chin. "This bone often breaks or gets crushed in hangings, especially with a short drop like Mr. Richards had from the top bunk in the jail cell."

Fenway nodded.

"But look at the way his bone was crushed," Dr. Yasuda continued. She walked over and clicked a button on her laptop and three photos of the hyoid bone, all from different angles, appeared on a projected image on the white wall behind her. "What do you notice about it?"

Fenway went over to the wall and studied the bone photographs. "The angle is wrong for hanging. It looks like there was direct pressure applied from the front, almost perpendicular to the neck."

"Yes, that's right. The bone was crushed from the front, with direct pressure."

"Did someone strangle Dylan with their hands?"

"Let's see." She walked over and pointed to a section of the crushed hyoid with the needle. "Does this seem like it could have been done with fingers or thumbs?"

Fenway looked at the photo, and studied it from all three angles.

"No," she finally answered the doctor. "It's too thin, and the crushing is consistent across the bone in a line. I think it looks like it was rope."

"Right again. As a matter of fact, indications are pretty good that the rope used to hang Mr. Richards was the murder weapon."

"Where do you think Dylan was when he was killed?"

"The physical evidence indicates Mr. Richards was lying supine when he was attacked and killed. The blood started to pool in the back of the head for about three to five minutes before his body was placed in an upright position and hanged." Dr. Yasuda mimed the physical movements. Fenway inwardly winced as the doctor continued. "The rope fibers match the marks on the skin, though there was some care given to make sure the hanging was done so the marks from the hanging would be in a similar location on the neck as the marks from the strangulation." The M.E. pointed to red marks on either side of the neck. "And although it's subtle, the angle of the hanging created a second set of rope marks close to the first, postmortem this time."

Fenway nodded. She could see exactly what Dr. Yasuda was talking about. "Whoever the killer is, they must be pretty strong to lift a grown man's dead body into a makeshift noose and short-drop him. I mean, Dylan wasn't tall—five-six or so, right?—but still, that's a good one hundred and fifty pounds to lift up as dead weight then drop."

"That's an astute observation, Miss Stevenson. I was hoping we'd get some clues with the type of rope used as the murder weapon. But we ran tests, and it's fairly standard issue, available at most home improvement stores. We ran recent orders through the system, and this particular brand of rope is also kept at many local law enforcement offices, Parks and Recreation, CHP, and, unfortunately, the Dominguez County Sheriff's Office."

"Unfortunately," Fenway repeated.

Dr. Yasuda nodded. "Since the death of Mr. Richards is now going to be ruled a homicide, and not a suicide, I believe Sheriff McVie will be one of the suspects. He found the body, and he was one of the only people who had access to the murder location, the victim, and the murder weapon."

Fenway felt her mouth go dry. "Do you think Sheriff McVie would have been able to lift the body and simulate the hanging?"

Dr. Yasuda didn't hesitate before answering. "It's likely. He's certainly strong enough to lift a hundred and fifty pounds."

Fenway thought about how McVie's strong arms had lifted her up off the sofa when they moved from the living room into the bedroom. *McVie was certainly strong enough*, Fenway thought: she outweighed Dylan Richards; she was certainly taller by four or five inches, and McVie had picked her up easily as he was kissing her, before he had gently, but forcefully, laid her on her back on the bed. She snapped back to what Dr. Yasuda was saying.

"At a dead weight, and given the necessary maneuvering he would have had to do to get Mr. Richards in the noose... I've seen people do a lot more physically demanding activities with significantly fewer physical gifts than the sheriff. Adrenaline and self-preservation are powerful stimulants."

"With that said," Fenway murmured, "yes, the sheriff could have done it." She paused. "But anyone could have gotten that rope, right? It's not like those supplies are under lock and key."

"Here they are. And there aren't a lot of people who have a key. You'll have to check if it's the same in Dominguez County."

"But anyone can go to a Home Depot."

Dr. Yasuda nodded. "You should tell the sheriff's lawyer that. Okay, now let's see how Trevor is coming along with the gun. Which is, this time, the correct caliber weapon."

They walked out through the double doors, up the stairs, and around the corner to the ballistics lab. Trevor was there, again, with the microscope and some safety goggles, holding a bullet with a pair of forceps.

"What do you have for us, Trevor?" Dr. Yasuda asked.

Trevor nodded in Fenway's direction. "Good morning, Miss Stevenson," he said, before looking back to Dr. Yasuda. "I haven't completed all the tests yet, but my initial assessments indicate this Smith & Wesson 4006 pistol was, in fact, the weapon that fired the bullet that killed Harrison Walker."

He started in on his presentation. He pointed out rotation marks on each of the bullets, and had a map of the inside of the chamber which made some of the marks.

"Hold on a second." Dr. Yasuda stopped Trevor at a photo where the gun sight was visible. "That's an adjustable sight."

"Yes, that's correct," said Trevor.

"Does this gun have a trigger play spring?" she said.

"Um." Trevor checked his notes. "No, I don't see anything like that."

"All right, that should make it a little easier to narrow things down." Dr. Yasuda turned to Fenway. "All of the model 4006 handguns came with a fixed sight and a trigger play spring—except for the ones issued to the California Highway Patrol for about 20 years. Those had an adjustable sight and no spring—like this one. The CHP changed to a newer model a couple of years ago, but this is a specific firearm."

Fenway looked at the adjustable sight. "You're saying this is a CHP officer's gun?"

Dr. Yasuda nodded. "If it isn't, it used to be. The CHP auctioned off their unwanted 4006s a few years ago, but there weren't too many of them auctioned off, and the state has done a pretty good job of keeping track of the ones that were sold."

"Not 'too many'? What does that mean? Ten? Twelve?"

Dr. Yasuda laughed. "Hundreds—but not thousands. It's a start. The database is pretty good. We'll be able to see which guns have been stolen, or are missing, or have been handed in when some of those cities have done buy-backs. That might narrow the list down to ten or twenty. Of course, it won't include guns that disappeared and didn't get reported."

Fenway tilted her head. "Really? Don't cops lose their badges over stuff like that?"

Dr. Yasuda shook her head. "You'd be surprised at how many guns assigned to law enforcement go missing every year. And no one gets fired."

"I can't say that makes me feel any better."

"There is something else here," Trevor said. "The numbers were filed off, true, but the filing job isn't the best. A few of the numbers are filed off pretty thoroughly, but some of them—it's possible that we might be able to lift the number. We've got some new chemical treatments now."

"That would be good," Fenway responded. "What about any fingerprints?"

"Not yet. The gun looks like it was wiped clean."

"Wiped clean?"

"Yes. Lots of abandoned guns are wiped clean. We're working on the inside of the gun. Probably didn't wipe off fingerprints there, although we often don't get anything useable from the inside."

"Hmm," Fenway mused. "Why would Dylan wipe the gun clean of fingerprints if he was going to bury it in his own garden?"

"I don't know," Dr. Yasuda said, "but if I had a nickel for every weird thing every criminal did, I'd buy my own island."

"Fair enough."

Dr. Yasuda had a few follow-up questions for Trevor, more for procedural review than anything else. Fenway thought Trevor answered Dr. Yasuda's questions with aplomb, although Dr. Yasuda didn't seem happy with a couple of his answers. When she was finished, she turned back to Fenway.

"Anything else, Miss Stevenson?"

Fenway shrugged. "I guess not."

Dr. Yasuda told her the official report wouldn't be ready for a few hours. When Fenway went out to the waiting area, Dr. Yasuda had already had some autopsy notes printed up for her. She thanked the M.E. and left into the bright sunshine.

CHAPTER NINETEEN

FENWAY WAS LOST IN THOUGHT ON THE DRIVE BACK TO ESTANCIA. SHE was almost on autopilot, with only the sound of the GPS voice.

She could feel the pieces starting to slip into place, even though there were twice as many murders to solve as the day before. It also looked increasingly likely she'd have to provide Sheriff McVie with an alibi that could wreck his marriage and career, and, Fenway feared, derail her plans in California before they even got off the ground.

She made the trip back in a little under an hour. Fenway walked from the parking garage to the office in the sunlight, which, a month ago, in rainy Seattle, she would have welcomed. Now, rather than enjoy the weather, she was impatient to get inside and do more research to figure out how the pieces would fit together.

Dez looked up as she entered. "Hey, Fenway. Any news?"

"You first. Anything come back from the phone records between Dylan and Lana?"

"We went back a year on both of their cell phones. Lana's home phone, too. Nothing between them, and nothing between their phones and any suspicious numbers. Lana called a lot of people after Carl was killed, but it was mostly extended family members, lawyers, the funeral home, florists, that kind of thing."

Fenway deflated slightly. "That wasn't what I was expecting."

"I *did* find a ton of texts, phone calls, and private social media messages between Dylan and Amy McVie, though. Going back about six months. Dylan didn't keep any of this stuff private. Since I was able to find out about Dylan and Amy so easily—I found all kinds of stuff in about ten minutes—then for sure I would have found something by now between Dylan and Lana."

"So it doesn't look like Dylan and Lana weren't sleeping together."

"Early indications, anyway. But that's not all. Since you said Carl uncovered Lana's affair with *someone*—not necessarily Dylan—I paid attention to any calls or texts that were regularly sent. I didn't see anything that looked like an affair to me—not from a younger man, not from an older man, not from a woman. Nothing. I also took a look at Lana's social media accounts, and looked to see if she had an account with any of the dating or affair sites. That'll take a little longer to get through, of course, but so far, no hits. It doesn't look like Lana was cheating at all."

"That's crazy." Then Fenway remembered who she got the information from. "Ah, crap. My father gave me bad information. Again."

Dez shrugged.

"He told me Carl hired a private investigator to look into the affairs. It might be worth seeing if Carl had any outgoing money to any P.I. firms locally, but if my dad lied about Lana's affair, I bet the P.I. doesn't exist either."

Dez nodded. "Okay. Now you."

Fenway leaned against the desk and pulled the notes out of her purse. "Dylan Richards was murdered. The killer tried to make it look like a suicide by hanging."

Dez pursed her lips and shook her head.

"And the gun they pulled out of Dylan's garden was a weapon custom-made for the California Highway Patrol, and it was the weapon that killed Walker."

"Ugh. Someone's going way far out of their way to set Dylan up."

"Let's not jump to conclusions yet, Dez. Dylan had motive—the video of Walker and Rachel."

"What?" Migs sprang up from his chair. "What video of Walker and Rachel?"

Fenway put her hand up. "Hold on, Migs," she said. "Dylan had the weapon. The CHP stopped using that gun a few years ago. Dylan could have bought it at auction or something."

Dez furrowed her brow. "Be careful about your conclusions, too, Fenway. Dylan didn't *have* the weapon. Dylan's *garden* had the weapon. Anyone could have jumped the fence and gotten in there. And the anonymous tip was awfully convenient."

"But Dylan lied about his alibi," Fenway pointed out.

"Yes," said Dez, "but a neighbor saw his truck in front of the sheriff's house."

"In front of the sheriff's house?" Migs exclaimed. "What was he doing at the sheriff's house?"

Fenway continued, "The neighbor said he wasn't sure it was Sunday night. Now pipe down, Migs. We're trying to figure this out."

"You guys don't tell me anything."

Dez pulled a sheet of paper out of a folder. "Plus, the report came back on Dylan's cell phone. It pinged cell towers right in the area of the McVies' house."

"Doesn't necessarily mean Dylan was there," Fenway pointed out.

"Enough for reasonable doubt for most juries, though."

Fenway looked at the floor and pinched the bridge of her nose, thinking. "We should interview Amy McVie."

"You have a death wish." Dez shook her head.

"That may be true, but we should still interview her. In fact, we should interview her before she finds out Dylan is dead. If we can do it so she convinces us he was with her, then I agree with you, Dez, someone is definitely trying to set Dylan up to take the fall."

"I can't believe you still doubt he's being set up," Dez said. "He was *murdered*, but someone staged it to look like a suicide. Come *on*. I don't have to have the sheriff's missus tell me they were sleeping together on Sunday night for me to know he's being set up."

Fenway looked at Migs. His eyes were big, and he had been holding his breath for about fifteen seconds. "See, Migs? This is why we don't tell you. Take a deep breath, man."

"You know they're going to look at the sheriff for Dylan's murder," Dez said.

"Yes, the M.E. said that to me, too."

"This isn't going to look good for him: arresting Dylan for murder when his own *wife* is Dylan's alibi, the sheriff actually finding Dylan's body, the murder weapon—a cop-issued murder weapon, might I add— conveniently planted, literally, on Dylan's property. And what exactly is the sheriff's alibi going to be?"

Fenway looked away. "I assume he was home with his wife."

Dez stared at Fenway, blinked, then stood up. "Come with me." She grabbed Fenway's elbow and pulled her into the conference room. She closed the door. "Now, Fenway, I'm going to tell you a funny story. Would you like to hear the funny story? Here it is. My niece lives in the apartment complex next to yours."

"Oh." Fenway tried not to wince. "That *is* funny."

"I know, right? I'd say it was a coincidence, but this is such a small town, I'm sure I know someone in just about every apartment complex around here. Anyway, I'm her favorite aunt. I'm the *cool* aunt. She's nineteen and she goes to the community college. Studying accounting. We sometimes go out to the movies, like yesterday. After such a stressful day, it was great to go to the movies with my niece."

"That sounds nice," Fenway said weakly.

"I dropped her off last night after the movie—it was around eleven thirty. That's why I don't look my best today, because I'm so tired after dropping off my niece at eleven thirty last night. Here's something else that's kind of funny: you know I can see right into the parking lot of your complex from my niece's apartment? And did you know that I know what car the sheriff drives?"

"I didn't know either of those things."

"No, I would guess you probably didn't." She folded her arms. "You were awfully *chipper* this morning, Fenway."

Fenway looked down at the floor.

"Listen." Dez dropped her voice. "I've only known you a few days. You seem to have a pretty good head on your shoulders—compared to the last couple of coroners, at least. And I hate to speak ill of the dead, but you're actually *engaged* with the job. Like, your brain is on. And I like that."

Dez shook her head. "And, I understand; I was young once. I see the sheriff look at you, and I know what he's looking at. But, girl, you got so much more to offer this department, and this county, than being a notch on the sheriff's bedpost." Dez sighed. "And, for the love of God, he's still a married man. Amy might be cheating on him with a man young enough to be her son, but it don't change the fact that Craig and Amy are still married. Get your head on straight, girl."

"He didn't seduce me, or anything." Fenway's tone was defensive. "I got shot at. I didn't want to be alone last night. He makes me feel safe. I wanted to do it."

"Oh, that is too much information." Dez put up her hand. "Just stop it. This gets out, and you're going to be the girl who sleeps her way into the job. That weakens all us women in the department. That weakens Rachel. And it validates all those piece-of-shit men who are going to hear about Walker and Rachel and think she was asking for it."

Fenway winced. "That's not fair, Dez."

"Of course it's not fair," Dez snapped. "There's a lot of shit that's not fair. But telling you *not* to sleep with the married sheriff is *not* unfair.

Sleeping with a married man, especially one you work with, is just stupid."

Fenway looked at Dez, whose face was angry and determined, although she was keeping her emotions mostly under the surface. Fenway couldn't figure out if she, herself, wanted to be angry back at Dez. But she didn't want them to fight. So, she swallowed hard. "Yeah. You're right, Dez. Yeah, it was probably a mistake."

"So don't do it again."

Fenway nodded.

"And as far as what you're going to do when the sheriff needs an alibi —let's hope it doesn't get to that point."

Dez started to step past her, but Fenway put her hand on Dez's shoulder. "Hold on a sec. Have you checked on Rachel? Has anyone told her about Dylan?"

Dez sighed. "No, I don't think so. I know her sister is with her."

"Look, I don't have a problem with her being out for a week or two. Or however long she needs, really. She's been through a lot, with the assault, and her husband getting arrested. And now it's going to come out, probably, that her husband was sleeping with the sheriff's wife, and that her husband was murdered, and I'm worried she's not going to be okay."

"I'll make sure her sister is taking good care of her."

"Maybe she should get out of town for a few days."

"On whose dime?"

"The department could pay for her to go to, I don't know, Sedona or something, for a couple of weeks. We don't want to get sued for a zillion dollars for employing a sexual predator."

Dez raised her eyebrows. "You think paying for her to go to Sedona for two weeks is going to stop her from suing the county?"

Fenway considered this. "No, I guess not. Probably not, anyway. But I'm still worried about her."

Dez nodded, then stepped past Fenway and opened the door.

Fenway followed Dez out into the main office. Migs was standing up at his desk, and he looked a little excited. Piper was standing next to him.

"Sorry," he said. "I didn't want to interrupt, but Piper found some emails on Walker's laptop."

Fenway managed to smile after her lecture from Dez. "Nice to see you again, Piper. I didn't realize what a techie bad-ass you are."

Piper blushed almost as red as her hair. "I don't know about *that*." Fenway saw Migs look at Piper, and he was obviously smitten. Fenway smiled wider.

"Okay, Piper, come around and show us what you found."

"All right." Piper picked up Walker's laptop and brought it over. She put it down and tucked her hair behind her ears with her long fingers. Fenway noticed she had fairly short, neatly trimmed nails, but no polish. "It looks like Walker was using an anonymizer for one of his browsers. But it also looks like he forgot to use it on a couple of occasions. He was trying to be all sneaky, but he was lazy. He had a private ZoothMail address— that's an encrypted email platform—and I think he usually used the anonymizer to access it. I can't tell yet if he was using the anonymizer for anything else, but he was definitely using it for this ZoothMail account." She clicked a few things and Walker's ZoothMail web page came up.

"How'd you get into his account?"

"That's the crazy part. He cached his username and password, if you can believe it." Piper giggled and put a hand in front of her mouth to stifle it. Fenway thought she saw Migs swoon a little. "All that anonymizer stuff, and he was too lazy to type in his username and password."

"Okay. What are we looking at?"

"There are a couple of interesting items here. It looks like this email account is communicating with only one other email address—this one." Piper clicked on the email address. It was a jumble of numbers and letters before the @ sign. "Now, I looked at the headers on this email address, and they've done a good job of obfuscating the IP address where this originated."

"So, we're nowhere?"

"No, no. I mean, if this is all we had, yes, we'd be nowhere." Piper pulled out a printout from the folder and thrust it in front of Fenway. "But look at the headers on the address the RAT software was sending the video feed to."

Fenway looked closely, from the screen to the paper and back. Both strings were jumbles of meaningless characters—but they were the same jumbles of meaningless characters.

"They're the same," she said.

"Yes." Piper nodded emphatically. "It's actually the exact same obfuscation the RAT tracking malware used."

Dez shook her head. "What does that mean?"

"It means the RAT malware and these emails came from the same person." Migs was so excited he was almost shouting.

"It's a high degree of certainty," Piper agreed.

Migs plowed on. "And it narrows down the possibilities, because if it's the same obfuscation, it can only be one of a handful of obfuscation tools, because most of the programs out there won't give the same result twice. The ones that do are cheap."

"I guess we now know the RAT software guy is cheap."

Piper nodded. "We might know who the email recipient is—and who the RAT hacker is—by the end of the day."

Fenway looked between their jubilant faces. "That's fantastic. No wonder you're excited. The way Migs talks about you, Piper, I thought he was exaggerating about how talented you are. Turns out he was right." Piper blushed again and mumbled a thank you. Fenway looked at Migs and winked.

"Okay," Dez said, "but what do the emails actually say? Is there anything in there that tells us anything?"

Piper typed a little more. "I think so. But let's take a look. I don't know what some of this stuff means."

She finished typing and then positioned the screen so Fenway could see. Dez leaned in over her shoulder.

From *92B7J6G9-13E9-41358*
To *HCW1-6DC19E60B485*
Received *1 May 18:21:56 -0800 PDT*
Subject *Re: Terms and meeting*

I accept your terms
Meet 2100 Sunday
Not at beach - Rte 326 at entrance to Coast H Park
Come alone
I will have paymt

"Think that's from the killer?" Migs asked Fenway.

"It certainly could be."

"I think it's pretty likely," said Dez.

"Okay, now here's the whole email thread from the beginning." Piper clicked off the last email and went to the 'Sent' folder. They read five emails between Walker and the unknown person/possible killer.

From *HCW1-6DC19E60B485*
To *92B7J6G9-13E9-41358*
Received *28 April 15:31:03 -0800 PDT*
Subject *Terms and meeting*

Changes you requested can be made
You can have file about 48 hours after payment
Price is 25
Meet at Lot A Guerrero St Beach tomorrow at 10 AM if you accept

From 92B7J6G9-13E9-41358
To HCW1-6DC19E60B485
Received 28 April 18:20:33 -0800 PDT
Subject Re: Terms and meeting

25 is more than twice what we discussed
Why go back on our agreement?

From HCW1-6DC19E60B485
To 92B7J6G9-13E9-41358
Received 29 April 17:20:08 -0800 PDT
Subject Re: Terms and meeting

You weren't at the beach this morning
You must want file to keep original conclusions

From 92B7J6G9-13E9-41358
To HCW1-6DC19E60B485
Received 30 April 04:43:17 -0800 PDT
Subject Re: Terms and meeting

Told you 25 is too much
You didn't respond
??

From HCW1-6DC19E60B485
To 92B7J6G9-13E9-41358
Received 30 April 15:31:03 -0800 PDT
Subject Re: Terms and meeting

I'm not negotiating
Higher than discussed originally

but your requested changes give me higher risk
You can say no but we both know what
a pain in the ass the investigators can be
if they see the conclusions in there now
If you accept meet me Sunday night

"Finished?" Piper asked them.

Fenway nodded.

"Just about." Dez read the screen for another five seconds. "Okay."

"What do you think, Dez?" Fenway asked.

"You're not going to like what I think."

Fenway remembered her mother, years before, struggling with a painting. They still lived in the tiny apartment at the time. One evening, Fenway came home from the library, and her mother was tired, but happy —Fenway thought she had had a breakthrough. One look at the painting, though, and Fenway knew her mother was on the wrong track. The focal point was odd. The perspective was off. And it was in a way that didn't look purposeful. Fenway remembered looking at her mother with trepidation. And her mother read her face. *Fenway, tell me. Tell me even if you think I don't want to hear it. Because I do want to hear it if it gets me closer to a great painting. Even if I have to start over.*

"I don't care if I don't like what you think, Dez. I want to hear if it gets us closer to finding out the truth."

Dez looked down. "I don't like it much either."

"Oh, you think it's my father," Fenway said.

She looked up. "We should go into the conference room again."

"Sorry Migs, sorry Piper." Fenway followed Dez, and they went in and closed the door. "So you *do* think it's my father."

Dez slowly shook her head. "I do not."

"You don't? I thought for sure you were going to say my father."

"I think it's Sheriff McVie."

Fenway's face fell. "Oh."

"I *said* you wouldn't like it."

"Okay. All right, yes, there are a lot of things pointing to McVie. But walk me through it."

Dez thought a moment. "It's obvious Walker was offering to alter the contents of the files. Something where the original file threatened the killer."

"Right. That's pretty evident. But what would be in the file that threatened McVie?"

"McVie is the one who led the investigation at the refinery after the incident. And The Owner has been known to grease wheels before," Dez continued. "Maybe there was evidence of negligence which McVie was paid to ignore. Maybe McVie screwed up some evidence collection. Maybe McVie looked the other way on some safety audit that was done before. It could be almost anything."

"Okay."

"It may not have even been real evidence. I mean, maybe the original file had real evidence that McVie was at fault for something, but I wouldn't put it past Walker to manufacture evidence specifically for purposes of blackmail."

"Yeah, I could see any of those scenarios being possible." Fenway was trying not to be defensive about McVie, but she could feel her hackles getting up.

"And maybe McVie scrimped and saved, maybe sold some stuff or cashed out some savings to get the ten or fifteen thousand. But when Walker upped it to twenty-five, where does a county sheriff get that kind of money?"

"Okay."

"All right. Now, McVie doesn't usually work Sundays, but we know he picked up a patrol shift for Callahan this past Sunday. So, he's driving around, doesn't have to be in any particular place."

"So, we've got motive and opportunity." Fenway held up two fingers. "Weapon?"

"It's a cop gun." Dez thought a moment. "Maybe the sheriff's office bought a couple at auction. Or he's got a buddy in the CHP."

"Dr. Yasuda is seeing who has those—and who has reported them missing. We should have that information soon enough. So, possible motive, definite opportunity, possible weapon."

"And a definite motive to get Dylan Richards away from his wife. McVie has access to the same phone records we do. If he had seen any of Amy's records, he would have known she was cheating."

Fenway nodded. "He knew. He knew, he just didn't think anyone else did."

"Well, there you go. And he might have stolen Dylan's truck, smashed it into the building and stolen the files. He would have known where all the cameras were to minimize detection."

"Do you think McVie is on the hook for Dylan's murder, too?"

Dez looked squarely at her. "You can probably answer this one better than me. What time did he leave your apartment? It was definitely after eleven thirty."

She blushed. "I don't know. I was exhausted after everything that happened yesterday. We fell asleep after the first time and, uh, we woke up again."

Dez made a face. "For the love of God, Fenway, I don't need to know the details."

"I don't know what time it was when he and I finally fell asleep for good. I woke up at six, and he was already gone."

"So, he could have left at any time?"

"I guess so."

"And he's got all the keys to the jail cell, and no one would think anything of him being there anyway. He'd know how to get in without anyone noticing. And the sheriff has every reason in the world to be in the jail anyway."

Fenway nodded. "But why kill Richards? McVie pretty much had him on a silver platter for the murder. I mean, I've seen cases where murder defendants have gotten convicted with a lot less than what they have on Dylan."

"Because, Fenway," Dez stressed, "we found his alibi. We found out Dylan was with McVie's wife during the murder—a fact no one would believe coming from Dylan, since he had already lied to the police."

"McVie's wife would corroborate, wouldn't she?"

"You haven't met her yet. She's kind of a piece of work. I don't know. I'm not sure she's the type of person who would come forward."

"I don't know either," Fenway said. "If she had any kind of feelings for this guy—and their affair went on for months, right?—wouldn't she feel obligated?"

"Or maybe McVie was infuriated with his wife's younger, better looking lover, and he decided he had to go. People make decisions like that, too."

There was a knock at the door. Migs stuck his head in. "Hey, it's past noon. I'm going to take Piper to lunch."

Fenway smirked at Migs.

"To thank her for all the work she's done for us," Migs stammered. His ears turned red.

"Have a good time." The door closed behind him. "Okay, Dez," Fenway said. "How do we go about proving that?"

"First, like you talked about earlier, we need to get Amy to admit Dylan was with her on Sunday night."

"Okay," Fenway said. "So, if Dylan was with Amy that night, he definitely wasn't the killer, and someone is trying to frame him."

"Right."

"And you think McVie is the most likely suspect?"

"Well," Dez paused. "I can't think of who else would want to frame Dylan."

"I can't either," Fenway admitted. "I guess I could see McVie planting the gun, but how would he plant the LAX long-term parking stub?"

Dez didn't answer.

"And what about the RAT software? If McVie sent those emails, then McVie also had Bradley install the spyware on Rachel's PC. Why would McVie want to spy on Rachel?"

"Maybe he wanted to spy on Walker, and that's the closest he could get."

"I don't know." Fenway shook her head. "I mean, I think a lot of it fits for sure, but a few things don't make sense."

"Maybe we haven't uncovered enough information yet." Dez grabbed her purse. "Let's go to step one and talk to Amy."

CHAPTER TWENTY

THEY GRABBED SANDWICHES AT THE DELI DOWN THE STREET. DEZ insisted on taking Fenway's new car, so Fenway insisted they eat at the deli before they headed out. As much as she wanted to get to the bottom of this case, she didn't want Dez's turkey avocado club to get smeared on her new seats.

Amy McVie worked at Coast Harbor Real Estate in Paso Querido, and Dez and Fenway arrived there just before one. The office was large, with overstuffed chairs in the waiting area, and what looked like hardwood floors. Dez showed her badge to the receptionist, and after a brief call, they were sent back. Amy was in her corner office, on the phone, pacing around her desk, but she waved them in.

She was about five foot four, dressed in a stylish business suit. Amy had a lithe, fit build, and her blonde hair cascaded in waves to her shoulders. As she walked, Fenway noticed the muscular, but still feminine, definition of her calves, as she paced in heels about as high as Fenway's, but more professional, without straps. Her skin was tanned, and she carried herself like someone who was comfortable being in charge. She had a small nose, but large green eyes, high cheekbones, and a determined expression.

Fenway looked at the shelves around the office: there were several pictures of Megan, a wedding photo with Craig, and two photos of Amy in a San Diego State soccer jersey; in one she was holding a trophy.

Amy hung up and turned to them. "I've got a house to show tomorrow at nine, and the staging company isn't happy." She motioned them to the chairs in front of her desk. "But whatever questions you have, I'm sure I can make a little time for you. Lord knows how many referrals you've given me, Dez."

"There've been a few for sure." Dez motioned to Fenway. "This is Fenway Stevenson, the new coroner. Fenway Stevenson, Amy McVie."

"Nathaniel's daughter, right?" Amy said. "Craig was really doing the hard sell to get you to replace Harrison." She smiled politely.

Dez closed the door behind her, then she and Fenway sat down in front of Amy's desk.

"So." Dez hesitated. "We have a few questions for you, Ms. McVie."

"Dez, please call me Amy."

"I'm not sure you'll be saying that after you hear our questions."

Amy looked up. "Did Craig say something to you? Whatever problems Craig and I are having, it's really none of your—"

Dez put her hand up. "I'm sorry, Amy. Let me ask the questions and then we can be on our way. We wouldn't be here if it weren't important." She cleared her throat. "We have a witness who puts Dylan Richards at your house on Sunday night, between eight o'clock and midnight. Can you tell us if Dylan was, in fact, there that night?"

Amy's eyebrows knitted. "Look, Craig is mad at me, I get that. Arresting Dylan for killing the coroner when he is clearly innocent—if I can be frank—it's a really shitty thing to do." She looked at Dez. "And you can tell him I said so. And basically forcing me to admit to adultery to save Dylan, just so it will be on the court records—that's really low."

Dez shook her head. "We don't really care about any of that. Dylan is our prime suspect, and I really don't think we should be wasting our time and energy if we can clear his name." She looked at Fenway. "No matter what Sheriff McVie thinks."

Fenway gave a slight nod.

Amy sniffed in disapproval. "I'm going to have to think about whether or not I'll admit to this in court, but yes. Dylan was at my house from about eight o'clock until well after midnight on Sunday. Craig called to say there was a body found in the woods, and he'd be home very late. I think Dylan left around two thirty." She smiled. "He wanted to go home a little earlier, because he had to work Monday morning, but I might have convinced him otherwise."

Fenway looked at Dez; she was trying not to make a face.

"Thanks, Amy." Dez got up from the chair. "That's all we needed." Fenway got up with her.

"So, you'll let Dylan go?" Amy asked.

Dez closed her eyes.

"Oh, Amy." Dez dropped her arms to her sides. "You haven't heard."

Amy stopped and swallowed. "Heard? Heard what?" Her voice was demanding, but had a hint of worry in it.

"Dylan was found in his cell this morning."

"'Found in his cell'? What does that mean?" Amy's voice wavered.

"I'm so sorry, Amy. He's dead."

Amy's face fell. She leaned forward, elbows on the desk, and covered her face with her hands. "No. No, Dylan can't be…" Her voice trailed off.

Dez took a step forward to the desk. "I'm really sorry to be the one to tell you."

"How?" Amy's voice broke.

"I'm sorry." Dez put her hand on Amy's shoulder. "I'm really sorry, Amy. I wish we could tell you, but we aren't allowed to comment on open investigations."

Fenway grabbed a box of tissues off the bookshelf and put them on her desk. "Do you need us to drive you home?"

Amy's breath caught, and she gasped a little, trying to keep control. "No. No, I told you, I have to deal with this house, and the buyers probably won't take 'my lover was murdered' as an excuse."

"We didn't say he was murdered," Dez said.

"Oh, give me a break," Amy snapped. "It wouldn't be an open investigation otherwise."

"We'll leave you alone then." Dez motioned with her head for the two of them to leave.

They left Amy's office and closed the door behind them. They walked in silence outside and got to the car.

"Okay," Fenway said on a hard exhale as they got into the Accord. She started it up, and looked to Dez. "Now what?"

"Paperwork. Lots of paperwork. Maybe I can pawn that off on Migs."

"Hey—isn't Bradley supposed to be coming in for his interview?"

Dez looked at her watch. "Yeah. Migs told us he'd be in town by two, right? We'll be able to get back in plenty of time."

Fenway was quiet for a minute. "The sheriff is still investigating the case."

"Yes."

"And you and I are now treating McVie like the chief suspect."

Dez blinked. "Yes."

"Is there any way to get the sheriff to stop investigating?"

"Ugh. That's going to be a political nightmare."

"I kind of figured," Fenway agreed, "but we can't have him anywhere near this case, can we?"

Dez crossed her arms and tapped her foot. "No, I suppose we can't."

"So, who can get the sheriff off this case? Do we have to have the state police take over? Or the state attorney general, or the FBI?"

"Aren't you taking the lead on the evidence? Tell him you've discovered a conflict of interest. He's the one who insisted no one who had an active file with the coroner could touch the office, not even for fingerprints. I bet he'd recuse himself."

"Yeah, I can tell him that," Fenway nodded. "But stuff like interrogating Bradley is a gray area. You only know for sure it's related to Walker's murder if you know the same person is behind both the RAT malware and the emails to Walker."

"Right. And McVie doesn't know about what we found on the laptop yet."

"But he will soon. And that's why I have to get him off the case sooner rather than later."

They rode in silence for another few miles.

"Man," Dez said, breaking their silence. "I can't *believe* you slept with him." Her tone was seething.

"I'm sorry!" Fenway exclaimed. "I said it was a mistake."

Dez was quiet again.

CHAPTER TWENTY-ONE

MIGS WAS WAITING FOR THEM AT THE ENTRANCE OF THE PARKING garage when they drove in. Fenway saw him and rolled down her window.

He rushed over, holding his tie down with one hand. "Bradley is back. I asked them to wait for you before they started. Mark is taking lead on it —I don't know if they've started or not."

"Crap. Migs, can you park the car?"

"Aw, Fenway, you gonna let that kid park your brand-new car?"

"Yes, Dez, I am. Now get out and let's get over there before they start without us."

They grabbed their purses, got out of the car, and started to hurry across the street. Dez, in her street shoes, easily passed Fenway in her high heels.

Fenway got over to the interview room to find the door closed. The observation room door was unlocked, though. Fenway opened it and found Dez and Sheriff McVie in there with two officers she didn't recognize. They all were looking through the one-way mirror into the interview room, watching Mark and the officer to whom she had given her moving truck's keys, Officer Callahan.

"Why aren't you in there asking him the questions?" Fenway whispered to McVie.

"Because Callahan really gets on Bradley's nerves. He's had to fix Callahan's computer a couple of times and got so frustrated with Callahan they almost got into a fistfight. So, we're hoping for some of that unhinged magic to pry loose who Bradley is getting money from." He reached forward to the wall and turned up the speaker a little so they could hear more clearly.

"I don't know what you guys are talking about," Bradley was saying. "I knew I'd have to deal with your stupid questions yesterday," he nodded to Callahan, "and I was like, screw it, I'm going to Vegas. Let Piper kiss up to you, Callahan. I didn't call in, I know, but I figured you wouldn't fire me since I'm the only one who knows how to close down ports on the firewall."

"Sure, I understand. But here's the thing, Bradley." Mark reached down next to him and pulled up several reports. "You may be the only one to deal with the firewall, but you're not the only who can run reports on it. And it looks to me like you've opened up some holes in the firewall you shouldn't have. It looks to me like you've been letting someone use their remote access virus—"

"Hang on, Sergeant." Callahan held up his hand. "I think Bradley would want you to call that type of malware a *Trojan horse*. Technically, it's not a virus." He turned to Bradley. "Am I correct? This is a Trojan horse, not a virus, right?"

Bradley sneered and looked at the floor.

"Please continue, Sergeant."

"Thanks, Callahan. At any rate, whatever it's called, you not only allowed it to be installed, you not only opened up the firewall ports so the traffic could go through, but you falsified the reports on all of it too."

"Maybe I should ask for my lawyer." Bradley folded his arms.

"Oh, you could certainly do that. Callahan, refresh my memory, what did we arrest Mr. Watermeier for?"

"I believe it was the invasion of privacy statute, Sergeant."

Bradley scoffed. "You know that's only for revenge porn and upskirt photos and stuff. You're not even accusing me of any of that perverted shit."

Callahan nodded. "Now, Sergeant, isn't Mr. Watermeier correct in saying this wasn't used for anything lascivious or dirty? Surely this is only punishable by firing, correct? This is obviously against our internal policies, but it cannot possibly meet the criminal standard—and besides, invasion of privacy is only a misdemeanor, right?"

"Impressive, Callahan. You're sure thinking like a defense attorney." Mark tapped his temple. "It sounds like Mr. Watermeier did his homework on this one."

"They're doing a good job playing off each other," Fenway whispered to McVie. "This is entertaining to watch."

"Shh," shushed McVie.

"But," Mark continued, "we're actually going to be filing some additional charges. We found out when the malware was installed, and when those ports were opened to allow it, and we can conclusively prove it was Mr. Watermeier who did it. So, we'll also be adding electronic eavesdropping charges."

"Ah." Callahan smiled knowingly.

"Bradley, you're a smart guy. You know what a *wobbler* is?"

"Yeah." Bradley's voice was miserable.

Callahan looked at Mark with a comically confused expression. He was clearly enjoying this. "A *wobbler*. I'm not sure I know what that is, Sergeant. But then, I'm not too bright. In fact, Mr. Watermeier can attest to me not being too bright. I think I need my memory refreshed on that one."

"Sure thing, Callahan. A *wobbler* is when the prosecutor can decide if they want to charge a crime as a misdemeanor or a felony."

"Oh, right!" Callahan exclaimed, smacking his forehead. "The misdemeanor is a maximum of six months. The felony is three years." He smiled. "That's quite a wobble."

"Callahan, is there anything you can think of that would make the prosecutor decide to charge this as a misdemeanor and not a felony?"

"Sure I can, Sergeant. I don't think we've let Bradley know that we have also seen several large cash deposits made every month since the time those firewall ports were opened. And even *I* know if Bradley, here, tells us who paid him to electronically eavesdrop on Rachel, the prosecutor will be a lot more lenient."

Mark swiveled his head slowly to look at Bradley. "What do you think, Bradley? You think you might want to tell us who it was who paid you?"

Bradley shifted uncomfortably in his seat. "He never told me his name."

"Did you see him?"

"Yeah."

Callahan picked up the folder in front of him. "It just so happens I've got some photos for you to look at." He got a six-photo array out of the folder and set it down in front of Bradley. Fenway saw the top right was a photo of Dylan Richards.

Bradley looked at them. "It wasn't any of these guys." He hung his head. "I told you, I don't know the guy's name. He sat behind me in the coffee shop one day and made the offer. I barely talked to him. The next day I went back to the coffee shop to meet him, and I thought he didn't show, but when I got home, I had an envelope full of cash in my laptop bag, and a note that identified what ports to open, and where to leave a flash drive for the anonymizer. I covered my tracks when I made the changes, too, because I knew it would raise red flags."

"Hey, Sergeant, covering his tracks—isn't that obstruction of justice?"

"Good question, Officer. It's a gray area in state law. Maybe not so gray with the feds, though. But I don't think Bradley is going to do anything to make us call the feds."

"I don't know. Bradley's a pretty smart guy. He's smarter than me, for sure. Maybe he thinks he's smarter than the feds."

Bradley looked wretched. "I'm telling you, I don't know who hired me. I've told you everything I know."

"Sit tight, Bradley. Callahan and I are going to go discuss this with the D.A. We'll let him know you *wanted* to cooperate, but you don't have any useful information." Mark stood up and turned to the door.

"Wait!" exclaimed Bradley. "That's it? Those six pictures are all you have? Isn't there, like, some big binder I can look through?"

Mark nodded. "Well, Bradley, that's the kind of stuff we like to hear. That *is* cooperation! I'm delighted to hear it. Callahan, why don't you get a couple of the binders for Mr. Watermeier to start on. Bradley, you hungry? You want anything to eat?"

They started talking about the kind of tacos Bradley wanted. Fenway figured Bradley would be busy with lunch and the binders for a couple of hours, at least—maybe more. She figured it was time to see if she could pull the sheriff off the case.

Fenway tapped the sheriff on the shoulder and motioned with her head for him to come outside with her. She let herself out of the viewing room and he followed.

They stopped in front of the coffee station and she turned to him, a serious look on her face. "I really don't want to tell you this."

McVie tilted his head.

Fenway lowered her voice. "I think you better recuse yourself from these investigations."

He looked annoyed. "Look, Fenway, just because you don't like what I had to say this morning—"

Fenway scoffed. "I sure as hell *didn't* like it. But that's not the issue. It's likely to come out that Dylan and Amy were having an affair, and if we don't pull you off the investigation *now*, whoever we *do* arrest will have more than reasonable doubt to throw out every piece of evidence you've touched."

McVie nodded. "I know I told you to treat everyone, even me, as a suspect, but when Dylan became the lead suspect—I don't know if you noticed—I haven't gone anywhere near the Walker investigation unless I've had to. Mark's the one who found the car. I didn't even go down to LAX."

"You had Dylan's Glock in your custody when we went to see the M.E."

McVie looked at the ground. "Yeah, but you saw how that turned out. You know I'm not trying to railroad him."

"Don't you see, though, Craig? That looks bad. It looks bad that you know these details. If you were trying to pin the murder on Dylan—which I guarantee is what the defense will argue—you had access to all the evidence. You might have hidden exculpatory evidence, or had Mark plant something to make it look like he did it."

"Yeah, well, there isn't going to be a defense now, is there?" McVie snarled. "I know you and I don't know each other very well, but accusing me of planting evidence with absolutely no foundation is pretty low."

"Craig, I'm not—"

"Stop it!" he barked. An officer at a desk nearby turned his head toward them. "Stop it, Fenway," he said more quietly. "I don't know what you're trying to do, but it feels like a coup." He took a few steps back and put his hand over his mouth and closed his eyes.

Fenway felt the awkward silence as she stood and waited. It felt like a long time to her.

McVie opened his eyes and dropped his hand to his side. "Okay, Fenway. I'm going to step away from the investigation completely in the hopes this doesn't become public. I'll continue with Bradley, and I'll stay far away from any car, or any laptop, or any stolen files."

Fenway rubbed her forehead. "You can't investigate Bradley either."

"What? I thought we *just* established that Dylan wasn't the one who paid Bradley. This looks to me like a separate case."

Fenway shook her head. "It's not. It's the same case."

McVie set his jaw. "Oh, I see what's going on."

She was quiet.

"I was afraid of this. Am I a suspect in Dylan's death, now?"

She paused. "I don't think you killed Dylan."

McVie stepped closer to Fenway, speaking softly. "I should hope not, as we were going for round two when Dylan killed himself." He stepped back and shook his head. "And you're thinking you don't want to tell anyone we were together last night, because Daddy would get mad and might not pay for your apartment anymore."

"That's not why, and you know it," she whispered, a hard edge in her voice. "Besides, you know it would be worse for you than for me; your wife doesn't know about last night, and sheriff is an *elected* position in this county. A man who sleeps with the much-younger woman he appointed might not get re-elected."

"So not only are you forcing me into a leave of absence, you're telling me I'm too old. I'll tell you something. The voters don't care that you're *much younger*, princess, they only care—" And he stopped suddenly.

Fenway's eyes narrowed. "They only care *what?*"

"Never mind."

She grabbed his wrist. "They only care that your ghosty-white ass fucked a *black girl?* Is that what you were going to say?"

"Let go of me."

"Or were you going to use another term besides '*black girl*'?" she hissed.

"I wasn't going to say anything like that," he snarled, shaking her loose. "Don't worry, Fenway. I'm done investigating any of this. With or without you. We're done." McVie looked her in the eye, then turned and stormed off.

CHAPTER TWENTY-TWO

FENWAY WATCHED HIM GO INTO THE BACK OFFICES. THEN SHE TURNED and left through the front door, past the strange look she thought she was getting from the desk officer who had raised his head when McVie raised his voice. She hoped he hadn't heard the other parts of their conversation.

She had to clear her head. She wanted to walk a circuitous loop around the city center buildings, through the plaza, but she knew it would be uncomfortable in her high heels. She started through the plaza anyway, then turned halfway through and headed back across the street. The memorial service was in a few hours, she remembered, and she needed to find out how to get to the church. As Fenway went inside her office building, she pulled the map up on her phone, but realized she didn't know what church it was.

"Hey, Migs." Her head was down as she stared at her phone. "Any more on the identity of the emailer from Piper?"

"No," a female voice said, "but they found Dylan's truck."

Startled, Fenway popped her head up. Rachel was sitting back at her desk.

"Rachel!" she exclaimed. "What are you doing here?"

"That's what I said when she came in," said Migs, sounding a little exasperated. "You should be at home, Rachel."

"Listen, Fenway," Rachel said with a guilty look on her face. "I know you were expecting me to be out all week, but if I don't have something to distract myself, I'm going to go crazy."

"No, Rachel, absolutely not. I can't let you do that."

Rachel's eyes were wide and doe-like. "Please, Fenway, I couldn't get Walker out of my head all weekend, and now I can't get the image of Dylan out of my head."

Fenway shook her head. "You need to give yourself some time. You need to be with family."

"Please. My dad hated Dylan."

"Rachel, come on. You've been through a lot this week. Don't you have arrangements you need to make?"

"Dylan's mom insisted on handling everything. I don't have anything to do but sit in our apartment feeling sorry for myself."

Fenway studied Rachel's face for a minute. She thought she could see the stress in her eyes, but she wasn't sure. Rachel looked away quickly. "I don't know if you're in shock, or what, but you need to take some time off."

"Listen, Fenway, if Dana Perino can brief the press with one eye, I can do my job after everything that happened to me this week."

"One eye?" Fenway cocked her head to the side.

"Yeah, remember at that press conference during the Iraq war? That one reporter threw his shoe at George W. Bush?"

"Vaguely..."

"Dubya ducked, and the shoe hit Dana in the eye."

Fenway was about to argue about how getting hit in the eye with a shoe is not the same thing as finding out your husband was arrested for murder, and then found dead in his cell, but she realized it would be counterproductive. Instead, she walked over to Rachel's desk.

"Be that as it may, Rachel, I don't know anyone who's been through what you've been through this week. I'm worried, frankly. You need to take care of yourself."

Rachel patted Fenway's hand. "I heard Lana Cassidy shot at you yesterday, and here *you* are back at work. In fact, I heard you kicked Lana's ass. If she had done her job, maybe none of this would have happened." She sighed. "Besides, you guys are super shorthanded right now. Piper's getting me a computer so I can do some tracking and get the latest info from the M.E. in San Miguelito. And there are still a ton of files to go through from that asshole's office."

Fenway thought for a minute. "If you need the distraction for a little bit, I guess you can stay today." The words were out of her mouth and she instantly regretted it. "If you feel tired, or overwhelmed, or stressed out, you go, okay? You don't even have to tell me. Promise me you'll go if you start feeling it."

Rachel waved her hand. "Fine, fine. And while I'm waiting for something to do, maybe we can go see Dylan's truck. They found it on a fire road about a mile off 326."

"Absolutely not." Fenway folded her arms. "You realize I'd get in a ton of trouble if I let you do that, right?"

"Figured I'd ask."

Fenway turned to Migs. "Migs, split up the file work with Rachel."

"Sure thing."

"I'm going to grab Dez and head to the truck. Rachel, do you know if there's a CSI team there?"

"That's what I heard. They're fingerprinting the truck and assessing the damage."

"Thanks. It's good to have you back, Rachel."

Fenway walked out of the office.

She heard a whisper behind her. "Fenway!"

She turned. Migs had followed her out.

"What is it?"

"You're really going to let Rachel stay?"

Fenway sighed. "I guess that wasn't the best idea," she admitted, "but she was so insistent. I think she's in denial."

"I don't feel right about it."

Fenway thought for a minute. "Okay, look, can you keep an eye on her? I think if she can finish out the day and keep her mind off everything, it will help her."

Migs looked skeptical, but nodded and went back in.

Fenway went back across the street and told Dez about the truck. Dez was in the observation room, watching Bradley eat his third taco.

"Not only did we find Dylan's truck," Fenway said, "but I also kicked McVie off the case."

"How did you do that?" Dez followed her out of the building.

"I basically told him he was a liability, and whoever we arrested would get everything he touched thrown out."

"You certainly don't lack balls, Fenway."

Fenway pursed her lips. "He didn't like it too much. Said I was accusing him of planting evidence."

"I guess I wouldn't like getting pulled off a case either, but I thought he'd take it a little better."

"Yeah."

Dez called in for the location of the truck, and once she heard it was on a fire road off the state highway, she decided to take a cruiser. "I'm not subjecting either one of our cars to the fire road," she said. Since Dez knew the roads better than Fenway, she went to the transportation department and got a sheriff's cruiser.

They drove to 326, then turned and drove north until they were about a half-mile from the entrance of Coast Harbor Park. There was an open metal gate on the left between a couple of fallen trees, and Dez pointed out a single pair of fresh tire tracks on the fire road behind the gate. "I think the CSI van is still here."

"How do you know?" Fenway asked.

"There would be two sets of tire tracks if they'd left. Come on, Fenway. Detective work 101."

They drove for a few minutes, taking the gravel road at about 20 miles an hour, until they saw the rooftop lights of the CSI van. They got out, with Fenway holding the side of the car for balance, tottering on her heels on the uneven surface. Dez looked at Fenway's black dress and heels again and shook her head.

Dez walked over to the CSI van. "Melissa, have you met our new coroner?"

The first tech didn't look up from her work. "New coroner, huh? I thought she was your prom date, Dez."

Dez suppressed a laugh. "How's the fingerprinting coming?"

"Plenty of fingerprints all over the place. We've lifted five sets so far."

"And Sergeant!" The second tech waved his hand from beside the truck. "You and the coroner might want to take a look at this."

Dez tut-tutted. "Mother mercy, it's the file drawer."

In the back seat of the truck was the missing drawer, and it was still full of files.

Fenway was still holding onto the side of the cruiser. "Dez, can you see if the Ferris Energy file is in the drawer?"

"Come on now, Prom Queen. You dressed too fancy to do real police work?"

Fenway glared at Dez, but managed to make it over to the truck without falling down. "I'm never coming to work in heels again," she muttered under her breath.

Dez already had her head in the truck. "So, Fenway, what do we expect to get out of this?" She lowered her voice so the techs couldn't hear her. "I mean, we think the sheriff is a suspect, and obviously we don't think Dylan was the one to drive his truck into the building, right? We think someone stole the truck and did it, right?"

"That's right."

"What do we think we're going to find in these files?" Dez already had a pair of latex gloves on. She handed Fenway a pair too.

"I guess it would depend on who smashed through the wall." Fenway pulled on the gloves.

"What if McVie stole the file?"

"I guess McVie could have been the one to steal the file," Fenway admitted. "He could have stolen the car, smashed through the wall, driven off, hidden the truck somewhere close, then gotten the cruiser to go get me. I guess we could time it—it'd be awfully close. But if he wanted to frame Dylan, I guess he could have."

"Okay. Let's suppose McVie did all that. Then he'd get the truck and dump it way out here. But why keep the files in the truck?"

"You said earlier McVie was the lead investigator on the accident at the refinery. Maybe he wanted to get rid of the evidence."

"So, he'd just destroy all the files, right?"

"I don't know, Dez. Maybe there's too much stuff in there related to *other* cases he worked on."

"I guess. I don't know, I thought if McVie did it, he would have taken the file and burned it, or trashed it. Or planted evidence in the file placing the blame on Dylan for something—so it would look like Dylan did it."

Fenway pursed her lips. "I don't think he'd do that. He got really upset when I suggested that he planted evidence."

"I wonder if the sheriff doth protest too much."

"Okay, the moment of truth." Fenway looked under the Fs until she found the Ferris Energy file. "It's still here. Let's see what's in it."

She opened it up. The file contained autopsy notes for both Carl Cassidy and Lewis Fairweather. Both men had died of "suffocation from bronchial hemorrhaging." The toxic fumes had done their work quickly. The toxicology report identified a chemical, that Fenway couldn't pronounce, as the culprit, and suggested both men were unconscious before their demise.

The investigator's notes were in the file as well, with separate pages of handwritten notes clipped to the autopsy forms, and toxicology reports, respectively. There were three sets of notes total.

One set was dated the day after the autopsy, which covered the material found on the controls for the fume disposal and ventilation systems that directed the toxic fumes into the room the two men were in. It stated the men shouldn't have been in the room at the time, and referenced a schedule of fumigation venting. The conclusions were that the men were in the room despite security controls, someone may have altered the schedule without company knowledge, and Ferris Energy, as a company, "could not be reasonably found to be at fault."

"That's a weird thing for the coroner to say," said Dez. "He's not supposed to offer legal opinions."

"Migs did say Walker was always going outside his depth on the legal issues, though."

"Yeah—but this is too much, even for him."

A second set of notes was dated about a week later. Those notes summarized the findings into Fairweather, covering his personal life, credit card and student loan debt, and family background.

The last set of notes was dated about a week later, detailing Cassidy's life. But the topics weren't the same: notes on Cassidy's EAP participation; detailed reports of an affair between Dylan Richards and Lana Cassidy; a statement from a private investigator; photos of a hotel out near Paso Querido; and photos of Dylan's truck parked outside a home identified as the Cassidy residence.

"If I'm reading this right," Fenway mused, "I'm supposed to conclude the person who was having an affair with Lana Cassidy somehow altered the ventilation system to kill Carl Cassidy? And Fairweather was collateral damage?"

"And Dylan Richards was that person."

"Right."

Dez had a confused look on her face. "This doesn't make any sense.

There would have to be a trail of phone calls if that affair actually happened, right?"

"I don't know. But this file has been out of our hands for a few days now. The thief could have tampered with it."

Dez examined the handwritten notes closely. "I can't tell. You see how these two sets of notes"—she indicated the Fairweather and Cassidy files —"are on different paper stock, with different color pens. Now, it looks like the handwriting is the same, but I can't be sure." The handwriting was printed, and not neatly. Some of the printed letters were connected to the next letter, in sort of a half-cursive, but there were no traditionally cursive shapes in the *b, s,* or *f* letters that would be expected in traditional cursive writing. The lowercase *g* letters were almost always connected to the next letter, an *r, a,* or *e.*

Fenway looked at the notes also. "Look here, Dez." She pointed to the page. "The loop of the *g* on this page and the loop of the *g* on this other page are of different sizes, but it does kind of look like they were written by the same person. Look, same shape of the uppercase *D*s here. And the crossbar on the *t*s and the uppercase *A*s are the same."

"Do we have any written notes from Walker to compare this to?"

Fenway selected a file from the front. *Ellsworth, James M.* "Let's look at this one."

"I remember this one," Dez said. "Drug overdose. Mother found his body in his apartment. It wasn't pretty."

Fenway thought the handwriting on this one looked less neat, although overall looked similar. But some of the quickly printed letters didn't connect the way they did in the Ferris Energy file. "Look at this." She pointed at the word *gastrointestinal.* "This *g-a* combination isn't connected. But the *g-a* combinations in the Cassidy notes are."

"It looks like Walker was in a hurry on this one. Not so much here."

"Yeah, but if you're in a hurry, aren't you *more* likely to connect letters, not less?"

Dez gave her a look. "You're asking me like I'm a handwriting expert. You need to get someone on Yasuda's team to look at this."

"I took a class a few months ago," Fenway said, "and I don't think these were written by the same person."

"Make sure you tell that to Yasuda. I'm sure she'll appreciate your educated opinion."

"All right, Dez, jeez. I'll let their handwriting expert deal with it."

Dez stuck her head out of the truck. "Did you guys find any finger-prints on the drawer?" she called.

"Wiped clean," the first tech called back. "Keep your gloves on for those files, though. We've got to take them back to the lab."

"Tag this Ferris Energy file for handwriting analysis, too. Prom Queen thinks it might be forged."

"Will do."

Dez and Fenway finished up with the truck. They looked between the seats, under the seats, and in the glove box. Dez did a lap around the truck, looking for any signs of additional damage. The crime scene techs were still scouring the surrounding brush for telltale signs of anything useful. Dez told the techs they were all finished up as Fenway wobbled back to the squad car.

"That was interesting." Fenway looked out the window as they started driving back down the fire road toward the highway. "What do you think?"

"As much crap as I gave you back there, Fenway, I think we have to consider the likelihood that those notes weren't written by Walker."

"Right. Are we thinking McVie?"

"I don't know. If it were McVie, wouldn't he know we'd catch on to the fake handwriting?"

"Maybe." Fenway said. "I was thinking more that the fake information doesn't really help McVie out."

"It does give Dylan the motive for crashing through the wall and stealing the files."

"Yeah, but it points people right in the direction of Dylan having an affair with a married woman." Fenway drummed her fingers on the door handle. "Wouldn't McVie have realized a good investigator would start digging? Wouldn't he have realized that would probably open a line of inquiry into Dylan's phone records, and then his affair with Amy would have come out? Wouldn't it make more sense if the files were missing altogether, as if Dylan had destroyed them?"

"I don't know." Dez shook her head. "Maybe it was an emotional decision for Craig. Maybe he wanted to show Amy she wasn't special to Dylan, and he wanted her to think Dylan did this with lots of other married women too. Maybe he thought getting rid of Dylan—and having Amy think he wasn't really in love with her—would somehow save his marriage." They arrived at the end of the fire road, and Dez turned back onto 326, heading back to the office. "Sometimes the emotional decision can outweigh logic."

Fenway nodded.

They traveled in silence for a while.

"Almost time for the memorial service, right?" Fenway said.

"Yeah. You'll finally be someplace today where those shoes aren't going to be a liability."

"You're going to it, right? I'm not sure where it's being held."

"The United Methodist on Santa Clarita Street."

CHAPTER TWENTY-THREE

AFTER THEY PULLED INTO THE PARKING LOT, DEZ SAID IT WAS GOING to be a scramble for them to drop off their paperwork and get over to the church in time. They got into the office at about a quarter to five. Migs was still there, but Mark and Rachel weren't.

Fenway stood in front of the counter where Migs was working. "Are Mark and Rachel already at the service?"

"Rachel is." Migs didn't look up from his keyboard. "Mark is still over at the sheriff's office, watching Bradley go through the mug shot binders. It's probably a long shot."

"When are you going?"

"Oh." Migs got a little red, and smoothed down his tie. "Piper told me there were some password-protected files on Walker's hard drive, and she thought she'd have it cracked by five. I thought you'd want to see them tonight, if they're important."

"Mm-hmm." Dez folded her arms. "Instead of going to your boss's funeral."

Migs didn't say anything. Fenway looked at Dez, who glared back at her.

Fenway sighed. "You know, Migs, those files can wait a little while for me to get back from the service."

"Um, okay, I guess I should go to Mr. Walker's funeral."

"Great," Dez said. "You can ride with us."

Migs closed the file he was working on. "We're going to have to hurry. There's going to be a ton of people there."

Fenway looked at the clock. "Give us ten minutes. We have to enter our notes into the system."

"That'll make us ten minutes late."

"Oh, now you're worried about being late? Go hang out with Piper for ten minutes if you're concerned about our punctuality."

Migs apparently didn't catch Fenway's sarcasm, because his face lit up and he was out the door before she even realized he was leaving.

There weren't a lot of entries to make, but the system was slow, and it took Dez and Fenway closer to fifteen minutes to finish up.

"Migs was right, we *are* going to be pretty late." Fenway saved the changes to the system and closed her laptop.

"These things never start on time. I wouldn't worry too much."

Fenway shuffled her papers together. "Binder clip?"

"Rachel has a few in her top left drawer."

She walked over to Rachel's desk and opened the top drawer. Fenway didn't see binder clips, but there was a bag from the office supply store. "Did Rachel put the binder clips in here?" She took the bag and looked inside.

There were five empty packages, torn open, all saying *FileMore USB Sticks 25 Value Pack*, and a receipt with the date and time stamp a few hours before.

Fenway looked on Rachel's desk. There was no laptop, but there were two cheap-looking 7-port USB hubs with prominent *Property of Estancia IT Dept* stickers.

"Find them?" Dez grabbed her purse.

"Oh shit, Dez."

"What?"

"Look." Fenway emptied out the bag with the packaging onto the desk.

"What are those?"

"Empty 25-packs of USB thumb drives." Fenway looked up at Dez. "Do you think Rachel copied the video of Walker assaulting her onto all those sticks?"

"Oh no."

"That's 125 USB drives. She wouldn't be distributing them at the service, would she?"

"I don't know, but if she *is* planning to do anything at the service, let's hope it hasn't started yet." Dez started out the door. "Let's go, Fenway, like *now*."

Fenway put down the bag and got her purse, following Dez quickly on the way out the door. "We'll take my car," Dez yelled at her over her shoulder.

"Yeah, you know where the church is." Fenway was trying unsuccessfully to keep up.

"Plus, you drive like my grandma." Dez took off at a sprint. By the time Fenway made it, clattering in her heels, to the ground floor of the parking garage, a Chevy Impala was squealing around the corner of the second-floor ramp. Dez came to a short stop in front of Fenway, who pulled the door open and jumped in.

The United Methodist Church was only about two miles away, near the outskirts of the town limits, but Fenway thought it took forever to get to the other side of the highway. As they got closer to the church, she could see the streets lined with cars on either side.

"Oh man, it's packed." She glanced at the clock on the dash—it was already five twenty-five.

"You're getting out." Dez pulled hard into the parking lot, which was completely full, and pulled the car up on the sidewalk next to the fire line. Fenway was out of the car, running—as best as she could—to the heavy, tall, wooden front doors of the church. She pulled the doors open and ran through the enormous carpeted foyer. Her heel caught on the carpet and she almost fell, but she regained her balance, and grabbed the door to the sanctuary, pulling it open.

The sanctuary was in the shape of a heptagon, with the chancel taking up the three sections directly across from Fenway. She stood at the top of an aisle with about twenty pews on either side. A man in a purple Damascene robe—Fenway assumed it was the reverend—was talking about how a young Harrison had met his wife.

A few people turned their heads to look at Fenway, but most of the attendees kept their attention on the speech. She did her best to smile in a slightly embarrassed way, even though she desperately wanted to find Rachel.

Although the rear pews were mostly empty, it was a well-attended service; the first ten rows were completely full. Fenway looked at one of the back rows. Every few feet, there was a paper program, with a picture of Harrison Walker, *A Celebration of Life* printed above the photo, and then Walker's full name, and birth and death dates below.

A USB stick was on top of each program in the row.

She looked at a few other pews. Wherever there was an empty seat with a program, there was a USB stick on top of it.

Fenway scanned the pews, but she didn't see the back of Rachel's head in any of them. A few rows in front of her, though, on the right-hand side, she saw her father.

As stealthily as she could, she started collecting the USB sticks from the empty seats. She picked up more than twenty drives as she walked through a few of the pews, and dropped them in her purse. Fenway looked around—there were many more, and it looked like everyone in a seat had already gotten a USB stick. She walked to the pew behind her father where there were a couple of open seats. Fenway scooted into one of them. She turned and looked up at the back of the sanctuary. There was a small rectangular window above the double doors. The window,

Fenway thought, might be the projection room. If the room contained a computer hooked up to a projector, Rachel might be in there. Fenway turned toward the back of her father's head and knelt down.

"Dad," she whispered. He jumped a little and turned to look at her. "I need your help. Follow me out the door and grab the USB drives on empty seats on the way out. I'll meet you in the foyer." She turned around and collected a few more drives before making her way to the back and out the door.

Dez was in the foyer, panting. Fenway suspected Dez had run all the way from wherever she parked.

"There are USB sticks on everyone's seat," Fenway whispered to Dez. "And I think everyone who's sitting down already has one."

Nathaniel Ferris came into the foyer. "Fenway? What is it?" He handed her a handful of USB sticks.

She held up one of the USB sticks. "These drives show Harrison Walker attempting to rape a woman. Attempting to rape Rachel, in fact."

"What are you talking about? Rachel was putting them down on all the seats right before the service. It's a video full of photos and music from Harrison's life."

"Is that what she told you it was?"

Ferris had a puzzled look on his face, and then he went white. "Oh no. Is that why Rob pulled Rachel out of there?"

"What? Why would Stotsky pull Rachel out of the memorial service?"

"Rachel is Rob's daughter, Fenway."

Fenway was floored. "Stotsky is the guy who wouldn't let Rachel go to Princeton? Who had a fit about her spending the semester in Costa Rica?"

Ferris had a blank look.

"You didn't know he was Rachel's dad?" Dez said.

"No clue," Fenway said.

Suddenly, it all came to her, like the last puzzle piece slipping into place.

"Okay, we need to find Rachel. And we need to get the rest of those drives. Where do you think Stotsky took her?"

Ferris paused. "I really don't have any idea, but I can't imagine they left the church. Rob and I came together in the limo. He wouldn't abandon me."

"He might choose his daughter over you, Dad."

"Why in the world would Rachel want to give a video of that to everyone?"

"I really can't talk about it right now. Where do you think they might have gone?"

"I—I don't know, Fenway."

"You can help me look for Rachel, Dad. Maybe they went to a conference room or an empty office. You look down here, I'll go upstairs."

Ferris nodded and started to walk down the hall.

"And I'll go in there and try to take as many of the sticks as I can," Dez said, turning toward the door of the sanctuary.

Fenway grabbed Dez's arm. "And we need to figure out how to get Stotsky down to the station," she said in a low voice. "Try to think of some excuse. I hope Bradley's still eating his tacos."

Dez got a light of recognition in her eyes, nodded to Fenway, and went into the sanctuary.

Fenway went to the stairway on the side of the foyer and took off her shoes so she could take the stairs two at a time. The hallway's balcony looked down into the foyer, with a door on the other side. It was roughly the right place for a room that might have a window over the sanctuary. She turned the door handle; it was locked. She put her ear to the door. She could hear a man talking.

She put her shoes down, took three of steps back, and then ran and smashed her shoulder against the door. Nothing. She wasn't sure how effective that would have been anyway, although she probably would have a good-sized bruise there the next day. She debated what to do next.

Then the door opened.

"What are you doing?" hissed the fiftyish man who opened the door, angrily. "Don't you know there's a service going on?" Behind him, a speaker was broadcasting the reverend's voice into the room.

"You didn't get a USB drive from a young woman, did you?" she hurriedly spit out. "Whatever you do, you can't play the video file on there!"

The man put his finger to his lips, and closed the door in her face. Fenway could hear it lock again. She had no idea if Rachel had gotten the USB drive into the projection room, and somehow convinced the man to play it, but it seemed Fenway couldn't do much about it.

She picked her shoes back up and turned down the hallway, looking for any open rooms where Rachel and Rob Stotsky might have gone.

The sanctuary may have been full, but the hallways were eerily quiet. All the rooms on either side of the hallway were empty. Fenway came to the end of the hallway and ran back to go to the other side of the projection room. Another quiet hallway, and the rooms again were devoid of people. She gave up and went back downstairs.

Dez was coming out of the sanctuary, carrying a paper bag, when Fenway arrived on the ground floor. "I couldn't get them all. I couldn't do it without calling attention to myself, and a few people didn't want to give them up. I even told them we found a computer virus on there, and still some people were saying they wanted to see the pictures of Walker." She shook the bag a little. "I got about 80 of them, but about 20 of them are with people who won't give them up."

"Did you see Stotsky?"

"No. Did you?"

Fenway shook her head.

And that's when they heard the voice of the reverend introduce a video of the life of Harrison Walker. They saw the lights under the door dim. And then they heard a video—the sounds of an office. Typing on a keyboard. And Fenway and Dez both opened the double sanctuary doors at the same time.

———

Rachel is on the screen, typing. She's in a light blue blouse, buttoned all the way up except for the top button. She looks tired.

The sound of the office door opening. Rachel looks up. She addresses someone off screen.

Mr. Walker, she says, if you're here to help me with the filing, I'm almost finished. Or did you want to take this up to the third floor yourself?

A gruff voice from offscreen. His voice sounds like he's been drinking. Don't play with me, Rachel. You and I both know what I'm here to help you with. And it's not filing, is it, sweetheart?

Rachel flinches in her chair and pushes it back from the desk as a man swoops in from the right side of the screen. He is on top of Rachel and her chair instantly. The viewer can only see the man's back—the back of his head, the back of his sports-coat, his backside as the coat rides up as he's bending over, pinning Rachel into her chair. At the bottom of the screen, he wedges his leg between her knees. His left hand holds her shoulder against the back of the chair. His right hand is not visible in the frame.

Rachel is screaming. No. Get off me. No.

The man is leaning his head over hers, whispering to her, inaudibly.

She keeps screaming. No. Get off me. Stop.

And she shakes her head from side to side, violently, and almost catches him under the chin. He leans back and then forward again. The chair tips back and crashes to the ground, with Rachel still in it, and with him on top of her. Most of Rachel and the man are offscreen, except for her feet and legs; they are flailing.

Rachel is yelling. Get off me. Get off me.

Then he bellows in pain. A sharp intake of breath. You bitch.

And then the sound of a punch. Rachel's legs and feet leave the screen. A blur of motion.

Rachel's voice off screen. You stay away from me.

The sound of keys, a pile of paper falling onto the floor. Walker's face now visible as he pulls himself up. You cut me. You little whore, you actually scratched me.

Rachel's voice again. You stay the hell away from me.

I don't want to see you again, you stupid bitch. Don't bother coming in on Monday. You're lucky I don't have you thrown out of here.

There is the sound of Walker spitting.

There is the sound of rapid footfalls and the door opening and closing.

The video stops.

———

The sanctuary stayed at low light. It was dead silent for what felt to Fenway like minutes.

Then the murmuring started in the front row.

Walker's widow got up; she looked to be in her fifties, and was dressed in a modest black pantsuit, paired with short black heels. From her black purse, she took out a pair of sunglasses and put them on. Then she turned, and purposefully walked up the aisle, past Dez and Fenway, and out of the sanctuary.

The reverend went over and started talking to the rest of the front row. They were keeping their tones low, but seemed to be speaking urgently. Fenway couldn't make out what they were saying, but the woman who had been sitting next to Walker's widow was getting louder and more angry-sounding as she spoke. The man who had been sitting on Walker's widow's other side was gesturing wildly with his hands; he seemed to be upset too.

The reverend stood up and cleared his throat. "Ladies and gentlemen," he announced in a loud, clear voice, "our service is over. Please exit out the sanctuary's rear doors."

The murmuring spread through the entire sanctuary. The lights came up a little more.

Fenway turned around to watch the attendees leave the room. She saw her father, still sitting in the back on the far left. She saw Rachel sitting two pews behind him, much closer to the center. Her jaw was set and she stared straight ahead, trancelike; she had a blank expression on her face. Her father—Stotsky—was in the pew in front of her, his head in his hands, his shoulders drooped.

Fenway looked back to the front; the woman and the man in the front row were still talking with the reverend. It looked like he was trying to calm them down, but failing.

Fenway went to the back pew and sat next to Rachel. "Hi," she said tentatively.

"Hi, Fenway. Are you going to arrest me?"

Fenway's brows knitted. "What for?"

"I don't know. I figured I'd probably be breaking some law by showing that video."

"I don't think so, but what do I know? I've only been on the job a couple of days. I don't even know California law that well."

Rachel was silent for a minute, then whispered, "I didn't mean to hurt my Dad. I wanted everyone to know Walker didn't deserve to have his life celebrated. I wanted everyone to know Walker was a rapist, and a predator, and that he wanted to ruin my life. But I didn't think how much it would hurt Dad if he saw that." She ran her hands through her hair. "To see that happen to his daughter." She shook her head. "I don't know what I would do if I were him. I don't know what I would think."

"I'm sorry, Rachel."

"And Dylan," she continued, "I wanted to make sure everyone knew Dylan killed Walker to *protect me*—not because of money, or anything like that." She blinked and looked down.

Fenway hesitated. "Well, Rachel, we actually don't think Dylan killed Walker after all."

Her head popped up. "What? What do you mean?"

"We have two witnesses who can put him miles away at that time.

Same with his phone—it triangulates from an area miles from where Walker was shot. Plus, some of the physical evidence doesn't match."

"I thought he and Parker were lying about where they were Sunday night."

Fenway hesitated again. She raised her head to look at Rachel's father. He was still slumped forward in his seat. But she thought he might be straining to listen to them. "Yes," she said, quietly, but loud enough for Stotsky to hear. "They were lying about where they were. But it wasn't anywhere near the murder scene."

Rachel's voice broke a little. "What was he doing? Where was he?"

Rob Stotsky flung himself around to face them. "I'll tell you where he was, Rachel," he said loudly, his voice cracking with emotion. "That creep was cheating on you. He was cheating on you with a sixteen-year-old girl."

Rachel's face fell.

Fenway saw the man in the front stop talking to the reverend and look at them.

"I don't want to hurt you, sweetie, but it's true," Stotsky continued. "Maybe, like Miss Stevenson said, maybe Dylan isn't a murderer. But he's a liar and a cheat and a *pedophile*, and he deserved to be locked up."

Fenway saw Rachel fold in on herself. She pulled her knees up and put her feet on the chair. She put her elbows on her knees, extending her arms, then put her head, face down, right between her elbows.

Fenway turned toward Stotsky. "I don't know what you heard, or where you heard it, Mr. Stotsky, but Dylan wasn't sleeping with a sixteen-year-old girl. He was sleeping with her *mother*."

"Her mother?"

"Yes, her mother. Who has definitely passed the age of consent."

Stotsky was silent.

"Dylan might have been a liar and a cheat," Fenway said, "but he wasn't a pedophile. For God's sake, have some decency."

Stotsky huffed. "You don't know what you're talking about. Either that or you're bald-faced lying to me right now."

"I've been working on this investigation since I came onboard, and I sure as hell *do* know what I'm talking about."

Stotsky looked from Fenway to his daughter—his daughter who was emotionally deteriorating in front of their eyes. "It's true," Rachel keened. "I knew he was cheating on me. Texting at random times. Not responding at weird times of the day. Not being at home, or with his brother when he said he would be." She sniffled. "And he *laughed* at me when I confronted him." She looked to Fenway. "Cheating with some teenager's mother? Like a forty-year-old?"

Fenway shrugged.

Rachel's brow crinkled. "But why wouldn't he say he was with her when I left the interrogation? Unless there was a reason he couldn't say anything." She looked Fenway in the eyes. "You know, don't you, Fenway?" she asked. "You know, and you're not telling me."

Fenway hesitated and looked down. "You've been through a lot this week."

"You need to tell me."

Fenway looked into Rachel's pleading eyes. "It's McVie's wife."

Rachel drew her breath in sharply. "Amy?"

Fenway nodded.

"Oh." She folded her hands over her heart and tightly shut her eyes. "Ouch. Oh."

"I'm sorry," Fenway said to Rachel, but she had one eye on the front of the sanctuary. The couple was getting more agitated, and the reverend looked stressed.

"Dylan and I went over to their house for New Year's. Amy served me hors d'oeuvres. I had too much champagne."

"Dylan really wasn't sleeping with the daughter?" Stotsky asked, incredulous.

Fenway shook her head. Stotsky went quiet again.

There was a bang at the front of the church.

"YOU!"

The man who had been sitting on the other side of Walker's widow had just slammed a hymnal onto the wooden pew. He looked a bit like Walker—same nose, same browline. His jaw was a little different, and his face was a little pinkish, where Walker had been ruddy.

He started up the aisle, looking directly at Rachel. Nathaniel Ferris took notice and stood up, but he looked unsure what to do.

"What right do you have to come in here and ruin this—don't *touch* me, Martha," he snapped at the horrified-looking woman next to him "—ruin this service? Do you feel *better* about yourself now?" He pointed at Rachel. "You think you can accuse a man like that and get away with it? I will sue you for every last penny you have."

"Doug, stop it," hissed Martha.

"I'm not going to let anyone ruin Harry's reputation," Doug called back to her, not taking his eyes off Rachel.

"Don't listen to him," Fenway whispered to Rachel. "You made no accusation. You just showed a tape. He can't sue you for anything. You didn't do anything wrong." She wasn't actually sure Rachel couldn't be sued, but she thought she should keep Rachel calm, and get them both out of there—hopefully with her dad in tow. "In fact, why don't we all leave the building?"

But Doug was incensed. "What are you two talking about? You talking about how you can steal money from the estate?"

Rob Stotsky stood up, his huge frame towering over the pew. "I think you're going to want to stop right there."

"Mind your own business," Doug said. "I'm talking to this bitch who thinks she can lie about my brother and get away with it."

Stotsky cracked his knuckles.

"Gentlemen." Fenway stepped next to Stotsky. "Don't fight. If you fight, I'm going to have to arrest you."

"Bullshit," Doug spat. "What are you, a teenager? I don't see a badge or gun." He motioned to Rachel. "You're trying to help this bitch steal my brother's money. You better get out of my way unless you want to get hurt too."

"Do *not* threaten my daughter," Stotsky said, in a menacing voice. He leaned forward, his massive frame blocking most of the aisle.

"Fighting in church is totally in bad taste anyway," Fenway said. "No one wants—"

And just as Fenway was hoping, Doug threw a punch.

Stotsky saw it coming and stepped back—Doug's fist missed Stotsky's jaw by a mile. Fenway was still standing next to Stotsky, though, and Doug's fist landed a glancing blow on her shoulder. It still hurt, and would likely bruise, but it wasn't bad.

Before Doug could take a step back, Fenway drove her left hand up under his chin and pushed forward with her whole body. Doug's punch had thrown his center of gravity off, so when Fenway drove forward, he twisted and fell awkwardly. She kept her hand on his chin and went down on top of him. Her knee was in his ribs when they hit the ground. Doug let out a painful wheeze.

"You assaulted a peace officer. Shall we go down to the station to sort this all out?" Fenway noticed how hard her heart was pounding. She looked up. Her father, the reverend, the woman who had been with Walker's widow, and the woman called Martha were all standing in the aisle about twenty feet away. Their eyes were big, like they couldn't believe what they saw.

"Rachel," Fenway said, "would you be a dear and go get Dez?"

"Um, sure." She went out the sanctuary doors.

"I'm going to sue you," Doug squeaked.

"I apologize for this happening in your church, Reverend," Fenway said, looking up at him. "It couldn't be helped."

Dez came in with Rachel following her. Fenway rolled Doug onto his stomach.

"This is starting to become a habit with you, Coroner." Dez took out her handcuffs. "Did this one have a gun too?"

"Just fists."

"I wasn't trying to hit *you*," Doug complained with a face full of floor. "I was trying to hit the big guy."

"He called Rachel a few names," she explained to Dez. "Mr. Stotsky didn't much care for it."

"You arresting him?"

Fenway looked from the man beneath her to Dez. "Yes. He punched me."

Fenway pushed herself up a bit so Dez could pull Doug's hands behind his back. "Keep this up," Dez deadpanned, snapping the cuffs on Doug, "and you're going to need to carry your own pair. All right, sir, what's your name?"

"I don't have to answer that."

"Suit yourself. We'll have to enter you as John Doe in the system. It'll take an extra day or two to process you that way, but I guess that's okay if you don't mind being a guest of the county."

"I think his name is Doug," Fenway said. "He said Harrison Walker was his brother."

Dez ignored her. "John Doe, you are under arrest for assault on a peace officer."

"I didn't know she was a peace officer."

Fenway looked at Dez. "I told him I could arrest him. He didn't believe me."

"We can sort this all out at the station." Dez helped Doug to his feet. "I'm going to call for a squad car. I can't take him into custody in my Impala. People who have just been arrested tend not to treat the back seat with the utmost care." She got on her radio to contact dispatch, and led Walker's brother out of the sanctuary.

Nathaniel Ferris looked at them leaving, then looked at Fenway. "I'll be right back." He followed them out.

Rachel watched all of them go. "Uh, thanks, Fenway. That was pretty bad-ass. Did you do the same kind of thing with Lana?"

Fenway nodded. "Well, Lana had a gun, but yeah."

Stotsky cleared his throat. "Rachel, you and I need to talk."

"Sorry, Dad. I'm not ready to talk to you right now."

Fenway looked at Rachel and her father. "Both of you need to give your witness statements to this little event. You can come down to the sheriff's office, give your statements, and then go talk, or not, as you see fit. And Rachel, you're on paid leave for two weeks. More if you need it. Go talk to a psychologist, or go sit on a beach, or something. After you give your statement tonight, I don't want to see you at the office."

Rachel shook her head. "I don't have the vacation time."

"After what happened to you at the office on Friday? On company time? I don't think it'll be a problem."

"Do I need to come down and give a statement too?" asked Stotsky. He had an annoyed look on his face.

"Absolutely."

He shook his head. "I've got to get Mr. Ferris home."

"I think my father can find his own way. If you want, you can even ride with me in Dez's Impala, although you have to promise not to mess up the back seat."

Ferris came back into the sanctuary and walked up to them. "They took Doug Walker out in handcuffs. This is a disaster. Doug is a lobbyist in Sacramento—this is awful for my business."

Fenway blinked at him. "You saw him punch me, Dad."

Ferris stopped. "I know he hit you, Fenway, but you *know* he was trying to hit Rob. And it barely touched you. You know emotions run high at these things. Why do that to a grieving relative? Really, Fenway? Handcuffs?"

"Thanks for your concern, Dad. I'll be fine." Fenway rubbed her shoulder. "Listen, Rob and Rachel both saw the guy hit me. We need to take their statements down at the sheriff's office. How about if Dez drives the four of us, and you meet us down there later tonight? I know you came with Rob—you okay going down there together and meeting us?"

"I saw the punch too," Ferris said. "Shouldn't I give my statement?"

Fenway couldn't see a way around it. "Sure, the more witnesses the better," she said.

Her father looked at his watch. "I've got to drop some paperwork off at the clerk's office, so I'm going that way anyway. What's it going to take, fifteen minutes?"

"I'm not sure I need to go, boss," Stotsky said.

"Don't be silly. We'll go in my car. We'll give our statements, we'll go get a steak dinner, we'll head back. You'll be home by eight."

"Rachel." Stotsky pulled her aside. "I really would like to talk with you."

She shook him off. "Dad, I know you didn't like Dylan, but have some respect. You were calling him a pedophile a few minutes ago."

"He *hurt* you." Stotsky raised his huge hand in front of his face and slowly made a fist. He stared at his fist for a minute, as if considering it for the first time. "He cheated on you, Rachel, maybe not with a teenaged girl, but he cheated on you. How am I *supposed* to act?"

Ferris walked over to Stotsky and put a hand on his shoulder. "Come on, Rob. We'll go drop off some paperwork with the county clerk—he told me he'd stay late—and then meet Fenway over at the sheriff's office."

Stotsky paused. "Okay."

They walked out into the foyer. Through the glass of the floor-to-ceiling front windows, they could see a police cruiser outside with its lights flashing, and Dez putting Doug Walker into the back of the squad car.

"The clerk's office shouldn't take us too long," Nathaniel Ferris said to Fenway, "so I think we'll be able to meet you by six thirty."

Fenway wanted to suggest that her father drop Stotsky off first, but she didn't want either of them to get suspicious. "Six thirty should be fine, Dad."

Ferris and Stotsky continued their walk toward the front door. Ferris nodded at Rachel. "You coming, too?"

Rachel looked at Fenway. "No, thanks. I'll catch a ride back with Fenway."

Ferris looked at Stotsky and nodded. "Okay. See you at the station."

Rachel and Fenway watched them walk out. The glass door swung shut behind them, and they turned right on the sidewalk towards the waiting limo. Then it was just the two of them, Rachel and Fenway, in the foyer.

"You're probably mad at me, Fenway."

Fenway gave her a sad smile. "No. No, I'm not. I can't imagine going through what you've gone through this past week. I have no idea how I would have handled it."

Rachel nodded and looked out the window as Dez slapped the top of the roof twice with her open hand and the cruiser pulled away.

"Actually." Fenway cleared her throat. "Actually, that's not true. I do know what I would do. Because I was in your situation once."

"What?"

"I was in college. He was my Russian Lit professor. He cornered me in his office and—" Fenway shook her head and looked down. "And I didn't say anything about it to anyone. I didn't tell my mom, or any of my friends. I didn't report it. I didn't think anyone would believe me. Or if they did, I thought they'd take his side." She took a deep breath. "But you didn't hide, Rachel. You didn't give in when Lana wouldn't do anything the first time. You recorded it. You kicked him in the knee and scratched his face, and you got away."

"I was lucky. He could have really hurt me."

Fenway nodded. "Yes, I guess you were lucky. But you also weren't ashamed. You copied that video onto a *hundred* USB sticks, and you got the projectionist to play the video at his memorial service so no one left here—no one left Harrison Walker's *own* memorial service—thinking he was anything but a rapist. I kind of envy you, Rachel. I wish I had had your mindset after it happened to me." Fenway looked up at the ceiling, above the second-floor hallway. Several long, pendulous rods came down from the ceiling, ending in a single ornamental silver light fixture. The light flared from the top and scattered itself throughout the foyer. "You were embarrassed when you told me a few nights ago. I was the first person you told, and you didn't know why." Fenway took a few steps back and leaned against the wall. "But I know why. Because you knew, deep inside, I was like you."

Fenway paused. "And, also, you're the first person *I've* told."

Rachel walked across the room and leaned up against the wall next to Fenway. "You said I wasn't ashamed, but I *was* ashamed. I still am." Tears welled in her eyes, but she fought them back. "But I did it anyway."

Dez pulled the door open. "Hey, everyone. Party at the sheriff's office. I'm driving."

CHAPTER TWENTY-FOUR

DEZ HAD PARKED A FEW BLOCKS AWAY, AND AFTER MAKING FUN OF Fenway's impractical heels yet again, the three of them got into the car and headed to the sheriff's office. They briefly discussed the idea of picking up some dinner, but they weren't hungry. And, more than anything, Fenway wanted to get Stotsky in front of Bradley to see if her hunch was right.

"It will be a little weird being in that interview room again," Rachel said.

Fenway shrugged. "It'll be over soon enough. And remember, after this, two weeks off. Take care of yourself."

The ride was quiet back to downtown, and they pulled into the parking garage about six fifteen.

"Okay, we're meeting your dad over at the sheriff's office in fifteen minutes." Fenway got out of the Impala. "Come into the office so I can finish up some paperwork before we head over there."

Migs and Piper were in the office when they arrived. Piper was sitting on the desk facing Migs, who was sitting in his office chair. Her long legs were dangling in front of him. They were both laughing.

Rachel raised her hand in greeting. "Hey Migs, hey Piper."

Migs looked at Dez. "I thought you were going to drive me to the service."

"Doesn't look like you're too sad about missing it."

Piper looked a little flustered; she dropped her smile and her ears turned a little red.

"Well," Migs asked Fenway, "do you have time to look at Walker's electronic files?"

Fenway thought for a moment. She was hoping she could connect more dots to Stotsky. "Do they say anything different than the files we've already looked at?"

Migs nodded. "It looks like Walker typed up all his handwritten notes into these computer files. We've been looking at all the files taken that night, and the handwritten notes match—not perfectly, because maybe he mistyped something, or in some cases a word or phrase is different. If there was a photo in the file, he typed up a short description of it, usually with an identification number. But content-wise, they're all consistent—nothing was changed that significantly altered the meaning of anything." Migs paused for dramatic effect, a little smirk on his face.

Then he dropped a file on the desk. "Except this one."

It was the Ferris Energy file.

Fenway shot Dez a look—hoping she'd get the message to look for evidence Stotsky tampered with the file. Dez folded her arms and nodded.

"All right, let's see the computer file, Migs." Fenway scooted around behind him and crouched a bit so she could see his screen. He clicked on an open window, and then launched the file. Dez came around to see the screen, and Rachel pulled a chair over for Piper.

"There are three sets of notes in the file." Piper pointed to the first set of notes on the screen. "So, there's one on Fairweather; this one matches pretty well—personal life stuff, a couple of typos in the computer version, but nothing significantly different."

Fenway didn't think Rachel should be in the room if her father's name showed up, but she couldn't think of how to get her out of the room without arousing her suspicion.

"This next one is a set of notes on Carl Cassidy," Piper continued. "This one is almost completely different. It's similar to the content of the Fairweather notes. A section on work history, a section on personal matters, a section on toxicology, notes on his criminal record—you see he had a drunk and disorderly about twenty years ago. And some notes on finances. But nothing on his employee assistance program. Nothing on any affair—not a single statement from any private investigator, not a single mention of a photo, not a single mention of Dylan. And Lana is mentioned as the spouse, in the list here from Carl's personal life, and her name pops up on a couple of financial accounts."

Dez patted Fenway on the shoulder. "Looks like you were right, Prom Queen. That note *was* forged."

Piper turned and looked at Dez. "Not just that one."

"What?" Fenway asked. "Not just Carl's?"

Migs shook his head. "Nope, not just Carl's."

Piper turned back to the screen. "In the last note, the hard copy in the physical folder didn't have a lot to say. Mostly, it said the company wasn't at fault. But Walker's notes *don't* say that. It says the fume ventilation system controls looked worn. And see this paragraph right here?"

Room in which decedents were found appears to be a hallway employees often used as a shortcut between work areas. A secured, air-sealed tank is about 30 meters away, and the gases vent into it, where they are treated with chemicals to break their toxicity. The venting was performed when people were in the hallway next to the ventilation duct, which is a breach of procedure, and the ventilation duct appears to have ruptured, flooding the hallway with toxic fumes. Ferris Energy appears to have been negligent in both its safety training, and maintenance, directly resulting in the death of both men.

Dez shook her head. "No wonder Lana was so ticked off at you, Fenway. I bet she thought you were going to cover this all up."

"You don't need to be a handwriting expert to see these notes are forged. Taking a quick look at these files, it looks to me like all of the notes in the Ferris Energy file were written by the same person, in a fairly decent, but detectable, imitation of Walker's handwriting." She pulled out the three handwritten pages and put them down on the desk side by side.

Rachel came over and looked over Piper's shoulder.

"Do we have any idea who forged them?" Fenway asked Piper.

"I haven't found anything yet."

Migs broke in. "But we might know soon enough anyway—I heard from the M.E." He picked up a file folder off his desk and looked through it. "Whoever filed the numbers off the gun that killed Walker did a pretty bad job. So far, they were able to raise every number but two with an acid treatment, and they think the other two might be visible if they leave the acid on overnight. They'll let us know tomorrow morning."

Fenway wracked her brain trying to remember where Stotsky had worked before becoming Ferris Energy's head of security. She thought she remembered Rachel saying it was the CHP. She bit her tongue—she wanted Rachel to confirm it, but couldn't risk it before Bradley met Stotsky.

Piper sat back in her chair. "And whoever murdered Walker wasn't aware the computer files would contradict the fake files. That, or they were hoping no one would find Walker's laptop."

"So, wait." Migs pointed to the paragraph in Walker's note reading *Ferris Energy appears to have been negligent in both its safety training, and maintenance.* "Is the 'conclusion' Walker was talking about in the other email? Ferris Energy was negligent?" He clicked through a few windows until he found what he was looking for. "Here's the email. 'I'm not negotiating. Higher than discussed originally but your requested changes give me higher risk. You can say no but we both know what a pain in the ass the investigators can be if they see the conclusions in there now.'"

"That makes sense." Fenway was now sure her father's company *was* involved—but was it Stotsky acting on his own? "The conclusion is that Ferris Energy is at fault for the accident—and the deaths of Cassidy and Fairweather—and that opens them up for all kinds of liability."

Dez leaned on the desk. "So, it makes sense that the person who messed with the files was from Ferris Energy, or hired by them. And it's likely the person who crashed Dylan's truck through the building was *also* someone from Ferris Energy, possibly the same someone. Not Dylan. Not Mc—" She stopped and glanced at Fenway. "Not anybody else."

Migs turned to Rachel. "But then why did someone from Ferris Energy put spyware on your computer? That doesn't make sense."

"What?" Rachel looked confused.

"Oh, right, you weren't here." Piper started to draw the connections on a blank piece of paper in front of her. "Okay, so Walker was emailing his killer, and, based on the email headers, it's the same person who installed spyware on your PC. And if someone from Ferris Energy swapped out the 'conclusions' in those files, it seems like Ferris Energy is involved in your spyware."

Migs interrupted. "But I don't get it. Why Rachel's computer? Why not put the spyware on Walker's machine? Why'd they pick Rachel, if they were planning on killing Walker?"

Dez glanced at Fenway and set her jaw.

Fenway looked at the clock on the wall. "All right, everyone. It's almost six thirty, and we need to meet Rachel's dad at the sheriff's office. We should check whether Bradley has identified who hired him in those mugshot binders. I have a feeling when we find who hired Bradley, this whole thing will fall into place."

"Excellent work, Piper." Dez walked back over to her desk. "Migs, thanks for bringing this to our attention."

Rachel, Dez, and Fenway were out the door and across the street minutes later.

———

Once the three of them were inside the sheriff's office, they went to the door of the interview room. It was still occupied, however; Bradley Watermeier was still going through the photos.

Dez and Fenway went into the observation room to see how much longer he would be. Rachel waited outside.

Bradley had obviously been at it for hours since they last saw him, and he looked exhausted. Callahan was sitting with Bradley, who had a stack of three binders on each side of him, and was going through a seventh binder in the middle.

"Looks like he's about half done," Fenway said.

"Look at you with the big brain, Prom Queen."

"All right, Dez." Fenway lowered her voice. "We need to get Bradley to get a look at Stotsky."

"Do you think Stotsky hired Bradley to put the RAT software on Rachel's computer?"

"Yes, I do. But we don't have enough evidence on Stotsky yet. I thought maybe there would be something in the file. And there's a lot in there that fits—but no direct evidence."

"That gun might be his. We might know tomorrow."

"I think he's starting to get suspicious. He could be in Mexico tomorrow. If Bradley identifies him, don't we have enough to hold him?"

"Probably," Dez nodded. "Okay. I can figure something out."

They stepped out of the observation room where Rachel was waiting.

Ferris and Stotsky came around the corner. Ferris gave Fenway a sideways hug. "Hi, sweetie. Are we going in the interview room again?"

"No, it's—" Fenway started.

"Yes," Dez interrupted. "I think the interview room is free."

Dez opened the interview room door. Bradley and Callahan were sitting at the table. Bradley's head turned—and he saw Stotsky standing behind Dez.

Stotsky looked back at Bradley.

"What the hell, Callahan?" Bradley shouted. "Did you set me up?"

Fenway moved behind Stotsky. "It was you."

In one quick, fluid motion, Stotsky turned and shoved Fenway aside. She tried to keep her balance but slammed against the wall and fell to the floor. Stotsky sprinted out of the room, heading for the front door. He was surprisingly fast.

Fenway was stunned, but managed to squeak out, "Stop him!" but her voice was too quiet. The officer at the front desk didn't look up. Stotsky was hurrying past him.

Dez jumped over Fenway and ran after Stotsky.

"Stop him!" Fenway yelled, finding her voice and getting to her feet. Stotsky was already out the door. Dez followed, but she was already several seconds behind.

"Go after him!" she yelled at the officer.

The officer stood up a little awkwardly, hand on his belt, rushed around the desk, and ran out the door after him.

Rachel's eyes were wide. "What just happened?"

"It was your dad, Rachel. Your dad is the one who hired Bradley. But not to spy on Walker—to spy on *you*."

"That's your *dad?*" Bradley said to Rachel, aghast. "He was using the spyware on *you?*" He stood up and walked out of the interview room. Callahan followed.

Rachel reached for a nearby chair and sat down. "Oh my God."

Fenway sat down next to Rachel. "He wasn't looking at that video for the first time at the memorial service," Fenway said, as gently as she could. "He had already seen it. He saw it the night it happened."

Rachel put her head in her hands. "It wasn't Dylan who saw the video and killed Mr. Walker to protect me. It was my dad."

Fenway turned to her father, who was standing stock-still, looking horrified. "Okay, Dad. Where did Stotsky go?"

"I—I don't know."

Fenway closed her eyes and took a deep breath. "You *do* know, Dad. You know where Stotsky would go if he were in trouble. And he's in trouble now. He's your head of security. Would he go to your office? Would he go home, grab as much stuff as he could, and then take off?"

Ferris shook his head.

Callahan had a confused look on his face. "What are you talking about?"

"That guy—Rachel's dad—was the one who hired me," Bradley said. "He hired me to put spyware on her computer."

"Why in the world would he do that?"

"Because he thinks I'm still a baby," Rachel snapped. "And he thinks I can't take care of myself. He wouldn't let me go to Princeton, he didn't want me to study a semester abroad, and as soon as I graduated, he set up a bunch of interviews in Estancia so I'd stay close to home. He wanted me to be an assistant manager in the apartment building you live in, Fenway. With a political science degree!"

Nathaniel Ferris turned to Rachel, and his eyes were soft. "He loves you. He's worried, probably more than he should be, sure, but his heart's always been in the right place."

Fenway felt nauseated. "Dad, we traced the spyware on Rachel's computer. And we traced an email setting up the time and place Walker was killed. They came from the exact same source—Rob Stotsky."

Ferris shuffled his feet. "You're not saying Rob killed Harrison Walker, are you?"

She looked up at her father and nodded. "Yes, Dad. That is exactly what I'm saying."

"No. No, no. Fenway, that can't be true. I've known the guy for years. He's no murderer."

"Come in here with me," Fenway demanded, grabbing her father's wrist and pulling him into the interview room, slamming the door behind her. She looked at her father. He looked a little surprised at her force-fulness.

She gritted her teeth. "You're telling me, Dad, this man, who was so overprotective of his adult daughter that he hired someone to *install spyware* on her work computer, saw Harrison Walker try to rape his daughter and *wouldn't* shoot him in the back the first chance he got?"

Ferris was silent.

"With a firearm *specifically* issued to the CHP. You hired him right out of the CHP, didn't you, Dad?"

He was still quiet.

"Has he had any questionable large expenses recently?"

"Well," Ferris said, rubbing the back of his neck, "there was a ten-thousand-dollar purchase order for security services two weeks ago. And last week Rob amended it to twenty-five thousand dollars. But he has big expenses all the time for security equipment and monitoring. I didn't think anything of it."

"Do you know where Stotsky was Sunday night?"

Her father stopped and pressed his lips together. "He and I were going to have dinner and discuss some work stuff. He told me he had some business with the apartments he had to take care of, and he begged off till later in the week."

Fenway nodded, seeing the wires in her father's brain finally connect-ing. "And instead, he was getting revenge on his daughter's rapist."

"Stop using that word, Fenway. That's an ugly word."

"I don't care if it's an 'ugly word,' Dad!" Fenway yelled. "I saw that footage and *I* wanted to shoot Harrison Walker in the back. And I barely know Rachel."

Ferris went quiet again.

"Okay, listen, Dad." She sighed. "Help me find him. Seriously, if you get a couple of overprotective parents on the jury, Stotsky might not serve a day in prison. Not for the murder, anyway."

"What do you mean? Is there something else?"

"I don't know, probably an obstruction of justice charge." She put her hands on her hips. "Because *someone* replaced Walker's original file—the original file said Ferris Energy was at fault for the accident that killed Carl Cassidy and Lewis Fairweather—with falsified documents. The falsified documents said Carl Cassidy's wife was having sex with Dylan Richards—trying to shift blame off your company for the accident."

"I don't know anything about that."

"We don't have anything *directly* implicating you, Dad. And our evidence that someone from your company did it is mostly circumstantial." She tapped him on the chest. "But when we get a warrant for Rob Stotsky's computer, we should be able to prove *he's* the one who sent the email to Walker discussing a bribe. *He's* the one who sent instructions to Walker on where to meet him Sunday night—the same spot where we found Walker's body. We're going to have the Ferris Energy head of security dead to rights." She gave him a pointed look. "And that might be far worse for your company than a Sacramento lobbyist who has to spend the night in jail for punching a peace officer."

Ferris suddenly got angry. "Goddammit, Fenway, this is *not* what I had in mind when I suggested Craig appoint you! You weren't supposed to rock the boat!"

Fenway got in her father's face and yelled back. "Did you think Stotsky covered his tracks so well none of the investigators here would find anything? Or maybe you think I'm too stupid to do this job competently!"

"No, no," he sputtered, "no, Fenway, that's not what I meant to say."

"Listen, Dad, it was *your* head of security who bribed one of *our* employees to put malware on Rachel's computer."

"If you think you can take that trust-fund kid's word over—"

"Dad! It's not up for discussion. Bradley identified Stotsky. Stotsky ran. I don't care what we can prove in court. I know it, you know it. And

I'm telling you, daughter to father, this looks really bad for your company, and it looks really bad for *you*."

Ferris set his jaw but didn't say anything.

"Stotsky bribed Bradley. Stotsky was illegally spying on one of our employees. And your buddy—Harrison Walker—sexually assaulted Stotsky's daughter in our office. This whole situation was set in motion by the people *you* hired, people *you* put in power."

"Harrison's not my buddy."

"You bankrolled his first campaign for coroner, so it's not like you just wave hello at the grocery store." Fenway folded her arms. "And, by the way, *your* head of security was trying to bribe Walker to change the findings in the file so Ferris Energy wouldn't be held responsible. If your political enemies find that out, they'll make it look like *you knew*. I bet Barry Klein would take out a full-page ad in every newspaper in California." She put her hands on the table. "In fact, not only would he make it look like you knew, he'll make it look like you planned the whole thing. He'll say your refinery is unsafe. He'll say you can't pass safety inspections. He'll say you killed two employees and tried to cover it up. And you will lose *everything*."

"I didn't know." Nathaniel Ferris's voice was quiet. "I didn't know about any of this."

"Are you sure?" Fenway leaned on the table and looked in his eyes. "Are you sure you didn't know about *any* of this?"

He stared at her, then broke her gaze and looked down.

"I knew the accident was probably due to our negligence," he admitted. "Our internal people said as much. And we reached out to the families to try to make it right, but the Cassidys wouldn't take our offer. They already had a lawyer involved. I asked some people on my staff to come up with solutions."

"Was Rob Stotsky one of those people?"

"I never told anyone to break the law."

She nodded. "And bribing Harrison Walker?"

"I didn't know about that. I didn't have anything to do with it."

"You turned a blind eye to twenty-five thousand dollars for unspecified security expenses."

"I trust the guy, Fenway."

"And breaking through the wall to steal the files in Walker's office?"

He hesitated.

"Okay, Fenway, I'm not proud of it. A couple of weeks ago, Rob and I were at the steakhouse. We were moaning about the fact that this file wasn't going to be good for us, and that the Cassidys could use it if they decided to sue us, which I think they would, and they might be successful with this information." He sighed. "I might have mentioned it would be great if someone broke down the wall and took the file. But it wasn't serious; I think I made a joke about the Kool-Aid man."

"Did you joke about anything else? Like shooting Walker, or killing Rachel's husband in his cell? Because, as coroner, the dead bodies are really what I'm most concerned about."

"No!" He lifted his head, defiant. "I had no idea!"

She nodded. "Okay, Dad. This might still be a salvageable situation for you and your precious energy company."

"Don't say it like that, Fenway."

She ignored him and pressed on. "If the story is that an overprotective father went blind with rage at his daughter's attacker and murdered him, that's a story that a lot of people can relate to. If it comes across powerfully enough in the media, you might be able to avoid the firestorm. Even if someone says, 'What about the accident? What about the files?' that's more boring. People in the media have the attention spans of goldfish. They'll glom onto the daddy-gets-revenge story."

He was quiet.

"But it's not *just* Walker. You've got one more dead body to deal with. And so does Stotsky. If it were just Walker, I could see the right jury finding him not guilty. But he killed Rachel's husband too, and even if a jury lets him off for the Walker murder, there's no way they're going to let him off for killing the guy he was trying to pin the Walker murder on."

"I don't know anything about him killing Rachel's husband."

"Stotsky knew how to bribe Bradley Watermeier. I bet he knew how to bribe one of the guards at the jail too," she said. "You know what I mean. Someone to let Stotsky go in for a few minutes to 'talk to him.' The M.E. says Dylan was killed by a really strong guy; they were thinking the sheriff could have done it. Bribing the guard probably cost a lot less than the twenty-five thousand dollars Walker was asking for to swap notes in the refinery accident file."

"I never—" Ferris started, and then stopped.

"You never *what?* You never authorized twenty-five grand as a payout? You never knew Walker had upped his price?" Fenway put her hands on her hips. "You want to rethink your answer on 'non-specific security expenses'?"

Her father wouldn't look at her.

"Dad, it's tough to say you're not in this up to your eyeballs. I've heard how powerful you are in this county, and how everyone kisses your ass around here. *I* may think you never crossed the line from bribery and negligence into murder, but, boy, your reputation is going to take a big hit."

He pursed his lips and put a hand over his eyes.

"I guess we can see how this goes," she continued, "but the faster we find Stotsky, the better."

"I *know* how this goes, Fenway. Barry Klein will talk to the D.A. and insist on giving Stotsky a deal to roll over on me. And, quite frankly, it won't matter if I've crossed the line into bribery or murder—or even *jaywalking*. There are people in this county who want to see me taken down. They'll say whatever they can to get me out of power."

"Oh, come on, Dad, you'd be able to get out of that. You must have good lawyers," she said.

"Not good enough for the court of public opinion. Listen, there are lines I've crossed, I'm sure. I'm a ruthless negotiator. I definitely don't want Carl Cassidy in the news, and I'm willing to pay his family a lot of money to keep it out of the media. Do I feel bad about what happened to Cassidy and Fairweather? Absolutely. Do I think I deserve to be out of business because of it? I do not." He slammed his hand down on the desk. "So, am I going to help you locate Stotsky? I don't think so. In fact, I hope he makes it out of the country before you catch him."

Nathaniel Ferris straightened his suit jacket. "Now, it's getting late. I'm getting hungry. And I think I have more important things to do than give my statement on a grieving brother who got a little too emotional at a funeral. I'm heading home."

He stomped out of the interview room. Fenway started to follow him, but he slammed the door after he walked out.

CHAPTER TWENTY-FIVE

FENWAY TOOK A DEEP BREATH AND OPENED THE DOOR. HER FATHER'S figure was disappearing down the hallway and out the front door. She stood there and watched him walk away angrily.

"Is he gone?"

She jumped. Dez had poked her head out of the observation room door.

"Sorry. We heard everything."

"We?" Fenway asked.

"Mark's in there, too. He was observing Bradley during the binder review."

"Where's Rachel?"

"We sent her home," Dez answered. "On top of everything she's been through this week, she just found out her dad is a murderer."

"We've got to get someone to stay with her. I'd be a complete mess if I were her."

"Her sister is still staying with her."

"She didn't do a good job keeping her out of trouble last time."

Dez shrugged.

The door to the observation room opened wider and Mark stepped out.

"Did Rachel give her statement before you guys sent her home?" Fenway asked.

"No," Mark replied. "She was pretty distraught about everything."

"Then I guess today is Doug Walker's lucky day. No one gave a witness statement, and the peace officer in question is too busy with a murder investigation to hold him."

Dez crossed her arms. "We could probably hold him for twenty-four hours. Bet he's never been in jail overnight before."

"The guy's just lost his brother, and now everyone knows his brother's a rapist." Fenway put her hands on her hips. "Maybe he's been through enough."

"Good thing you're not running in November, or you'd get pegged as soft on crime," Mark smirked.

"Ha ha. All right—so where are we on catching Stotsky? Was that officer able to catch him?"

Dez shook her head. "The officer didn't see him. He got away."

Fenway shook her head. "Maybe put an APB on his car? Airports, train stations, get someone at his house?"

"Already done." Mark nodded. "I'll go see if they've made any progress." Mark took off toward dispatch.

Dez pulled Fenway aside. "Maybe you should call McVie. Tell him he's off the hook. He's good at coordinating this kind of stuff. He's been involved in manhunts before."

Fenway nodded. Dez went out the front doors back toward the coroner's building.

Fenway took her purse off the chair and took her cell phone out. She went through *Recent Calls* until she found McVie's number.

It rang once, twice, three times, four times. The voicemail came on. She hung up.

Fenway texted him.

Stotsky killed Walker and Dylan
He's on the run
Need u to help find him

She saw the three dots flashing for a second, indicating he was writing a response. And then they disappeared.

Fenway thought about some of the things she had told the sheriff earlier. In hindsight, she didn't think she liked some of the things she had said. In fact, she wasn't proud of the way she had *acted*, either.

But Fenway realized some of those things—asking McVie to step down from the investigation—was simply the best thing for the county. It was a hard thing to do, and it certainly didn't help her relationship with the sheriff, professionally or romantically, but the situation could have been handled with a little more empathy on her side. She looked back at how she had jumped down McVie's throat when he mentioned anything she felt even a little threatened by. But did that mean she deserved the cold shoulder from McVie? No.

Well, maybe.

She sent another text.

Please

It took a minute, but the three little dots appeared again. Then:

Station in 30 minutes

Fenway had been holding her breath, and she let out a huge exhale. The sheriff would be back in half an hour and would be coordinating the manhunt for Rob Stotsky.

She went into the dispatch room. Mark was still there.

"Hi, Sergeant. Did a uniform take Rachel home?"

He blinked at her. "Yes, I think so."

"Did the uniform stay with her? Stotsky was asking her several times to talk and she refused. If he thinks this is his last chance to talk with her, he may try to contact her."

One of the dispatchers raised her hand. "On it."

"And we've already notified the local airports." Mark put his hands on his hips. "But Stotsky has resources, right? He has access to a couple of private planes."

"Ferris Energy planes?"

"Yes."

"Okay, where are those planes? Local airstrip?"

"They've got a Challenger 350 housed at the Estancia Airport," another dispatcher said. "I think they have a turboprop, too."

Fenway shook her head. "I remember when Dad bought that stupid jet," she said. "Can you check and see if they've filed a flight plan?"

"Sure. I can check the computer."

Fenway paused. "If they were trying to get Stotsky across the Mexican border, they wouldn't file a flight plan, would they?"

The dispatcher hesitated. "If they were crossing an international border, technically, they'd have to."

"They'd have to? What if they didn't?"

He paused. "Um, it's a fine of about a thousand dollars."

Mark laughed. "That will sure put the fear of God into them."

Fenway nodded. "We need people at the airports, bus stations, train stations."

"The rideshare apps, too," said Mark. "I think we're setting up a watch on his credit card transactions and ATM withdrawals."

"There's always the taxis," Fenway suggested. "He could give a cab driver a thousand bucks to go to Tijuana. Or even a regular person with a regular car who needs the cash."

"Let's at least not make it easy for him," Mark said. "If he gets by us, let's make sure he doesn't do it by boarding a Greyhound bus, or a United flight. If he's in the wind, so be it, but let's make sure it's not because we overlooked anything."

The dispatchers got on their phones and computers. Soon, they were giving his information to all the local airports, including the small airfields. His information—and he had a lot of it—was readily available in his old CHP file.

"There were a couple of partials in Walker's car," Mark said. "We would have found him out eventually. Maybe not today, but eventually."

Fenway nodded. "Okay. Have we posted someone at Stotsky's house?"

"On their way. He lives up in the hills above Camino Pablo. It'll take our officer another ten minutes to get there, at least. But even if Stotsky got in a car as soon as he left the station, I think the officer would still beat him there."

"You think he'd be prepared enough for this to have a go bag? Money, fake passport, all the stuff you see in CIA movies?"

Mark shook his head. "The CHP isn't the CIA. I mean, maybe he was smart enough to know he might not get away with it, so he might have had something set up, I guess, but I think most people overestimate their own ability to fool the police."

"And there's an officer with Rachel?"

"Yes," the first dispatcher said from behind the sergeant. "I got ahold of him. He just got to her apartment. He's outside her door now."

"Okay." Fenway took a deep breath.

For a few minutes, there was only the sound of the dispatchers on the phone with Amtrak, then the Estancia Municipal Airfield, then Vandevoort Regional Airfield, then the bus station in Estancia, then the one in San Miguelito, then Uber, then Lyft, then some company Fenway had never heard of before ("they're a new SoCal startup," the second dispatcher assured her).

"Dammit," Fenway muttered. "His office. He might have a stash of cash, or a go bag at his office."

Mark looked skeptical. "Stotsky probably wouldn't risk that. He wouldn't be able to get in and out in a hurry there."

"He might not have to. Security might not let us into the building. They all report up to him, don't they? They'd at least delay us as long as possible. We'd probably need warrants, court orders, subpoenas, whatever."

"But Stotsky wouldn't be able to leave."

"He might already have been there and gone," Fenway said. "If that's where he went, Stotsky could still escape and be in Tijuana before the bars close."

"We'll get a couple of deputies there," the first dispatcher said to Fenway, and called out on the radio.

"And I got a flight plan," the second dispatcher said. "It's the Challenger. It's at Estancia, headed to Burbank. Leaves in twenty minutes."

"Let's go." Mark grabbed his sportscoat from the back of the chair, and he was out the door.

"Can I come?" Fenway called after him.

"Hurry."

She kicked off her high heels and picked them up along with her purse, and rushed after Mark. Dispatch was on the radio immediately asking all available units to respond.

She followed Mark out to the squad car area. The sun had set, and the sky was rapidly darkening.

He slid into the front seat of a cruiser. He had already started the car by the time Fenway got in the passenger seat.

"I probably shouldn't have let you come." Mark turned hard, tires squealing, siren wailing as he exited the lot.

"So why did you let me?"

"Because I like you. And you haven't said anything about me being gay."

Fenway paused. "What the hell does that have to do with anything?"

"Exactly." Mark accelerated through a green light. "You don't have a firearm, do you?"

"No."

"Know how to shoot one?"

"Not really," she admitted.

"You should probably learn."

She snorted a laugh. "Yeah, well, I was waiting until my second week."

"You're funny. Especially when you're scared out of your mind."

She hung on as they took a corner at seventy, joining another cruiser with its lights and siren also going full blast. They caught a little bit of air going on the ramp to the freeway, which Fenway thought was thrilling. Mark was a good driver, and when she thought the car might start careening out of control, he was calm, and the tires kept their grip. They passed through traffic without any close calls.

She saw the exit for the airport and braced herself as they crossed three lanes of traffic to get off the freeway. Mark and the other cruiser ran the red light past a few stopped cars, and they headed down the airport road.

Mark pointed out the window. "The private aircraft are housed on the other side of the airport."

"I haven't been here since I was a kid. I don't even remember it."

They passed freight, and the United entrance, and turned into General Aviation. There was a chain-link fence, which the security team had left open for them, and beyond that, the tarmac.

"There should be a bullhorn in the trunk," Mark shouted over the roar of a plane overhead. "When we stop, get out of the car and get down. I'll open the trunk. You stay down and get to the rear of the car. The bullhorn will be in a red and white box in a nook on the right side of the trunk. Get it, and come around the left side, where I'll be waiting. Remember, stay down the whole time."

A white and blue Bombardier Challenger 350 was parked at an

unusual angle, with an airport security SUV blocking its path. Two security officers were crouched down behind the vehicle.

The sergeant screeched the cruiser to a stop. "Now!"

Fenway threw open the door and awkwardly rolled out of the car. She left her shoes and purse inside. Even though night had fallen, the tarmac was still warm on her feet. She crawled around to the back.

She raised the trunk lid with one hand and put her head up to look for the red and white box. It was on the right side, like Mark said. It took her a few tries to get the box open, but she finally undid the catches and took the electronic bullhorn out. She shuttled around the left side, crouching again, and gave him the bullhorn.

"Get back. This side is more exposed. Go behind the trunk and stay down."

Fenway followed his instructions. She shuttled halfway around the left rear fender when he switched the bullhorn on.

Mark's voice boomed across the asphalt of the tarmac. "This is Sergeant Mark Trevino with the Dominguez County Sheriff. Anyone on board the aircraft, come out with your hands on top of your head." She glanced around. Both officers from the other patrol car were kneeling behind the side of the cruiser with guns trained on the airplane, steadying their aim with both hands.

She stole a glance forward and Mark had his gun drawn too, and was also in a crouch behind the car, one hand holding his firearm, and one hand holding the bullhorn.

"Come out with your hands on top of your head," he repeated.

A few seconds later, the door to the plane swung down. The pilot, hands on top of his head, came out. Next was a blonde woman in a crisp skirt and a tank blouse, maybe thirty-five years old.

"Ugh," Fenway mumbled. "Charlotte."

Next—and last—was Nathaniel Ferris.

They all stood on the runway with their hands on top of their heads.

Even from this distance, Fenway could tell her father was unhappy. Charlotte didn't look pleased either.

"Everyone out of the airplane!" Mark's voice rang through the bullhorn.

Ferris yelled a response. Fenway couldn't hear it over the engines.

Mark looked at the other officers and did a few movements with his hand. They ran toward the aircraft and went up the stairs. About three minutes later they returned. "All clear," Mark's radio crackled.

He started walking up to Ferris. Fenway followed, barefoot.

"Robert Stotsky isn't on this plane?" Mark shouted.

"No." Ferris was angry and defiant. "What the hell, Fenway? You knew where we were going. We didn't make any secret about it."

Then it struck her. That's why he had dinner with her last night—which to Fenway seemed like an eternity ago—instead of over the weekend. "Burbank. You and Charlotte are going to the movie premiere this weekend in Hollywood."

Ferris took his hands off his head, pursed his lips, and nodded.

Fenway turned to the officers who had searched the plane. "Guys, this plane has an access door to the luggage area inside, near the bathroom. Did you see if anyone was hiding in there?"

Her father's face scrunched up in anger.

They looked at each other. "No, ma'am. We'll go check that out right now."

"Did you really think I'd fly Stotsky somewhere?" Ferris shook his head in disappointment.

"You told me you wanted him to make it out of the country before we caught him."

"Rooting for someone to escape the law isn't a crime, but being an accessory after the fact is." He set his jaw. "You may not like some of the decisions I make, Fenway, but you know where the line is with me."

"Most of the time."

He laughed, a harsh, sarcastic laugh. "Yes. Most of the time."

Fenway looked at Charlotte and nodded in greeting. "Hi, Charlotte."

Charlotte still had her hands on her head. "I know we don't see each other often, Fenway, but next time, you can just stop by the house for dinner. You don't have to pull us out of our plane with the whole sheriff's department just because you miss your daddy and me."

Fenway tilted her head and smiled sardonically at Charlotte. She hated that Charlotte was only seven years older than she was, and she hated that Charlotte had replaced her mother, and she hated Charlotte's smart-ass comments.

Mark's radio crackled again. "Clear."

He holstered his weapon. "Sorry, folks. You're free to go."

Charlotte took her hands off her head. "Finally."

Nathaniel Ferris looked at Fenway. "If you weren't my daughter, I'd have my lawyers on you like you wouldn't believe." He shook his head. "I'm starting to really regret recommending you." He turned back toward the plane.

The airport security people got back in their cars and drove away. Fenway started walking back to the police cruiser with Mark, the other two headed back to their cars as well.

"Sorry," Mark said. "That's rough, the stuff your dad said."

"I don't know. My father can be kind of hard on me sometimes, but I'd probably be just as pissed off as he was if the situation were reversed." She stopped and looked back at the plane, which was again starting to taxi around. "And you know, even if I *had* remembered they were going to the movie premiere, I'd have still stopped their plane and checked it for Stotsky."

"How'd you know about the luggage compartment?"

"My father bought a ten-million-dollar jet, but didn't pay my mom a cent in alimony or child support. I got a little obsessed with that plane for a while."

Mark nodded.

"Do you think my father suggested I fill in as coroner because he thought I was too naïve, or too incompetent to see when he was doing shady stuff?"

Mark smiled. "I don't spend a lot of time thinking about your father. I hear stuff, sure, but I don't really give a damn about most of it."

"Well, that's probably for the best. Maybe I should do more of that."

They got to the cruiser. Mark put away the bullhorn while Fenway got in the passenger seat. She watched the small jet start to gain speed. It started to rise off the ground, then it was airborne. Its lights flickered in a regular pattern, and it was quickly out of her field of vision.

Her phone rang. She dug it out of her purse.

"Fenway Stevenson," she answered.

"Hi, Fenway, this is Dr. Yasuda."

"Dr. Yasuda, hi." She put her finger in her other ear as Mark got in the car and started it up.

"Listen, I got the message you had a credible suspect before I left for the evening. A former CHP officer named Robert Stotsky. Is that correct?"

Mark turned the car around and headed back to the station.

"That's right. I thought we might have caught him, but he wasn't on the plane we stopped."

"I thought you'd want to know we were able to lift the serial number off the gun. It's a match to the one issued to Robert Stotsky when he was with the California Highway Patrol."

"And he never handed it in?"

"No report on what happened to it." She could hear Dr. Yasuda clicking on her computer. "There are about twenty guns similarly listed as *whereabouts unknown*, although most of those officers are still with the CHP."

"I heard we had some partial prints, too?"

"Yes, from both inside the car and the gun."

"Wasn't the gun wiped clean?" Fenway asked.

"The outside was, but we got partials from whoever cleaned the gun last. And both sets of partials match the fingerprints in Stotsky's file. Not sure how well it would stand up in court."

"I don't know if it will ever come to that. We had a witness identify Stotsky, and Stotsky fled. He might be in the wind. That's why we're at the airport."

"I understand the suspect is a rather large man? His CHP file says six foot, five inches tall," Dr. Yasuda said.

"Yes. Everything seems to be falling into place."

Dr. Yasuda perked up. "Oh, speaking of falling into place, I have something on Dylan Richards."

Fenway felt her shoulders sag. "Ugh."

"Oh, you'll have to forgive my morbid sense of humor. It comes out at the worst times." The doctor stifled a laugh. "So, Richards. You'll remember I told you someone, like Sheriff McVie, could have physically staged the scene with enough adrenaline? Someone with Robert Stotsky's physical size would be more easily able to do it, even without a surge of adrenaline."

"Do we have any evidence that can directly link Stotsky to Dylan's murder?"

"Not as of yet, but we're working on it." She lowered her voice. "And, I must say, I'm relieved Sheriff McVie isn't the main suspect anymore."

Oh no, Fenway thought. *Sheriff McVie. He's been waiting at the station for me. Probably for a while now.*

"I rather like him," Yasuda continued. "One of the few law enforcement officers I've met who actually respects the M.E.'s office."

Fenway swallowed hard and nodded.

Mark pulled into the transportation lot at the station. Fenway said goodbye to Dr. Yasuda and hung up the phone. She collected her purse, put her shoes back on, and went inside with Mark.

Sheriff McVie was talking with Celeste Salvador, the officer who had interviewed Fenway after Lana attacked her, in the station. It looked like she was updating him on the case.

Fenway walked up to him when Celeste finished.

"Hey, McVie." Fenway tried a tentative smile.

McVie was all business. "Hi, Fenway. Looks like Stotsky didn't have a car here—he was getting a ride with your dad. We're tracking down the driver now to see if he saw anything or drove him anywhere."

"The driver is probably en route between the airport and my father's house."

He nodded. "Yeah, I heard what happened over the radio."

Fenway looked down at her shoes. "I'm sorry."

McVie pulled her aside and lowered his voice. "Listen, when we were arguing earlier? I wasn't going to say anything like what you were thinking. I was going to say *the daughter of the most powerful man in the county*. But I thought that would offend you. I never thought you were afraid I'd say something, well, a lot more offensive."

She half-smiled. "I've made some really shitty assumptions about what you were thinking today, and some stuff you were going to say."

"Yeah."

"Anyway, I'm sorry," she said genuinely. "It's been an insane couple of days."

McVie paused. "I told Amy I knew about her and Dylan. She, uh, she brought up a ton of emotional stuff. It's not just the cheating. She's really unhappy."

"Yeah. Dez and I, we interviewed her earlier. We had to tell her Dylan was dead." She looked down again. "She was devastated. I'm sorry you're going through this. I know how much divorce sucks."

McVie raised his head. "Oh, Fenway, we're not getting a divorce."

She looked back up at him. "What?"

"Not yet, anyway. We decided to work on our relationship. We're setting up marriage counseling. We've got a ton of work to do, but Amy and I aren't giving up—it's hard enough on Megan as it is."

"Oh."

Fenway wasn't sure what she was feeling. Part of her knew spending the night with him was a mistake, but part of her still wanted him to leave his wife. She could rationalize it—Amy had been cheating on Craig with a much younger man (younger than Fenway, even). The affair had gone on for a while, too, and it probably would have gone on for much longer if Harrison Walker hadn't gotten killed. But, no matter how she rationalized it, and even though she thought it was a bad idea, she still wanted McVie to want her. She still wanted more nights with him.

"Did you tell her about me?"

He paused. "No. No, I didn't tell her about us. She thinks I slept in the office last night. I didn't really see any need to tell her otherwise."

"So, you and I are done?"

He shifted his weight from foot to foot, slightly uncomfortable. " I certainly liked that you and I seemed to work really well together. Professionally. Before, you know."

"Yeah."

"I don't know. I'd kind of like to forget either of us did what we did last night." He looked in Fenway's eyes. "I'd like us to be the kind of sheriff and coroner who can work together effectively. Bounce ideas off each other. Call each other on our bullshit. We were doing it well. For a couple of days, anyway."

Fenway nodded solemnly. "And even if we can't, you only have to put up with me for a few more months."

"You never know. Life is full of surprises."

"Okay," she answered, not really knowing what else to say.

They were silent for a while.

McVie put his hand on her arm. "Listen, why don't you go have dinner with Rachel? Get some take-out or something. I'll call you if we have any updates on Stotsky's whereabouts. If not, you've had a long day. Go home and get some sleep."

Fenway nodded. McVie squeezed her arm gently and then patted her on the shoulder in a friendly kind of way, as if he were encouraging her during a basketball game. Fenway did, however, catch his eyes going down her legs, and looking at her strappy high heels back on her feet. He was trying to be subtle about it, but Fenway noticed his gaze lingering.

She thought about chasing McVie through the plaza. Tottering on the gravelly road to Dylan's pickup. Running down the hallways of the church. Keeping up with Mark to get in the squad car. And, finally, McVie's gaze lingering on her sexy shoes.

Yeah, Fenway thought, *totally* not *worth it*.

CHAPTER TWENTY-SIX

FENWAY WALKED BACK TO THE CORONER'S SUITE. DEZ WAS ON THE phone, talking in a hushed but angry voice. Fenway went to Rachel's desk and plucked a business card from its holder; her mobile number was on it. Dez hung up, almost slamming the receiver back on its cradle.

"You'd think I was telling the lieutenant *himself* he was wanted for murder!"

"What was that all about, Dez?"

"The CHP. They acted like I was blaming *them* for Stotsky. I had to talk to three different people before they agreed to set up a road check on either side of Estancia on the freeway."

"The blue wall?"

Dez shook her head and pointed a finger at Fenway. "Ordinarily, Fenway, I'd tell you—again!— you watch too many cop shows, but man! It sure seemed like we were getting the runaround there."

"A CHP-issued gun was used by a former CHP officer to kill a peace officer," Fenway pointed out. "It can't look good."

"Letting him get away with it would look worse. I had to threaten to call a reporter to ask them why their former officers are above the law."

"You've got a reporter who would do that?"

Dez gave her a look. "You'd be surprised by what I've got, girl."

"I'm sure I would. But it's been a good hour since he walked out the door here. Isn't it a little late?"

"You never know. He didn't have a car here, so he might spent an hour or two getting transportation."

"Okay." Fenway drummed her fingers on the desk. "Dez, where do *you* think Stotsky is right now? Still in town?"

Dez paused. "I don't know, Fenway. If I were Stotsky, I'd get out of town as fast as I could. But then again, as soon as I'd heard of any kind of break in the case, I would have taken off. Grabbed as much cash as I could, liquidated everything, gone to Mexico, or Panama, or Morocco."

"But?"

Dez thought for a moment. "Obviously Stotsky stuck around because he cares about his daughters. He might think, what good is it to protect Rachel if I'm never going to see her or her sister again?"

"Yeah."

"When Bradley recognized him, or sure he would have tried to leave town. But without a car, and with us getting to the airports, train stations, and bus stations so quick, he might not have been able to yet."

Fenway nodded. "True."

"With his connections, though," Dez continued, "I'm almost sure he would have been able to find *some* way out. A sympathetic friend or one of his direct reports at Ferris Energy hiding him in the trunk and driving to Tijuana. Getting a disguise, or a fake ID, and getting a train ticket." She stood up from her chair and started to pace, lost in thought. "Ferris Energy has a second plane, too. We're not sure where it is. It might be on its way to Mexicali with Stotsky onboard."

"Are we talking to any of Stotsky's friends or colleagues?"

Dez looked up. "Come on, Fenway, how many resources do you think we have? We've got a good twenty people in motion on this right now, not including those ass-draggers at the CHP. We can't get any more coverage on it without leaving the sheriff's office empty."

Fenway sighed. "I bet he's gone. I bet we missed him. He'd have just needed to take a car on any road out of the county, besides the freeway. Even with the freeway—he had a good twenty minutes to get out."

Dez folded her arms. "Man, I know we couldn't have really done anything, but I hate it when they get away."

"We can contact L.A. county, San Miguelito, maybe even Monterey, right?"

"We can. But the more time that passes, the larger the radius we have to search, the more places he can be, the higher the chance of him getting away. If we had grabbed him at the station, we'd have him. Once I let him out the door, the chances of him getting away got much higher."

Fenway looked at Dez. "Don't tell me you blame yourself for Stotsky getting away."

Dez waved her hand at Fenway, as if shooing a fly.

Fenway stared at the ceiling. "Okay, I spoke with McVie. He suggested I get a couple hours away from the station. I think I may get some takeout and go have dinner with Rachel tonight. He thought it would be good for her to have someone to talk with."

"Yeah, someone who's not her sister," Dez agreed. "I talked to Rachel before I called the CHP. Her sister had all kinds of questions about their dad—the fact that he's the main suspect probably complicates things, and she kept asking Rachel over and over, you know, picking at the scab. Rachel finally had to send her home." Dez paused. "Rachel likes Italian. Zorro's over on Broadway. She likes the penne arrabiata."

"Thanks." Fenway went in the conference room and closed the door. She dialed Rachel's mobile number. It rang three times before she picked up.

"Hello?"

"Hi, Rachel, it's Fenway. I know I told you to take some time off, but

I thought maybe I could get some takeout for us tonight, and we could hang out."

"Don't you have to work? Isn't my dad still on the run?"

"We haven't found him yet. I talked to a few people here. We think he's out of Dominguez County by now."

"My dad's pretty smart. If anyone could get out of the county, he could."

"Yeah, that's what I think, too," Fenway agreed with a sigh.

Rachel was silent for a moment. "So, takeout?"

"If you're up for it."

"Actually, that sounds great. I've got to tell you, I need to get out of the house. The cop outside my door is nice and all, but he made my sister nervous, and she was asking all kinds of questions about my dad. I had to send her home."

"You want to go to a sit-down place somewhere?"

"Maybe I can pick up dinner and come over to your place? I don't want to be by myself right now, but I also don't want to be around a ton of people."

Fenway shrugged on her end of the line. "Um, sure. I mean, I just moved in, so the apartment's not really in the best shape for entertaining, but what the hell."

"I think I'll be fine. Hey, is the officer going to follow me over?"

"I don't think so." Fenway paused. "We thought your dad might come to see you, maybe go to your apartment."

"I don't think he'll try to find me. I made it pretty clear I didn't want to talk to him."

"Okay. And I agree, I think it would be good for you to get out if you're going a little stir crazy."

"Excellent," Rachel said, and Fenway could hear the smile in her voice. "Okay, so there's this awesome Italian restaurant called Zorro's."

"I've heard that's a good place." *Wow, Dez pays attention to everything.*

"It's a little ways down Broadway, but they have the *best* penne arrabiata."

Fenway smiled into the receiver. "That sounds great. I'm still at work, so I can pick it up after I leave."

"Oh, don't worry about it. It's on the way to your house, plus I know the owners and I haven't seen them in a while. They usually give me some free stuff when I go—garlic bread, tiramisu, something like that."

"You okay to be in a crowd? It *is* Friday night."

"It'll be a quick in-and-out. I'll be fine," Rachel assured her. "What do you want? They've got a good veggie lasagna, and their pastas are great."

"I'll get the penne arrabiata, too."

"Awesome! You'll love it. I'll call it in and pick it up in about half an hour. I should be at your house by seven forty-five."

"See you then."

This would be Fenway's first dinner with another person in her new place; beers with McVie didn't count. She had her plates and silverware unpacked, and she still had two beers left. For one of the first times since moving to Estancia, Fenway felt like she might belong. She had a similar feeling during that first lunch McVie, and again at the office with Dez. And, despite Rachel's awkward confession the evening they met, she and Rachel might be forging a friendship.

Fenway left the conference room. "Okay, Dez, I'm heading out for a while—dinner with Rachel, like McVie suggested. He said he'd keep me up to date on what's happening. You let me know too, okay?"

"Sure. I want to follow up on Stotsky's financials anyway. I got wind he might have an offshore account."

"Okay. If that's the case, he *will* want to leave the country."

"He's probably halfway there already." Dez heaved a sigh. "Say hi to Rachel for me. Hope she's doing okay."

"I'll do that. I can't believe it's been the longest workday of my life and I've done it all in these stupid heels." Fenway kicked out her foot, inspecting the shoes in question.

"Yeah," Dez said. "That'll teach you to try to look sexy for a married man."

"Gosh, thanks, Dez." Fenway rolled her eyes.

"Soak in some Epsom salts, girl. It's magic."

Fenway walked out of the office and out the doors. The sun had dipped behind the horizon, and the sky was stippled with pinks and purples. It had been a long ten hours since Fenway got to work—not as long as either McVie or Dez, but still grueling and emotionally draining—but the beautiful sky, the brisk sea air, and the promise of a great Italian meal almost made up for it all.

She nearly walked past her car in the parking garage, not recognizing it right away in the pale yellow light, but she stopped after she passed the car, shook her head, and turned around.

Fenway saw a large man walking up from the front of the garage, silhouetted by the harsh entrance light behind him. She felt a chill run up her back—was it Stotsky?

Fenway took her keys out of her purse, putting a key between the second and third fingers of her closed fist. The man came closer.

She heard a car start up behind her and spun around. A Ford pickup turned its headlights on.

The stranger was the parking lot attendant. He smiled at Fenway and nodded, walking past her to the stairwell on the second floor.

Fenway exhaled. The pickup truck passed her.

It was enough to rattle her. She took her phone out of her purse and put the flashlight on. She shined it in the back seat. Nothing. She shined it in the front seat. Still nothing. She took her remote out and popped the trunk. The lid slowly raised, but the trunk was empty. She crouched down a few feet from the car and shined her light underneath the car. There was nothing but concrete.

Fenway stood up. She walked around to the back of the car, closed the trunk, and unlocked the door.

She got in, and checked the back seat one more time: still nothing. She started up the car and drove out of the garage.

Fenway turned the radio on and some old Michael Jackson was playing. She made the short trip back to her apartment complex and looked at her watch. She still had about fifteen minutes before Rachel was supposed to be there. It would give her a chance to get out of the black dress and the sexy but increasingly uncomfortable high heels, and put on some sweats and her sheepskin slippers.

She got out of the car. Fatigue overwhelmed her as she climbed the single flight of stairs to the second floor. She got to the landing, walked to her apartment, and reached out to put the key in the deadbolt.

The door was open a crack.

She gasped.

The door flung open.

Rob Stotsky came at her with a black flannel scarf.

Fenway tried to scream but the scarf—*her* scarf—covered her mouth. Her keys fell from her hand. In a quick, fluid movement, Stotsky grabbed the ends of the scarf behind her head and tightened, gagging her. He swung her around into the apartment by her head, and slammed the door shut.

Fenway tried to shout again, but the scarf covered the sound. Stotsky pulled harder, and, using the scarf for leverage, pushed her down to her knees. Her purse fell to the floor. One of her heels came off. Then he shoved her down onto the floor on her stomach, her head turned to the side, the scarf pushed up almost over her nose. Her dress slid up to the tops of her thighs, and she briefly thought of the Russian Lit professor again.

"Oh, Fenway," he growled. "If only you had let me leave."

Stotsky put a knee on the small of her back. Her breath went out of her.

"I was about to empty my bank account. I had my train ticket. I would have been in Tijuana by midnight, and you would have never seen me again."

Fenway struggled but couldn't move.

"But you had to mess everything up for me, didn't you? Putting a gold on my cards. Getting an officer to watch for me at the train station."

She could barely breathe.

"I saw how you took down that crazy guy in the church," he hissed in her ear. "I'm not going to underestimate you like he did."

Fenway was a tall woman, but Stotsky outweighed her by at least a hundred pounds. She didn't think she could take him down—not without help.

"Here's what's going to happen to Fenway Stevenson, the girl who killed the goose that laid the golden egg," he whispered in her ear. "You're going to give me your car keys. It'll be tougher to track a car that doesn't have plates yet. You're going to get in the trunk. Then we're going to Mexico, and your father is going to wire me all the money I need. Then, and only then, will I let you go."

Fenway saw her high heel was next to her right hand. She wondered if she could grab it without Stotsky noticing.

"Now, you're not going to do anything stupid, right, Fenway? You're probably just as useful to me dead, but if your dad insists on proof of life before sending me the money, I'd like to be able to give it to him."

"Mm-hmm," Fenway wheezed through the gag.

"Swear on your mother's grave," he sneered.

That knocked the breath out of her almost as much as his knee in her back.

"Swear it!" He pulled the scarf down.

"I swear," she gasped.

"Where are the keys?" he said.

Fenway realized he hadn't seen her drop them out on the landing.

"In my purse," she lied.

"Where's your purse?"

"I don't know. I dropped it."

Stotsky grabbed a handful of her hair. "Where did you drop it, damn it?"

"When you first threw me in here. I dropped it. Maybe over by the kitchen island."

He pulled. "There's nothing by the kitchen island."

"Ow—then I don't know."

"Tell me where you dropped your purse!" he hissed.

"I dropped my purse when you spun me around. I didn't see where it went."

He increased the pressure on the small of her back. "You are *such* a pain in my ass." He let go of her hair, stuffed the scarf back in her mouth, straightened up, still on top of her, and turned his head away, looking for the purse on the floor.

Something in his voice told Fenway she would not survive the trip to Mexico. Once Stotsky had his money from her father—assuming Ferris would even send it—Stotsky would have far less trouble killing her and getting rid of her body than letting her go.

Fenway scooted her right hand up and laid it on top of her shoe. He didn't notice.

"Under the kitchen table," he sighed. The tone of his voice made her think he saw the purse. "Don't move or I'll kill you."

Fenway was waiting for him to take his weight off her back so she could drive hard up into him and swing around with her shoe, the sharp heel out. She thought about where his head might be, and whether or not she could hit his temple.

But Stotsky was thinking ahead. He grabbed the scarf tied around her face, then picked her head up quickly and slammed it into the kitchen floor.

It surprised her, and it hurt. Her ear rang where it smashed against the floor.

It might have briefly incapacitated her, except the floor was cheap linoleum, not hardwood or tile. It hurt, but it didn't knock her out. Her lip curled.

He rose to a squatting position over her and started to stand.

She pushed herself up fast. She arched her back fast, then twisted to her left, the high heel in her right hand. Stotsky was off balance and barely caught himself on the table.

She swung hard; the heel caught his left cheek and ripped a big flap of skin off, slicing across his face.

He roared in pain.

Fenway scrambled out from between his legs.

He grabbed at her with his right hand, then dropped to his knees and clipped her right hip. It was enough to knock her down, as she fell she kicked out with her left foot—the foot still in the other high heel—and caught him in the mouth, splitting his lip. He grabbed for her ankles but missed.

She scooted back and stood across the kitchen from him.

The knife block.

It was next to the microwave, out of both of their reaches. Maybe out of his line of sight, too. Could she grab the big knife before he noticed?

But he was closer than Fenway was. Maybe he'd get to her before she got to the knives. Fenway's high heel would have to do for now.

Kneeling, he spat a wad of blood onto the floor. He snarled although his lip and cheek bled badly. He touched the wound on his cheek and glared at the blood on his fingers. "I'm still taking your car."

She pulled off the scarf. "But you're not going to take me." Fenway held the high heel as menacingly as she possibly could.

Keeping his eyes on her, he backed up to where her purse had come to rest under the kitchen table. He pulled it in front of himself and dumped everything out. He rifled through the mints and coins and hand lotion. He recoiled slightly when he touched the tampons. Fenway thought for a brief second he might use them to soak up the blood on his face, but no.

"Where are you keys?" he growled.

Fenway sprang toward the knife block. Stotsky hesitated, and she grabbed the big chef's knife—the good one her mother had bought her for her twenty-fifth birthday—and she swiped at him before he could get to the knife block.

She missed, and he jumped back.

"Get out of my house," Fenway seethed at him.

"I'm going to kill you."

"*Get out!*" she screamed.

And then she kept screaming. Fenway wanted everyone in the building to come. She wanted someone to call the cops.

He lunged at Fenway and she thrust the knife at him. But he knocked it out of her hand, and it clattered to the floor.

He grabbed her wrist and spun her around, and suddenly Fenway was in a choke hold.

He squeezed her neck and she couldn't breathe.

Grabbing at his arm, she scratched him hard.

He grimaced, but tightened his grip.

She couldn't get air.

The door burst open.

It was Rachel—holding a .22 pistol.

"Let her go." Rachel's voice was high-pitched and wavering.

Stotsky spun Fenway around to face her. "Rachel," he said, "Rachel, listen to me."

"You're killing her. Let her go, or I'll put a bullet in you."

"Rachel—"

"I'm not kidding, Dad. You know I'm a good shot. You trained me yourself."

In the distance, faintly, the sound of sirens wafted up through the open door.

"After everything I've done for you." Stotsky's grip relaxed just enough so Fenway could get a shallow breath.

"You killed my husband."

"He didn't love you," Stotsky spat. "He was cheating on you. You deserve so much better."

"Maybe so, Dad, but that's not up to you. And I can't let you kill anyone else."

His tone changed, like he was negotiating. "Okay, okay, I won't. But you've got to let me go. I'll go to Mexico. You won't have to see me again. Fenway needs to tell me where her car keys are. Then I'll leave."

The sirens were getting closer.

"Deal, Fenway?" Rachel said.

She struggled in his grip for a second. "Fine," Fenway choked out.

"You've gotta let Fenway go, Dad."

"Tell me where the keys are, Fenway."

She felt she didn't have a choice. "On the landing. I dropped them on the ground as soon as you opened the door."

"Good." Stotsky started to drag Fenway out of the kitchen. He tightened his chokehold on her.

"Dad! What the hell are you doing?"

"Taking what I came for, Rachel. I don't expect you to understand. I've worked all my life for this, and I need Fenway so I can get the money I'm owed." He coughed, a wet, bloody cough, then swung Fenway in front of him, still in the choke hold, and half-pushed, half-dragged her to the front door, toward Rachel.

The sirens got louder.

"Get away from her." Rachel tightened her two-hand grip on the .22.

Fenway locked eyes with Rachel. Rachel, barely holding onto her emotions, stared back. Fenway was going to do something crazy—and Rachel knew it. Fenway and Stotsky were only about two feet away from the front door jamb, about five feet in front of Rachel.

"I'm sorry, Rachel, but it's her or me. I'm going to leave, and you're not going to stop me."

Fenway suddenly swung her right foot up, put it against the door jamb, and pushed backward with everything she had.

Stotsky lost his balance, he let go of Fenway's neck, and they both went down. Fenway fell half on top of him.

He quickly rolled onto his stomach and grabbed the knife on the floor. Fenway scrambled to her feet and Stotsky held the knife out threateningly.

"You're coming with me, Fenway, and I'll cut you if I have to."

Bang.

Stotsky's right shoulder snapped back. A pop of blood.

Bang.

His upper arm tensed. Another pop of blood.

He screamed and dropped the knife. It clattered away.

Fenway turned her head. Rachel still held the gun with both hands, smoke curling from the barrel. A tear was running down her cheek.

"Goddammit, Daddy!" she screamed. "Don't make me shoot you again! Get down on the ground!"

"You shot me." His voice was weak and incredulous.

"Get down on the ground!"

Stotsky, holding his right arm with his left, got down on his knees.

"On your stomach."

"Rachel—"

"*ON YOUR STOMACH!*" she screamed.

He grimaced when he put weight on his arm, but he got on his stomach on the kitchen floor.

Rachel kept the gun trained on her father. Her hands were surprisingly still. The sirens were close now.

Fenway leaned against the wall and slumped to the floor. She looked at her hands; they were shaking much more than Rachel's were.

Dez burst in, followed by Sheriff McVie, with Mark and Celeste right behind him. Fenway kept shaking. Rachel still held the gun trained on her father, on his stomach, bleeding from wounds in his arm, his cheek, his mouth. Mark handcuffed him.

Dez gently took the gun from Rachel's hands. Rachel put her head on Dez's shoulder and Dez hugged her. Rachel started to sob; her whole body seemed to give out at once and Dez held her up, stroking the back of her head while she cried.

McVie crouched down in front of Fenway. "Fenway, are you okay?"

She looked McVie in the face, his serious face, with his alabaster skin and his freckles.

Stay with me tonight, she wanted to say, but didn't.

"No. I'm not okay. I'm not even close to okay."

He nodded.

"We're going to need you and Rachel to tell us what happened."

"He was waiting for me when I got home," she started. "The building manager reports to him. He obviously had a key. That didn't even occur to me."

"It didn't occur to *any* of us."

"Well, then, you're pretty awful cops."

McVie smiled. "Yeah."

"He wanted my car because it doesn't have plates yet. He wanted to kidnap me so my dad would wire him money in Mexico."

McVie nodded. "If he kept off the freeway, he might have gotten to the border."

"I don't think he would have let me go after he got the money. I think he would have killed me."

McVie put his hand on her shoulder. "You want to go over what happened?"

She grabbed his hand and put it against her cheek.

"Fenway?"

"Give me a few minutes."

Rachel was talking, trying to catch her breath. Dez was still holding her.

"...so after I got the take-out," Rachel said, between sobs, "I got to the apartment complex, and as soon as I opened the car door, I heard Fenway scream. *Get out. Get out.* She was screaming it over and over. And I left the food in the car, and grabbed the gun from the glove compartment, and ran upstairs. Fenway's keys were outside the door, and there were noises and yelling inside, and I pushed the door open and pointed the gun at him."

"Come on." McVie squeezed Fenway's hand. "We should move to another room. I can't have you hearing this before I take your statement."

He led her into her bedroom and shut the door.

She sat on the bed.

"I'm just taking your statement," he said, gently but with conviction.

"I know."

And she told him everything.

PART FIVE
SATURDAY

CHAPTER TWENTY-SEVEN

MCVIE TOOK FENWAY'S STATEMENT AND LEFT HER BEDROOM. MARK came in and asked how she was doing. She nodded, not looking directly at him. He put his hand on her shoulder; she grabbed it and held on for a minute. He squeezed back before letting go and quietly leaving the room.

Dez found Stotsky's "go bag" behind the chair in the living room. It had a fake passport, and about five hundred dollars in cash. There were a couple of changes of clothes too.

The police stayed for over an hour. Rachel went down with the police, and came back with the two orders of penne arrabiata from her car.

Rachel and Fenway didn't eat the penne that night. Their stomachs were all knotted up. Neither of them wanted to be alone. Rachel cried a few more times. They talked about Dylan. They talked about what Rachel could do about the logistics of his memorial, his burial; letting his parents be involved. They talked about Amy and Dylan's affair. They talked about what he ever saw in her, and Fenway let Rachel insult Amy and call her old. Rachel cried some more.

At about eleven thirty, Rachel helped Fenway clean the blood off the kitchen floor. They talked a little more. Fenway told Rachel to see a therapist, and she nodded. Exhaustion was taking over, and Rachel wound up crashing on the sofa. The pasta stayed in the fridge.

Fenway got a blanket and put it over Rachel. She started to walk away, but then stepped back and tucked the blanket gently in under the sofa cushions. She watched Rachel sleep for a minute, then went to her room.

Fenway slept through some disturbing dreams, but didn't wake up until almost noon. She woke up disoriented and saw Rachel had left a note saying she had gone home to call her mother-in-law and figure out how to deal with Dylan's death.

Fenway decided to go for a walk. She grabbed some water, and put her trail running shoes on, which felt like heaven after spending the day before in the high heels—those beautiful, sexy, life-saving heels.

She walked down past the complex to the dead end, to the short, white, wooden fence with the reflectors. She turned on the well-worn dirt path and walked out into the trees. Past the first grove of trees, she got to the small clearing, and then she walked to the second grove of trees. She heard a sound that wasn't quite a rustling; it sounded like rapid but muted clicking. She looked up into the trees and there were thousands upon thousands of monarch butterflies. They were on their way north, and the trees were so full of orange it looked like autumn.

Fenway watched the butterflies for about ten minutes, then she walked through the second grove of trees, up the grassy area, and she sat at the short drop off, looking out over the sandy beach and the Pacific a few hundred feet beyond.

She thought of her mother's painting and promised herself she would go to Seattle and get it out of storage the first chance she got. She thought she might put it on the wall across from her bed, so it would be the first thing she saw every day.

Fenway stopped at the Coffee Bean on the way back. She had already ordered her latte when she saw Sheriff McVie and his wife—Craig and Amy. They were sitting down together; Amy was leaning forward, elbows on the table; Craig was leaning back, frowning; his arms were folded.

Craig saw her and immediately brightened as he waved her over. Fenway wanted to pretend she didn't see them, but it was obvious she had. She said hi, and she smiled and told them she had gone on a walk down to the ocean, and it cleared her head, and yes, it was a little weird still being in the apartment where it all happened, but she thought she was doing okay.

The television mounted on the wall behind Amy was tuned to an entertainment channel, and there were movie stars on the red carpet.

"Hey, look," Craig said. "Isn't that your dad behind the interviewer?"

Fenway looked, and sure enough it was. Her father was in a black-on-black tuxedo, looking pleased with himself, and Charlotte looked nauseatingly gorgeous in a shimmery silver dress with a plunging neckline.

"Stotsky's going in front of the district attorney on Monday," Craig said. "Doesn't look like your dad is too worried about him cutting a plea deal."

They chatted a little longer. Fenway got the sense Amy didn't want her to stay, so she said goodbye and walked out of the coffee shop with most of her dignity.

She got home and took a shower. As she finished drying off, it hit her again, like a train, that her mother was gone. She wished she had her mother there the night before to hold her the way Dez had been holding Rachel.

She sat down on the sofa and put her feet up. She knew she should be starting her reading for her final forensics class, but she wanted to let the memory of the last few days wash over her. She hadn't even gotten her first paycheck yet—it would come the next Friday—but she liked her job. She didn't like getting shot at, or getting put in a choke hold, but she liked going through those files, seeing the bullet casings, talking theories of the crime with Dez and Dr. Yasuda, researching the gunshot residue— and she especially liked when she found out Stotsky was Rachel's father, and seeing all the puzzle pieces fit together almost perfectly in her head.

She sighed. Although this coroner position was temporary, maybe after she finished her forensics program, she'd look into some other options besides nursing; maybe a crime-scene analyst, or even a job in Dr. Yasuda's office.

Fenway called Rachel, who had gotten back from seeing Dylan's mother. She told Fenway the two of them had cried together and made phone calls and set up the memorial and the cremation.

Rachel didn't want to be in the apartment she shared with Dylan—she couldn't bring herself to put anything away yet, she said. His clothes were still in the closet, his toothbrush was still on the bathroom counter, and everything made her both sad for his death and angry at his betrayal.

"I called my friend Jordan to see if she wanted to go to a movie tonight," Rachel said, "but she was weird. It's like she didn't know what to say to me."

They made plans for Rachel to come over to Fenway's at eight o'clock that night, watch a stupid romantic comedy, and eat the penne from the night before.

"Is this what my life is going to be like from now on?" Rachel asked.

"I don't know," Fenway said. "I really don't know."

WANT MORE FENWAY?

The Fenway Stevenson Mysteries
Book One: *The Reluctant Coroner*
Book Two: *The Incumbent Coroner*
Book Three: *The Candidate Coroner*
Book Four: *The Upstaged Coroner*
Book Five: *The Courtroom Coroner*
Book Six: *The Watchful Coroner*

Anthology
Short story: "The Coroner and the Body in the Bath"
in the Mystery Anthology *12 Shots*

Collection
Books 1–3 of *The Fenway Stevenson Mysteries*

Dez Roubideaux
Bad Weather

To order more books in the Fenway Stevenson series, go to
www.books2read.com/rl/fenway

Sign up for **The Coroner's Report**,
Paul Austin Ardoin's newsletter:
www.paulaustinardoin.com

I hope you enjoyed reading this book as much as I enjoyed writing
it. If you did, I'd sincerely appreciate a review on your favorite book
retailer's website, Goodreads, and BookBub. Reviews are crucial for
any author, and even just a line or two can make a huge difference.